THE SAVAGE ALTAR

Åsa Larsson

Translated by Marlaine Delargy

PENGUIN BOOKS

PENGUIN BOOKS

Published by the Penguin Group
Penguin Books Ltd, 80 Strand, London WC2R 0RL, England
Penguin Group (USA) Inc., 375 Hudson Street, New York, New York 10014, USA
Penguin Group (Canada), 90 Eglinton Avenue East, Suite 700, Toronto, Ontario, Canada M4P 2Y3
(a division of Pearson Penguin Canada Inc.)
Penguin Ireland, 25 St Stephen's Green, Dublin 2, Ireland (a division of Penguin Books Ltd)
Penguin Group (Australia), 250 Camberwell Road, Camberwell, Victoria 3124, Australia
(a division of Pearson Australia Group Pty Ltd)
Penguin Books India Pvt Ltd, 11 Community Centre, Panchsheel Park, New Delhi – 110 017, India
Penguin Group (NZ), 67 Apollo Drive, Rosedale, North Shore 0632, New Zealand
(a division of Pearson New Zealand Ltd)
Penguin Books (South Africa) (Pty) Ltd, 24 Sturdee Avenue, Rosebank, Johannesburg 2196, South Africa

Penguin Books Ltd, Registered Offices: 80 Strand, London WC2R 0RL, England

www.penguin.com

First published in Sweden by Albert Bonniers as *Solstorm* 2003
First published in the United States of America by Bantam Dell as *Sun Storm* 2006
First published in Great Britain by Viking as *The Savage Altar* 2007
Published in Penguin Books 2008
1

Copyright © Åsa Larsson, 2003
Translation copyright © by The Bantam Dell Publishing Group,
a division of Random House, Inc. 2003
All rights reserved

ISBN: 978-0-141-02471-4

It grows like a tree of rage
behind my brow
with flashing red leaves, blue leaves, white!
A tree
still quivering in the wind

And I will crush
your house, and nothing
will be unfamiliar to me,
not even
what is human

Like a tree from the inside
forces its way out
and crushes
the skull

And glows
like a lantern deep in the forest
deep in the darkness

Göran Sonnevi

THE SAVAGE ALTAR

And evening came and morning came, the first day

When Viktor Strandgård dies it is not, in fact, for the first time. He lies on his back in the church called The Source of All Our Strength and looks up through the enormous windows in its roof. It's as if there is nothing between him and the dark winter sky up above.

You can't get any closer than this, he thinks. When you come to the church on the mountain at the end of the world, the sky will be so close that you can reach out and touch it.

The Aurora Borealis twists and turns like a dragon in the night sky. Stars and planets are compelled to give way to her, this great miracle of shimmering light, as she makes her unhurried way across the vault of heaven.

Viktor Strandgård follows her progress with his eyes.

I wonder if she sings? he thinks. Like a lonely whale beneath the sea?

And as if his thoughts have touched her, she stops for a second. Breaks her endless journey. Contemplates Viktor Strandgård with her cold winter eyes. Because he is as beautiful as an icon lying there, to tell the truth, with the dark blood like a halo round his long, fair, St. Lucia hair. He can't feel his legs anymore. He is getting drowsy. There is no pain.

Curiously enough it is his previous death he is thinking of as he lies there looking into the eye of the dragon. That time in the late winter when he came cycling down the long bank toward the cross-roads at Adolf Hedinsvägen and Hjalmar Lundbohmsvägen. Happy and redeemed, his guitar on his back. He remembers how the wheels of his bicycle skidded helplessly on the ice as he tried desperately to brake. How he saw the woman in the red Fiat Uno coming from the right. How they stared at each other, the realization in the other's eyes; now it's happening, the icy slide toward death.

With that picture in his mind's eye Viktor Strandgård dies for the second time in his life. Footsteps approach, but he doesn't hear them. His eyes do not have to see the gleam of the knife once again. His body lies like an empty shell on the floor of the church; it is stabbed over and over again. And the dragon resumes her journey across the heavens, unmoved.

Monday, February 17

Rebecka Martinsson was woken by her own sharp intake of breath as fear stabbed through her body. She opened her eyes to darkness. Just between the dream and the waking, she had the strong feeling that there was someone in the flat. She lay still and listened, but all she could hear was the sound of her own heart thumping in her chest like a frightened hare. Her fingers fumbled for the alarm clock on the bedside table and found the little button to light up the face. Quarter to four. She had gone to bed four hours ago and this was the second time she had woken up.

It's the job, she thought. I work too hard. That's why my thoughts go round and round at night, like a hamster on a squeaking wheel.

Her head and the back of her neck were aching. She must have been grinding her teeth in her sleep. Might as well get up. She wound the duvet around her and went into the kitchen. Her feet knew the way without her needing to switch on the light. She put on the coffee machine and the radio. Bellman's music played over and over as the water ran through the filter and Rebecka showered.

Her long hair could dry in its own time. She drank her coffee while she was getting dressed. Over the weekend she had ironed her clothes for the week and hung them up in the wardrobe. Now it was Monday. On Monday's hanger was an ivory blouse and a navy blue Marella suit. She sniffed at the tights she'd been wearing the previous day; they'd do. They'd gone a bit wrinkly around the ankles, but if she stretched them and tucked them under her feet it wouldn't show. She'd just have to make sure she didn't kick her shoes off during the day. It didn't bother her; it was only worth spending time worrying about your underwear and your tights if you thought somebody was going to be watching you get undressed. Her underwear had seen better days and was turning gray.

An hour later she was sitting at her computer in the office. The words flowed through her mind like a clear mountain stream, down her arms and out through her fingers, flying over the keyboard. Work soothed her mind. It was as if the morning's unpleasantness had been blown away.

It's strange, she thought. I moan and complain like all the other young lawyers about how unhappy the job makes me. But I feel a sense of peace when I'm working. Happiness, almost. It's when I'm not working I feel uneasy.

The light from the street below forced its way with difficulty through the tall barred windows. You could still make out the sound of individual cars among the noise below, but soon the street would become a single dull roar of traffic. Rebecka leaned back in her chair and clicked on "print." Out in the dark corridor the printer woke up and got on with the first task of the day. Then the door into reception banged. She sighed and looked at the clock. Ten to six. That was the end of her peace and quiet.

She couldn't hear who had come in. The thick carpets in the

corridor deadened the sound of footsteps, but after a while the door of her room opened.

"**A**m I disturbing you?" It was Maria Taube. She pushed the door open with her hip, balancing a mug of coffee in each hand. Rebecka's copy was jammed under her right arm.

Both women were newly qualified lawyers with special responsibility for tax laws, working for Meijer & Ditzinger. The office was at the very top of a beautiful turn-of-the-century building on Birger Jarlsgatan. Semi-antique Persian carpets ran the length of the corridors, and here and there stood imposing sofas and armchairs in attractively worn leather. Everything exuded an air of experience, influence, money and competence. It was an office that filled clients with an appropriate mixture of security and reverence.

"By the time you die you must be so tired you hope there won't be any sort of afterlife," said Maria, and put a mug of coffee on Rebecka's desk. "But of course that won't apply to you, Maggie Thatcher. What time did you get here this morning? Or haven't you been home at all?"

They'd both worked in the office on Sunday evening. Maria had gone home first.

"I've only just got here," lied Rebecka, and took her copy out of Maria's hand.

Maria sank down into the armchair provided for visitors, kicked off her ridiculously expensive leather shoes and drew her legs up under her body.

"Terrible weather," she said.

Rebecka looked out the window with surprise. Icy rain was hammering against the glass. She hadn't noticed earlier. She couldn't remember if it had been raining when she came into work. In fact, she couldn't actually remember whether she'd walked or taken the Underground. She gazed in a trance at the rain pouring down the glass as it beat an icy tattoo.

Winter in Stockholm, she thought. It's hardly surprising that you shut down your brain when you're outside. It's different up at home, the blue shining midwinter twilight, the snow crunching under your feet. Or the early spring, when you've skied along the river from Grandmother's house in Kurravaara to the cabin in Jiekajärvi, and you sit down and rest on the first patch of clear ground where the snow has melted under a pine tree. The tree bark glows like red copper in the sun. The snow sighs with exhaustion, collapsing in the warmth. Coffee, an orange, sandwiches in your rucksack.

The sound of Maria's voice drew her back. Her thoughts scrabbled and tried to escape, but she pulled herself together and met her colleague's raised eyebrows.

"Hello! I asked if you were going to listen to the news."

"Yes, of course."

Rebecka leaned back in her chair and stretched out her arm to the radio on the windowsill.

Lord, she's thin, thought Maria, looking at her colleague's rib cage as it protruded from under her jacket. You could play a tune on those ribs.

Rebecka turned the radio up and both women sat with their coffee cups cradled between their hands, heads bowed as if in prayer.

Maria blinked. It felt as if something were scratching her tired eyes. Today she had to finish the appeal for the county court in the Stenman case. Måns would kill her if she asked him for more time. She felt a burning pain in her midriff. No more coffee before lunch. You sat here like a princess in a tower, day and night, evenings and weekends, in this oh-so-charming office with all its bloody traditions that could go to hell, and all the pissed-up partners looking straight through your blouse while outside, life just carried on without you. You didn't know whether you wanted to cry or start a revolution but all you could actually manage was to drag yourself home to the TV and pass out in front of its soothing, flickering screen.

It's six o'clock and here are the morning headlines. A well-known religious leader around the age of thirty was found murdered early this morning in the church of The Source of All Our Strength in Kiruna. The police in Kiruna are not prepared to make a statement about the murder at this stage, but during the morning they have revealed that no one has been detained so far, and the murder weapon has not yet been found. . . . A new study shows that more and more communities are ignoring their obligations, according to Social Services. . . .

Rebecka swung her chair round so quickly that she banged her hand on the windowsill. She turned the radio off with a crash and at the same time managed to spill coffee on her knee.

"Viktor," she exclaimed. "It has to be him."

Maria looked at her with surprise.

"Viktor Strandgård? The Paradise Boy? Did you know him?"

Rebecka avoided Maria's gaze. Ended up staring at the coffee stain on her skirt, her expression closed and blank. Thin lips, pressed together.

"Of course I knew of him. But I haven't been home to Kiruna for years. I don't know anybody up there anymore."

Maria got up from the armchair, went over to Rebecka and pried the coffee cup from her colleague's stiff hands.

"If you say you didn't know him, that's fine by me, but you're going to faint in about thirty seconds. You're as white as a sheet. Bend over and put your head between your knees."

Like a child Rebecka did as she was told. Maria went to the bathroom and fetched paper towels to try to save Rebecka's suit from the coffee stain. When she came back Rebecka was leaning back in her chair.

"Are you okay?" asked Maria.

"Yes," answered Rebecka absently, and looked on helplessly as Maria started to dab at her skirt with a damp towel. "I did know him," she said.

"Well, I didn't exactly need a lie detector," said Maria without looking up. "Are you upset?"

"Upset? I don't know. Frightened, maybe."

Maria stopped her frantic dabbing.

"Frightened of what?"

"I don't know. That somebody will—"

The telephone burst in with its shrill signal before Rebecka could finish. She jumped and stared at it, but didn't pick it up. After the third ring Maria answered. She put her hand over the receiver so that the person on the other end couldn't hear her, and whispered:

"It's for you and it must be from Kiruna, because there's a Moomintroll on the other end."

When Inspector Anna-Maria Mella's telephone rang, she was already awake. The winter moon filled the room with its chilly white light. The birch trees outside the window drew blue shadow pictures on the walls with their bent and aching limbs. As soon as the phone started to ring, she picked it up.

"It's Sven-Erik—were you awake?"

"Yes, but I'm in bed. What is it?"

She heard Robert sigh and glanced in his direction. Had he woken up? No, his breathing became deep and regular again. Good.

"Suspected murder in The Source of All Our Strength church," said Sven-Erik.

"So? I'm on desk duty since Friday, in case you've forgotten."

"I know"—Sven-Erik's voice sounded troubled—"but bloody hell, Anna-Maria, this is something else. You could just come and have a look. The forensic team will be finished soon, and we can go in. I've got Viktor Strandgård lying here, and it looks like a slaughterhouse. I'd guess we've got about an hour before every bloody TV station is here with cameras and the whole circus."

"I'll be there in twenty minutes."

There's a turn-up, she thought. Sven-Erik ringing to ask me for help. He's changed.

Sven-Erik didn't answer, but Anna-Maria heard his suppressed sigh of relief just before he put the phone down.

She turned to Robert and gazed at his sleeping face. His cheek was resting on the back of his hand and his red lips were parted slightly. She found it irresistibly sexy that a few strands of gray had started to appear in his straggling moustache and at his temples. Robert himself used to stand in front of the bathroom mirror looking anxiously at his receding hairline.

"The desert is spreading," he would say ruefully.

She kissed him on the mouth. Her stomach got in the way, but she managed it. Twice.

"I love you," he assured her, still asleep. His hand fumbled under the sheet to draw her close, but by then she had already managed to sit upright on the edge of the bed. All of a sudden she was desperate for a pee. Her bladder was bursting all the time. She'd already been to the bathroom twice during the night.

Quarter of an hour later Anna-Maria climbed out of her Ford Escort in the car park below The Source of All Our Strength church. It was still bitterly cold. The air pinched and nipped at her cheeks. If she breathed through her mouth her throat and lungs hurt. If she breathed through her nose the fine hairs in her nostrils froze when she inhaled. She wound her scarf around to cover her mouth and looked at her watch. Half an hour max; any longer and the car wouldn't start. It was a big parking lot with spaces for at least four hundred cars. Her light-red Escort looked small and insignificant beside Sven-Erik Stålnacke's Volvo 740. A radio car was parked next to

Sven-Erik's Volvo. Apart from that there were only a dozen or so cars, completely covered in snow. The forensic team must have gone already. She started to walk up the narrow path to the church on Sandstensberget. The frost lay like icing on the birch trees, and right at the top of the hill the mighty Crystal Church soared up into the night sky, surrounded by stars and planets. It stood there like a gigantic illuminated ice cube, shimmering with the Aurora Borealis.

All bloody show, she thought as she struggled up the bank. This lot are rolling in money; they ought to be giving some of their cash to Save the Children instead. But I suppose it's more fun to sing gospel songs in a huge church than to dig wells in Africa.

In the distance she could see her colleagues Sven-Erik Stålnacke, Sergeant Tommy Rantakyrö and Inspector Fred Olsson outside the church door. Sven-Erik, bareheaded as usual, was standing quite still, leaning slightly backwards with his hands deep in the warm pockets of his fleece. The two younger men were bounding about like excited puppies. She couldn't hear them, but she could see Rantakyrö's and Olsson's eager chatter coming out of their mouths like white bubbles. The puppies barked happily in greeting as soon as they caught sight of her.

"Hi," yapped Tommy Rantakyrö, "how's it going?"

"Fine," she called back cheerfully.

"Soon we'll be saying hello to your stomach first, then you'll turn up quarter of an hour later," said Fred Olsson.

Anna-Maria laughed.

She met Sven-Erik's serious gaze. Small icicles had formed in his walrus moustache.

"Thanks for coming," he said. "I hope you've had breakfast, because what's in there won't exactly give you an appetite. Shall we go in?"

"Do you want us to wait for you?"

Fred Olsson was stamping his feet up and down in the snow. He was looking from Sven-Erik to Anna-Maria and back again. Sven-Erik was supposed to be taking over during Anna-Maria's leave, so technically he was in charge now. But since Anna-Maria was here as well it was a bit difficult to know who was making the decisions.

Anna-Maria kept quiet and looked at Sven-Erik. She was only there to keep him company.

"It would be good if you could hang on," said Sven-Erik, "so we don't suddenly get somebody coming along who has no business here before the body has been collected. But by all means come and stand inside the door if you're cold."

"Hell no, we can stand outside, I just wondered, that's all," Fred Olsson assured them.

"No problem." Tommy Rantakyrö grinned with blue lips. "We're men after all. Men don't feel the cold."

Sven-Erik went into the church right behind Anna-Maria and pulled the heavy door shut behind them. They walked slowly through the cloakroom, slumbering in the twilight. Long ranks of empty coat hangers rattled like an out-of-tune glockenspiel, set in motion by the draught as the cold air outside met the warmth inside. Two swing doors led into the main body of the church. Sven-Erik instinctively lowered his voice as they went in.

"It was Viktor Strandgård's sister who rang the main office around three. She'd found him dead and she used the phone in the pastor's office."

"Where is she? At the station?"

"Well, no. We don't know where she is. I left instructions to get somebody out there looking for her. There was nobody in the church when Tommy and Freddy got here."

"What did the technicians say?"

"Look but don't touch."

The body was lying in the middle of the central aisle. Anna-Maria stopped a little way from it.

"Fucking hell," she burst out.

"I did tell you," said Sven-Erik, who was standing just behind her.

Anna-Maria pulled a little tape recorder from the inside pocket of her jacket. She hesitated for a moment. She usually spoke into it rather than making notes. But this wasn't really her case. Maybe she ought to keep quiet and just sort of go along with Sven-Erik?

Don't go making everything so complicated, she told herself, and switched on the tape recorder without even looking at her colleague.

"The time is five thirty-five," she said into the microphone. "It's the sixteenth, no seventeenth, of February. I'm standing in The Source of All Our Strength church and looking at someone who, as far as we know at the moment, is Viktor Strandgård, generally known as the Paradise Boy. The dead man is lying in the middle of the aisle. He appears to have been well and truly slit open, because he absolutely stinks and the carpet beneath the body is wet. This wetness is presumably blood, but it's a little difficult to tell because he is lying on a red carpet. His clothes are also covered in blood and it isn't possible to see very much of the wound in his stomach; it does seem, however, that some of his intestines are protruding, but the doctor can confirm that later. He's wearing jeans and a jumper. The soles of his shoes are dry and the carpet under his shoes is not wet. His eyes have been gouged out. . . ."

Anna-Maria broke off and switched off the tape recorder. She moved round the body and bent over the face. She had been about to say that he made a beautiful corpse, but there were limits to what she could think aloud in front of Sven-Erik. The dead man's face made her think of King Oedipus. She had seen the play on video at school. At the time she hadn't been particularly affected by the scene where he put out his own eyes, but now the image came back to her with remarkable clarity. She needed to pee again. And she mustn't forget about the car. Best get going. She switched on the tape recorder again.

"The eyes have been gouged out and the long hair is covered in blood. There must be a wound to the back of the head. There is a cut on the right of the neck, but no bleeding, and the hands are missing. . . ."

Anna-Maria turned inquiringly to Sven-Erik, who was pointing toward the rows of chairs. She bent down with difficulty and looked along the floor among the chairs.

"Oh, I see, one hand is lying three meters away under the chairs. But where's the other?"

Sven-Erik shrugged.

"None of the chairs has been overturned," she continued. "There are no indications of a struggle; what do you think, Sven-Erik?"

"No," replied Sven-Erik, who disliked speaking into the tape recorder.

"Who took the photos?"

"Simon Larsson."

Good, she thought. That meant they would have good pictures.

"Otherwise the church is tidy," she went on. "This is the first time I've been in here. There are hundreds of frosted lamps along those sections of the walls that are not made of glass bricks. How high would it be? Must be more than ten meters. Huge windows in the roof. Blue chairs in rows, straight as a die. How many people would fit in here? Two thousand?"

"Plus the pulpit," said Sven-Erik.

He wandered round and allowed his gaze to sweep over every surface like a vacuum cleaner.

Anna-Maria turned and looked at the pulpit towering behind her. The organ pipes soared upward and met their own reflection in the windows in the roof. It was an impressive sight.

"There isn't really very much more to add," said Anna-Maria hesitantly, as if some idea might work its way up from her subconscious and creep out through a gap in the syllables as she spoke. "There's something . . . something that makes me feel frustrated when I look at all this. Besides the fact that this corpse is in the worst state I've ever seen—"

"Hey, you two! His lordship the assistant chief prosecutor is on his way up the hill."

Tommy Rantakyrö had stuck his head in through the doorway.

"Who the hell rang him?" asked Sven-Erik, but Tommy had already disappeared.

Anna-Maria looked at him. Four years ago when she became team leader Sven-Erik had hardly spoken to her for the first six months. He had been deeply hurt because she had got the job he wanted. And now that he'd found his feet as her second in command, he didn't want to take that extra step forward. She made a mental note to give him a pep talk later. But now he'd just have to manage by himself. Just as Assistant Chief Prosecutor Carl von Post stormed in through the door, she gave Sven-Erik an encouraging look.

"What the fuck is going on here?" yelled von Post.

He yanked off his fur hat and his hand went up to his mane of curly hair from sheer force of habit. He stamped his feet. The short walk up from the car park was enough to turn his feet to ice in his smart shoes from Church's. He strode up to Anna-Maria and Sven-Erik but recoiled when he caught sight of the body on the floor.

"Oh, bloody hell," he burst out, and looked anxiously down at his shoes to check whether he might have got them dirty.

"Why didn't somebody ring me?" he went on, turning to Sven-Erik. "From now on I'm taking over the investigation, and you can expect a serious talk with the chief if you've been keeping me in the dark."

"Nobody's been keeping you in the dark, we didn't know what had happened and we still don't really know anything," ventured Sven-Erik.

"Crap!" snapped the prosecutor. "And what the hell are you doing here?"

This was directed at Anna-Maria, who was standing in silence gazing at Viktor Strandgård's mutilated arms.

"I rang her," explained Sven-Erik.

"I see," said von Post through clenched teeth. "So you rang her, but not me."

Sven-Erik said nothing, and Carl von Post looked at Anna-Maria, who raised her eyes and met his gaze calmly.

Carl von Post clamped his teeth together so hard that his jaws ached. He'd always had a problem with this midget of a police-woman. She seemed to have her male colleagues on the Investigation squad by the balls, and he couldn't work out why. And just look at her. One meter fifty at the most in her stocking feet, with a long horse's face which more or less covered half her body. At the moment she was ready for a circus freak show with her enormous belly. Like a grotesque cube, she was as broad as she was tall. It just had to be the inevitable result of generations of inbreeding in those little isolated Lapp villages.

He waved his hand in the air as if to waft away his sharp words and started on a new tack.

"How are you feeling, Anna-Maria?" he asked, pasting on a gentle and sympathetic smile.

"Fine," she answered without expression. "And you?"

"I reckon we'll have the press round our ears in maybe an hour or so. It'll be all hell let loose, so tell me what you know so far about the murder and the dead man; all I know is that he was a religious celebrity."

Carl von Post sat down on one of the blue chairs and pulled off his gloves.

"I'll let Sven-Erik tell you," said Anna-Maria in a laconic but not unfriendly tone. "I'm supposed to be on desk duty until my time comes. I came along with Sven-Erik because he asked me to, and because two pairs of eyes see more than... well, you know all that. And now I need to pee. If you'll excuse me."

She noticed with satisfaction the pained smile on von Post's face as she went off to the bathroom. To think that the word "pee" could offend his ears quite so much. She wouldn't mind betting that his wife made sure she directed the stream of liquid onto the porcelain when she peed so his delicate little ears wouldn't be troubled by the sound of piddling. Bloody man.

"Well," said Sven-Erik when Anna-Maria had disappeared, "you can see things for yourself, and we don't know much more. Somebody has killed him. And they've done it very thoroughly, I must say. The dead man is Viktor Strandgård, or the Paradise Boy as he's known. He's the main attraction in this huge church community. Nine years ago he was involved in a terrible car accident. He died at the hospital. His heart stopped and everything, but they got him back, and he could tell them all about what had happened during the operation and when they were trying to resuscitate him, that the doctor had dropped his glasses and so on. And then he said he'd been in heaven. He met angels, and Jesus. Anyway, one of the nurses who'd been involved in the operation was saved, and the woman who ran into him, and suddenly the whole of Kiruna was one big revivalist meeting. The three biggest free churches joined together to make one new church, The Source of All Our Strength. The congregation grew and in recent years they've built this church, started their own school and their own nursery, and held huge revivalist meetings. Tons of money is pouring in, and people come here from all over the world. Viktor Strandgård is—or was, I should say—employed by the church full-time, and he's written a best seller. . . ."

"Himlen Tur och Retur, *Heaven and Back*."

"That's the one. He's their golden calf, he's been in all the papers, even *Expressen* and *Aftonbladet*, so there's bound to be a lot written now. And the TV cameras will be up here."

"Exactly," said von Post, and stood up, looking impatient. "I don't want anyone leaking information to the press. I'll take over all contact with the media and I want you to report to me on a regular basis; anything that emerges during interrogation and so on, is that clear? Everything is to be passed on to me. When the journalists start asking questions you can say I'll be holding a press conference on the steps of the church at twelve midday today. What's your next move?"

"We need to get hold of the sister, she was the one who found the body; then we need to speak to the three pastors. The medical examiner is on his way from Luleå; he should be here any minute now."

"Good. I want a report on the cause of death and a credible version of the course of events leading up to it at eleven-thirty, so be by the phone then. That's all. If you're done here I'll just take a look around on my own for a bit."

"Oh, come on," said Anna-Maria to Sven-Erik Stålnacke. "This has got to be better than sitting around interviewing pissed-up snowmobile riders."

Her Ford Escort wouldn't start, and Sven-Erik was giving her a lift home.

It was just as well, she thought; he needed encouragement so that he didn't get fed up with the job.

"It's that bastard von Pisspot," Sven-Erik replied with a grimace. "As soon as I have anything to do with him I just feel like saying sod the lot of it, and just going through the motions every day until it's time to go home."

"Well, don't think about him now. Think about Viktor Strandgård instead. The lunatic who killed him is out there somewhere, and you're going to find him. Let that pompous old fool scream and shout and talk to the newspapers. The rest of us know who actually does all the work."

"How can I not think about him? He's watching me like a hawk all the time."

"I know."

She looked out through the car window. The houses still lay sleeping in the darkness of the streets, with just an occasional light in a window. The orange paper Advent stars were still hanging here and there. This year nobody had burned to death. There had been fights and the usual dose of misery, but no worse than usual. She felt slightly sick. Hardly surprising. She'd been up for a good hour and had eaten nothing. She realized she wasn't concentrating on what Sven-Erik was saying, and rewound her memory to catch up. He'd asked how she'd managed to work with von Post.

"We never actually had that much to do with each other," she said.

"Look, I could really do with your help, Anna-Maria. There's going to be a hell of a lot of pressure on those of us working on this case, without that bully on top of everything else. I could do with a colleague's support right now."

"That sounds like blackmail to me." Anna-Maria couldn't help laughing.

"I'll do whatever it takes. Blackmail, threats. In any case, it's good for you to get a bit of exercise. You could at least be there and talk to the sister when we find her. Just help me get started."

"Fine, ring me when you've found her."

Sven-Erik bent forward over the steering wheel and looked up at the night sky.

"Just look at the moon," he said with a smile. "I should be out there hunting foxes."

In Meijer & Ditzinger's offices Rebecka Martinsson took the telephone from Maria Taube.

A Moomin troll, Maria had said. But there was only one Moomintroll. The image of a snub-nosed face suddenly materialized on the
inside of her eyelids.

"Rebecka Martinsson."

"It's Sanna. I don't know if you've heard it on the news already,
but Viktor's dead."

"Yes, I heard it just now. I'm sorry."

Without thinking, Rebecka picked up a pen from the table and
wrote, "Say no! NO!" on a yellow Post-it note.

On the other end of the phone Sanna Strandgård took a deep
breath.

"I know we haven't kept in touch lately, but you're still my closest friend. I didn't know who to call. I was the one who found Viktor in the church, and I . . . but perhaps you're busy?"

Busy? thought Rebecka, and felt confusion rising in her like mercury in a hot thermometer. What kind of question is that? Did Sanna seriously think that anybody could answer that question?

"Of course I'm not busy when it involves something like this," she answered gently, pressing her hand to her eyes. "Did you say you found him?"

"It was terrible." Sanna's voice was quiet and flat. "I got to the church at about three in the morning. He was supposed to have come over to me and the girls for a meal in the evening, but he never turned up. I just thought he'd forgotten. You know what he's like when he's alone in the church, praying; he forgets what time it is and where he is. I often tell him, 'You can be that sort of Christian when you're a young guy, and you're not responsible for any kids. I have to take the chance when I can, and say a prayer sitting on the toilet.' "

She was quiet for a moment, and Rebecka wondered whether she had realized that she was talking about Viktor as if he were still alive.

"But then I woke up in the middle of the night," said Sanna, "and I had the feeling that something had happened."

She broke off and began to hum a psalm. The Lord is My Shepherd.

Rebecka fixed her eyes on the flickering text on the screen in front of her. But the letters jumped out of their places, regrouped and formed a picture of Viktor Strandgård's angelic face covered in blood.

Sanna Strandgård was talking again. Her voice was like thin September ice. Rebecka recognized that voice. Cold black water swirled under the shining surface.

"They'd cut off his hands. And his eyes were, well, it was all so strange. When I turned him over the back of his head was completely . . . I think I'm going mad. And the police are looking for me. They came to the house early this morning, but I told the girls to be as quiet as mice, and we didn't open the door. The police probably believe I murdered my own brother. Then I took the girls and left. I'm so scared of cracking up. But that's not the worst thing."

"No?" asked Rebecka.

"Sara was with me when I found him. Well, Lova was too, but she was sleeping in the sledge outside the church. And Sara is in total shock. She won't speak. I've tried to reach her, but she just sits and stares out through the window and tucks her hair behind her ears."

Rebecka could feel her stomach tying itself in knots.

"For God's sake, Sanna. Get some help. Ring the Psychiatric Service and tell them it's an emergency. Both you and the girls could do with some support at the moment. I know it sounds dramatic, but—"

"I can't, you know I can't," wailed Sanna. "Mum and Dad will say I've gone mad and they'll try to take the girls away from me. You know what they're like. And the church is totally against psychologists and hospitals and all that. They'd never understand. I daren't talk to the police, they'll just make everything worse. And I daren't answer the phone in case it's some reporter; it was difficult enough when the revival first started, with everybody ringing up and saying he was hallucinating and he was crazy."

"But you do understand that you can't just stay away," pleaded Rebecka.

"I can't cope with this, I can't cope with this," said Sanna as if she were talking to herself. "I'm very sorry I rang and disturbed you, Rebecka. You get on with your work now."

Rebecka swore to herself. Shit, shit, shit.

"I'll come," she sighed. "You have to let the police interview you. I'll come up and go with you, okay?"

"Okay," whispered Sanna.

"Can you manage to drive the car? Can you get to my grandmother's house in Kurravaara?"

"I can ask someone to give me a lift."

"Good. There's never anyone there in the winter. Take Sara and Lova. You remember where the key is. Get the fire going. I'll be there this afternoon. Can you manage until then?"

Rebecka stared at the telephone when she had put the receiver down. She felt empty and confused.

"Unbelievable," she said to Maria Taube in an exhausted voice. "She didn't even have to ask me."

Rebecka looked down at her watch. Then she closed her eyes, breathed in through her nose and straightened her head at the same time, then breathed out through her mouth and let her shoulders drop. Maria had seen her do it many times. Before negotiations and important meetings. Or when she was sitting working in the middle of the night with a deadline hanging over her.

"How do you feel?" asked Maria.

"I don't think I want to find out."

Rebecka shook her head and let her gaze fly out through the window to avoid Maria's troubled eyes. She bit her lips hard from the inside. It had stopped raining.

"Listen, kid, you shouldn't work so bloody hard," said Maria gently. "Sometimes it's a good idea just to let go and scream a bit."

Rebecka clasped her hands on her lap.

Let go, she thought. What happens if you find out you keep on falling? And what happens if you can't stop screaming. Suddenly you're fifty. Pumped full of drugs. Shut up in some mental hospital. With the scream that never stops inside your head.

"That was Viktor Strandgård's sister," she said, and was surprised at how calm she sounded. "Evidently she found him in the church. It seems as if she and her two daughters could do with some help right now, so I'm going to take some time off and go up there for a few days. I'll take my laptop and work from up there."

"This Viktor Strandgård, he was something big up there?" asked Maria.

Rebecka nodded.

"He had a near-death experience, and then there was a kind of religious explosion in Kiruna."

"I remember," said Maria. "It was in the evening papers. He'd been to heaven, and he said that if you fell over, it didn't hurt; the ground just sort of received you into its embrace. I thought it sounded lovely."

"Mmm." Rebecka went on, "And he said he'd been sent back to this earthly life to tell everyone that God had great plans for Christianity in Kiruna. A great revival was coming, and it would spread from the north over the whole world. Wonders and miracles would happen if the churches would only unite and believe."

"Believe in what?"

"In the power of God. In the vision. In the end all those who believed in everything joined together to form a new church, The Source of All Our Strength. And then the whole of copper red Kiruna turned into one big revivalist meeting. Viktor wrote a book that was translated into loads of languages. He stopped studying and started preaching. They built a new church, the Crystal Church; it was supposed to make people think of the ice church and the ice sculptures they build in Jukkasjärvi every winter. Above all, it wasn't meant to remind anyone of the Kiruna church, which is really dark inside."

"And what about you? Were you part of all this?"

"I was already a member of the Mission church before Viktor's accident. So I was there from the start."

"And now?" asked Maria.

"Now I'm a heathen," said Rebecka with a mirthless smile. "The pastors and the elders requested that I leave the church."

"But why?"

"It's a long story; some other time."

"Okay," said Maria hesitantly. "What do you think Måns is going to say when you tell him you're taking some leave at such short notice?"

"Nothing. He's just going to kill me, tear me limb from limb and feed my body to the fish in Nybroviken. I'll have to talk to him as soon as he gets in, but first I'll ring the police in Kiruna so they don't pull Sanna in for questioning; she won't be able to cope with that."

Assistant Chief Prosecutor Carl von Post stood at the door of the Crystal Church and stared at the people who were getting on with the business of packing up Viktor Strandgård's body. The police surgeon, Senior Medical Examiner Lars Pohjanen, was drawing heavily on a cigarette as usual, mumbling orders to Anna Granlund, the autopsy technician, and two burly men with a stretcher.

"Try and loop his hair up so it doesn't get caught in the zip. Pull the plastic round the whole thing and try to keep the intestines inside the body when you lift it. Anna, can you sort out a paper bag for the hand?"

A murder, thought von Post. And a sodding awful murder. Not some miserable bloody tale of an alky who finally kills the old woman more or less by mistake after a week on the booze. A terrible murder. Worse than that—the terrible murder of a celebrity.

And it was all his. It belonged to him. All he had to do was take the helm, let the whole world switch on the spotlights and sail straight into fame. And then he could get away from this pit. He had never meant to stay here, but his qualifications had only been good enough to get a place with the court in Gällivare. Then he'd got a job with the prosecutor's office. He'd applied for plenty of jobs in Stockholm, but without success. All of a sudden the years had gone by.

He stepped to one side to let the men carrying the stretcher, with its well-sealed gray plastic body bag, pass by. Senior Medical Examiner Lars Pohjanen came limping behind, shoulders slightly hunched as if he were cold, eyes fixed on the ground. The cigarette was still dangling from the corner of his mouth. His hair was usually plastered over his shiny bald head; now it was hanging tiredly down over his ears. Anna Granlund was just behind him. She was carrying a paper bag containing Viktor Strandgård's hand. When she caught sight of von Post her lips tightened. He stopped them on their way out.

"So?" he said challengingly.

Pohjanen looked uncomprehending.

"What can you tell me at this stage?" asked von Post impatiently.

Pohjanen took his cigarette between his thumb and his index finger and drew heavily on it before he allowed it to leave his thin lips.

"Well, I haven't actually performed the autopsy yet," he answered slowly.

Carl von Post could feel his pulse rate rising. He wasn't going to stand for anybody being obstructive or awkward.

"But surely you must have noticed something already? I want ongoing reports and detailed information at all times."

He snapped his fingers as if to illustrate the speed with which all this information was to be passed on.

Anna Granlund looked at the snapping fingers; it occurred to her that she used exactly the same gesture to her dogs.

Pohjanen stood in silence, looking at the floor. The sound of his breathing, slightly too fast, quietened only when he raised the cigarette to his lips and inhaled with great concentration. Carl von Post met Anna Granlund's fierce gaze.

You can stare, he thought. A year ago at the police Christmas party you were giving me a very different look. For God's sake, I'm surrounded by spastics and morons. Pohjanen looked worse now than before the operation and his sick leave.

"Well, then?" he said challengingly, when he thought the doctor had been silent for long enough.

Lars Pohjanen looked up and met the prosecutor's raised eyebrows.

"What I know at this moment," he said in his rasping voice, which was not much more than a loud whisper, "is that first of all he's dead, and that secondly death was probably due to externally applied force. That's all, so you can let us pass now, sonny."

The prosecutor saw how the corners of Anna Granlund's mouth twitched downward in an attempt to suppress a smile as they walked past him.

"When will I get the autopsy report?" snapped von Post as he followed them to the door.

"When we've finished," replied Pohjanen, and let the church door slam shut in the assistant chief prosecutor's face.

Von Post raised his right hand and caught the swinging door; at the same time he was forced to root in his inside pocket with his left hand because his cell phone had started to vibrate.

It was the girl from the police switchboard.

"I've got a Rebecka Martinsson on the line saying she knows where Viktor Strandgård's sister is and she wants to arrange a time for an interview. Tommy Rantakyrö and Fred Olsson have gone to look for the sister, so I didn't know whether to put her through to them or to you."

"You did exactly the right thing; put her through to me."

Von Post allowed his gaze to wander up the aisle of the church as he waited for the call to be connected. It was evident that the architect had had a clear vision in mind: the long red handwoven carpet ran along the nave right up to the choir stalls, and on either side stood rows of blue chairs with wavy contours on the back. It made you think immediately of the Bible story of the parting of the Red Sea. He began to stroll up the aisle.

"Hello," said a woman's voice on the telephone.

He answered with his name and title, and she went on.

"My name is Rebecka Martinsson. I'm calling on behalf of Sanna Strandgård; I understand that you wish to speak to her with regard to the murder."

"Yes; you have information about where we can find her."

"Well, not exactly," continued the polite and almost too well-spoken voice. "Since Sanna Strandgård wishes me to accompany her to the interview, and since I am in Stockholm at the moment, I wanted to check with whoever is in charge of the investigation to see if it would be more convenient for us to come in this evening, or if tomorrow would be better."

"No."

"Sorry?"

"No," said von Post, not bothering to hide his irritation, "it isn't convenient this evening and it isn't convenient tomorrow. I don't know whether you've quite grasped this, Rebecka Whatever-your-name-is, but this is actually an ongoing murder investigation, for which I am responsible, and I want to talk to Sanna Strandgård right now. I think you should advise your friend not to stay in hiding, because I'm quite prepared to issue a warrant for her arrest in her absence and to post her as wanted by the police straightaway. As for you, there is a crime called obstructing the police in the course of their duty. If you're convicted you can end up in prison. So now I would like you to tell me where Sanna Strandgård is."

For a few seconds there was silence. Then the young woman's voice could be heard again. She spoke extremely slowly, almost drawling, and she was clearly exercising considerable self-control.

"I'm afraid there has been a slight misunderstanding. I am not ringing to ask your permission to come in for an interview with Sanna Strandgård at a later stage, but to inform you that she intends to cooperate fully with the police and that an interview cannot take place before this evening at the earliest. Sanna Strandgård and I are not friends. I am a lawyer with Meijer & Ditzinger; I don't know whether you are familiar with the name up there—"

"Well, actually, I was born in—"

"And I'd think twice about making threats," the woman interrupted von Post's attempt to pass a comment. "Any attempt to frighten me into telling you where Sanna Strandgård is seems to me to be bordering on professional misconduct, and if you issue her name as wanted by the police without her being an actual suspect, simply because she is waiting to be interviewed until her legal representative can be present, I can guarantee that a notice from the Justice Department will be heading your way."

Before von Post could answer, Rebecka Martinsson continued, her tone of voice suddenly friendly.

"Meijer & Ditzinger doesn't wish to cause any difficulties. We normally have a very good working relationship with the Prosecution Service; at least that is our experience in the Stockholm area. I hope you will permit me to guarantee that Sanna Strandgård will present herself for an interview as agreed. Let's say eight o'clock this evening at the police station."

She put the phone down.

"Shit," exclaimed Carl von Post as he realized that he had trodden in some blood and something sticky; he didn't want to think about what that might be.

He rubbed his shoes along the carpet on the way to the door, feeling slightly sick. He'd deal with that stuck-up cow when she turned up tonight. Now, however, it was time to get ready for the press conference. He rubbed his hand over his face. He needed a shave. In three days he would meet the press with just a little stubble, looking for all the world like an exhausted man giving his all in the hunt for a murderer. But today he needed to be clean shaven, hair just a little tousled. They'd love him. They just wouldn't be able to help themselves.

Måns Wenngren, a lawyer and a partner with Meijer & Ditzinger, sat behind his desk and looked at Rebecka Martinsson with a sour expression. Her whole attitude annoyed him. She didn't look defensive, with her arms folded over her chest. Instead her arms were hanging straight down by her sides as if she were standing in the ice-cream queue. She had explained the situation and was waiting for an answer. Her expressionless gaze rested on the erotic Japanese woodcut on the wall. A young man, so young that he still had long hair, was kneeling in front of a woman, a prostitute, both with their sexual organs exposed. Other women usually tried to avoid looking at the graphic representation, nearly two hundred years old. Måns Wenngren could often see how their eyes were instinctively drawn to the picture, like curious dogs sniffing the air. But they never sniffed for long. They dropped their eyes straightaway, or forced themselves to look somewhere else in the room.

"How many days will you be away?" he asked. "You're entitled to two days off with pay for family circumstances, will that be enough?"

"No," replied Rebecka Martinsson. "And it isn't my family; I'm what you might call an old friend of the family."

Something in the way she spoke gave Måns Wenngren the feeling that she was lying.

"Unfortunately I can't say for sure how long I'll be away," said Rebecka, looking him calmly in the eye. "I've got quite a bit of holiday owing and—"

She broke off.

"And what?" continued her boss. "I hope you're not about to start talking to me about overtime, Rebecka, because I'd be very disappointed in you. I've said it before and I'll say it again, if you lot feel you can't cope with the work during normal hours, then by all means resign. Any overtime is voluntary and unpaid. Otherwise I might just as well let you disappear on a year's sabbatical with pay."

He added the last sentence with a conciliatory laugh, but quickly resumed his censorious expression when she didn't even give a hint of a smile in return.

Rebecka regarded her boss in silence before she replied. He had started to read some papers lying in front of him, but in a preoccupied manner, as if to indicate that her audience was now at an end. The day's post lay in a neat pile. A few bits and pieces from Georg Jensen stood to attention along the edge of the desk. No photos. She knew that he had been married and had two grown-up sons. But that was all. He never mentioned them. No one else talked about them either. You found out about things slowly in the office. The senior partners loved to gossip, it was true, but they were sensible enough to gossip only with each other, not with the juniors or associates. The secretaries were far too timid to dare to reveal any secrets. But now and again somebody got a bit too drunk at a party and said something they shouldn't, and gradually you became one of those in the know. She knew that Måns drank too much, but then practically everybody who met him in the street knew that. He actually looked quite good, with his dark curly hair and his blue husky-dog eyes.

Although he was starting to look a bit frayed at the edges. Bags under his eyes and a bit overweight. He was still one of the very best in the country when it came to taxation cases, both criminal and civil. And as long as he brought in the cash, his colleagues were happy to let him drink in peace. It was the money that mattered. Presumably it would be too expensive for the firm to help somebody to stop drinking. A rehab clinic and sick pay, that would cost money, then on top of that there was the loss of income for the firm. His situation was probably the same as many others'. When you drank, your private life was the first thing to fall apart.

She still felt the prickle of humiliation when she thought about last year's office Christmas party. Måns had danced and flirted with all the other female lawyers during the evening. Toward the end of the party he had come over to her. Crumpled, drunk and full of self-pity, he had put his hand round the back of her neck and made a rambling speech that had ended in a pathetic attempt to get her to go home with him, or maybe just into his office, who knows. After that she was at least clear about what she was in his eyes. The last resort. The one you have a go at when you've tried everybody else and you're half a millimeter from unconsciousness. Since then relations between Rebecka and Måns had been frosty. He never laughed or chatted in a natural way with her as he did with the others. She communicated with him mostly via e-mail and notes placed on his desk when he wasn't in. This year she hadn't gone to the Christmas party.

"We'll call it holiday, then," she said without a hint of a smile. "And I'll take the laptop and do some work from up there."

"Fine, it's all the same to me," said Måns, his voice heavy with regret. "After all, it's your colleagues who'll have a heavier workload. I'll give Wickman's to somebody else."

Rebecka forced herself not to clench her fists. Bastard. He was punishing her. Wickman's was her client. She had brought in the business, she had developed an excellent relationship with them, and as soon as the tax arrears assessment was out of the way, they were going to start preparing the legal transfer of the small company to the younger members of the family. Besides which, they liked her.

"Do whatever you think is appropriate," she answered with an almost imperceptible shrug, and allowed her eyes to wander along the fringes of the Persian rug. "You can reach me via my e-mail address if anything comes up."

Måns Wenngren felt the urge to go up to her, grab hold of her hair, yank her head backwards and force her to look him in the eye. Or just give her a slap.

She turned to leave the room.

"So how are you getting up there?" he asked before she got through the door. "Do they have flights all the way up to Kiruna, or will you have to catch the reindeer caravan in Umeå?"

"There are flights," she replied neutrally.

Just as if she had taken his question completely seriously.

Inspector Anna-Maria Mella leaned back in her office chair and looked listlessly at the documents spread out in front of her. Stale and old. Investigations that had ground to a halt. Unsolved cases: robberies from shops, stolen cars—all several years old. She picked up the folder nearest to her. Domestic violence, a nasty one, but the woman had later withdrawn the charge and insisted that she'd fallen down the stairs.

That was a bloody awful case, thought Anna-Maria, remembering the unpleasant photographs taken at the hospital.

She picked up another file. Stolen tires from a firm down on the industrial estate. A witness had seen someone cutting the wire fence and loading the tires onto his Toyota Hilux, but during a later interview the witness was suddenly unable to remember a single thing. It was as clear as daylight that he'd been threatened.

Anna-Maria sighed. There was no money for witness protection or anything else when it came to a few poxy tires being nicked. She typed "Toyota Hilux" into the computer and made a note of the owner's name. Petty criminals, little tyrants who take whatever they want. It was more than likely that she would come across him in some other context in the future. She ran a multiple query on the owner. Convictions for assault and illegal possession of a firearm. He was also listed as a suspect several times.

Pull yourself together, she told herself. Don't just sit here opening and closing files and surfing databases.

She put the tire theft to one side. They weren't going to get anywhere with that one. The prosecutor might as well drop it. From the coffee machine outside her door she could hear the sound of a plastic cup dropping down and the loud whine as it was filled with that wretched instant machine coffee. For a while she hoped it might be Sven-Erik, and that he might come in with some news about Viktor Strandgård. But then she heard the steps disappearing down the corridor; it must be somebody else.

"Don't even think about it," she said half out loud, and reached for another folder from the pile.

Her gaze immediately strayed away from the text and wandered aimlessly over the desk. She looked sadly at the mug of cold tea. The very thought of coffee almost made her throw up at the moment. But she'd never been a tea drinker either. It just stood there and went cold, every time. And Coke made her stomach too gassy.

When the phone rang she snatched up the receiver. She thought it would be Sven-Erik, but it was Lars Pohjanen, the medical examiner.

"I've finished the initial autopsy report," he said in his rasping coffee percolator voice. "Do you want to come down?"

"Well, Sven-Erik's in charge of this one," she said hesitantly. "And von Post."

Pohjanen's voice became irritated.

"I've no intention of hunting all over town for Sven-Erik, and his lordship the prosecutor can read the report. I'll pack up and get back to Luleå, then."

"No, damn it. I'll come," said Anna-Maria, just as she heard the conversation at the other end being cut off with a click.

I hope the old bastard heard that, she thought as she pulled on her leather boots. He'll probably have gone by the time I get to the hospital.

She found Lars Pohjanen in the hospital security guards' smoking room. He was slumped on a sturdy green seventies sofa. His eyes were closed, and only the glowing cigarette in his hand gave any indication that he might be awake, or even alive.

"So," he said without opening his eyes, "aren't you interested in Viktor Strandgård, deceased? I would have thought this was just up your street, Mella."

"I'm supposed to be pushing paper until I have the baby," she said, standing in the doorway. "But it's better if I talk to you before you go, rather than nobody doing it."

He gave a croaky laugh that turned into a feeble cough, opened his eyes and fixed her with his piercing blue gaze.

"You're going to dream about him at night, Mella. Come and talk it through, otherwise you're going to be running round with the pram interrogating suspects while you're on maternity leave. Shall we?"

He made an exaggerated gesture, inviting her into the autopsy room.

The room where the autopsies were held was very neat. A clean stone floor, three stainless-steel tables, red plastic boxes stacked according to size under the sink, two hand basins where Anna Granlund made sure there was a constant supply of spotlessly clean hand towels. The dissection table had been sluiced down and dried off. Out in the sluice room the dishwasher was running. The only thing that made you think of death was a long line of ID-marked transparent plastic jars containing gray or light brown bits of brain or internal organs, preserved in formalin so that tests could be carried out on them at a later stage. And Viktor Strandgård's body. He was lying on his back on one of the tables. An incision ran across the back of his head from one ear to the other, and the whole of his scalp had been drawn away from his skull up over the forehead to expose his cranium. Two long wounds ran across his stomach and were held together with rough sutures. One had been made by the autopsy technician in order to allow an examination of the internal organs. There were also several short wounds on the body; Anna-Maria had seen marks like these before. Knife wounds. He was clean, stitched up and sluiced down, pale under the fluorescent lights. It bothered Anna-Maria to see his slender body lying naked on the cold steel table. She had kept her fleecy jacket on.

Lars Pohjanen pulled on a green surgical gown, shoved his feet into his worn old clogs, which bore only vestiges of the white they had once been, and slipped on his thin, supple rubber gloves.

"How are the kids?" he asked.

"Jenny and Petter are fine. Marcus is suffering from a broken heart and is mostly just lying on his bed with his headphones on, developing tinnitus."

"Poor kid," said Pohjanen with genuine sympathy, and turned to Viktor Strandgård.

Anna-Maria wondered whether he meant Marcus or Viktor Strandgård.

"Do you mind?" she asked, and took her tape recorder out of her pocket. "So the others can listen later."

Pohjanen shrugged his shoulders in agreement. Anna-Maria switched on the tape recorder.

"Chronologically," he said. "First a blow to the back of the head with a blunt instrument. You and I are not really in a position to try and turn him over, but you can see it on here."

He took out a computer slide and clipped it on to the X-ray light box. Anna-Maria looked at the images in silence, thinking of the black-and-white ultrasound pictures of her baby.

"You can see the split in the skull here. And the subdural bleed. Just here."

The doctor's finger traced a dark area on the pictures.

"It might have been possible to save his life if he had suffered only the blow to the head, but probably not," he said.

"Your murderer is most likely right-handed," continued Pohjanen. "Then, after the blow to his head, he receives these two stab wounds to the stomach and the chest."

He pointed to two of the wounds on Viktor Strandgård's body.

"It's impossible to speculate about the height of the perpetrator from the blow to the back of the head, and unfortunately there are no clues from the stab wounds either. They were delivered from above, so it's my guess that Viktor Strandgård was on his knees when he received those wounds. Either that, or the perpetrator is immensely tall, like an American basketball player. But I would presume that Strandgård suffered the blow to his head first. Bang."

The doctor smacked his own bald head to illustrate the blow.

"The blow makes him fall to his knees—there are no grazes or hematomas on the knees, but the carpet was quite soft—and then the killer stabs him twice. That's why the angle of entry is sloping from above. So it's difficult to say anything about his height."

"So he died from the blow and the two stab wounds?" asked Anna-Maria.

"Yes," continued Pohjanen, suppressing a cough. "This stab wound through the wall of the rib cage splits the seventh rib bone on the left-hand side, opens the pericardium—"

"The peri—?"

"The heart sac, the right ventricle, the heart chamber. This causes a bleed into the heart and the right lung. With the second blow the knife cut through the liver and caused a bleed into the abdominal cavity and the peritoneum."

"Did he die immediately?"

Pohjanen shrugged his shoulders.

"What about the rest of his injuries?" asked Anna-Maria.

"He sustained those after death. All this damage to the torso and belly with a sharp object. These blows came from directly in front and were delivered after the moment of death. I would guess that Viktor Strandgård was lying on his back at the time. There's also this long gash which opened up the stomach."

He pointed at the long reddish blue wound in the stomach, which was now held together with rough stitches.

"And the eyes?" asked Anna-Maria, gazing at the gaping holes in Viktor Strandgård's face.

"Look at this," said Pohjanen, slotting in another X-ray plate. "Just here! Can you see this splinter that's come away from the cranium right inside the eye socket? And here! I hardly noticed it at first, but then I rinsed out the socket and looked at the skull itself. There are marks where something has scraped against the skull on the edge of the eye sockets. The murderer pushed the knife into the eyes and twisted it. Gouged them out, you could say."

"What the hell was he trying to do?" exclaimed Anna-Maria with feeling. "And the hands?"

"They were also removed after death. One was still at the scene."

"Fingerprints?"

"Maybe on the wrist stumps, but it's up to the forensic lab in Linköping to sort that out. I don't hold out much hope, though. There are a couple of decent marks around the wrists where somebody has gripped them hard, but as far as I can see, there aren't any prints. I think Linköping will say that the person who cut off the hands was wearing gloves."

Anna-Maria felt her courage fail. She was seized by a strong desire to catch the murderer. All of a sudden she felt as if she couldn't bear it if the investigation was just shelved in some archive in a few years' time. Pohjanen was right. She would probably dream about Viktor Strandgård.

"What kind of knife was it?" she asked.

"Some kind of biggish hunting knife. Too broad for a kitchen knife. It wasn't double-edged."

"What about the blunt object that hit him on the back of the head?"

"Could have been anything at all," said Pohjanen. "A spade, a large stone..."

"Isn't it odd that he was hit from behind with a weapon and then stabbed from the front?" asked Anna-Maria.

"You're the detective," said Lars Pohjanen.

"Maybe there was more than one person," wondered Anna-Maria out loud. "Anything else?"

"Not at the moment. No drugs. No alcohol. And he hadn't eaten for several days."

"What? Several days?"

Anna-Maria herself found it necessary to eat every two hours.

"He wasn't dehydrated, so it wasn't some kind of stomach bug or anorexia or anything like that. But he seems to have ingested only liquids. The lab will be able to tell you what else was in his stomach. You can switch off the tape recorder."

He passed over a copy of the preliminary autopsy report. Anna-Maria clicked off the tape recorder.

"I don't like guessing," said Pohjanen, clearing his throat. "At least not when there's a record."

He nodded in the direction of the tape recorder, which disappeared into Anna-Maria's pocket.

"But the cuts on the wrists were very neat," he went on. "You're looking for a hunter, Mella."

"So this is where you are," came a voice from the doorway.

It was Sven-Erik Stålnacke.

"Yes," replied Anna-Maria, and realized she was embarrassed in case her colleague thought she'd gone behind his back. "Pohjanen rang and he was just about to leave and..."

She stopped, angry that she'd tried to explain herself and to make excuses.

"That's fine," said Sven-Erik cheerfully. "You can tell me all about it in the car. We've got problems with our pastors. Hell, I've been looking everywhere for you. In the end I asked Sonja on the switchboard who'd phoned you. We need to go now."

Anna-Maria glanced questioningly at Pohjanen; he shrugged his shoulders and raised his eyebrows at the same time, as if to say that their business was finished.

"I see Luleå got hammered by Färjestad." Sven-Erik smirked as a parting shot to the doctor, at the same time hustling Anna-Maria along with him.

"Go on, rub it in," sighed Lars Pohjanen, fumbling in his pocket for a cigarette.

The plane to Kiruna was almost full. Hordes of foreign tourists off to drive a dog team and spend the night on reindeer skins in the ice hotel at Jukkasjärvi jostled for space with rumpled business-men returning home clutching their free fruit and newspapers.

Rebecka sank down and fastened her seat belt. The murmur of voices, the synthetic ping as the signs lit up and went off overhead and the humming of the engines lulled her into a restless sleep. She slept for the whole journey.

In her dream she is running across a cloudberry bog. It is a hot August day. The heat of the sun is making the moisture rise from the bog. Sweat and midge repellent are pouring down her forehead and into her eyes. It stings. There are tears in her eyes. A black cloud of midges creeps into her nostrils and ears. She can't see. Someone is chasing her. They're right behind her. And as always in her dreams, her legs won't carry her weight. They have no strength and the bog is waterlogged. Her feet sink deeper and deeper into the peat moss and someone, or something, is chasing her. Now she can't lift her foot. She's sinking into the bog. She tries to shout for her mummy, but only a faint sound comes from her throat. Then she feels a hand, heavy on her shoulder.

"I'm sorry, did I frighten you?"

Rebecka opened her eyes and saw a flight attendant bending over her. The woman smiled a little uncertainly and took her hand from Rebecka's shoulder.

"We're preparing to land in Kiruna; I'll have to ask you to put the back of your seat into the upright position."

Rebecka's hand flew up to her mouth. Had she been dribbling? Or worse, screaming? She didn't dare look at her neighbor, but turned to look out into the darkness. It was down there. The town. It shone like a jewel glittering at the bottom of a well, its lights surrounded by the darkness of the mountains. It felt like a blow to the stomach— and the heart.

My town, she thought, the melancholy of seeing it again blending with happiness, rage and fear in a strange mixture.

Twenty minutes later she was sitting in the rented Audi on the way down to Kurravaara. The village lay fifteen kilometers outside Kiruna. As a child she had often traveled the whole way from Kiruna down to the village on her kick sledge. It was a happy memory. Especially in the late winter when the road was covered with a wonderful layer of thick, shining ice, and nobody spoiled it with sand, salt or grit.

The moon lit up the snow-covered forest around her. The snow-drifts along the sides of the road formed a frame.

It's not right, she thought, I shouldn't have let them take this away from me. Before I go back I'm going to bloody well get the kick sledge out and have a go.

From when should I have started to handle things differently? she thought as the car swept through the forest. If I could go back in time, would I have to go right back to the first summer? Or even further back? In that case it would have to be that spring. When I first met Thomas Söderberg. When he visited my class at the Hjalmar Lundbohm School. Even then I should have behaved differently. I should have seen through him. Not been so bloody naïve. The others in the class must have been much smarter than me. Why weren't they tempted?

"Hi, everyone, may I introduce Thomas Söderberg. He's the new pastor at the Mission church. I've invited him along as a representative of the free churches."

It is Margareta Fransson who is speaking, the Religious Studies teacher.

She's smiling all the time, thinks Rebecka, why is she doing that? It isn't a happy smile, it's just submissive and conciliatory. And she buys all her clothes from A Helping Hand, an ideologically run boutique that sells products made by a women's collective in the Third World.

"You've already met Evert Aronsson, a priest from the Church of Sweden, and Andreas Gault from the Catholic Church," continues Margareta Fransson.

"I think we should be allowed to meet a Buddhist or a Muslim or something," says Nina Eriksson. "Why do we only get to meet a load of Christians?"

Nina Eriksson is the class spokeswoman and chief busybody. Loud and clear, her voice echoes round the classroom. Many support her statement and murmur in agreement.

"There isn't such a wide choice in Kiruna," Margareta Fransson apologizes halfheartedly.

Then she hands over to Thomas Söderberg.

He looks good, you have to admit. Dark brown curly hair, and long black eyelashes. He laughs and jokes, but from time to time he becomes totally serious. He's young to be a priest—or pastor, as he says. And he's wearing jeans and a shirt. He draws on the board. The picture of the bridge. It's all about how Jesus gave up his life for them. Built a bridge to God. Because God so loved the world that he gave up his only son. He addresses the class with the friendly "du" form, although he is talking to twenty-four people at the same time. He wants them to choose life. Say yes. And he answers all the questions they put to him at the end. At some of the questions he falls silent for a while. He frowns and nods thoughtfully. As if it's the first time anyone has asked these questions. As if they have given him something to think about. Much later Rebecka realizes that it was far from the first time he'd heard those questions. That the answers had been prepared a long time ago. But the person who asks the questions is made to feel special.

He ends the visit with an invitation to the Mission church summer gathering in Gällivare. Three weeks' work and Bible studies, no pay but free board and lodging.

"Dare to be curious," he urges them. "You can't be sure the Christian faith isn't for you unless you've found out what it really stands for."

Rebecka thinks he's looking straight at her as he speaks. She looks straight back at him. And she can feel the fire.

The snowplow had cleared the road right up to her grandmother's gray cottage. There was a light upstairs. Rebecka lifted out her suitcase and the supermarket carrier bag of food. She had shopped on the way. Maybe they wouldn't need it, but you never know. She locked the car.

That's the sort of person I am now, she thought. The sort of person who locks things.

"Hello!" she called when she got inside.

There was no answer, but presumably Sanna and the children had closed the upstairs door leading to the staircase, so they wouldn't have heard her.

She put down what she was carrying and took a walk around downstairs without switching on the lights. It had the characteristic smell of an old house. Lino and dampness. Musty. The furniture stood there like a collection of tired ghosts, pressing themselves against the walls in the darkness, covered with grandmother's hand-stitched linen sheets.

She went upstairs carefully, afraid of falling; the melted snow under the soles of her boots had made them slippery.

"Hello," she shouted up the stairs, but there was no reply this time either.

Rebecka opened the door to the upstairs flat and went into the narrow, dark hallway. When she bent down to unzip her boots something black came flying at her face. She screamed and tumbled backwards. Two cheerful yelps and the black thing turned out to be a lovely little dog. A pink tongue took the opportunity to acquaint itself with her face. Two more encouraging yaps and then the dog licked her again.

"Virku, come here!"

A girl of about four appeared in the open doorway. The dog did a little pirouette on Rebecka's stomach, danced over to the girl, gave her a lick, then pranced back to Rebecka. But by then Rebecka had managed to get to her feet. The dog shoved its nose into the bag of groceries instead.

"You must be Lova," said Rebecka, switching on the hall light and edging the dog away from the carrier bag with her foot at the same time.

The light fell on the girl. She had a blanket wrapped around her, and Rebecka realized it was cold in the house.

"Who are you?" asked Lova.

"My name's Rebecka," she replied briefly. "Let's go in the kitchen."

She stopped at the door and looked at the kitchen, dumbstruck. The chairs had been turned over. Grandmother's rag rug was screwed up under the kitchen table. Virku scampered up to a pile of sheets that had presumably been covering the furniture. She growled and shook them playfully. There was a powerful smell of Ajax and soap. When Rebecka looked more closely, she could see that the floor was smeared with cleaning fluid.

"What on earth!" she exclaimed. "Whatever has been going on here? Where are your mother and your big sister?"

Lova pointed at the sofa bed in the alcove. A girl of about eleven sat there, wearing a long gray sheepskin coat, maybe Sanna's. She looked up from her magazine with narrowed eyes, her mouth a thin compressed line. Rebecka felt a stab in her heart.

Sara, she thought. She's got so big. And so like Sanna. The same blond hair, but hers is straight like Viktor's.

"Hi," said Rebecka to Sara. "What's Lova been up to? Where's Sanna?"

Sara shrugged her shoulders, making it clear that it wasn't her job to keep an eye on her little sister or tabs on her mother.

"Mummy got cross," said Lova, tugging at Rebecka's sleeve. "She's in the bubble. She's lying down in there."

She pointed at the bedroom door.

"Who are you?" asked Sara suspiciously.

"My name's Rebecka, and this is my house. Partly mine anyway." She turned to Lova.

"What do you mean, 'in the bubble'?"

"When she's in the bubble she doesn't speak and she doesn't look at us," explained Lova, and couldn't help tugging at Rebecka's buttons again.

"Oh, God," sighed Rebecka, shrugging off her coat and hanging it on a hook in the hall.

It really was freezing in the house. She must get the fire going.

"I know your mummy," said Rebecka, starting to pick up the chairs. "My grandparents lived here when they were alive. Have you got soap in your hair as well?"

She looked at Lova's hair, hanging in sticky clumps. The dog sat down and tried to reach round and lick its back. Rebecka crouched down and called to the dog in the same way as her grandmother used to call the dogs at home.

"Here, girl!"

The dog came straight over to her and showed her submissiveness by attempting to lick Rebecka's mouth. Rebecka could see now that she was some sort of spitz crossbreed. The thick black coat stood out like a woolly frame round the narrow feminine head. Her eyes were black, shining with happiness. Rebecka ran her hands through the fur and sniffed at her fingers. They smelled of carbolic.

"Nice dog," she said to Sara. "Is she yours?"

Sara didn't answer.

"Two-thirds belong to Sara and one-third belongs to me," said Lova, as if she had learned it by heart.

"I want to talk to Sanna," said Rebecka, and stood up.

Lova took her hand and led her into the other room. The accommodation on the upper floor consisted of the big kitchen with the alcove for the sofa bed, and another room. This had been the children's bedroom. Grandmother and Grandfather had slept in the alcove in the kitchen. Sanna was lying on her side on one of the beds, her knees drawn up so that they were almost touching her chin. Her face was turned to the wall, and she was wearing only a T-shirt and a pair of flowery cotton knickers. Her long blond angel hair was spread over the pillow.

"Hello, Sanna," said Rebecka carefully.

The woman on the bed didn't reply, but Rebecka could see that she was breathing.

Lova picked up a blanket that was lying folded at the foot of the bed and spread it over her mother.

"She's in the bubble," she whispered.

"I understand," said Rebecka through clenched teeth.

She poked Sanna hard in the back with her forefinger.

"Come with me," said Rebecka, and took Lova back into the kitchen.

Virku trotted after them once she had checked that her mistress, lying immobile and silent on the bed, was in no danger.

"Have you had anything to eat?" asked Rebecka.

"No," replied Lova.

"You and I used to know each other when you were little," said Rebecka to Sara.

"I'm not little," shouted Lova. "I'm four!"

"Now, this is what we're going to do," decided Rebecka. "We're going to tidy up in the kitchen, I'll cook us a meal, then we'll heat up some water on the stove and we'll wash Lova and Virku."

"And I need a new top," said Lova. "Look!"

She opened the blanket and revealed a soap-smeared T-shirt.

"And you need a new top," sighed Rebecka, exhausted.

An hour later Lova and Sara were sitting eating sausage and mashed potato. Lova was wearing a pair of jeans belonging to one of Rebecka's cousins and a washed-out pale red top with cartoon characters on the front. Virku was sitting at their feet waiting patiently for her share. The wood in the stove crackled and sparked.

Rebecka glanced at the clock. Seven already. And she and Sanna had to go to the police station. The stress gnawed at her stomach.

Sara sniffed at Lova's top.

"You smell disgusting," she said.

"No she doesn't," said Rebecka with a sigh. "The clothes smell a bit funny because they've been folded up in a drawer for such a long time. But her own are even worse, so we'll just have to put up with it. Give Virku your leftover sausage."

She left the girls in the kitchen, went into the other room and closed the door.

"Sanna," she said.

Sanna didn't move. She lay in exactly the same position as before, her face turned to the wall.

Rebecka went over to the bed and stood there with her arms folded.

"I know you can hear me," she said harshly. "I'm not the same person I used to be, Sanna. I've become nastier and more impatient since then. I have no intention of sitting by you, stroking your hair and asking you what's wrong. You can get up right now and get some clothes on. Otherwise I shall take your daughters straight to Social Services and tell them that you're unable to look after them at present. Then I'll get the next plane back to Stockholm."

Still no answer. Not a movement.

"Okay," said Rebecka after a while.

She took a deep breath as if to indicate that she had finished waiting around. Then she turned and walked toward the kitchen door.

That's it, then, she thought. I'll ring the police and tell them where she is. They can carry her out of the house.

Just as she placed her hand on the door handle she heard Sanna sit up on the bed behind her.

"Rebecka" was all she said.

Rebecka hesitated for half a second. Then she turned round and leaned on the door. She folded her arms again. Like somebody's mother: Now let's get this sorted out once and for all.

And Sanna was like a little girl, chewing on her lower lip, pleading with her eyes.

"Sorry," she mumbled in her husky voice. "I know I'm the worst mother in the world and an even worse friend. Do you hate me?"

"You've got three minutes to put your clothes on and get yourself out here to eat something," ordered Rebecka, and marched out.

Sven-Erik Stålnacke had parked outside the hospital Emergency department. Anna-Maria leaned on the car door when he fumbled in his jacket pocket for the keys. It wasn't that easy to take deep breaths when the air was so cold it actually took your breath away, but she had to try and relax. Her stomach had grown as hard as a snowball on the short walk from the autopsy out to the car.

"The Church of All Our Strength has three pastors," said Sven-Erik, groping in his other pocket. "They have informed us that they are available to receive the police for the purpose of interrogation. They are setting aside one hour, no more. And they have no intention of being interrogated individually; all three of them will talk to us together. They say they wish to cooperate, but—"

"But they have no intention of cooperating," supplied Anna-Maria.

"What the hell do you do?" wondered Sven-Erik. "Go in hard, or what?"

"No, because then the whole community will just shut up like a giant clam. But you have to wonder why they're not prepared to speak to us one-on-one."

"No idea. One of them did explain. Gunnar Isaksson, his name was. But I hadn't a clue what he was talking about. Maybe you can ask when we meet them. Bloody hell, Anna-Maria, I should have had them dragged out of bed first thing this morning."

"No," replied Anna-Maria, shaking her head thoughtfully. "You couldn't have done anything differently."

The Aurora Borealis was still swirling its veils of white and green across the sky.

"It's just unbelievable," she said, tipping her head backwards. "It's been like this all winter. Have you ever known anything like it?"

"No, but it's these sun storms," replied Sven-Erik. "It looks fantastic, but any day now they're bound to decide it causes cancer. We should probably be walking around with a silver parasol to protect us from the radiation."

"Now, that would really suit you," laughed Anna-Maria.

They got into the car.

"On that particular subject," Sven-Erik went on, "how are things with Pohjanen?"

"I don't know, it wasn't really the right time to ask."

"No, of course not."

He can ask Pohjanen himself, thought Anna-Maria crossly.

Sven-Erik parked below the church and they began to walk up the hill. The piles of snow by the side of the path had disappeared, and the tracks of both people and dogs crisscrossed the snow all around the church. The whole area had been searched for the murder weapon, in the hope that whoever had murdered Viktor Strandgård would have thrown away the weapon outside the church, or perhaps buried it in a mound of snow. But nothing had been found.

"What if we don't find a weapon," said Sven-Erik, slowing down as he noticed that Anna-Maria was out of breath. "Can you get a conviction for murder these days if there's no technical proof?"

"Just remember what happened to the guy everybody said had murdered Olof Palme," puffed Anna-Maria.

Sven-Erik gave a hollow laugh.

"Oh, that's made me feel so much better."

"Have you found the sister yet?"

"No, but von Post says he's arranged for her to come in at eight o'clock this evening to be interviewed, so we'll see what comes of that."

Anna-Maria Mella and Sven-Erik Stålnacke entered the church of The Source of All Our Strength at ten minutes past five in the afternoon. The three pastors were sitting in a row right at the front of the church, their faces turned toward the altar. There were also three other people in the church. A middle-aged woman was dragging an unwieldy vacuum cleaner as it droned and roared over the carpets. Anna-Maria thought she looked skinny in her old-fashioned tights and a pale lilac knitted cotton sweater that almost came down to her knees. From time to time the woman had to switch off the vacuum cleaner and get down on her hands and knees to pick up bits of rubbish that were too big for the hose. Then there was another middle-aged woman, much more elegant, in a smart skirt, well-pressed blouse and matching cardigan. She was walking up and down the rows of chairs and placing a photocopied sheet on each seat. The third person was a young man. He appeared to be wandering aimlessly around, talking to himself. He held a Bible in his hand. Every so often he stopped in front of a chair, reached out his hand and seemed to be talking to it in an agitated manner, but no sound came from his lips. Or he stopped dead, raised the Bible up toward the ceiling and gabbled out loud a series of phrases that were completely incomprehensible to Sven-Erik and Anna-Maria. When they walked past him, he gave them a filthy look. The blood-soaked rug was still lying in the aisle, but someone had moved the chairs so that it was easy to get by without walking where the body had been.

"So, this is the Holy Trinity, then," said Sven-Erik in an attempt to lighten the atmosphere as the three pastors rose to greet them, their faces serious.

None of them gave the slightest hint of a smile.

When they were seated Anna-Maria jotted down their names with a short description in her notebook so that she'd remember afterward who was who and who said what. A tape recorder was out of the question. It was probably going to be difficult enough to get anything out of them as it was.

"Thomas Söderberg," she wrote, "dark, good-looking, trendy glasses. Forty-something. Vesa Larsson, forty-something, the only one who isn't wearing a suit and tie. Flannel shirt and leather waistcoat. Gunnar Isaksson. Pudgy, beard. About fifty."

She thought about their handshakes. Thomas Söderberg had pressed her hand firmly, met her eyes steadily and held on for a moment. He was used to inspiring trust. She wondered how he would react if the police indicated that they didn't quite believe something he said. His suit looked expensive.

Vesa Larsson's handshake was flaccid. He wasn't used to shaking hands. When their hands met he had actually made his greeting through a brief nod that preceded the handshake, and he was already looking at Sven-Erik.

Gunnar Isaksson had nearly crushed her hand in his. And it wasn't the unconscious strength you sometimes find in men.

He's just afraid of seeming weak, thought Anna-Maria.

"Before we start I'd like to know why you wish to be interviewed together," asked Anna-Maria by way of introduction.

"This thing that's happened is just terrible," said Vesa Larsson after a short silence, "but we feel very strongly that the church must stand together in the days to come. This applies to us, the three pastors, most of all. There are powerful forces that will attempt to sow discord, and we intend to give these forces as few openings as possible."

"I quite understand," said Sven-Erik in a tone of voice that conveyed quite clearly that he didn't understand in the slightest.

Anna-Maria looked at Sven-Erik as he pushed his lips forward, his moustache protruding like a big scrubbing brush beneath his nose.

Vesa Larsson fiddled with a button on his leather waistcoat and glanced sideways at Thomas Söderberg. Thomas Söderberg didn't look at him, but nodded thoughtfully at what had just been said.

Aha, thought Anna-Maria, Pastor Söderberg approves of Vesa's reply. It isn't difficult to see who's pulling the strings in this particular setup.

"Can you explain how the church is actually organized?" asked Anna-Maria.

"God is at the top," replied Gunnar Isaksson in a loud voice full of faith, pointing upward. "The church has three pastors, that's us, and five elders. If we were to compare it with a company, you could say that God is the owner, we three are the managing directors and the elders form the board."

"I thought you wanted to talk to us about Viktor Strandgård," interrupted Thomas Söderberg.

"We'll get to that, we'll get to that," Sven-Erik assured him, almost humming.

The young man with the Bible had stopped beside a chair, and he was praying in a loud voice and waving his hands at the empty seat. Sven-Erik looked confused.

"Could I just ask...?" he said, jerking his thumb toward the young man.

"He's praying for this evening's service," explained Thomas Söderberg. "Speaking in tongues can seem a little strange when you're not used to hearing it, but I can promise you it isn't some kind of hocus-pocus."

"It's important that the church is prepared with the spirit world," explained Pastor Gunnar Isaksson, stroking his thick, well-groomed beard.

"I understand," said Sven-Erik again, looking helplessly at Anna-Maria.

His moustache was almost at a ninety-degree angle to his face.

"So, tell us about Viktor Strandgård," said Anna-Maria. "What kind of person was he? What did you think of him, Pastor Larsson?"

Pastor Vesa Larsson looked troubled. He swallowed vigorously before answering.

"He was dedicated. Very humble. Loved by everyone in the church community. He simply allowed himself to be used by God. Despite his, how shall I put it, elevated status within our community, he wasn't slow to serve, even when it came to practical matters. He was on the church cleaning rota, so you'd often see him dusting these chairs. He made posters for our services. . . ."

"Looked after the children," added Gunnar Isaksson. "We have a rolling program so that parents with very young children can listen in a completely focused way to the word of God."

"Like yesterday, for example," Vesa Larsson continued. "He didn't join everyone for coffee after the service, instead he stayed here to tidy the chairs. That's the disadvantage of not having pews, it can soon look a mess if you don't put the chairs back into neat rows."

"That must be a huge job," said Anna-Maria. "There's an awful lot of chairs in here. Nobody stayed behind to help him?"

"No, he said he wanted to be alone," said Vesa Larsson. "Unfortunately we never lock the door when someone is in here, so some madman must have . . ."

He broke off and shook his head.

"Viktor Strandgård seems to have been a gentle soul," said Anna-Maria.

"Yes, you could say that." Thomas Söderberg smiled sadly.

"Do you know if he had any enemies, or had fallen out with anyone?" asked Sven-Erik.

"No, no one," replied Vesa Larsson.

"Did he seem worried about anything? Anxious?" Sven-Erik went on.

"No," replied Vesa Larsson again.

"What kind of work did he do for the church? He was a full-time employee, wasn't he?" asked Sven-Erik.

"He did the work of God," replied Gunnar Isaksson pompously, with considerable emphasis on "God."

"And by doing the work of God he brought some money into the church," Anna-Maria commented in measured tones. "What happened to the money from his book? What will happen to it now that he's dead?"

Gunnar Isaksson and Vesa Larsson turned to their colleague, Thomas Söderberg.

"I don't quite see what any of this has to do with your murder investigation?" Thomas Söderberg inquired in a friendly tone.

"Just answer the question, please," Sven-Erik replied amiably, but with an expression on his face that brooked no argument.

"Viktor Strandgård made over all royalties from his book to the church long ago. After his death any income will continue to go to the church. So nothing will change."

"How many copies of the book have been sold?" asked Anna-Maria.

"Over a million, including translations," replied Pastor Söderberg dryly, "and I still don't really see—"

"Have you sold anything else?" asked Sven-Erik. "Posters or anything?"

"This is a church, not Viktor Strandgård's fan club," said Thomas Söderberg sharply. "We don't sell pictures of him, but a certain amount of income has been generated from other sources—for example, video sales."

"What sort of videos?"

Anna-Maria adjusted her position on the chair. She needed a pee.

"We've taped sermons given by the three of us, or Viktor Strandgård, or guest preachers. Meetings and services have also been recorded," replied Pastor Söderberg as he removed his glasses and took a spotless little handkerchief out of his trousers pocket.

"You record your services on video?" asked Anna-Maria, altering her position on the chair yet again.

"Yes," answered Vesa Larsson, since Thomas Söderberg appeared to be too busy polishing his glasses to reply.

"There was a service here yesterday," said Anna-Maria, "and Viktor Strandgård was there. Was that recorded on video?"

"Yes," replied Pastor Larsson.

"Right, we want that tape," Sven-Erik said firmly. "And if there's a service tonight, we'd like that tape as well. In fact, we'll have all the tapes for the last month—what do you think, Anna-Maria?"

"Good idea," she answered briefly.

They looked up as the noise of the vacuum cleaner stopped. The woman who was cleaning had switched it off and gone over to the well-dressed woman; they were whispering to each other and looking over toward the pastors. The young man had sat down on one of the chairs and was leafing through his Bible. His lips were moving constantly. The well-dressed woman noticed that the conversation between the pastors and the police had ground to a halt, and seized the opportunity to come over.

"Sorry to interrupt," she said politely, and when no one stopped her she went on, facing the pastors. "Before this evening's service, what shall we do about . . ."

She fell silent and gestured with her right hand toward the blood-stained spot where Viktor Strandgård had lain.

"As the floor isn't varnished, I don't think we'll be able to scrub away every single trace. . . . Perhaps we could roll up the rug and put something else over the spot until we get a new one."

"That will be fine," answered Pastor Gunnar Isaksson.

"Just leave it, Ann-Gull, my dear," interrupted Pastor Söderberg, glancing almost imperceptibly at Gunnar Isaksson at the same time. "I'll deal with all that shortly. Just leave it for now. The police will soon be finished with us, I imagine?"

This last remark was directed at Anna-Maria and Sven-Erik. When they didn't reply, Thomas Söderberg gave the woman a smile that seemed to indicate that their conversation was at an end for the time being. She disappeared like a willing handmaiden and went back to the other woman. Soon the vacuum cleaner was droning again.

The pastors and the detectives sat in silence, staring at one another.

Typical, thought Anna-Maria angrily. Untreated wooden floor, thick handwoven rug, chairs instead of pews. It all looks lovely, but it's got to be damned difficult to keep clean. Good job they have so many obedient women who clean for God for free.

"There is a limit to how much time we can spare," said Thomas Söderberg.

His voice had lost all trace of warmth.

"We have a service here this evening and I'm sure you will understand that we have a considerable amount of preparation to do," he said when there was no reply from the two detectives.

"So," said Sven-Erik thoughtfully, as if they had all the time in the world, "if Viktor Strandgård didn't have enemies, I'm sure he must have had friends. Who was closest to Viktor Strandgård?"

"God," replied Pastor Isaksson with a triumphant smile.

"His family, of course, his mother and father," said Thomas Söderberg, ignoring his colleague's comment. "Viktor's father, Olof Strandgård, is chairman of the Christian Democrats and a local councillor. The church has a significant number of representatives on the local council, principally through the Christian Democrats, the largest party among the middle classes in Kiruna. Our influence throughout the whole community is growing steadily, and we expect to have a majority at the next election. We are also relying on the police not to do anything that might damage the trust we have built up among the electorate. And then there's Viktor's sister, Sanna Strandgård—have you spoken to her?"

"No, not yet," replied Sven-Erik.

"Just be careful when you do; she's a very fragile person," said Pastor Söderberg.

"And then I should include myself," continued Thomas Söderberg.

"Were you his confessor?" asked Sven-Erik.

"Well," said Thomas Söderberg, smiling once again, "we don't call it that. Spiritual mentor, perhaps."

"Do you know whether Viktor Strandgård was intending to make some kind of revelation before he died?" asked Anna-Maria. "Something about himself, perhaps? Or about the church?"

"No," replied Thomas Söderberg after a second's silence. "What could it have been?"

"Excuse me," said Anna-Maria as she stood up. "But I must just pop to your bathroom."

She left the men and went to the bathroom right at the back of the church. She had a pee, then sat for a while resting her gaze on the white-tiled walls. One thought was pounding in her head. During her years with the police she had learned to recognize the signs of stress. Everything from sweating to dizziness. People were usually nervous when they were talking to the police. But it was when they started trying to hide their stress that it became interesting to watch them.

And there was one particular sign of stress that you only got one chance to catch. It only happened once. And she'd just heard it. Immediately after she'd asked whether Viktor Strandgård was intending to reveal something before he died. One of the three pastors, she hadn't managed to work out which one, had taken a deep breath. Just once. Caught his breath.

"Shit," she said aloud, and was surprised at how good it felt to swear secretly in church.

It didn't necessarily mean a damned thing. Someone breathing. It's obvious there's something going on. Show me the board of a large organization where there isn't. Even in the police. And this lot aren't as pure as the driven snow either.

"But that doesn't make them murderers," Anna-Maria continued her discussion with herself as she flushed the toilet.

But there were other inconsistencies. Why, for example, had Vesa Larsson said that nothing was troubling Viktor Strandgård if Thomas Söderberg was supposed to be his "spiritual mentor," and therefore must have been the one who knew him best?

When Sven-Erik and Anna-Maria left the church and were making their way down to the car park, the woman who had been vacuuming came running after them. She had only socks and clogs on her feet, and half ran, half slid down the slope to catch them.

"I heard you asking if he had any enemies," she panted.

"Yes?" asked Sven-Erik.

"He did," she said, seizing Sven-Erik's arm in a viselike grip. "And now he's dead, the enemy will be even stronger. I myself can feel how I am beset by the foe."

She let go of Sven-Erik and flung her arms around herself in a vain attempt to keep out the bitter cold. She hadn't put on any sort of coat or jacket. She bent her knees slightly to keep her balance on the slope. If she leaned backwards even slightly the clogs began to slip.

"Beset?" asked Anna-Maria.

"By demons," said the woman. "They want to make me start smoking again. I used to be possessed by the tobacco demon, but Viktor Strandgård laid hands upon me and freed me."

Anna-Maria looked at her, completely exhausted. She couldn't cope with a mad person right now.

"We'll make a note of it," she said tersely, and started to walk toward the car.

Sven-Erik stayed where he was and took his notebook out of the inside pocket of his fleece.

"He was the one who killed Viktor," said the woman.

"Who?" asked Sven-Erik.

"The Prince of Demons," she whispered. "Satan. He is trying to force his way in."

Sven-Erik shoved the notebook back in his pocket and took hold of the woman's ice-cold hands.

"Thank you," he said. "Now, why don't you go back inside, so you don't freeze to death."

"I just wanted to tell you about it," the woman called after them.

Inside the church the pastors were engaged in a loud discussion.

"We can't do it like this!" shouted Gunnar Isaksson agitatedly, dogging Thomas Söderberg's footsteps as he walked around the black bloodstain on the floor and moved the chairs so that the dark impression of Viktor Strandgård's death ended up almost as if it were in the middle of a circus ring.

"Yes, we can," said Thomas Söderberg calmly, and, turning toward the well-dressed woman, he went on:

"Take the rug away from the aisle. Leave the bloodstain as it is. Go and buy three roses and place them on the floor. I want the church rearranged completely. I shall stand beside the spot where he died and preach. I want the chairs in a circle."

"You'll have the congregation all around you," squeaked Gunnar Isaksson. "Do you expect people to sit and look at your back?"

Thomas Söderberg went over to the pudgy little man and placed his hands on his shoulders.

You little shit, he thought. You're not a gifted enough orator to speak in an arena. A theater. A marketplace. You have to have everybody sitting right there in front of you, and a lectern to hang on to if it gets tricky. But I can't let your inadequacy get in my way.

"Remember what we said, brother," said Thomas Söderberg to Gunnar Isaksson. "We must hold fast now. I promise you this will work. People will be allowed to weep, to call out to God, and we— God—will triumph tonight. Tell your wife to bring a flower to place on the spot where his body lay."

The atmosphere will be incredible, thought Thomas Söderberg.

He made a mental note to get several more people to bring flowers and lay them on the floor. It would be just like the spot where Olof Palme was murdered.

Pastor Vesa Larsson was still sitting in exactly the same spot as during the conversation with the police, leaning forward. He took no part in the heated discussion, but sat there with his face buried in his hands. He might possibly have been crying, it was difficult to see.

Rebecka and Sanna were sitting in the car on the way into town. Gray pine trees, weighed down with snow, swept past in the beam of the headlights. The uncomfortable silence was like a shrinking room. The walls and the ceiling were moving inward and downward. With each passing minute it became more difficult to breathe properly. Rebecka was driving. Her eyes flicked back and forth between the speedometer and the road. The intense cold meant that the road wasn't slippery at all, despite being covered with packed snow.

Sanna sat with her cheek resting on the cold window, winding a lock of her hair tightly around her finger.

"Can't you just say something," she said after a while.

"I'm not used to driving on roads like this," said Rebecka. "I find it difficult to talk and drive at the same time."

She could hear how obvious the lie was, as clear as a reef just below the surface of the water. But it didn't matter. Perhaps that's what she wanted. She looked at the clock. Quarter to eight.

Don't start anything, she told herself firmly. You've rescued Sanna. Now you have to row her to the shore.

"Do you think the girls will be all right?" she asked.

"They'll have to be," replied Sanna, straightening up in her seat. "And we won't be long, will we? I daren't ring anybody to ask for help; the fewer people who know where I am, the better."

"Why?"

"I'm frightened of journalists. I know what they can be like. And then there's Mum and Dad . . . but let's talk about something else."

"Do you want to talk about Viktor? About what happened?"

"No. I'll be telling the police soon anyway. We'll talk about you, that'll calm me down. How are things with you? Is it really seven years since we saw each other?"

"Mmm," replied Rebecka. "But we've had the odd chat on the phone."

"To think you've still got the house in Kurravaara."

"Well, Uncle Affe and Inga-Lill don't think they can afford to buy me out. I think they're annoyed because they're the only ones putting work and money into the house. But on the other hand, they're the only ones getting any pleasure out of it as well. I'd like to sell it really. To them or to somebody else, it's all the same to me."

She wondered whether what she had just said was true. Did she really get no pleasure from her grandmother's house, or from the cottage in Jiekajärvi? Just because she was never there? Just the thought of the cottage, the idea that there was somewhere that belonged to her, far away from civilization, deep in the wilderness, beyond marsh and forest, wasn't that a kind of pleasure in itself?

"You look, how shall I put it, really smart," said Sanna. "And sure of yourself, somehow. Of course, I always thought you were pretty. But now you look as if you've come straight out of one of those TV series. Your hair looks great too. I just let mine grow wild, then cut it myself."

Sanna ran her fingers through her thick, pale curls with an air of self-assurance.

I know, Sanna, thought Rebecka angrily. I know that you're the fairest in all the land. And that's without spending a fortune on haircuts and clothes.

"Can't you just chat a bit," whined Sanna. "I feel absolutely terrible, but I did say sorry. And I'm just rigid with fear. Feel my hands, they're freezing."

She took one hand out of its sheepskin glove and reached toward Rebecka.

She's not right in the head, thought Rebecka furiously, keeping her hands firmly clamped on the wheel. She's totally fucking crazy.

Feel my hand, Rebecka, it's shaking. It's really cold. I love you so much, Rebecka. If you were a boy I'd fall in love with you, did you know that?

"That's a nice dog you've got," said Rebecka, making an effort to keep her voice calm.

Sanna drew back her hand.

"Yes," she said. "Virku. The girls love her. We got her from a Sami lad we know. His father wasn't looking after her properly. Not when he was drinking, at any rate. But he didn't manage to ruin her. She's such a happy dog, and so obedient. And she really loves Sara, did you notice that? How she keeps putting her head on Sara's knee. It's really nice, because the girls have been so unlucky with pets over the last year or so."

"Oh?"

"Yes—well, I don't know if 'unlucky' is the right word. Sometimes they're just so irresponsible. I don't know what it is with them. Last spring the rabbit escaped because Sara hadn't shut the cage door properly. And she just refused to admit it was her fault. Then we got a cat. And in the autumn that disappeared. Although that was nothing to do with Sara, of course. That's just the way it is with cats that live outside. It probably got run over or something. We've had gerbils that have disappeared as well. I daren't think where they've gone. They're probably living in the walls and under the floor, slowly but surely chewing the house to bits. But Sara and Lova, they drive me mad. Like before, when Lova got soap and washing-up liquid all over herself and the dog. And Sara just sits there watching, not taking any responsibility. I just can't cope. Lova's always making a mess. Anyway, let's talk about something less depressing."

"Just look at the Aurora Borealis," said Rebecka, leaning forward over the steering wheel and glancing up at the sky.

"It's been amazing this winter. It's because there are storms on the sun, I'm sure that's why. Doesn't it make you want to move back up here?"

"No, maybe—oh, I don't know!"

Rebecka laughed.

The Crystal Church could be seen in the distance. It looked like a spaceship, hovering in the sky above the streetlights. Soon the houses were much closer together as the country road turned into an urban street. Rebecka dipped her headlights.

"Are you happy down there?" asked Sanna.

"I'm nearly always working," answered Rebecka.

"What about the people, though?"

"I don't know. I don't feel at home with them, if that's what you're asking. It feels as if I'm moving away from simple relationships all the time. You learn to look in the right direction when you drink a toast, and to write and say thank you for inviting me within the accepted time limit, but you can't hide who you are. So you feel just a little bit like an outsider all the time. And you always feel a little bit resentful of society people, the ones with money. You never really know what they think of you. They're so bloody nice to everybody, whether they like a person or not. At least up here you know where you are with people."

"Do you?" asked Sanna.

They fell silent, each lost in her own thoughts. They passed the churchyard and approached a garage with a snack bar.

"Shall we get something to drink?" suggested Rebecka.

Sanna nodded and Rebecka pulled in. They sat in the car without saying a word. Neither of them made a move to get out and buy something, and neither of them looked at the other.

"You should never have moved," said Sanna unhappily.

"You know why I moved," said Rebecka, turning her head away so that Sanna couldn't see her face.

"I think you were the only person Viktor really ever loved, did you know that?" Sanna burst out. "I don't think he ever got over you. If you'd stayed..."

Rebecka spun around. Rage flared up in her like a burning torch. She was trembling and shaking, and the words that came out of her mouth were broken and jerky. But they came out. She couldn't stop them.

"Just stop right there," she screamed. "Just shut the fuck up and we'll get this sorted out once and for all."

A woman with an overweight Labrador retriever on a lead stopped dead when she heard Rebecka's scream, and she peered curiously into the car.

"I haven't the faintest idea what you're talking about," Rebecka went on, without lowering her voice. "Viktor was never in love with me, he was never even keen on me. I never want to hear a single word about it again. I don't intend to take any responsibility for the fact that he and I didn't end up together. And I certainly don't intend to take responsibility for the fact that he was murdered. You're not fucking right in the head if that's what you've come up with. Please feel free to carry on living in your parallel universe, but leave me out of it."

She fell silent and pounded on the side window. Then she banged her head with both hands. The woman with the dog looked alarmed, took a step backwards and disappeared.

For God's sake. I must calm down, thought Rebecka. I'm in no fit state to drive the car. I'll have us off the road.

"That's not what I meant," whined Sanna. "I've never blamed you for anything. If anyone's to blame, it's me."

"What for? Viktor's murder?"

Something inside Rebecka stopped and pricked up its ears.

"Everything," mumbled Sanna. "The fact that you were forced to move away. Everything!"

"Pack it in!" spat Rebecka, filled with a new rage that swept away the shaking and turned her legs to ice and iron. "I have no intention of sitting here, patting you on the shoulder and telling you none of it was your fault. I've done that a hundred times already. I was an adult. I made my choice and I took the consequences."

"Yes," said Sanna obediently.

Rebecka started the car and screeched out onto Malmvägen. Sanna raised her hands to her mouth as an oncoming car tooted angrily at them. From Hjalmar Lundbohmsvägen they could see the mining company's offices glowing in front of the mine. Rebecka was struck by the fact that they no longer seemed so big. When she used to live in the town, the offices had always been massive. They passed the town hall with its stiff tiled façade, its remarkable clock tower outlined against the sky like a black steel skeleton.

What I said was true, thought Rebecka. He was never in love with me. Although I can understand everybody thinking he was. That's what we let them think, Viktor and me. It began that very first summer. During the summer church with Thomas Söderberg in Gällivare.

In the end there are eleven young people attending the summer church. They are to live, work and study the Bible together for three weeks. Pastor Thomas Söderberg and his wife, Maja, are leading the group. Maja is pregnant. She has long, shiny hair, doesn't wear makeup and always looks so sweet and cheerful. But sometimes Rebecka sees her move to one side and press her fist into the small of her back. And sometimes Thomas puts his arms around her and says:

"We can manage without you. Go and lie down and have a little rest."

She usually looks at him with relief and gratitude. It's hard work, being the unpaid wife of a pastor.

Maja's sister, Magdalena, is there too, helping out. She does everything quickly, like a cheerful mouse. She can play the guitar, and teaches them hymns.

Viktor and Sanna are among the eleven. Everyone notices them straightaway. They are very much alike. They both have long, fair hair. Sanna's is *naturally curly. Her snub nose and big eyes give her face a doll-like expression.*

She'll still look like a child when she's eighty, thinks Rebecka, and forces herself not to stare.

Sanna is the only one of the young people who is a committed Christian. She's only seventeen, and has a small child with her. Sara, who is three months old.

"Jesus and I have an exciting, loving relationship," says Sanna with a crooked smile.

They have different kinds of belief, Sanna and Thomas Söderberg. Thomas demonstrates his belief in several different ways.

"The word 'belief,'" he says, "means the same as to rely on, to be convinced of. If I say 'I believe in you, Rebecka,' then I mean that I'm convinced you will fulfill my expectations of you."

"I don't know," Sanna protests. "I think that to believe is simply to believe. Not to know. To have doubts, sometimes. But still to invest in your relationship with God. To listen for his whisper in the forest."

Viktor leans forward and ruffles his big sister's hair.

"The whispering and sighing is all in your head, Sanna," he says, and laughs.

He doesn't believe. But he likes to discuss things. He often wears his long fair hair in a knot on top of his head. His skin is so fair it almost tips over into pale blue. The other girls look at him, but he soon finds a way of keeping them at bay. He plays a game with Rebecka.

Rebecka isn't stupid. She soon realizes that the way he looks at her doesn't mean anything, and that she isn't allowed to reciprocate the quick caresses of her hair or her hand. She learns to sit still and pretend to be the object of his unrequited longing. She doesn't come out of the game empty-handed. Viktor's admiration gives her a higher status among the other girls in the group. She has outplayed them, and that brings respect.

During their Bible study the views of Thomas and the participants are quite different at the beginning. The young people don't understand. Why is homosexuality a sin? How can it be that the Christian faith is the only true faith? What will happen to all the Muslims, for example—will they all go to hell? Why is it wrong to have sex before marriage?

Thomas listens and explains. You have to choose, he explains. Either you believe in the whole of the Bible, or you can pick out different bits and just believe those, but what kind of faith would that be? Insipid and toothless, that's what.

They sit on the jetty by the lake during the light summer nights and swat the mosquitoes that land on their arms and legs. They discuss and consider. Sanna is secure in her God. Rebecka feels as if she is standing in the middle of a raging torrent.

"It's because you have been called," says Sanna. "He wants you. If you don't say yes now, you could be lost forever. You can't postpone your decision until later, because you might never feel this longing again."

When the three weeks are up, all except two of the participants have given themselves to God. Among those newly saved are Viktor and Rebecka.

"**W**hat about you and Viktor, then?" Thomas asks Rebecka when the summer church is almost over. "What's going on between you two?"

He and Rebecka are walking to the local supermarket to buy some milk. Rebecka breathes in the wonderful aroma of warm, dusty asphalt. She's pleased that Thomas wanted to come with her. Most of the time she has to share him with everyone else.

"I don't know," says Rebecka hesitantly as she decides not to tell the truth. "He might be interested, but I haven't time for anyone but God in my life right now. I want to invest one hundred percent in Him for a while."

She breaks a thin twig from a birch tree as they walk by. The fragile green leaves smell like a happy summer. She puts a leaf in her mouth and chews.

Thomas grabs a leaf as well and pops it in his mouth. He smiles.

"You're a sensible girl, Rebecka. I know that God has great plans for you. It's a wonderful time when you've just fallen in love with God. It's good that you're making the most of it."

She heard Sanna's voice, at first from a long way off, then close by. Sanna's hand on her upper arm.

"Look," squeaked Sanna. "Oh, no."

They had arrived at the police station. Rebecka had parked the car. At first she couldn't see what Sanna was looking at. Then she saw the reporter running toward their car with a microphone at the ready. A man was standing behind the reporter. He lifted the video camera toward them like a black weapon.

In the Crystal Church, Pastor Gunnar Isaksson's wife, Karin, sat with her eyes half closed, pretending to pray. There was an hour to go before the evening's meeting. On the stage at the front, the gospel choir was warming up. Thirty young men and women. Black trousers. Lilac sweatshirts with an explosion of yellow and orange and the word "Joy" on the front.

Once she had been so in love with this church that it almost hurt. The divine acoustics. Like now. Long, drawn-out notes swirling up toward the ceiling, then cascading down to a depth only the bass voices could reach. The warm light. The polar night outside the immense glass windows. A bubble of God's strength amid the darkness and the cold.

The musicians on the electric and bass guitars were tuning their instruments. There was a dull thud as the lighting technician switched on the spotlights on the stage. The boys who were looking after the sound were struggling with a microphone that was refusing to work. They were talking into it, but you couldn't hear anything, and then all of a sudden it gave a piercing whistle.

Her arms itched. This morning the rash had been angry and red. She wondered if it could be psoriasis. Just as long as Gunnar didn't catch sight of it. She didn't want his intercession.

They had rearranged the furniture in the church. The chairs had been placed around the spot where Viktor had been lying. It looked just like the circus. She looked at her husband, sitting in the front row. His thick neck bulging over the white shirt collar. Next to him sat Thomas Söderberg, trying to concentrate before the evening's sermon. She saw how Gunnar was forcing himself to look down at the Bible, determined not to distract the other man, only to forget himself and start babbling. His right hand shot out and started to paint pictures in the air with great sweeping strokes.

After Christmas he had decided to lose some weight. This afternoon he had skipped lunch. She had sat at the kitchen table twirling spaghetti around her fork, while he stood at the sink eating three pears. His broad back bending over the draining board. Slurping and gobbling. The sound of the pear juice dripping into the sink. His left hand pressing his tie against his stomach.

She looked at the clock. In a quarter of an hour he would leave his place at Thomas Söderberg's side, sneak off to the car, drive into town and eat a hamburger in secret. Come back with his mouth full of spearmint gum.

Lie to somebody who cares, she thought. I don't.

In the beginning he had been a different man. He'd been filling in as caretaker at Berga School, where she'd been working as a teacher. And she'd been to college, he thought that was wonderful. It was an energetic and very obvious courtship. Made-up errands to the staff room when she had a free lesson. Fun and laughter and an endless stream of bad jokes. And beneath all this, an insecurity that moved her. The delighted comments of her colleagues. How he clapped his hands with pleasure when she'd had her hair cut, or bought a new blouse. She watched him with the children in the playground. They liked him. A kind caretaker. It didn't bother her then that he didn't read books.

It was later, when he found himself in the shadow of Thomas Söderberg and Vesa Larsson, that the urge to assert himself was aroused.

But then she started to go with him to the Baptist church. At the time it was a church threatened with extinction. No, that was wrong, it was doomed to extinction. The members of the congregation looked as though they'd just dropped in for a rest on the way to the grave. Signe Persson, his gossamer-fine transparent hair carefully waved. His scalp shining through, pink with brown patches. Arvid Kall, once a loader for the LKAB mining company. Now half asleep in a pew, his huge hands lying powerless on his knees.

Naturally they hadn't been able to afford a pastor; there was hardly enough money to heat the church. Gunnar Isaksson ran the church community like a one-man business. Mended and maintained what they could afford. Sighed over the rest. For example, the damage caused by the damp in the cloakroom. The wall that bellied out like a swollen corpse. The wallpaper that kept peeling off. The idea was that members of the congregation should take it in turns to preach; services were held every other Sunday. Since nobody else volunteered, Gunnar Isaksson stepped in.

There was no kind of thread to be found in his sermons. He drove here and there at random through the landscape of the free church he'd known since his youth. But still the routine was always very similar, with obligatory stops in well-known places, such as "the Spirit of God descending like a dove," "Behold, I am making all things new" and "Those who drink of the water that I will give them." Without exception the journey always ended with a revivalist call to the cooperative souls sitting there, saved long ago.

One consolation was that things weren't much better in the other churches around the town. God's temple in Kiruna: a dilapidated hovel where the stale air stood completely still.

Gunnar stood up and came toward the exit. Slowed down to show respect as he passed the place where Viktor Strandgård's body had lain. A pile of flowers and cards was already lying there. He gave her a brief smile and a wink. A sign that appeared to mean he was just going to the bathroom, or to have a quick word with someone in the cloakroom.

He wasn't stupid. Not in the least. The very fact that he'd managed to get where he was today. Right at the top of the church, along with Thomas Söderberg and Vesa Larsson. Without any formal training as a pastor. Without any talent as a fisher of men. That very fact demanded a certain talent.

She remembered when Gunnar had told her that the Mission had a new pastor. A young married couple.

A week or so later Thomas Söderberg came to a service in the Baptist church. Sat in the second row nodding in agreement throughout Gunnar's sermon. Encouraging smiles. Serious consideration. His wife, Maja, like a model pupil by his side.

They stayed for coffee afterward. Gray winter darkness outside. Clouds full of snow. The day dwindling before it had even arrived properly.

Maja talked loudly and slowly into Arvid Kalla's ear. Asked Edit Svonni for her recipe for sugar biscuits.

Thomas Söderberg and Gunnar having an animated conversation with two of the church elders. Switching between serious nodding of heads and loud laughter, like a well-rehearsed, perfectly coordinated dance. United in brotherhood.

And the obligatory question to the southerners: How do you like it up here? The darkness and the cold? They answered as one: They absolutely loved it. They certainly weren't missing the slush and the rain. They'd be celebrating the next family Christmas in Kiruna.

That was all it took. The fact that they didn't feel they'd been banished to a distant place beyond the bounds of tolerance. No whining or complaining about the biting wind or the darkness that creeps into your soul. The answers made the congregation's faces soften.

When they'd gone, Gunnar said to her: "Nice people. He's got lots of ideas, that boy."

That was the last time he called Thomas Söderberg, ten years younger than him, "that boy."

Two weeks later she met Thomas Söderberg in town. She was pushing the pram through a blizzard. Andreas was two and a half months old, and would only sleep in the pram. She pushed him up and down the streets of Kiruna. Dragging the two-year-old, Anna, like a fretful bundle. Hands and feet freezing.

She felt dreadful. Exhaustion filled her like a gray, rising dough. At any moment she might just burst and go under. She hated Gunnar. Kept losing her temper with Anna. Just wanted to cry all the time.

Thomas came walking up behind her. Laid his left hand on her left shoulder. Caught up with her at the same time. For a second, just as he drew level with her, it was as if he had his arm around her. Half an embrace for a fraction of a second too long. When she turned her head he was smiling broadly. Greeted her as if they were old friends. Said hi to Anna, who clung fast to Karin's legs and refused to answer. Peeped at Andreas, who was sleeping like an angel from God in his warm outfit.

"I keep trying to convince Maja that we ought to have children," he confessed, "but . . ." He didn't finish the sentence. Sighed deeply and let the smile fade away. Then he regained his good humor. "I do understand her," he said. "It's you women who bear the heaviest load. It'll happen when it's meant to happen."

Andreas moved in the pram. It was time to go home and feed him. She wanted to invite Thomas back for lunch, but didn't dare ask. He walked part of the way with her. It was so easy to talk. New topics of conversation just popped up by themselves, attaching themselves to the old ones like the links of a chain. At last they were standing by the crossroads where they had to part company.

"I would like to do more for God," she said. "But the children. They take all the strength I have, and a little bit more."

The snow was whirling around them like a hail of sharp arrows. Made him blink. An archangel with dark curly hair wearing a blue padded jacket made of some kind of synthetic crackling material that looked cheap. Jeans tucked into high-heeled leather boots. Knitted cap, homemade, with an Inca pattern. She wondered if it was Maja who was so creative. Maja, who didn't want children.

"But, Karin," he said, "don't you understand that you are doing exactly what God wants? Looking after the children. That's the most important thing of all right now. He has plans for you, but right now . . . right now you must be with Anna and Andreas."

Six months later he had held the first summer church. A little flock of newly saved children waddled behind him like ducklings. Imprinting him as their spiritual parent. One of them was Viktor Strandgård.

She, Gunnar, Vesa Larsson and his wife, Astrid, were invited to share in the happiness when they held a baptism for the believers. Gunnar swallowed his bitter jealousy and went along. He knew how to join the winning team. At the same time he started the endless comparisons. The desire to try to shine himself. His face took on a cunning expression.

She wasn't without blame herself. Hadn't she said to her husband a thousand times: "Don't let Thomas walk all over you. He can't be allowed to decide everything."

She had convinced herself that she was supporting her husband. But wasn't the truth that she'd actually wanted him to be someone else?

Thomas Söderberg got up and walked over to the gospel choir. He was wearing a black suit. Normally his ties were colorful, verging on bold. This evening it was a discreet gray. An upside-down exclamation mark inside his jacket.

He carried his wealth as easily as he had once carried his—not poverty, she thought, his lack of money. Two people living on a pastor's wage. But it never seemed to bother them. Not even when they had children.

Then things changed. He stood there now in his fine wool suit, talking to the choir. Said what had happened was terrible. One of the girls began to sob loudly. Those standing closest to her put their arms around her.

It was okay to cry, said Thomas. It was all right to grieve. But—and here he took a deep breath and uttered each word separately, with a short pause in between—it was not okay to lose. Not okay to go backwards. Not okay to sound the retreat.

She couldn't face listening to the rest. Knew more or less how it would sound.

"Hi, Karin. Where's Gunnar?"

Maja, Thomas Söderberg's wife, sat down beside her. Long, shiny, sandy-colored hair. A little discreet makeup. No lipstick. No eyeshadow. Just a little bit of mascara and blusher. Not that Thomas had anything against women wearing makeup, but Karin guessed that he preferred to see his own wife without. A few years ago Maja had wanted to have her hair cut short, but Thomas had put his foot down.

"He was here a minute ago. I'm sure he'll be back shortly."

Maja nodded.

"And where are Vesa and Astrid?" she asked.

Taking a tough line on attendance tonight. Karin raised her eyebrows and shook her head in reply.

"It's really important that everyone sticks together at a time like this," said Maja quietly.

Karin looked at the red rose lying on Maja's knee.

"Are you going to put that with the others?"

Maja nodded.

"Yes, but I'll wait until the meeting is under way. I can't grasp what's happened. It's just so unreal."

Yes, it is unreal, thought Karin. What's going to happen without Viktor?

Viktor, who refused to cut his hair or wear a suit. Who turned down a pay raise and made Thomas give the money to Médecins Sans Frontières instead. She remembered seven years ago, when she'd gone to a conference in Stockholm. How surprised she'd been when she saw so many young men who looked exactly like Viktor. On the underground and in cafés. Ugly knitted or crocheted hats. Soft shoulder bags. Jeans slung low on narrow hips. Suede jackets from the sixties. The slow, nonchalant walk. A kind of anti-fashion reserved for the good-looking and the confident.

Viktor had belonged to the court surrounding Thomas Söderberg, but he had never become a copy of Thomas. More his opposite. Without possessions, without ambition. Abstemious. Although the latter was perhaps because Rebecka Martinsson had crushed him in her madness. It was hard to know.

Maja leaned toward her. Hot breath hissing in her ear.

"Aha, here comes Astrid. But where's Vesa?"

Pastor Vesa Larsson's wife, Astrid, pushed her way in through the door of the Crystal Church. On the stage, Thomas Söderberg was leading the gospel choir in prayer before the evening service.

The trek up the hill from the car park had made her blouse wet and sticky under her arms. Just as well she had a cardigan over the top. She hastily wiped under her eyes with her index finger just in case her mascara had run. She'd once seen herself on one of the church video recordings. It had been snowing when she'd walked to the church, and on the film she had been going around with the collection bag like a trained panda. Since then she always checked in the mirror. But now the cloakroom was full of people and she was so stressed.

A pile of flowers and cards lay in the central circle.

Viktor is dead, she thought.

Tried to make it seem real.

Viktor is actually dead.

She caught sight of Karin and Maja. Maja was waving eagerly. No chance of escape. The only thing to do was to go over to them. They were wearing dark suits. She had rummaged in her wardrobe and tried things on for an hour. All her suits were red, pink or yellow. She had one dark suit. Navy blue. But she couldn't zip up the skirt. Finally she settled on a long knitted cardigan that made her look thinner and disguised her hips and bottom. But looking at Karin and Maja, she felt like a mess. A sweaty mess.

"Where's Vesa?" whispered Maja, before she'd even managed to sit down.

Friendly smile. Dangerous eyes.

"Ill," she replied. "Flu."

She could see they didn't believe her. Maja closed her mouth and breathed in through her nose.

They were right. Her whole body was telling her that she didn't want to sit there, but she sank down on the chair next to Maja.

Thomas had finished the prayer with the choir and was walking over to them.

So I shall have to answer to him as well, she thought.

She felt a pang as Thomas placed his hand on Maja's arm and greeted her with a quick, warm smile. Then he asked about Vesa. Astrid replied again: ill; flu. He gazed at her sympathetically.

Poor me, having such a weak husband, she thought.

"If you're worried about him, go home," said Thomas.

She shook her head obediently.

"Worried." She tried out the word.

No, she should have been worried several years ago. But at the time she'd been fully occupied with the children and the house being built. And by the time she discovered that she had reason to worry, it was already too late and time to begin grieving. To get over the grief of being abandoned in her marriage. Learn to live with the shame of not being good enough for Vesa.

It was the shame. That was what made her sit next to Maja, although she didn't want to. Made her stand in front of the freezer with the door open, stuffing herself with frozen cakes when the children were at school.

They did still sleep with each other, although it was rare. But it happened in the dark. In silence.

And this morning. The kids had gone off to school. Vesa had been sleeping in the studio. When she brought in the coffee he was sitting on the edge of the bed in his flannel pajamas. Unshaven, eyes tired. Deep lines around the corners of his mouth. His long, fine artist's hands resting on his knees. The floor around the bed littered with books. Expensive, beautifully bound art books with thick shiny pages. Several about icons. Thin paperbacks from their own publishing firm. In the beginning Vesa had designed the covers. Then he'd suddenly decided he didn't have the time.

She had put the tray of coffee and sandwiches down on the floor. Then she had crept up behind him, kneeling on the bed. His hips between her thighs. She had let her dressing gown fall open and pressed her breasts and her cheek against his back while her hands caressed his firm shoulders.

"Astrid," was all he said.

Troubled and suffering. Filled her name with apologies and feelings of guilt.

She had fled to the kitchen. Switched on the radio and the dishwasher. Picked up Baloo and wept into the dog's fur.

Thomas Söderberg leaned down toward the three women and lowered his voice.

"Have you heard anything about Sanna?" he asked.

Astrid, Karin and Maja shook their heads.

"Ask Curt Bäckström," said Astrid. "He's forever trailing around after her."

The pastors' wives turned their heads like periscopes. It was Maja who first caught sight of Curt. She waved and pointed until he reluctantly got up and shambled over to them.

Karin looked at him. He always seemed so anxious. Walked a bit hesitantly. Almost sidling along. As if it might appear too aggressive to approach head-on. Looked at them out of the corner of his eyes, but always glanced away if you tried to meet his gaze.

"Do you know where Sanna is staying?" asked Thomas Söderberg.

Curt shook his head. Answered as well, just to be on the safe side: "No."

He was obviously lying. There was fear in his eyes. At the same time, they were resolute. He didn't intend to reveal his secret.

Like a dog that's found a bone in the woods, thought Karin.

Curt looked furtively at them. Almost crouching. As if Thomas might suddenly shout "Away" and hit him on the muzzle.

Thomas Söderberg looked disturbed. He twisted his body as if he were trying to shake off the pastors' wives.

"I just want to know that she's all right," he said. "Nothing must happen to her."

Curt nodded, and his gaze slid over the seats, which were beginning to fill up. He held up the Bible in his hands and pressed it to his chest.

"I want to bear witness," he said quietly. "God has something to say."

Thomas Söderberg nodded.

"If you hear anything from Sanna, tell her I was asking about her," he said.

Astrid looked at Thomas Söderberg.

And if you hear anything from God, she thought, tell Him I'm asking about Him all the time.

Måns Wenngren, Rebecka Martinsson's boss, got home late going on early. He'd spent the evening at Sophie's, treating two young ladies to drinks, along with a representative for one of the law firm's clients, a computer company specializing in industrial IT that had recently floated on the stock exchange. It was pleasant to deal with that kind of client. Grateful for every cent you managed to keep away from the tax collector. The clients who'd been accused of tax evasion or dubious book-keeping weren't usually that keen on sitting in a bar with their lawyer. They sat and drank at home instead.

After Sophie's had closed Måns had shown one of the young ladies, Marika, his nice office, then he had put little Marika in a cab with some money in her hand, and himself in another cab.

When he walked into the dark apartment on Floragatan he thought as usual that he ought to move to something smaller. It was hardly surprising that every time he came home he felt, well, however it was he felt when the apartment was so bloody desolate.

He threw his gray cashmere coat on a chair and flicked on every light on his way to the living room. As he was hardly ever home before eleven at night, the video timer was always set to record the news. He switched on the video, and as Channel 4's news titles rolled he went into the kitchen and opened the refrigerator.

Ritva had been shopping. Good. It must be her easiest job, cleaning his flat and making sure there was fresh food in. He never made a mess, except on the rare occasions he invited people back. The food Ritva bought was usually untouched when it was replaced with fresh. He presumed she took the old stuff home to her family before it went off. It was an arrangement that suited him perfectly. He ripped open some milk and drank straight from the carton, one ear on the news. The murder of Viktor Strandgård was the top story.

That's why Rebecka went up to Kiruna, thought Måns Wenngren, heading back into the living room. He sank down on the sofa in front of the TV, the carton of milk in his hand.

"The religious celebrity Viktor Strandgård was found murdered this morning in the church of The Source of All Our Strength in Kiruna," announced the newsreader.

She was a well-dressed middle-aged woman who used to be married to someone Måns knew.

"Hi there, Beate, how's things?" said Måns, raising the milk carton to the screen in a toast and taking a deep draught.

"According to police sources, Viktor Strandgård was found by his sister, and those same sources report that the murder was extremely brutal," continued the newsreader.

"Come on, Beate, we know all that," said Måns.

He suddenly became aware of how drunk he was. He felt stupid, his head full of cotton wool. He decided to have a shower as soon as the news was finished.

They were showing a report on the murder now. A male voice was speaking over pictures. First of all, pale blue wintry pictures of the impressive Crystal Church up on the hill. Then shots of the police shoveling their way through the area around the church. They'd also used some clips from one of the church gatherings, everyone singing, and gave a short summary of who Viktor Strandgård was.

"There is no doubt that this incident has aroused strong feelings in Kiruna," continued the reporter's voice. "This was made very clear when Viktor Strandgård's sister, Sanna Strandgård, arrived at the police station to be interviewed, accompanied by her lawyer."

The picture was showing a snow-covered car park. A breathless young female reporter dashed up to two women who were climbing out of a red Audi. The reporter's red hair stuck out from under her cap like a fox's brush. She looked young and energetic. It was dark, but you could make out a boring redbrick building in the background. It couldn't be anything other than a police station. One of the women getting out of the Audi had her head down, and all you could see of her was a long sheepskin coat and a sheepskin hat pulled well down over her eyes. The other woman was Rebecka Martinsson. Måns turned up the volume and leaned forward on the sofa.

"What the . . . ?" he said to himself.

Rebecka had told him she was going up there because she knew the family, he thought. Saying she was the sister's lawyer must be a mistake.

He looked at Rebecka's set face as she walked quickly toward the police station, her arm firmly around the other woman, who must be Viktor Strandgård's sister. With her free arm she tried to fend off the woman with the microphone who was trotting along after them.

"Is it true that his eyes had been gouged out?" asked the female reporter in a broad Luleå accent.

"How are you feeling, Sanna?" she went on when she got no reply. "Is it true the children were with you in the church when you found him?"

When they got to the entrance of the police station, the fox placed herself resolutely in front of them.

"My God, girl," sighed Måns. "What's going on here? Hard-hitting American journalism à la Lapland?"

"Do you think it might have been a ritual killing?" asked the reporter.

The camera zoomed in on her glowing, agitated cheeks, then there was a close-up of Rebecka's and the other woman's faces in profile. Sanna Strandgård was holding her hands up to her face like blinkers. Rebecka's gray eyes glared straight into the camera first of all, and then she looked straight at the reporter.

"Get out of the way," she said sternly.

The words and the expression on Rebecka's face stirred an unpleasant memory in Måns' head. It had been at the firm's Christmas party the previous year. He'd been trying to chat and be pleasant, and she'd looked at him as if he were something you might find while cleaning out the urinals. If he remembered rightly, that was exactly what she'd said to him as well. In the same stern voice.

"Get out of the way."

After that he'd kept his distance. The last thing he wanted was for her to feel embarrassed and resign. And he didn't want her getting any ideas either. If she wasn't interested, that was fine.

All at once things were happening very quickly on the screen. Måns paid closer attention, kept his finger poised over the pause button on the remote control. Rebecka raised her arm to get past, and suddenly the reporter had vanished out of the picture. Rebecka and Sanna Strandgård more or less climbed over her and went into the police station. The camera followed them, and the reporter's furious voice could be heard over the clip.

"Ow, my arm. Christ, did you get that on film?"

The voice of the male reporter from Channel 4 could be heard once again.

"The lawyer is with the well-known firm of Meijer & Ditzinger, but no one at the office was prepared to comment on this evening's events."

Måns was shocked to see an archive picture of the company's offices. He pressed the pause button.

"Too fucking right," he swore, getting up from the sofa in such a rush that he spilt milk all over his shirt and trousers.

What the hell was she up to? he thought. Was she really acting as this Sanna Strandgård's lawyer without telling the firm? There must have been some sort of misunderstanding. Her judgment couldn't be that poor.

He grabbed his cell phone and keyed in a number. No reply. He pressed the bridge of his nose with his right index finger and thumb and tried to think straight. As he was walking into the hall to fetch his laptop he tried another number. No reply there either. He felt sweaty and out of breath. He opened up the computer on the table in the living room and started the video again. Assistant Chief Prosecutor Carl von Post was speaking outside The Source of All Our Strength.

"Damn it," swore Måns, trying to start up the computer and holding his cell phone clamped between his shoulder and his ear at the same time.

His hands felt clumsy and agitated.

Måns found the earpiece and was able to make calls and start up the computer at the same time. Every number rang without anyone picking up the receiver. No doubt the phones had been red hot after the evening news. The other partners were no doubt wondering how the hell one of his tax lawyers could be up there flattening journalists one after the other. He checked his phone and found that he had fifteen messages. Fifteen.

Carl von Post was looking straight at Måns from the television screen and explaining how the investigation was proceeding. It was the usual stuff about how the search was in full swing, door-to-door inquiries, interviewing members of the congregation, looking for the murder weapon. The prosecutor was elegantly dressed in a gray wool coat with matching gloves and scarf.

"Bloody clotheshorse," commented Måns Wenngren, failing to grasp that von Post was wearing virtually the same as he was.

Finally someone picked up the phone. It was the husband of one of the female partners, and he wasn't happy. She had remarried the much younger man, who lived well off his successful lawyer wife while he pretended to be studying, or whatever the hell he was supposed to be doing.

He doesn't need to sound quite so miserable, thought Måns.

When his colleague came on the line the conversation was very short.

"We can meet right away, can't we?" said Måns crossly. "What do you mean, the middle of the night?"

He looked at his Breitling. Quarter past four.

"Okay, then," he said. "We'll meet at seven instead. Early breakfast meeting. We'll need to try and get hold of the others as well."

When he had finished the conversation he sent an e-mail to Rebecka Martinsson. She hadn't answered the phone either. He shut down the computer, and as he stood up he could feel his trousers sticking to his legs. He looked down and discovered the milk he'd spilt all over himself.

"That bloody girl," he growled as he pulled his trousers off. "That bloody girl."

And evening came and morning came, the second day

Inspector Anna-Maria Mella is sleeping restlessly in the darkest hour of the night. Clouds cover the sky, and the room is pitch-black. It is as if God himself has cupped His hand over the town, just as a child places his hand over a scuttling insect. No one who has joined the game shall escape.

Anna-Maria tosses her head from side to side to escape the voices and faces from yesterday that have occupied her sleep. The child kicks angrily in her stomach.

In her dream Prosecutor Carl von Post pushes his face toward Sanna Strandgård and tries to force answers from her that she cannot give. He presses her and threatens to interrogate her daughters if she cannot answer. And the more he asks, the more she closes down. In the end she appears to remember nothing.

"What were you doing in the church in the middle of the night? What made you go there? You must remember something, surely? Did you see anyone else there? Do you remember calling the police? Were you angry with your brother?"

Sanna hides her face in her hands.

"I don't remember. I don't know. He came to me in the night. Suddenly Viktor was standing by my bed. He looked sad. When he just dissolved I knew something had happened. . . ."

"He dissolved?"

The prosecutor looks as if he doesn't know whether to laugh or give her a slap.

"Hang on, so you were visited by a ghost and you realized something had happened to your brother?"

Anna-Maria whimpers so much that Robert wakes up. He raises himself on his elbow and strokes her hair.

"Ssh, Mia-Mia," he soothes her. He says her name over and over again, stroking her straw-colored hair until suddenly she gives a deep sigh and relaxes. Her face softens and the whimpering stops. When her breathing is calm and even once more, he goes back to sleep.

Those who know Carl von Post probably believe he is sleeping well tonight. That he has eaten his fill of attention and golden dreams of what the future holds in her glorious lap. He should be sleeping in his bed with a contented smile on his face.

But Carl von Post is tossing and turning as well. His jaws are clamped together so that the surfaces of his teeth grind impotently against one another. He always sleeps like this. The events of the day have not saved him.

And Rebecka Martinsson. She is in a deep sleep on the sofa bed in the kitchen of her grandparents' house. Her breathing is calm and regular. Virku has kindly come to lie beside her, and Rebecka is sleeping with her arm around the dog's warm body, her nose buried in the black woolly coat. There is not a sound from the outside world. No cars and no planes. No loud late-night revelers and no winter rain hammering against the windowpanes. In the bedroom Lova mumbles in her sleep, and presses closer to Sanna. The house itself creaks and groans a little, as if it were turning over in its long winter sleep.

Tuesday, February 18

Just before six o'clock Virku woke Rebecka by pushing her nose into Rebecka's face.

"Hello, you," whispered Rebecka. "What do you want? Time for a pee?"

She fumbled for the lamp by the bed and switched it on. The dog scampered toward the door, gave a little whimper, turned back to Rebecka and nudged her face with her nose again.

"I know, I know."

She sat up on the edge of the bed, but kept the blanket wound around her. It was cold in the kitchen.

Everything in here is my grandmother, she thought. It's as if I've been sleeping beside her in the kitchen sofa bed, allowed to stay in the warm bed while she lit the stove and put the coffee on.

She could see Theresia Martinsson sitting at the table rolling her morning cigarette. Her grandmother used newspaper instead of the expensive cigarette papers you could buy. She would tear the margin carefully down one page of the previous day's *Norbottenskuriren*. It was wide and free from print, ideal for her purpose. She scattered a few strands of tobacco over it and rolled a thin cigarette between her thumb and forefinger. Her silvery hair was well tucked in under a head scarf, and she was wearing her blue-and-black-checked nylon overall. Out in the barn the cows were calling to her. "Hello, *pikku-piika*," she used to say with a smile. "Are you awake?"

Pikku-piika. Little maid.

Virku yelped impatiently.

"Yes, in a minute," answered Rebecka. "I'm just going to light the stove."

She had slept in woolen socks, and with the blanket still wrapped around her she went over to the old kitchen stove and opened the door. Virku sat down patiently and waited. From time to time she gave a tentative little whine, just to make sure she wasn't forgotten.

Rebecka took a sharp Mora knife and with a practiced hand shaved sticks from one of the logs by the stove. She laid two logs on top of some birch bark and the sticks, and lit them. The fire quickly took hold. She pushed in a birch log that would burn a little longer than the pine, and closed the door.

I should spend more time thinking about my grandmother, she thought. Who was it who decided it was better to concentrate on the present? There are many places in my memory where grandmother lives. But I don't spend any time there with her. And what does the present have to offer?

Virku was whimpering and doing a little pirouette by the door. Rebecka pulled on her clothes. They were ice cold, and made her movements rapid and jerky. She pushed her feet into a pair of Lapp boots that were standing in the hallway.

"You'll have to be quick," she said to Virku.

On her way out she switched on the lights outside the house and the barn.

It had turned a little milder. The thermometer was showing minus fifteen, and the sky was pressing down, shutting out the light of the stars. Virku squatted down a short way off and Rebecka looked around. The ground had been cleared of snow right up to the barn. Around the house the snow had been shoveled up against the walls to provide insulation against the cold.

Who's done the shoveling? Rebecka wondered. Could it be Sivving Fjällborg? Is he still clearing the snow for Grandmother, even though she's gone? He must be around seventy now.

She tried to peer through the darkness at Sivving's house on the opposite side of the road. When it was lighter she would look to see if it still said "Fjällborg" on the mailbox.

She wandered along beside the wall of the barn. The outside light glittered on the roses of rime frost on the barred windows. At the other end was her grandmother's greenhouse. Several broken panes stared hollow-eyed and accusing at Rebecka.

You ought to be here, they said. You ought to look after the house and the garden. Look how the putty has given up. Just imagine what the roof tiles must look like under the snow. They've cracked and come loose. And your grandmother was so particular. So hardworking.

As if Virku could read her gloomy thoughts, she came scampering across the garden behind Rebecka through the darkness and barked happily.

"Hush," laughed Rebecka. "You'll wake up the whole village."

Immediately a couple of answering barks came from far away. The black dog listened carefully.

"Don't even think about it," warned Rebecka.

Maybe she should have brought a lead.

Virku looked at her happily and decided Rebecka would do very well as a companion for a dog in the mood for a game. She burrowed playfully down into the feather-light snow with her nose, came back up again and shook her head. Then she invited Rebecka to join in by plonking her front paws on the ground and sticking her bottom up in the air.

Come on, then, said her shiny black eyes.

"Right, then!" shouted Rebecka cheerfully, and lunged at the dog.

She immediately fell over. Virku flew at her like an arrow, jumped over her like a performing dog in a circus, spun around and half a second later was standing in front of Rebecka, her pink tongue lolling out of her laughing mouth and demanding that Rebecka get up and try again. Rebecka laughed and set off after the dog again. Virku hurtled over the piled-up snow and Rebecka clambered after her. They both sank into the untouched snow behind, a meter deep.

"I give up," panted Rebecka after ten minutes.

She was sitting on her bottom in a snowdrift. Her cheeks were glowing red, and she was covered in snow.

When they got back in, Sanna was up and had put the coffee on. Rebecka pulled off her clothes. The outer layers soon got wet from the melting snow, and the clothes nearest her skin were already soaked in sweat. She found a Helly Hansen T-shirt and a pair of Uncle Affe's long johns in a drawer.

"Nice outfit," sniggered Sanna. "It's good to see you've adapted to the classic look up here so quickly."

"The baggy Gällivare look suits any figure," replied Rebecka, wiggling her bottom so that the loose seat of the long johns flapped about.

"God, you're thin," exclaimed Sanna.

Rebecka straightened up at once and poured herself a cup of coffee in silence, her back toward Sanna.

"And you look so sort of dried-up," Sanna went on. "You ought to take more care what you eat and drink."

Her voice was gentle and concerned.

"Still," she sighed when Rebecka didn't respond, "it's lucky for the rest of us that most men like a girl with something to get hold of. Although of course I think it's really attractive to be flat-chested like you."

Well, lucky me, thought Rebecka sarcastically. At least you think I look good.

Her silence made Sanna babble nervously.

"Just listen to me," she said. "I sound like a real mother hen. I'll be asking you next if you're getting your vitamins."

"Do you mind if I put the news on?" asked Rebecka.

Without waiting for a reply she went over to the television and switched it on. The picture was grainy. There was probably snow on the aerial.

An item about the embezzlement of some EU funds was followed by the murder of Viktor Strandgård. The voice of the reporter explained that the police were following the usual procedures in their hunt for the murderer, and as yet there was no obvious suspect. Pictures followed one another in rapid succession. Police and dogs searching the area outside the Crystal Church as they looked for the murder weapon. Assistant Chief Prosecutor Carl von Post talking about door-to-door inquiries, interviews with members of the church and those attending the service. Then Rebecka's red Audi appeared on the screen.

"Oh, no!" exclaimed Sanna, crashing her coffee cup down on the table.

"Viktor Strandgård's sister, who found the dead man at the scene of the crime, also arrived under somewhat dramatic circumstances to be interviewed at the police station last night."

The whole incident was shown, but on the morning news almost all the sound had been removed, except for Rebecka's stifled "Get out of the way." It emerged that the reporter had reported the lawyer for assault, before the anchorman in the studio exchanged a few words with the weatherman about the forecast that would follow the break.

"But you couldn't see how aggressive and horrible that reporter was!" said Sanna in amazement.

Rebecka felt a burning pain in her midriff.

"What is it?" asked Sanna.

What do I say? thought Rebecka, and slumped down on a chair by the kitchen table. That I'm afraid of losing my job. That they'll freeze me out until I'm forced to resign. When she's lost her brother. I ought to ask her about Viktor again. Ask if she wants to talk about it. I just don't want to get drawn into her life and her problems again. I want to go home. I want to sit at the computer writing an analysis of income tax set against pension contributions.

"What do you think happened, Sanna?" she asked. "To Viktor. You said he'd been mutilated. Who could have done something like that?"

Sanna squirmed uncomfortably.

"I don't know. That's what I told the police. I really don't know."

"Weren't you scared when you found him?"

"I wasn't thinking like that."

"What were you thinking, then?"

"I don't know," said Sanna, and put her hands on her head as if to console herself. "I think I screamed, but I'm not sure about that either."

"You told the police Viktor woke you up, and that's why you went there."

Sanna lifted her eyes and looked straight at Rebecka.

"Do you really think that's so strange? Have you started to believe that everything stops because your body no longer works? He was standing by my bed, Rebecka. He looked so sad. And I could see that it wasn't him, not physically anyway. I knew something had happened."

No, I don't think it's strange, thought Rebecka. She's always seen more than the rest of us. A quarter of an hour before somebody came to visit completely unannounced, Sanna would put the coffee on. "Viktor's on his way," she'd sometimes say.

"But..." began Rebecka.

"Please," begged Sanna, "I really don't want to talk about it. I daren't. Not yet. I've got to keep it together. For the girls' sake. Thanks for coming up. Even though you've got your career to think about. You might think we've lost touch, but I think about you loads. It gives me strength just to know that you're down there."

Now Rebecka was squirming.

Stop it, she thought. We're not friends. Her opinion of me used to mean so much. The fact that she said I was an important part of her life. But now... now it feels as if she's spinning a web around my body.

Virku was the first to hear the sound of the snowmobile, interrupting them with a sharp bark. She pricked up her ears and looked out of the window.

"Is somebody coming?" asked Rebecka. She wasn't sure where the noise came from, but thought it sounded as if the snowmobile was idling not far from the house. Sanna leaned her forehead against the windowpane and shaded her eyes with her hands so that she could see past her own reflection.

"Oh, no," she exclaimed with a nervous laugh, "it's Curt Bäckström. He was the one who gave us a lift out here. I think he's got a bit of a thing about me. But he's really good-looking. A bit like Elvis, somehow. Might suit you, Rebecka."

"Stop right there," said Rebecka firmly.

"What? What have I done?"

"You've been doing it for as long as I've known you. You attract endless brainless admirers, and then announce that they might suit me. Thanks but no, thanks."

"I do apologize," said Sanna in an offended voice. "I'm sorry if people I know and associate with aren't good enough or smart enough for you. And how can you call him brainless? You don't even know him."

Rebecka went over to the window and looked out at the yard.

"He's sitting on his snowmobile, it's practically the middle of the night, and he's staring at the house you're staying in, instead of coming to the door," she said. "I rest my case."

"Besides, it's not my fault if some men are attracted to me," Sanna went on. "Or maybe you agree with Thomas and think I'm a whore."

"No, but you can damn well stop making comments about my appearance or offering me your cast-off admirers."

Rebecka grabbed her travel bag and rushed into the bathroom. She banged the door so hard that the little red wooden heart that said "Here It Is" swung violently.

"Ask him to come up," she shouted out to the kitchen. "He can't sit out there in the cold like an abandoned dog."

God, she thought as she locked the door. Sanna's witless admirers. Sanna's loose way of dressing. It's not my problem anymore. But it upset Thomas Söderberg. And at the time, when Sanna and I used to share an apartment, in some peculiar way it was my responsibility.

"I would like you to speak to Sanna about her clothes," Thomas Söderberg says to Rebecka.

He is displeased with her. She can feel it in every pore. And it is as if she is being crushed to the ground. When he smiles, heaven opens and she can feel God's love, even though she cannot hear His voice. But when Thomas has that disappointed look in his eyes, it is as if a light goes out inside her. She becomes nothing more than an empty room.

"I have tried," she defends herself. "I've told her that she must think about how she dresses. That her necklines shouldn't be so low cut. And that she should wear a bra, and longer skirts. And she understands, but . . . it's as if she doesn't see what she's putting on in the mornings. If I'm not there to keep an eye on her when she's getting dressed, she just forgets, somehow. Then I meet her in town and she looks like . . ."

She hesitates, the word "whore" sticks in her throat. Thomas wouldn't like to hear that word from her mouth.

". . . well, I don't know what she looks like," she goes on. "You ask her what on earth she's got on and she looks at herself in amazement. She doesn't do it on purpose."

"I don't care whether she does it on purpose or not," Thomas Söderberg says harshly. "As long as she can't dress decently I can't let her take any kind of leading role in the church. How can I let her bear witness, or sing in the choir, or lead the prayers, when I know that ninety percent of all the men who are sitting there listening are just staring at her nipples sticking out under her top, and the only thing they can think about is shoving a hand between her legs."

He stops speaking and looks out through the window. They are sitting in the prayer room at the back of the Mission church. The clear light of the late winter sun pours in through the high, narrow windows. The church is in an apartment block designed by Ralph Erskine. The people of Kiruna call the brown concrete building "The Snuffbox." And consequently the church becomes known as the Lord's Pinch. Rebecka thinks the church was more attractive before. Spartan and austere. Like a monastery, with its concrete walls, its concrete floor and the hard pews. But Thomas Söderberg had the fixed pulpit removed, and replaced it with a movable one made of wood. At the same time he had a wooden floor laid at the front. So that it wouldn't be so depressing. And now the church looks just like any other free church.

Thomas lets his gaze wander up to the ceiling, where there is a huge patch of damp. It always appears in the early spring, when the snow on the roof begins to melt.

It is his way of falling silent and not meeting her eyes that makes Rebecka understand. Thomas Söderberg is angry with Sanna because she is tempting him as well. He too is one of those men who want to shove their hand inside her knickers and . . .

Fury bursts out like a burning rose in her breast.

Bloody Sanna, she swears to herself. You little slag.

She knows it isn't easy to be a pastor. Thomas is tempted in every possible way. The foe would like nothing better than to catch him in a trap. And he has a weakness when it comes to sex. He was quite open about this with the young people in the Bible study group.

She remembers how he told them about a visitation by two angels.

Without being able to help himself, he had been attracted to one of them. And she had known it.

"That would be the worst thing that could happen," the angel had said. "I would become the opposite of myself. As much of the darkness as I am now of the light."

Sanna knocked timidly on the bathroom door.

"Rebecka," she said. "I'm going to go down and ask Curt to come up. You are going to come out of there, aren't you? I don't really want to be alone with him, and the girls are asleep. . . ."

When Rebecka came out, Curt Bäckström was sitting at the table. He held his mug of coffee with both hands when he drank. He lifted it carefully from the table, and at the same time lowered his head so that he wouldn't have to lift it too high. He had kept his boots on, and just shrugged off the upper part of his snowmobile overalls so that they hung down below his waist. He glanced sideways at Rebecka and said hello without meeting her eyes.

Where's the resemblance to Elvis? thought Rebecka. Two eyes and a nose in the middle of his face? His hair, of course. And his moody expression.

Curt had black, wavy hair. His thick fur hat had pressed it down so that it was plastered to his forehead. The outer corners of his eyes had a slight downturn.

"Wow," exclaimed Sanna, looking Rebecka up and down. "You look fantastic. It's really strange, because it's only a pair of jeans and a sweater, and it looks as if you've just pulled any old thing out of the wardrobe. But it's just so obvious it's top-quality stuff.

"Sorry," she went on, her hand covering an embarrassed smile. "I wasn't supposed to comment on your appearance."

"Like I said, I just wanted to see how you were," said Curt to Sanna.

He pushed the coffee mug away slightly to indicate that he was about to leave.

"I'm fine," replied Sanna. "Well, I say fine . . . but Rebecka has been an enormous support to me. If she hadn't come up here and gone with me to the police station, I don't know if I could have done it."

Her hand flew out and lightly brushed Rebecka's arm.

Rebecka saw the muscles under the skin around Curt's mouth stiffen. He pushed back his chair to stand up.

Well done, Sanna, thought Rebecka. Tell him how nicely dressed I am. What a support I've been. And touch me just to make sure he understands how close we are to each other. So you've put some distance between you and him, and the only one he's angry with is me. Like the pawn placed in front of a threatened queen on the chessboard. But I'm not your damned chaperone. The pawn is handing in her resignation.

She quickly placed her hand on Curt's back.

"No, you stay there," she said. "Keep Sanna company. She can find some bread and something to put on it and you can both have some breakfast. I've got to go down to the car to fetch my cell phone and laptop. I'll sit downstairs, make a few calls and send some e-mails."

Sanna followed her with an inscrutable gaze as she went into the hall to put on her heavy boots. They were wet, but she was only going the short distance to the car. She could hear Sanna and Curt talking quietly at the kitchen table.

"You look tired," said Sanna.

"I've been up all night praying in the church," replied Curt. "We've started a chain of prayer, so there's somebody praying all the time. You ought to go. Put yourself down just for half an hour. Thomas Söderberg has been asking about you."

"But you didn't tell him where I was, did you?"

"No, of course not. But you really shouldn't stay away from the church now, you should find your refuge in it. And you ought to go home."

Sanna sighed. "I just don't know who I can rely on anymore. So you mustn't tell anybody where I am."

"I won't. And if there's anyone you can rely on, Sanna, it's me."

Rebecka appeared in the doorway just in time to see Curt's hands working their way across the table to find Sanna's.

"My keys," said Rebecka. "Both my car keys and the key to the house are missing. I must have dropped them in the snow when I was playing with Virku."

Rebecka, Sanna and Curt hunted for the keys in the snow with their torches. It hadn't started to get light yet, and the cones of light swept across the garden, the snowdrifts and the footprints left in the deep snow.

"This is just hopeless," sighed Sanna, burrowing aimlessly where she was standing. "Keys can sink really deep if the snow isn't packed."

Virku went to stand beside Sanna and starting digging like something possessed. She found a twig and shot off with it.

"And you can't trust that one either," said Sanna, gazing after Virku, who had been swallowed up by the darkness within a couple of meters. "She might have picked them up in her mouth and carried them off, if she couldn't find anything else interesting."

"You and Curt might as well go back inside with the dog," said

Rebecka, trying to hide her annoyance. "The girls might wake up, and soon I won't know which tracks are mine and which are yours."

Her feet were icy cold and damp.

"No, I don't want to go in," whined Sanna. "I want to help you find your keys. We'll find them. They've got to be here somewhere."

Curt was the only one who seemed to be in a good mood. It was as if the darkness gave him some protection against his shyness. And the exercise and the fresh air had made him wake up.

"It was just unbelievable last night!" he told Sanna excitedly. "God was just reminding me of His power all the time. I was completely filled by Him. You should go to the church, Sanna. When I prayed, I could feel His strength pouring over me. I could speak fluently in tongues. *Shakka baraj.* And my soul was dancing. Sometimes I sat down and just let the Bible fall open where God wanted me to read. And it was all about promises for the future. Bang, bang, bang. He was just bombarding me with promises."

"You might like to pray that I find my keys," muttered Rebecka.

"It was just as if He was burning some of the words from the Bible into my eyes with a laser," Curt went on. "So that I would pass them on. Isaiah 43:19: 'Behold, I will do a new thing; now it shall spring forth; shall ye not know it? I will even make a way in the wilderness, rivers in the desert.' "

"You could pray yourself that you find your keys," said Sanna to Rebecka.

Rebecka laughed. It sounded more like a snort.

"Or Isaiah 48:6," droned Curt. " 'Thou hast heard, see all this; and will ye not declare it? I have showed thee new things from this time, even hidden things, and thou didst not know them.' "

Sanna straightened up and shone her torch straight into Rebecka's eyes.

"Did you hear what I said?" she asked in a serious voice. "Why don't you pray for your keys yourself?"

Rebecka raised her hand against the blinding light.

"Stop it!" she said.

"And I think God showed me every single place in the New

Testament where it says you can't pour new wine into old bottles,"
said Curt to Virku, who was now standing at his feet and appeared to
be the only one listening to him. "Because then they crack. And
everywhere it says you can't mend an old garment with a piece of
new cloth, because then the new cloth rips along with the old, and
the tear is worse."

"If you want us to pray to find your keys, we'll do it," said Sanna,
without shifting the light from Rebecka's face. "But don't you stand
there and pretend God would listen to my prayers and Curt's more
than yours. Don't trample the blood of Jesus under your feet."

"Pack it in, I said," hissed Rebecka, pointing her torch at Sanna's
face.

Curt fell silent and looked at them both.

"Curt," asked Rebecka, staring straight into the dazzling beam of
Sanna's torch, "do you believe God listens equally to everyone's
prayers?"

"Of course," he said, "there is never anything wrong with His
hearing, but there can be obstacles in the way of His will being done,
and obstacles in the way of prayers being answered."

"What if you don't live according to His will, for example. Surely
God can't work in your life in the same way then?"

"Exactly."

"But then that's just some kind of doctrine," exclaimed Sanna in
despair. "Where's the grace in that? And God Himself, what do you
imagine He thinks of that kind of read-the-Bible-say-your-prayers-
for-an-hour-a-day-and-you'll-have-successful-faith doctrine? I pray
and read the Bible when I long for Him. That's how I'd want to be
loved. Why should God be any different? And all this about living according to His will. Surely that should be one of our goals in life. Not
a way of winning the star prize for effective praying."

Curt didn't answer.

"Sorry, Sanna," said Rebecka eventually, lowering her torch. "I
don't want to fight about Christian faith. Not with you, at any rate."

"Because you know I'll win," said Sanna with a smile in her voice,
and lowered her torch as well.

They stood in silence for a moment, looking at the pools of light on the snow.

"This business with the keys is going to drive me mad," said Rebecka eventually. "Stupid dog! It's all your fault!"

Virku barked in agreement.

"Don't you listen to her," said Sanna, throwing her arms around Virku's neck. "You're not a stupid dog! You're the best, most wonderful dog in the whole wide world. And I love you to bits." She hugged Virku, who reciprocated these declarations of affection by trying to lick Sanna's mouth.

Curt stared jealously at them.

"It's a rented car, isn't it?" he asked. "I can drive into town and pick up the spare keys."

He was talking to Sanna, but it was as if she couldn't hear him. She was completely taken up with Virku.

"I'd really appreciate that," Rebecka said to Curt.

Not that you could care less whether I appreciate it or not, she thought, contemplating the slump of his shoulders as he stood behind Sanna, waiting for her to pay him some attention.

Sivving Fjällborg, she thought then. He's got a spare key to the house. At least he used to have. I'll go and see him.

It was quarter past seven when Rebecka walked into Sivving Fjäll-borg's house without ringing the doorbell, just as she and her grandmother had always done. There was no light in any of the windows, so he was presumably still asleep. But that couldn't be helped. She switched on the light in the little hallway. There was a rag rug on the brown lino floor, and she wiped her feet on it. She had snow over the tops of her boots as well, but she couldn't get much wetter now. A staircase led up to the top floor, and next to it was the dark green door down to the boiler room. The kitchen door was closed. She shouted upstairs into the darkness.

"Hello!"

A low bark came at once from the cellar, followed by Sivving's strong voice.

"Quiet, Bella! Sit! Now! Stay!"

She heard footsteps on the stairs, then the cellar door opened and

Sivving appeared. His hair had turned completely white, and he might have gone a bit thin on top, but otherwise he hadn't changed at all. His eyebrows were set high above his eyes, making him look as if he were always about to discover something unexpected or to hear some good news. His blue-and-white-checked flannel shirt just about buttoned over his paunch, and was tucked well into a pair of combat trousers. The brown leather belt holding up the trousers was shiny with age.

"It's Rebecka!" he exclaimed, a huge smile splitting his face.

"Come, Bella!" he called over his shoulder, and in a trice a pointer bitch came galloping up the stairs.

"Well, hello there," said Rebecka. "Is it you that's got such a deep voice?"

"She's got a really manly bark," said Sivving. "But it keeps the people trying to sell raffle tickets and the like away, so I'm not complaining. Come on in!"

He opened the kitchen door and switched on the light. Everything was terribly neat, and it smelled slightly musty.

"Sit down," he said, pointing to the rib-backed settee.

Rebecka explained why she was there, and while Sivving fetched the spare key she looked around. The freshly washed green-and-white-striped rag rug was in precisely the right place on the pine floor. Instead of an oilcloth on the table, there was a beautifully ironed linen cloth, decorated with a little vase of beaten copper, holding dried buttercups and everlasting flowers. There were windows on three sides, and from the window behind her you could see her grandmother's house. In daylight, of course. All you could see at the moment was the reflection of the pine lamp hanging from the ceiling.

When Sivving had given her the keys he sat down at the opposite side of the table. Somehow he didn't look quite at home in his own kitchen. He was perched on the very edge of the red-stained chair. Bella didn't seem able to settle either, but was wandering about like a lost soul.

"It's been a long time." Sivving smiled, looking closely at

Rebecka. "I was just about to have my first cup of coffee. Would you like one?"

"Please," said Rebecka, sketching out a timetable in her head.

It wouldn't take more than five minutes to pack her case. Tidying up, half an hour. She could catch the ten-thirty plane, provided Curt turned up with the car keys.

"Come on," said Sivving, getting up.

He went out of the kitchen and down the cellar steps, with Bella at his heels. Rebecka followed them.

Everything was cozy and homely in the boiler room. A made-up bed stood against one wall. Bella climbed straight into her own bed, which was next to it. Her water and food bowls were sparkling clean, newly washed. There was a washstand in front of the water heater, and an electric hot plate stood on a little drop-leaf table.

"You can pull up that stool," said Sivving, pointing.

He took down a little coffeepot and two mugs from a string shelf on the wall. The aroma from the tin of coffee blended with the smell of dog, cellar and soap. A pair of long johns, two flannel shirts and a T-shirt with "Kiruna Truck" on it were hanging on a washing line.

"I must apologize," said Sivving, nodding toward the long johns. "But then, I wasn't expecting such an elegant visitor."

"I don't understand," said Rebecka in bewilderment. "Do you sleep down here?"

"Well, you see," said Sivving, running his hand over the stubble on his chin as he carefully counted scoops of coffee into the pot, "Maj-Lis died two years ago."

Rebecka muttered a few words of sympathy in reply.

"It was stomach cancer. They opened her up, but all they could do was stitch her back together. Anyway, the house was too big for me. The kids had moved out long ago, and with Maj-Lis gone too . . . First of all I stopped using the top floor. The kitchen and the little bedroom downstairs were enough. Then Bella and I realized that we were only using the kitchen. So then I moved the TV into the kitchen and slept in there, on the sofa bed. And stopped using the bedroom."

"And in the end you moved down here."

"Well, it's much less cleaning. And the washing machine and the shower were down here. I bought that little fridge. It's big enough for me."

He pointed toward a little fridge in the corner with a plate rack on top of it.

"But what does Lena say, and . . ." Rebecka fumbled for the name of Sivving's son.

"Mats. Ah, the coffee's ready. Well, Lena makes a lot of noise and plays hell and reckons her dad's lost the plot. When she comes to visit with the kids, they run about all over the house. And in some ways that's good, because otherwise I might as well sell up. She's moved to Gällivare, and she's got three boys. But they're getting quite big now, and starting to live their own lives. They do like fishing, though, so they usually come over quite a bit in the spring to fish through holes in the ice. Milk? Sugar?"

"Black."

"Mats is divorced, but he's got two kids. Robin and Julia. They usually come on the holidays and so on. What about you, Rebecka? Husband and children?"

Rebecka sipped at the hot coffee. It went all the way to her cold feet.

"No, neither."

"No, I suppose they wouldn't dare come near you. . . ."

"What do you mean?" laughed Rebecka.

"Your temperament, my girl," said Sivving as he got up and fetched a packet of cinnamon buns from the fridge. "You've always been a bit fierce. Here, have a bun. God, I remember that time you lit a fire in the ditch. You were a tiny little thing. Stood there like a policewoman with your hand raised when your grandmother and I came running. 'Stop! Don't come any closer!' you shouted, full of authority, and you were so cross when we put the fire out. You were going to grill fish on it."

Sivving was laughing so much, he had to wipe away a tear at the memory. Bella raised her head and barked happily.

"Or the time you threw a stone at Erik's head because you weren't allowed to go with the lads on their raft," Sivving went on, laughing so that his stomach quivered.

"All barred by the statute of limitations." Rebecka smiled as she gave Bella a piece of her bun. "Is it you who's been clearing the snow over at Grandmother's?"

"Well, it's nice for Inga-Lill and Affe to be able to do other things when they come here. And I need the exercise."

He patted his stomach.

"Hello!"

They heard Sanna's voice on the stairs. Bella jumped up, barking.

"Down here," called Rebecka.

"Hi," said Sanna, and came down. "It's okay, I like dogs."

She was speaking to Sivving, who was holding on to Bella's collar. She bent down and let Bella sniff at her face. Sivving looked serious.

"Sanna Strandgård," he said. "I read about your brother. It was a terrible thing. I'm sorry."

"Thank you," said Sanna, her lap full of friendly dog. "Rebecka, Curt rang. He's on his way with the keys."

Sivving stood up.

"Coffee?" he asked.

Sanna nodded and accepted a thick china mug with a pattern of brown and yellow flowers around the top. Sivving offered her the bag of buns so that she could dunk one in her coffee.

"They're good," said Rebecka. "Who's been baking? Was it you?"

Sivving's reply was an embarrassed grunt.

"Oh, that's Mary Kuoppa. She can't cope with the idea that there's a freezer somewhere in the village that isn't full of decent buns."

Rebecka smiled at his pronunciation of "Mary." He said it so that it rhymed with "Harry."

"The poor woman's called Mary, surely?" said Sanna, and laughed.

"Well, that's what the teacher at our school thought too," said Sivving, brushing a few crumbs off the cloth; Bella licked them up straightaway. "But Mary just used to stare out of the window and pretend she didn't realize he was talking to her when he said 'Maaaary.' "

This time he sounded like a bleating sheep. Rebecka and Sanna started giggling, and looked at each other like a couple of schoolgirls. Suddenly it was as if all the awkwardness between them had been swept away.

I still care about her, in spite of everything, thought Rebecka.

"Wasn't there somebody in the village called Slark?" she asked. "After the parents' idol, Slark Gabble?"

"No," laughed Sivving, "that must have been somewhere else. There's never been anybody called Slark in this village. Then again, when your grandmother was young she knew a girl she felt really sorry for. She was very delicate when she was born, and because they didn't think she was going to survive, they got the schoolteacher to do an emergency baptism. The teacher was called Fredrik Something-or-other. Anyway, the little girl lived, and then of course she was to be baptized properly by the priest. Of course, the priest understood only Swedish, and the parents only spoke Tornedalen Finnish. So the priest picked up the child and asked the parents what she was to be called. The parents thought he was asking who had baptized the child, so they answered, 'Feki se kasti,' it was Fredrik who baptized her. And so the priest wrote 'Fekisekasti' in the church register. And you know how people respected the priest in those days. The child was called Fekisekasti for the rest of her life."

Rebecka glanced at the clock. Curt was bound to be here by now. She could catch the flight, even if there wasn't an awful lot of time.

"Thanks for the coffee," she said, and stood up.

"Are you off?" asked Sivving. "Was it just a flying visit?"

"Arrived yesterday, leaving today," replied Rebecka with a brief smile.

"You know how it is with these career women," said Sanna to Sivving. "Always on the move."

Rebecka pulled on her gloves with jerky movements.

"This wasn't exactly a pleasure trip," she said.

"I'll hang the key up in the usual place," she went on, turning to Sivving.

"Come back in the spring," said Sivving. "Drive out to the old cottage at Jiekajärvi. Do you remember in the old days, when we used to go up there? Your grandfather and I took the snowmobile. And you and your grandmother and Maj-Lis and the kids skied all the way."

"I'd like to do that," said Rebecka, and discovered that she was telling the truth.

The cottage, she thought. It was the only place grandmother allowed herself to sit still. Once the berries picked that day had been cleaned. Or the birds that had been shot had been plucked and drawn.

She could see her grandmother now, absorbed in reading a story while Rebecka played cards or a board game with her grandfather. Because the cottage got so damp when nobody was there, the pack of cards had swollen to double its size. The board game was warped and uneven, and it was difficult to balance the pieces on it. But it didn't matter.

And the feeling of security, falling asleep as the adults sat chatting around the table beside you. Or slipping into dreams to the sound of Grandmother washing up in the red plastic bowl, with the heat radiating from the stove.

"It was good to see you," said Sivving. "Really good. Wasn't it, Bella?"

Rebecka gave Sanna and the children a lift home and parked out-side the apartment block where Sanna lived. She would have preferred to say a quick good-bye in the car and drive off. Quick good-byes in cars were good. If you were sitting in the car it was difficult to hug. Particularly if you were wearing a seat belt. So you escaped the hugs. And in a car there were other things to talk about, apart from "We must meet up again soon" and "We mustn't leave it so long next time." A few words about not forgetting the bag on the backseat and not forgetting the bag in the boot and "Are you sure you've got everything now?" Then, once the car door had chopped off the rest of the unspoken sentences, you could wave and put your foot down without an unpleasant taste in your mouth. You didn't have to stand there like an idiot stamping your feet up and down while your thoughts went round and round like a swarm of midges, trying to find the right words. No, she'd stay in the car. And not undo her seat belt.

But when she stopped the car Sanna jumped out without a word. A second later, Virku followed her. Rebecka felt she had to get out as well. She turned her collar up above her ears, but it gave no protection against the cold, which immediately worked its way under the fabric and fastened itself to her earlobes like two clothes pegs. She looked up at Sanna's apartment. A little block made of panels of forest green wood, with a red tin roof. The snowplow hadn't been around for a long time. The few parked cars had left deep tracks in the snow. An old Dodge was hibernating under a snowdrift. She hoped she wouldn't get stuck on the way out. The building was owned by LKAB, the mining company. But only ordinary people lived here, so LKAB saved money by not using the snowplow as often as they should. If you wanted to get the car out in the mornings, you had to clear the snow yourself.

Sara and Lova were still sitting in the backseat. Their hands and elbows kept meeting in some nonsense rhyme that Sara had mastered to perfection; Lova was making a huge effort to learn it. Every so often she got it wrong, and they both exploded into giggles before starting all over again.

Virku was running around like a mad thing, taking in all the new smells with her little black nose. Circled around two unfamiliar parked cars. Read with interest a haiku that next door's dog had drawn on the white snowdrift in golden yellow sign language; she seemed flattered. Followed the irritating trail of a mouse that had disappeared under the front steps where she couldn't follow.

Sanna tipped her head back and sniffed the air.

"It smells like snow," she said. "It's going to snow. A lot."

She turned toward Rebecka.

She's just so like Viktor, thought Rebecka, catching her breath.

The transparent blue skin, stretched over the high cheekbones. Although Sanna's cheeks were slightly rounder, like a child's.

And the way she stands, thought Rebecka. Just like Viktor. Head always slightly crooked, leaning to one side or the other, as if it were a little bit loose.

"Right, well, I'd better get going, then," said Rebecka, trying to start her good-byes, but Sanna was squatting down and calling to Virku.

"Here, girl! Come here, there's a good girl!"

Virku came hurtling through the snow like a black glove.

It's just like a picture from a fairy tale, thought Rebecka. The sweet little black dog, her coat tipped with tiny snow crystals. Sanna, a wood nymph in her knee-length gray sheepskin coat, her sheepskin hat on top of her thick, wavy blond hair.

There was something about Sanna that gave her the ability to relate to animals. They were somehow alike, Sanna and the dog. The little bitch who'd been mistreated and neglected for years. Where had all her troubles gone? They'd simply been washed away and replaced by sheer joy at being able to push her nose into freshly fallen snow, or to bark at a frightened squirrel in a pine tree. And Sanna. She'd only just found her brother hacked to death in the church. And now she was standing in the snow playing with the dog.

I haven't seen her shed a single tear, thought Rebecka. Nothing touches her. Not sorrow, not people. Presumably not even her own children. But it isn't actually my problem any longer. I have no debt to pay. I'm leaving now, and I'm never going to think about her or her children or her brother or this pit of a town ever again.

She went over to the car and opened the back door.

"Out you come, girls," she said to Sara and Lova. "I've got a plane to catch."

"Bye, then," she called after them as they disappeared up the steps to the door of the building.

Lova turned and waved. Sara pretended not to hear.

She pushed aside the forlorn feeling as Sara's red jacket vanished through the door. A picture from the time when she lived with Sanna and Sara lit up a dark space in her memory. She was sitting with Sara on her lap, reading a story. Her cheek resting against the little girl's soft hair. Sara pointing at the pictures.

That's just the way it is, thought Rebecka. I'll always remember. She's forgotten.

Suddenly Sanna was standing beside her. The game with Virku had brought warm, pale pink roses to her blue cheeks.

"But you must come up and have something to eat before you go."

"My plane leaves in half an hour, so . . ."

Rebecka finished the sentence by shaking her head.

"There'll be other planes," pleaded Sanna. "I haven't even had a chance to thank you for coming up. I don't know what I'd have done if—"

"That's okay." Rebecka smiled. "I really do have to go."

Her mouth continued to smile and she stretched out her hand to say good-bye.

It was a way of marking the moment, and she knew it as she slid her hand out of her glove. Sanna looked down and refused to take her hand.

Shit, thought Rebecka.

"You and I," said Sanna without raising her eyes. "We were like sisters. And now I've lost both my brother and my sister."

She gave a short, mirthless laugh. It sounded more like a sob.

"The Lord giveth and the Lord taketh away. Blessed be the Lord."

Rebecka steeled herself against a sudden impulse to throw her arms around Sanna and comfort her.

Don't try this with me, she thought angrily, letting her hand drop. There are certain things you can't fix. And you definitely can't do it in three minutes while you're standing out in the cold saying good-bye.

Her feet were starting to feel cold. Her Stockholm boots were far too flimsy. Her toes had been aching. Now it felt as though they were starting to disappear. She tried to wiggle them a bit.

"I'll ring when I get there," she said, getting into the car.

"You do that," said Sanna without interest, fixing her eyes on Virku, who had squatted down by the wall to answer a message left in the snow.

Or maybe next year, thought Rebecka, and turned the key.

When she looked in the rearview mirror she caught sight of Sara and Lova, who had come back out onto the steps.

There was something in their eyes that made the ground beneath the car shift.

No, no, she thought. Everything's fine. It's nothing. Just drive.

But her feet wouldn't release the clutch and step on the accelerator. She stopped, her eyes fixed on the little girls at the top of the steps. Saw their wide eyes, saw them shouting something to Sanna that Rebecka couldn't hear. Saw them raise their arms and point up at the apartment, then quickly lower them as someone came out of the building.

It was a uniformed policeman, who reached Sanna in a few rapid steps. Rebecka couldn't hear what he said.

She looked at her watch. It was pointless even to try to catch the plane. She couldn't go now. With a deep sigh, she got out of the car. Her body moved slowly toward Sanna and the policeman. The girls were still standing on the steps and leaning over the snow-covered railings. Sara's gaze was firmly fixed on Sanna and the policeman. Lova was eating lumps of snow that had stuck to her gloves.

"What do you mean, house search?"

Sanna's tone of voice made Virku stop, and approach her mistress uneasily.

"You can't just go into my home without permission? Can they?"

The last question was directed at Rebecka.

At that very moment Assistant Chief Prosecutor Carl von Post came out, followed by two plainclothes detectives. Rebecka recognized them. It was that little woman with a face like a horse—what was her name, now? Mella. And the guy with a walrus moustache. Good God, she thought moustaches like that had gone out in the seventies. It looked as if somebody had glued a dead squirrel under his nose.

The prosecutor went up to Sanna. He was holding a bag in one hand, and he fished out a smaller transparent plastic bag. Inside it was a knife. It was about twenty centimeters long. The shaft was black and shiny, and the point curved upward slightly.

"Sanna Strandgård," he said, holding the bag with the knife just a little too close to Sanna's face. "We've just found this in your residence. Do you recognize it?"

"No," replied Sanna. "It looks like a hunting knife. I don't hunt."

Sara and Lova came over to Sanna. Lova tugged at the sleeve of Sanna's sheepskin coat to get her mother's attention.

"Mummy," she whined.

"Just a minute, chicken," said Sanna absently.

Sara nestled into her mother and pressed against her so that Sanna was forced to step backward with one foot so as not to lose her balance. The eleven-year-old followed the prosecutor's movements with her eyes and tried to understand what was going on between these serious adults standing in a circle around her mother.

"Are you absolutely certain?" von Post asked again. "Take a good look," he said, turning the knife over.

The cold made the plastic bag crackle as he showed both sides of the weapon, holding up first the blade and then the shaft.

"Yes, I'm certain," answered Sanna, backing away from the knife. She avoided looking at it again.

"Perhaps the questions could wait," said Anna-Maria Mella to von Post, nodding toward the two children clinging to Sanna.

"Mummy," repeated Lova over and over again, tugging at Sanna's sleeve. "Mummy, I need a pee."

"I'm freezing," squeaked Sara. "I want to go in."

Virku moved anxiously and tried to press herself between Sanna's legs.

Picture number two in the book of fairy stories, thought Rebecka. The wood nymph has been captured by the villagers. They have surrounded her and some are holding her fast by her arms and tail.

"You keep hand towels and sheets in the drawer under the sofa bed in the kitchen, isn't that right?" von Post continued. "Are you also in the habit of keeping knives among the towels?"

"Just a minute, honey," said Sanna to Sara, who was pulling and tugging at her coat.

"I need a pee," whimpered Lova. "I'm going to wet myself."

"Do you intend to answer the question?" pressed von Post.

Anna-Maria Mella and Sven-Erik Stålnacke exchanged glances behind von Post's back.

"No," said Sanna, her voice tense. "I do not keep knives in the drawer."

"What about this, then," continued von Post relentlessly, taking another transparent plastic bag out of the larger bag. "Do you recognize this?"

The bag contained a Bible. It was covered in brown leather, shiny with use. The edges of the pages had once been gilded, but now there was very little of the gold color left, and the pages of the book were dark from much thumbing and leafing. A variety of bookmarks protruded from everywhere: postcards, plaited laces, newspaper clippings.

With a whimper Sanna sank down helplessly and sat there in the snow.

"It says Viktor Strandgård inside the cover," von Post continued mercilessly. "Could you tell us whether it's his Bible, and what it was doing in your kitchen? Isn't it true that he had it with him everywhere he went, and that he had it in the church on the last night of his life?"

"No," whispered Sanna. "No."

She pressed her hands against the sides of her face.

Lova tried to push Sanna's hands away so that she could look into her mother's eyes. When she couldn't do it, she burst into tears, inconsolable.

"Mummy, I want to go," she sobbed.

"Get up," said von Post harshly. "You're under arrest on suspicion of the murder of Viktor Strandgård."

Sara turned on the prosecutor. "Leave her alone," she screamed.

"Get these children away from here," von Post said impatiently to Tommy Rantakyrö.

Tommy Rantakyrö took a hesitant step toward Sanna. Then Virku rushed forward and placed herself in front of her mistress. She lowered her head, flattened her ears and bared her sharp teeth with a low growl. Tommy Rantakyrö backed off.

"Right, I've had just about enough of this," said Rebecka to Carl von Post. "I want to make a complaint."

Her last remark was directed to Anna-Maria Mella, who was standing beside her and gazing up at the surrounding buildings. At every window the curtains were twitching inquisitively.

"You want to make a—" said von Post, interrupting himself with a shake of the head. "As far as I'm concerned, you can come along to the station for questioning with regard to a complaint of assault made against you by a television reporter from Channel 4's Norrbotten news."

Anna-Maria Mella touched von Post lightly on the arm.

"We're starting to get an audience," she said. "It wouldn't look very good if one of the neighbors rang the press and starting talking about police brutality and all the rest of it. I might be mistaken, but I wouldn't be surprised if the old guy in the flat up there to the left was filming us with a video camera."

She pointed up at one of the windows.

"It might be best if Sven-Erik and I leave, so it doesn't look as if there's a whole army of us here," she went on. "We can go and ring forensics. I assume you want them to go over the flat?"

Von Post's upper lip was twitching with displeasure. He tried to look in through the window Anna-Maria Mella had pointed at, but the flat was completely dark. Then he realized he might be staring straight into the lens of a camera, and hastily looked away. The last thing he wanted was to be linked to police brutality, or to be censured in the press.

"No, I want to talk to the forensics guys myself," he replied. "You and Sven-Erik can take Sanna Strandgård in. Make sure the flat's sealed.

"We'll speak again," he said to Sanna before jumping into his Volvo Cross Country.

Rebecka noticed the look on Anna-Maria Mella's face as the prosecutor's car disappeared.

Well, I'll be damned, she thought. Horse face tricked him. She wanted him out of here, and . . . Hell, she's smart.

As soon as Carl von Post had left, silence reigned. Tommy Rantakyrö stood there uncertainly waiting for a sign from Anna-Maria or Sven-Erik. Sara and Lova were on their knees in the snow with their arms around their mother, who was still sitting on the ground. Virku lay down by their side and chomped on lumps of snow. When Rebecka bent down to stroke her, she thumped her tail just to show that everything was all right. Sven-Erik gave Anna-Maria a questioning look.

"Tommy," said Anna-Maria, breaking the silence, "can you and Olsson seal the flat? Mark the kitchen tap so nobody uses it until the forensics team has been in."

"Hi," Sven-Erik said gently to Sanna. "We're really sorry about all this. But we're stuck with the situation now. You have to come with us to the station."

"Can we drop the children off somewhere?" asked Anna-Maria.

"No," said Sanna, raising her head. "I want to speak to my lawyer, Rebecka Martinsson."

Rebecka sighed.

"Sanna, I'm not your lawyer."

"I want to talk to you anyway."

Sven-Erik Stålnacke glanced uncertainly at his colleague.

"I don't know—" he began.

"Oh, please!" snapped Rebecka. "She's being detained for questioning. Not arrested with limited access. She has every right to speak to me. Stand here and listen, we're not going to be talking about any secrets."

Lova whimpered in Sanna's ear.

"What did you say, honey?"

"I've wet my knickers," howled Lova.

Every gaze was turned on the little girl. It was quite true, a dark stain had appeared on her old jeans.

"Lova needs dry trousers," said Rebecka to Anna-Maria Mella.

"Listen to me, girls," said Anna-Maria to Sara and Lova. "Why don't you come upstairs with me and we'll find some dry trousers for Lova, then we'll come back down to your mum. She won't go anywhere till we come back. I promise."

"Go on, do what she says," said Sanna. "My precious little girls. Fetch some clothes for me too. And Virku's food."

"I'm sorry," said Anna-Maria to Sanna. "Not your clothes. And the prosecutor will want to send everything you're wearing to Linköping."

"That's okay," said Rebecka quickly. "I'll sort some new clothes out for you, Sanna. All right?"

The girls disappeared inside with Anna-Maria. Sven-Erik Stålnacke squatted down a little way from Sanna and Rebecka and talked to Virku. They seemed to have a lot in common.

"I can't help you, Sanna," said Rebecka. "I'm a tax specialist. I don't deal with criminal cases. If you need a public defender, I can help you get hold of someone good."

"Don't you understand?" mumbled Sanna. "It has to be you. If you won't help me, I don't want anybody. God can look after me."

"Just stop it, please," begged Rebecka.

"No, you stop it," said Sanna angrily. "I need you, Rebecka. And my children need you. I don't care what you think of me, but now I'm begging you. What do you want me to do? Get down on my knees? Say you've got to do it for old times' sake? It has to be you."

"What do you mean, the children need me?"

Sanna grabbed hold of Rebecka's jacket with both hands.

"Mum and Dad will take them away from me," she said, pain in her voice. "That mustn't happen. Do you understand? I don't want Sara and Lova to spend even five minutes with my parents. And now I can't stop it. But you can. For Sara's sake."

Her parents. Images and thoughts fought their way to the surface of Rebecka's mind. Sanna's father. Well dressed. Perfect manners. With his soft, sympathetic manner. He'd gained considerable popularity as a local politician. Rebecka had even seen him on national television from time to time. In the next election he would probably be on the list of parliamentary candidates for the Christian Democrats. But underneath the warm façade was a pack leader, hard as nails. Even Pastor Thomas Söderberg had deferred to him and shown him respect over many issues within the church. And Rebecka remembered with distaste how Sanna had told her—with a lightness of tone, as if the whole thing had happened to someone else—how he had always killed her animals. Always without warning. Dogs, cats, birds. She hadn't even been allowed to keep an aquarium her primary-school teacher had given her. Sometimes her mother, who was completely under his thumb, had explained that it was because Sanna was allergic. Another time it might be because she hadn't been working hard enough at school. Most of the time she got no explanation at all. The silence was such that it was not possible even to form the question. And Rebecka remembered Sanna sitting with Sara on her knee when she was small and didn't want to go to sleep. "I'm not going to be like them," she'd said. "They used to lock my bedroom door from the outside."

"I need to speak to my boss," said Rebecka.

"Are you staying?" asked Sanna.

"For a while," replied Rebecka in a strangled voice.

Sanna's expression softened.

"That's all I'm asking," she said. "And how long can it take—after all, I'm innocent. You don't believe I did it, do you?"

An image of Sanna walking along in the middle of the night, the bloodstained knife in her hand illuminated by the street lamps, formed in Rebecka's head.

But then, why did she go back? she thought. Why would she have taken Lova and Sara to the church to "find" him?

"Of course not," she said.

Case number, total hours. Case number, total hours. Case number, total hours.

Maria Taube sat in her office at the law firm Meijer & Ditzinger filling in her weekly time sheet. It looked good, she decided, when she added up the number of debited hours in the box at the bottom. Forty-two. It was impossible to make Måns happy, but at least he wouldn't be unhappy. She'd worked more than seventy hours this week in order to be able to debit forty-two. She closed her eyes and flipped down the back of her chair. The waistband of her skirt was cutting into her stomach.

I must start doing some exercise, she thought. Not just sit on my backside in front of the computer, comfort eating. It's Tuesday morning. Tuesday, Wednesday, Thursday, Friday. Four days left until Saturday. Then I'll do some exercise. And sleep. Unplug the phone and go to bed early.

The rain pattered against the window, sending her to sleep. Just as her body had decided to give in and rest for a little while, just as her muscles relaxed, the telephone rang. It was like being woken up by a kick in the head. She sat bolt upright and grabbed the receiver. It was Rebecka Martinsson.

"Hi, kid!" exclaimed Maria cheerfully. "Hang on a minute."

She rolled her chair away from the table and kicked the office door shut.

"At last!" she said when she picked up the phone again. "I've been trying to ring you like mad."

"I know," replied Rebecka. "I've got hundreds of messages on my phone, but I haven't even started listening to them. It's been locked in the car, and . . . no, I haven't got the energy to tell you the whole miserable story. I assume one or two might be from Måns Wenngren, who's presumably absolutely furious?"

"Mmm, well, I'm not going to lie to you. The partners have had a breakfast meeting about what was on the news. They're not very happy about Channel 4 showing pictures of the office and talking about angry lawyers. They're buzzing about like bees today."

Rebecka leaned against the steering wheel and took a deep breath. There was a painful lump in her throat that made it difficult to say anything. Outside, Virku, Sara and Lova were playing with a rug that was hanging on the line. She hoped it belonged to Sanna and not one of the neighbors.

"Okay," she said after a while. "Is there any point in speaking to Måns, or does he just want my resignation on his desk?"

"God, no. You've got to talk to him. As I understand it, most of the other partners wanted to talk about how to get rid of you, but that wasn't on Måns' agenda at all. So you've still got a job."

"Cleaning the toilets and serving coffee?"

"Wearing nothing but a thong. No, seriously, Måns seems to have really stuck up for you. But it was just a misunderstanding, wasn't it, you acting as lawyer for the Paradise Boy's sister? You were just with her as a friend, weren't you?"

"Yes, but something's just happened and . . ."

The car window had misted up, and Rebecka rubbed at it with her hand. Sara and Lova were standing on top of a pile of snow talking to each other. There was no sign of Virku. Where had she got to?

"I need to discuss this with Måns," she said, "because I can't talk for much longer. Can you put me through?"

"Okay, but don't let on you know anything about the meeting."

"No, no—how did you find all this out anyway?"

"Sonia told me. She was sitting in."

Sonia Berg was one of the secretaries who had been at Meijer & Ditzinger the longest. Her finest attribute was the ability to remain as silent as the grave about the firm's affairs. Plenty of people had tried to pump her for information, and had been met with her particular cocktail of unwillingness, irritation and well-simulated incomprehension as to what the person wanted. At secret meetings— for example, to do with mergers—it was always Sonia who took the minutes.

"You're unbelievable," said Rebecka, impressed. "Can you get water out of stones as well?"

"Getting water out of stones was the foundation course. Getting Sonia to talk is advanced plus. But don't talk to me about impossible tricks. What have you done to Måns? Given a voodoo doll a lobotomy or something? If I'd been on TV flattening journalists, I'd be staked out in his torture chamber experiencing my last agonizing twenty-four hours in this life."

Rebecka laughed mirthlessly.

"Working for him in the near future is going to be a bit like that. Can you put me through?"

"Sure, but I'm warning you, he might have stuck up for you, but he's not happy."

Rebecka wound up the window and shouted to Sara and Lova, "Where's Virku? Sara, go and find her and stay where I can see you. We're going soon.

"Is he ever happy?" she said into the phone.

"Is who ever happy?"

Måns Wenngren's chilly voice could be heard at the other end.

"Oh, hi," said Rebecka, trying to pull herself together. "Er, it's Rebecka."

"I see" was all he said.

She could hear him breathing hard through his nose. He had no intention of making it easy for her, that much was clear.

"I just wanted to explain that it was a misunderstanding, this idea that I was acting for Sanna Strandgård."

Silence.

"I see," drawled Måns after a while. "Is that all?"

"No . . ."

Come on, thought Rebecka, giving herself a pep talk. Don't get upset. Just say what has to be said and hang up. Things can't get any worse.

"The police have found a knife and Viktor Strandgård's Bible in Sanna Strandgård's flat," she said. "They've detained Sanna as a murder suspect; they've just driven off with her. I'm standing outside her flat at the moment. They're just sealing it off. I'm going to take her daughters to school and day care."

The irritated breathing at the other end of the phone stopped, and Rebecka permitted herself a pause before she went on.

"She wants me to defend her, refuses to have anybody else, and I can't say no. So I'll be staying up here for the time being."

"You've got a bloody nerve," exclaimed Måns Wenngren. "You go behind my back. Embarrass the firm on television and all over the papers. And now you're intending to take on a case outside the terms of your employment. It's a competitive act, and grounds for dismissal, you do know that?"

"Måns, don't you understand, I want to take the case as a member of the firm," said Rebecka agitatedly. "But I'm not asking for permission. I can't back out of this. And I can do it—I mean, how difficult can it be? I'll sit in on a few interviews, there probably won't be too many. She doesn't know anything and she can't remember anything. They've found the murder weapon—if it was the knife—and Viktor's Bible in her flat. She was in the church just after it happened. There isn't a hope in hell of anybody getting her off if it gets to court. If they do decide to prosecute, which is not what I expect, I hope somebody who specializes in criminal law would back me up—Bengt-Olov Falk or Göran Carlström. There'll be a lot of press interest, and some publicity on the criminal side would be good for the firm—you know that. It might be company law and tax cases that bring in the big money, but it's the big crime cases that make a firm well known in the papers and on TV."

"Thank you," said Måns deliberately. "You've already made a start on publicity for the firm. Why the hell didn't you get in touch with me when you flattened that journalist?"

"I didn't flatten her," Rebecka defended herself. "I was trying to get past her and she slipped—"

"I haven't finished!" hissed Måns. "I've wasted an hour and a half this morning sitting in a meeting about you. If I'd had my way, I'd be asking for your resignation. Fortunately for you, other people were in a more forgiving frame of mind."

Rebecka pretended she hadn't heard. "I need some help with that journalist. Can you get in touch with the news team and get her to withdraw her complaint?"

Måns gave an astonished laugh. "Who the hell do you think I am? Don Corleone?"

Rebecka scrubbed at the car window again.

"I was only asking," she said. "I've got to go. I'm looking after Sanna's two kids, and the youngest is taking all her clothes off."

"Well, let her get on with it," said Måns crossly. "We're not finished yet."

"I'll ring or send you an e-mail later. The kids are outside and it's bitter. A four-year-old with double pneumonia is the last thing I need right now. Bye."

She hung up before he managed to say anything else.

He didn't tell me I couldn't do it, she thought with relief. He didn't tell me I couldn't carry on, and I haven't lost my job. How come it was so easy?

Then she remembered the children and hurled herself out of the car.

"What on earth are you doing?" she screamed at Sara and Lova.

Lova had taken off her jacket, gloves and both jumpers. She was standing there in the snow with her hat on her head, her upper body bare except for a tiny white cotton vest. Tears were pouring down her face. Virku was looking anxiously at her.

"Sara said I looked like an idiot in the jumper I borrowed from you," sobbed Lova. "She said I'd get teased at nursery."

"Put your clothes on at once," said Rebecka impatiently.

She grabbed hold of Lova's arm and forced her into the jumpers. The child sobbed inconsolably.

"It's true," said Sara mercilessly. "She looks ridiculous. There was a girl at our school who had on a jumper like that one day. The boys got hold of her and pushed her head down the toilet and flushed it till she nearly drowned."

"Leave me alone!" bawled Lova as Rebecka dressed her by sheer force.

"Get in the car," said Rebecka in a tight voice. "You are going to nursery and to school."

"You can't force us," screamed Sara. "You're not our mother!"

"You want to bet?" growled Rebecka, lifting the two screaming children into the backseat. Virku hopped in after them, turning round and round anxiously on the seat.

"And I'm hungry," wailed Lova.

"Exactly," yelled Sara. "We haven't had any breakfast, and that's neglect. Give me your cell phone, I'm going to ring Granddad."

She grabbed Rebecka's phone.

"Like hell you are," snapped Rebecka as she snatched back the phone.

She leapt out of the car and flung open the back door.

"Out!" she ordered, dragging Sara and Lova out of the car and throwing them down on the snow.

Both children fell silent immediately, and stared at her with big eyes.

"It's true," said Rebecka, trying to control her voice. "I'm not your mother. But Sanna has asked me to look after you, so neither you nor I has any choice. We'll make a deal. First we'll drive to the café in the bus station and have breakfast. Because it's been such a terrible morning, you can order anything you want. Then we'll go buy some new clothes for Lova. And for Sanna too. You can help me choose something nice for her. Now get in the car."

Sara didn't speak, just looked down at her feet. Then she shrugged and got in the car. Lova climbed in after her and the older girl helped her little sister with the seat belt. Virku licked the salty tears off Lova's face.

Rebecka Martinsson started the car and reversed out of Sanna's yard.

Please, God, she thought for the first time in many years. Please help me, God.

The redbrick houses on Gasellvägen were neatly arranged along the street like pieces of Lego. Snow-covered hedges, piles of snow and kitchen curtains covering the lower part of the windows protected them from anybody who might look in.

And this family is going to need that, thought Anna-Maria Mella as she and Sven-Erik Stålnacke got out of the car outside Gasellvägen 35.

"You can actually feel the neighbors' eyes on the back of your neck," said Sven-Erik, as if he'd read her thoughts. "What do you think Sanna and Viktor Strandgård's parents might have to tell us?"

"We'll see. Yesterday they didn't want to see us, but once they heard their daughter had been taken in for questioning they rang and asked us to come."

They stamped the snow off their shoes and rang the doorbell.

Olof Strandgård opened the door. He was well groomed and

articulate as he invited them in. Shook hands, took their coats and hung them up. Late middle age. But with no sign of middle-age spread.

He's got a rowing machine and weights down in the cellar, thought Anna-Maria.

"No, no, please keep them on," said Olof Strandgård to Sven-Erik, who had bent down to take off his shoes.

Anna-Maria noticed that Olof Strandgård himself was wearing well-polished indoor shoes.

He led them into the lounge. One end of the room was dominated by a Gustavian-style dining suite. Silver candlesticks and a vase by Ulrika Hydman-Vallien were reflected in the dark mahogany surface of the table. A small reproduction crystal chandelier hung from the ceiling. At the other end of the lounge was a suite consisting of a pale, squashy corner sofa made of leather, and a matching armchair. The coffee table was made of smoky glass with metal legs. Everything was spotlessly clean and tidy.

Kristina Strandgård was slumped in the armchair. Her greeting to the two detectives who had turned up in her living room was distracted.

She had the same thick, pale blond hair as her children. But Kristina Strandgård's hair was cut in a bob following the line of her jaw.

She must have been really pretty once upon a time, thought Anna-Maria. Before this absolute exhaustion got its claws into her. And that didn't happen yesterday, it happened a long time ago.

Olof Strandgård leaned over his wife. His voice was gentle, but the smile on his lips didn't reach his eyes.

"Perhaps we should give Inspector Mella the comfortable chair," he said.

Kristina Strandgård shot up out of the chair as if someone had stuck a pin into her.

"I'm so sorry, yes, of course."

She gave Anna-Maria an embarrassed smile and stood there for a second as if she'd forgotten where she was and what she was supposed to be doing. Then she suddenly seemed to come back to the present, and sank down on the sofa next to Sven-Erik.

Anna-Maria lowered herself laboriously into the proffered armchair. It was far too low and the back wasn't sufficiently upright to be comfortable. She turned the corners of her mouth upward in an attempt at a grateful smile. The baby was pressing against her abdomen, and she immediately got heartburn and a pain in her lower back.

"Can we get you anything?" asked Olof Strandgård. "Coffee? Tea? Water?"

As if she had been given a signal, his wife shot up again.

"Yes, of course," she said with a quick glance at her husband. "I should have asked."

Both Sven-Erik and Anna-Maria waved dismissively. Kristina Strandgård sat down again, but this time she perched on the very edge of the sofa, ready to leap to her feet again if something came up.

Anna-Maria looked at her. She didn't look like a woman who'd just lost her child. Her hair was newly washed and blow-dried. Her polo-neck sweater, cardigan and trousers were all in toning shades of sandy brown and beige. Her makeup wasn't smudged around her eyes or mouth. She wasn't wringing her hands in despair. No screwed-up tissues on the coffee table in front of her. Instead, it was as if she'd shut out the outside world.

No, actually, thought Anna-Maria, suddenly feeling uncomfortable. She isn't shutting out the outside world. She's shutting herself in.

"We appreciate the fact that you were able to come straightaway," said Olof Strandgård. "We heard just a little while ago that you'd taken Sanna in for questioning. You must realize it's a mistake. My wife and I are extremely concerned."

"I understand," said Sven-Erik. "But perhaps we could take one thing at a time. If we ask some questions regarding Viktor first, we can talk about your daughter afterward."

"Of course," said Olof Strandgård with a smile.

Well done, Sven-Erik, thought Anna-Maria. Take command now,

otherwise the visit will be over before we've got an answer to anything.

"Could you tell us about Viktor," said Sven-Erik. "What kind of person was he?"

"In what way is this information likely to be of assistance in your investigation?" asked Olof Strandgård.

"It's a question we always ask," said Sven-Erik, not allowing himself to be provoked. "We have to try and build a picture of him, since we didn't know him when he was alive."

"He was gifted," said his father seriously. "Extremely gifted. I suppose that's what any parent would say about their child, but if you ask his teachers they'll confirm what I say. He got top grades in every subject, and he was highly musical. He had the ability to focus. On his schoolwork. On guitar lessons. And after the accident he focused one hundred percent on God."

He leaned back on the sofa and pulled his right trouser leg up a fraction before crossing his right leg over the left.

"It was no easy calling God laid upon the boy," he went on. "He put everything else to one side. Left school, and gave up his music. He preached and prayed. And he had a burning conviction that the revival would come to Kiruna, but he was also convinced that this could only happen if the free churches joined together. United we stand, divided we fall, as they say. At that time there was no sense of community between the Pentecostal church, the Mission church and the Baptist church, but he was determined. Only seventeen when he got the call. He more or less forced the pastors to start meeting and praying together: Thomas Söderberg from the Mission church, Vesa Larsson from the Pentecostal church and Gunnar Isaksson from the Baptist church."

Anna-Maria squirmed in the armchair. She was uncomfortable, and the baby was boxing with her bladder.

"He got his calling in connection with his accident?" she asked.

"Yes. The boy was riding his bike in the middle of winter, and he was hit by a car. Well, you're from Kiruna, you know the rest. The church just kept on growing, and we were able to build the Crystal Church. It's just as well known as the lad himself. We had some really famous singers at the Christmas concert there in December."

"How was your relationship with him?" asked Sven-Erik. "Were you close?"

Anna-Maria could see how Sven-Erik was making a real effort to draw Kristina Strandgård in with his questions, but she was staring blankly at the pattern on the wallpaper.

"Our family is very close," said Olof Strandgård.

"Was he going out with anybody? Did he have other interests outside the church?"

"No, as I said, he decided to put everything else in life to one side for the time being, and to work only for God."

"But didn't that worry you? Not having anything to do with girls, or any hobbies?"

"No, not at all." Viktor's father laughed, as if he found what Sven-Erik had just said utterly ridiculous.

"Who were his closest friends?"

Sven-Erik looked at the photographs on the walls. Above the television hung a large photograph of Sanna and Viktor. Two children with long, silvery blond hair. Sanna's in ringlets. Viktor's straight as a waterfall. Sanna must have been in her early teens. It was quite clear that she was refusing to smile for the photographer. There was something defiant in the turned-down corners of her mouth. Viktor's expression was also serious, but natural. As if he was sitting and thinking about something else altogether, and had forgotten where he was.

"Sanna was thirteen and the boy was ten," said Olof, who had noticed Sven-Erik looking at the photograph. "It's obvious how much he looked up to his sister. Wanted to have long hair just like hers from when he was little, and screamed like a stuck pig if his mother ever came near him with the scissors. At first he got teased in school, but he wanted it long."

"His friends?" prompted Anna-Maria.

"I'd like to think the family were his closest friends. He and Sanna were very close. And he idolized the girls."

"Sanna's daughters?"

"Yes."

"Kristina," said Sven-Erik.

Kristina Strandgård jumped.

"Is there anything you'd like to add? About Viktor," he explained when she looked at him questioningly.

"What can I say," she said uncertainly, glancing at her husband. "I haven't really got anything to add. I think Olof described him perfectly."

"Have you got an album of clippings about Viktor?" asked Anna-Maria. "I mean, he was in the papers quite a bit."

"There," said Kristina Strandgård, pointing. "That big brown album on the bottom shelf."

"May I borrow it?" asked Anna-Maria, getting up and taking it off the shelf. "You'll have it back as soon as possible."

She held on to the album for a moment before putting it on the table in front of her. She was desperate to get another image of Viktor into her head, instead of the white lacerated body with its eyes gouged out.

"It would be very helpful if you could write down the names of people who knew him," said Sven-Erik. "We'd like to talk to them."

"It'll be a very long list," said Olof Strandgård. "The entire population of Sweden knew him. And more."

"I mean those who knew him personally," said Sven-Erik patiently. "We'll send somebody to pick up the list this evening. When was the last time you saw your son alive?"

"On Sunday evening, at the Songs of Praise Service in the church."

"That would be the Sunday evening preceding the murder, then. Did you speak to him?"

Olof Strandgård shook his head sorrowfully.

"No, he was part of the intercession group, so he was busy all the time."

"When was the last time you met and had time to talk?"

"On Friday afternoon, just about two days before—" Viktor's father broke off and looked at his wife.

"—You'd cooked some food for him, Kristina; it was Friday, wasn't it?"

"Definitely," she replied. "The Miracle Conference was just starting. And I know he forgets to eat, always puts others before himself. So we went round to his house and filled up the freezer. He thought I was being a mother hen."

"Did he seem worried about anything?" asked Sven-Erik. "Was anything bothering him?"

"No," answered Olof.

"He obviously hadn't eaten for some considerable time when he died," said Anna-Maria. "Do you have any idea why that might be? Could it have been because he'd just forgotten to eat?"

"Presumably he was fasting," replied his father.

I'll need to find the bathroom in a minute, thought Anna-Maria.

"Fasting?" she asked, concentrating on not wanting to go. "Why?"

"Well," said Olof Strandgård, "it says in the Bible that Jesus fasted for forty days in the desert and was tempted by the devil before He appeared in Galilee and chose the first disciples. And it says that the apostles prayed and fasted when they were choosing the elders for the first churches and handing them over to God. In the Old Testament, Moses and Elijah fasted before they received God's revelations. Presumably Viktor felt that he had an important role during the Miracle Conference, and wanted to sharpen his concentration beforehand through fasting and prayer."

"What is this Miracle Conference?" asked Sven-Erik.

"It started on Friday evening and finishes next Sunday evening. Seminars during the day, and services in the evenings. It's all about miracles. Faith healing, wonders, prayers being answered, various spiritual gifts of grace. Wait a minute."

Olof Strandgård got up and went out into the hall. After a while he came back with a shiny colorful folder in his hand. He passed it to Sven-Erik, who leaned toward Anna-Maria so that she could look at it.

It was an invitation in folded A4 format. The soft-focus pictures showed happy people with their hands raised. In one picture a laughing woman was holding up her child. In another, Viktor Strand-gård was praying for a man who was on his knees, his hands raised toward heaven. Viktor's index and middle fingers rested on the man's forehead, and his eyes were closed. The text explained that the semi-nars would be dealing with topics including "You Have the Power to Demand That Your Prayers Are Answered," "God Has Already Con-quered Your Illness," and "Release Your Spiritual Gifts of Grace." There was also information about the evening services, where you could dance in the spirit, sing in the spirit, laugh in the spirit and see God work miracles in your own life and the lives of others. And all for four thousand two hundred kronor, excluding board and lodging.

"How many participants are there in the conference?" wondered Sven-Erik.

"I can't tell you exactly," said Olof, betraying a hint of pride, "but somewhere around two thousand."

Anna-Maria could see Sven-Erik calculating how much the church had made from the conference.

"We need a list of participants," said Anna-Maria. "Who should we get in touch with?"

Olof Strandgård gave her a name, and she made a note of it. Sven-Erik could get somebody to check it against police records.

"How was his relationship with Sanna?" asked Anna-Maria.

"I'm sorry?" said Olof Strandgård.

"Could you describe their relationship?"

"They were brother and sister."

"But that doesn't necessarily mean that they had a good relation-ship," Anna-Maria persisted.

Olof took a deep breath.

"They were the best of friends. But Sanna is a fragile person. Sen-sitive. Both my wife and I, and our son, have had to take care of her and the girls on many occasions."

There's a hell of a lot of talk about how fragile she is, thought Anna-Maria.

"What do you mean by 'sensitive'?" she asked, and noticed Kristina squirm slightly.

"This isn't easy to talk about," said Olof. "But there are times when she finds it difficult to cope as an adult. Difficult to maintain the boundaries for the girls. And sometimes she's found it difficult to look after them and herself, hasn't she, Kristina?"

"Yes," replied his wife obediently.

"She has actually spent a whole week lying in a darkened room," Olof Strandgård went on. "We took care of the girls then, and Viktor sat and fed Sanna with a spoon, like a child."

He paused and gazed steadily at Anna-Maria.

"She wouldn't have been able to keep the girls without the support of the family," he said.

Okay, thought Anna-Maria. You really do want to convince us of how frail and weak she is. Why? A neat and tidy family like you should be trying to keep a low profile about something like this, surely.

"Don't the girls have a father?" she asked.

Olof Strandgård sighed.

"Of course," he said. "She was only seventeen when she had Sara. And I..."

He shook his head at the memory.

"...I insisted they get married. They had to go before the highest authority, as they say. But the promise they made before God didn't stop the young man from abandoning his wife and child when Sara was only one. Lova's father was a passing weakness."

"Can you give me their names? We'd like to get in touch with them," said Sven-Erik.

"Certainly. Ronny Björnström, Sara's father, lives in Narvik. At least, we think so. He doesn't have any contact with his daughter. Sammy Andersson, Lova's father, died two years ago in a tragic snowmobile accident. He was driving over a lake in early spring and the ice didn't hold. Terrible thing."

No, that's it, if I'm going to avoid doing it in the armchair, thought Anna-Maria, heaving herself up.

"I'm sorry, but could I...?" she began.

"In the hall on the right," said Olof Strandgård, getting up as she left the room.

The bathroom was as pristine as the rest of the house. It smelled of something synthetic and flowery. Presumably from one of the aerosols on top of the cupboard. In the toilet bowl hung a little container with something blue in it that ran down along with the water when you flushed.

Clean, clean, clean, thought Anna-Maria as she walked back through the hall to the living room.

"We're very worried about the fact that Rebecka Martinsson has our girls," said Olof Strandgård once she was settled in the armchair again. "They must be shocked and terrified by what's happened. They need a calm, secure environment."

"That isn't something the police can get involved in," said Anna-Maria. "Your daughter is responsible for the care of her children, and if she has handed them over to Rebecka Martinsson, then—"

"But I'm telling you, Sanna isn't reliable. If it hadn't been for my wife and me, she wouldn't have custody of them today."

"It still isn't a police matter," said Anna-Maria in neutral tones. "It's Social Services and the courts who decide to remove custody from unsuitable parents."

The softness in Olof Strandgård's voice disappeared instantly.

"So we can't expect any help from the police, then," he snapped. "I shall of course be contacting Social Services if necessary."

"But don't you understand," Kristina Strandgård suddenly burst out. "Rebecka tried to split up the family before. She'll do everything she can to turn the girls against us. Just like she did with Sanna that time."

The last comment was addressed to her husband. Olof sat with his jaws clamped shut, staring out of the window. His whole body was rigid, his hands clenched on his knees.

"What do you mean by 'with Sanna that time'?" asked Sven-Erik gently.

"When Sara was three or four, Sanna and Rebecka Martinsson

shared a flat," Kristina Strandgård went on, her voice strained. "She tried to break up the family. And she is an enemy of the church and of God's work in this town. Do you understand how it makes us feel, knowing our girls are in her power?"

"I understand," said Sven-Erik sympathetically. "How exactly did she try to break up the family and work against the church?"

"By—"

A look from her husband made her swallow the rest of the sentence.

"By what?" probed Sven-Erik, but Kristina Strandgård's face had turned to stone, and her eyes were fixed on the shiny surface of the glass table.

"It's not my fault," she said in a broken voice.

She repeated it over and over again, her gaze on the table, not daring to look up at Olof Strandgård.

"It's not my fault, it's not my fault."

Is she defending herself to her husband, or is she accusing him? thought Anna-Maria.

Olof Strandgård became his gentle, considerate self once again. He placed his hand lightly on his wife's arm to silence her, then stood up.

"I think this has been a bit too much for us," he said to Anna-Maria and Sven-Erik, and the conversation was at an end.

When Sven-Erik Stålnacke and Anna-Maria Mella emerged from the house, the doors of two cars parked in the street flew open. Out jumped two reporters equipped with microphones wrapped in thick woolen socks. A cameraman was right behind one of them.

"Anders Grape, Radio Sweden's local news team," said the first one to reach them. "You've arrested the Paradise Boy's sister—any comment on that?"

"Lena Westerberg, TV3," said the one who had the cameraman in tow. "You were first on the scene of the murder—can you describe what it looked like?"

Sven-Erik and Anna-Maria didn't reply but jumped into the car and drove off.

"They must have asked the neighbors to tip them off if we turned up," said Anna-Maria; in the rearview mirror she could see the journalists walking up to the parents' house and ringing the doorbell.

"Poor woman," said Sven-Erik as they pulled out onto Bävervägen. "He's a cold bastard, that Olof Strandgård."

"Did you notice he never mentioned Viktor by name? It was 'the lad' and 'the boy' the whole time," said Anna-Maria.

"We need to talk to her sometime when he's not home," said Sven-Erik thoughtfully.

"You should do that," said Anna-Maria. "You've got a way with women."

"How come so many pretty women end up like that?" asked Sven-Erik. "Fall for the wrong kind of guy and sit at home like miserable prisoners once the kids have moved out."

"I'm sure there aren't more pretty ones who end up like that than any other sort," said Anna-Maria dryly. "But the pretty ones get all the attention."

"What are you going to do now?" asked Sven-Erik.

"Have a look at the album, and at the videos from the church," replied Anna-Maria.

She looked out through the car window. The sky was gray and leaden. When the sun couldn't fight its way through the clouds, it was as if all the colors disappeared, and the town looked like a black-and-white photograph.

"But this just isn't acceptable," said Rebecka, looking in through the cell door as the guard unlocked it and let Sanna Strandgård out into the corridor.

The cell was narrow, and the stone walls were painted an indeterminate shade of beige with splashes of black and white. There was no furniture in the tiny room, just a plastic mattress placed directly on the floor and covered in paper. The reinforced window looked out over a path and apartment blocks with a façade of green corrugated tin. It had a stale, sour smell of dirt and drunkenness.

The guard accompanied Sanna and Rebecka to the interview room. Three chairs and a table stood by a window. As the women sat down, the guard went through the bags of clothes and other bits and pieces Rebecka had brought with her.

"I'm so glad they're letting me stay here," said Sanna. "I hope they don't take me to the proper jail in Luleå. For the girls' sake. I've got to be able to see them. They've got furnished holding cells, but they were all occupied, so I had to go in the drunks' cell for the time being. But it's really practical. If anybody's been sick or something, they just hose it down. It'd be good if you could do that at home. Out with the hose, sluice it all down, and the Friday housework would be done in a minute. Anna-Maria Mella, you know, the little pregnant one, said there should be a normal cell today. It's nice and light. From the window in the corridor you can see the mine and Kebnekaise, did you notice?"

"Oh, yes," said Rebecka. "Just get a makeover expert round here and a family with three children can move in shortly and sit there beaming."

The guard handed the bags to Rebecka with a nod, and left the room. Rebecka passed them to Sanna, who rummaged through them like a child on Christmas Eve.

"What gorgeous clothes," smiled Sanna, her cheeks flushed with pleasure. "Look at this jumper! Pity there isn't a mirror in here."

She held up a red scoop-neck jumper with a shiny metallic thread running through it, and turned to Rebecka.

"Sara chose that one," said Rebecka.

Sanna dipped into the bags again.

"And underwear and soap and shampoo and everything," she said. "You must let me give you some money."

"No, no, it's a present," insisted Rebecka. "It didn't cost that much. We went to Lindex."

"And you've got books out of the library. And bought sweets."

"I bought a Bible too," said Rebecka, pointing to a small bag. "It's the new translation. I know you prefer the 1917 version, but you must know that one by heart. I thought it might be interesting to compare."

Sanna picked up the red book, turning and twisting it several times before opening it at random and flicking through the thin pages.

"Thank you," she said. "When the Bible Commission's translation of the New Testament came out, I thought all the beauty of the language had been lost, but it'll be interesting to read this one. Although it feels odd, reading a completely new Bible. You get used to your own, all the underlining and the notes. It might be really good to read new ways of putting things, and to have pages without any notes. No preconceptions."

My old Bible, thought Rebecka. It must be in one of the boxes up in the loft in Grandmother's barn. I can't have thrown it away, surely? It's like an old diary. All the cards and newspaper cuttings you put in it. And all the embarrassing places underlined in red, they give a lot away. "As the hart longs for flowing streams, so longs my soul for Thee, O God." "In the day of my trouble I seek the Lord, in the night my hand is outstretched and grows not weary, my soul refuses to be comforted."

"Did it go all right with the girls today?" asked Sanna.

"In the end," replied Rebecka tersely. "I got them to school and nursery anyway."

Sanna bit her lower lip and opened the Bible.

"What is it?" asked Rebecka.

"I'm just thinking about my parents. They might go and pick them up."

"What is this thing with you and your parents?"

"Nothing new. It's just that I got tired of being their property. You must remember how things were when Sara was little."

I remember, thought Rebecka.

Rebecka runs up the stairs to the flat she shares with Sanna. She's late. They should have been at a children's party ten minutes ago. And it takes at least twenty minutes to get there. More, probably, now that it's snowed. Maybe Sanna and Sara have gone without her.

Please, please, she thinks, and notices that Sara's winter shoes aren't in the entrance hall. If they've gone, I don't have to have a guilty conscience.

But Sanna's boots are there. Rebecka opens the door and takes a deep breath, so she can get through all the explanations and excuses whirling around in her head.

Sanna is sitting on the floor in the hallway, in the dark. Rebecka almost falls over her, sitting there with her knees drawn up to her chin and her arms around her legs. And she is rocking back and forth. As if to console herself. Or as if the very rhythm could keep terrible thoughts at bay. It takes a while for Rebecka to reach her. To get her to talk. And the tears come at the same time.

"It was Mummy and Daddy," sobs Sanna. "They just came and took Sara. I said we were going to party and we were going to have lots of fun this weekend, but they wouldn't listen. They just took her with them."

Suddenly she gets angry and hammers on the wall with her fists.

"What I want doesn't matter," she screams. "They don't take any notice of what I say. They own me. And they own my child. Just like they used to own my dogs. There was Laika—Daddy just took her away from me. They're so frightened of being alone with each other, they just—"

She breaks off and the rage and the tears turn into a long, drawn-out wail from her throat. Her hands fall helplessly to the floor.

"They just took her," she whimpers. "We were going to make a gingerbread house, you and me and Sara."

"Ssh," says Rebecka, stroking the hair from Sanna's face. "It'll be all right. I promise."

She dries the tears from Sanna's cheeks with the back of her hands.

"What kind of mother am I?" whispers Sanna. "I can't even defend my own child."

"You're a good mother," Rebecka reassures her. "Listen to me, it's your parents who've done something wrong. Not you."

"I don't want to live like this. He just comes in with his spare key and takes what he wants. What could I do? I didn't want to start screaming and pulling at Sara. She'd have been terrified. My little girl."

A picture of Olof Strandgård forms in Rebecka's head. His deep, reassuring voice. Not used to being contradicted. His permanent smile above the starched shirt collar. His cardboard cutout wife.

I'll kill him, she thinks. I'll kill him with my bare hands.

"Come along," she says to Sanna, in a voice that brooks no disagreement.

And Sanna gets ready and goes with her like an obedient child. She drives the car to where Rebecka wants to go.

Kristina Strandgård opens the door.

"We've come to collect Sara," says Rebecka. "We're going to a party and we're already forty minutes late."

Fear flashes through Kristina's eyes. She glances over her shoulder into the house, but doesn't move to let them in. Rebecka can hear that they have guests.

"But we agreed that Sara was coming to us this weekend," says Kristina, trying to catch Sanna's eye.

Sanna looks obstinately at the ground.

"As I understand it, you didn't agree anything of the sort," says Rebecka tersely.

"Just a minute," says Kristina, biting her lip nervously.

She disappears into the lounge, and after a while Olof Strandgård appears in the doorway. He is not smiling. His eyes bore into Rebecka first. Then he turns to his daughter.

"What's this nonsense?" he growls. "I thought we had an agreement, Sanna. It doesn't do Sara any good being dragged from pillar to post. I find it very disappointing that you keep making her pay the price for your whims and fancies."

Sanna hunches her shoulders, but still stares stubbornly at the ground. Snow is falling onto her hair, forming a helmet of ice around her head.

"Are you going to answer when you're spoken to, or can't you even manage to show me that much respect?" says Olof in a tightly controlled voice.

He's afraid of causing a scene when they've got guests, thinks Rebecka.

Her heart is pounding, but still she takes a step forward. Her voice is shaking as she stands up to Olof.

"We're not here for a discussion," she says. "Now, either you fetch Sara, or I will go straight to the police with your daughter and report you for abduction. I swear on the Bible, I'll do it. And before I do it, I'll force my way into your living room and play hell. Sara is Sanna's daughter, and she wants her. Your choice. You can fetch her, or the police will."

Kristina Strandgård peers anxiously over her husband's shoulder.

Olof Strandgård smiles scornfully at Rebecka.

"Sanna," he says to his daughter in a commanding voice, without taking his eyes off Rebecka. "Sanna."

Sanna looks down at the ground. Almost imperceptibly she shakes her head.

And then it happens. Olof's mood changes abruptly. His expression becomes concerned and hurt.

"Come in," he says, backing into the hall.

"If it was so important to you, you only had to say," says Olof to Sanna, who is dressing Sara in her snowsuit and boots. "I can't read your mind. We thought it might be nice for you to have a weekend to yourself."

Sanna puts on Sara's hat and gloves in silence. Olof is talking quietly, afraid the guests will hear.

"You didn't need to come here threatening and carrying on," he insists.

"This really isn't like you, Sanna," whispers Kristina, but she is looking daggers at Rebecka, who is leaning against the front door.

"Tomorrow we're getting the locks changed," says Rebecka as they walk to the car.

Sanna is holding Sara in her arms and says nothing. Holding her as if she'll never let her go.

God, I was so angry, thought Rebecka. And it wasn't even my own anger. It was Sanna who should have been angry. But she just

Fiction collection

Sc-fi
Fantasy
Romance
Adventure
Bestsellers
Prize winners
Historical fiction
Crime/thrillers/mystery
Modern contemporary
fiction

Quick reads

couldn't do it. And we changed the locks, but two weeks later she'd given her parents a spare key.

Sanna grabbed hold of her arm to bring her back to the present.

"They're going to want to have the girls while I'm in here," she said.

"Don't worry," said Rebecka absently. "I'll speak to the school."

"How long do I have to stay here?"

Rebecka shrugged her shoulders.

"They can't hold you for questioning for longer than three days. Then the prosecutor has to make an application for your arrest. And that has to be heard no more than four days after you were taken in for questioning. So that's Saturday at the latest."

"Will I be arrested then?"

"I don't know," said Rebecka uncomfortably. "It doesn't look good, finding Viktor's Bible and that knife in your kitchen."

"But anybody could have put them there when I went to church," exclaimed Sanna. "You know I never lock the door."

She fell silent, fingering the red jumper.

"What if it was me?" she said suddenly.

Rebecka found it hard to breathe. It was as if they'd run out of air in the tiny room.

"What do you mean?" she asked.

"I don't know," whimpered Sanna, pressing her hands against her eyes. "I was asleep, I don't know what happened. What if it was me? You've got to find out."

"I don't know what you mean," said Rebecka. "If you were asleep . . ."

"But you know what I'm like! I forget things. Like when I fell pregnant with Sara. I didn't even remember that Ronny and I had slept together. He had to tell me. And how good it was. I still can't remember. But I got pregnant, so it must have happened."

"Okay," said Rebecka slowly. "But I don't believe it was you. Blank spots in your memory don't mean you can kill somebody. But you need to think."

Sanna looked at her questioningly.

"If it wasn't you," said Rebecka deliberately, "then somebody planted the Bible and the knife there. Somebody wanted to put the blame on you. Somebody who knows you never lock the door. Do you understand what I'm saying? Not some oddball who's wandered in off the street."

"You've got to find out what happened," said Sanna.

Rebecka shook her head. "That's up to the police."

Both of them stopped talking and looked up as the door opened and a guard poked his head in. It wasn't the same one who had shown them to the visitors' room. This one was tall and broad-shouldered, with a cropped, military haircut. Rebecka still thought he looked like a lost boy as he stood in the doorway. He gave Rebecka an embarrassed smile and handed Sanna a small paper bag.

"Sorry to disturb you," he said. "But I'm off duty soon and I . . . I just thought you might like something to read. And I bought you some sweets."

Sanna smiled at him. An open smile, eyes sparkling. Then she quickly lowered her eyes, as if she was embarrassed. Her eyelashes brushed her cheeks.

"Thank you so much," she said. "You're really kind."

"It's nothing," said the guard, shifting his weight from one foot to the other. "I just thought you might get a bit bored in here."

He was quiet for a moment, but when neither of the young women spoke, he went on.

"Yes, well, I'd better be off, then."

When he'd gone Sanna looked in the bag he'd given her.

"You bought much better sweets," she said.

Rebecka gave a resigned sigh.

"You don't have to think my sweets are better," she said.

"But I do, though."

A fter visiting Sanna, Rebecka went to find Anna-Maria Mella. Anna-Maria was sitting in a conference room in the police station and eating a banana as if somebody were about to take it off her. In front of her on the table lay three apple cores. In the far corner of the room stood a television showing a video of an evening service at the Crystal Church. As Rebecka came into the room, Anna-Maria greeted her cheerfully. As if they were old friends.

"Would you like some coffee?" she asked. "I went to get some, but I don't know why. Can't face it at the moment..."

She finished the sentence by pointing to her stomach.

Rebecka remained standing by the door. The past was coming to life inside her. Set in motion by the faces on the flickering screen. She clung to the door frame. Anna-Maria's voice reached her from far away.

"Are you all right? Sit down."

On the screen Thomas Söderberg was addressing his congregation. Rebecka sank down onto a chair. She could feel Anna-Maria Mella's thoughtful gaze on her.

"This is from the service before the night he was murdered," said Anna-Maria. "Do you want to watch a little bit?"

Rebecka nodded. She was thinking she ought to say something by way of explanation. Something about not having eaten, or whatever. But she remained silent.

Behind Thomas Söderberg, the gospel choir was standing guard. Some of them shouted out in agreement as he spoke. His message was accompanied by shouts of "Hallelujah" and "Amen" from both the choir and the congregation.

He's changed, thought Rebecka. Before, he used to wear a striped shirt with a mandarin collar from Arbetarboden, jeans and a leather waistcoat. Now he looks like a stockbroker in his Oscar Jacobsson suit and trendy glasses. And the congregation is made up of cheap H & M copies of this image of success.

"He's a talented speaker," commented Anna-Maria.

Thomas Söderberg was switching rapidly between relaxed jokes and intense seriousness. His theme was opening your heart to the spiritual gifts of grace. Toward the end of the short sermon he invited everyone present to come forward and allow themselves to be filled with the Holy Spirit.

"Step forward and we will pray for you," he said, and as if they had been given a sign, Viktor Strandgård, the two other pastors from the church and some of the elders were standing by his side.

"*Shabala shala* amen," Pastor Gunnar Isaksson called out. He was marching back and forth, waving his hands. "Step forward, you who are tortured by sickness and pain. It is not the will of God that you should remain in your sickness. There is someone among us who suffers with migraine. The Lord sees you. Come forward. The Lord says that one of our sisters has problems with a stomach ulcer. God intends to put an end to your suffering. You will not need tablets anymore. The Lord has neutralized the corrosive acid in your body. Come forward and accept the gift of healing. Hallelujah."

A crowd of people surged forward. Within a few minutes there was a mass of people in ecstasy around the altar. Some were lying on the floor. Others stood like swaying grass, their hands stretched upward. They were praying, laughing, weeping.

"What are they doing?" asked Anna-Maria Mella.

"Falling under the power of the spirit," replied Rebecka curtly. "Singing, speaking and dancing in the spirit. Soon some of them will start to prophesy. And the choir will start singing hymns to accompany the whole thing."

The choir began to sing in the background, and more and more people surged forward. Many danced their way to the front as if they were drunk.

The camera frequently zoomed in on Viktor Strandgård. He was holding his Bible in one hand and praying fervently for a stout man on crutches. A woman was standing behind Viktor with her hands held up toward his hair, also praying. As if she were filling herself with God's power.

Viktor went up to a microphone and started to speak. He began in his usual way.

"What shall we talk about?" he asked the congregation.

He always preached like this. He prepared himself by praying. Then the congregation was permitted to decide what he should speak about. Much of the sermon was a conversation with those who were listening to him. This had also made him famous.

"Tell us about heaven," shouted someone from the congregation.

"What can I tell you about heaven?" he said with a tired smile. "Buy my book instead, and read it. Come on! Something else."

"Tell us about success!" said someone else.

"Success," said Viktor. "There are no shortcuts to success in the kingdom of God. Think of Ananias and Sapphira. And pray for me. Pray for that which my eyes have seen, and shall see. Pray that the strength of God will continue to flow from Him through my hands."

"What was that he said just now?" asked Anna-Maria. "Ana . . ."

She shook her head impatiently before she went on.

". . . and Sapphira, who were they?"

"Ananias and Sapphira. They're in the Acts of the Apostles," replied Rebecka, without taking her eyes off the television screen. "They stole money from the first church, and God punished them by killing them."

"Wow, I thought God only struck people dead in the Old Testament."

Rebecka shook her head.

When Viktor had been speaking for a while, the prayers of intercession continued. A man of about twenty-five wearing a hooded top and loose-fitting, well-worn jeans, pushed his way forward to Viktor Strandgård.

That's Patrik Mattsson, thought Rebecka. He's still there, then.

The man seized Viktor's hands, and just before the camera switched to the gospel choir, Rebecka saw Viktor jerk backwards and snatch his hands away from Patrik Mattsson.

What happened there? she thought. What's going on between those two?

She glanced at Anna-Maria Mella, but she was bending down and rummaging though a box of videotapes on the floor.

"This is the tape from yesterday evening," said Anna-Maria as she popped up from behind the desk. "Would you like to watch a little bit?"

On the tape from the evening following the murder, Thomas Söderberg was preaching again. The wooden floorboards beneath his feet were stained brown from the blood, and there were piles of roses on the floor.

The performance was serious; he was fired up. Thomas Söderberg exhorted the members of the congregation to arm themselves in readiness for spiritual conflict.

"We need the Miracle Conference more than ever now," he proclaimed. "Satan shall not gain the upper hand."

The congregation answered with cries of "Hallelujah!"

"This just can't be true," said Rebecka, shocked.

"Think carefully about who you can rely upon," shouted Thomas Söderberg. "Remember: 'He who is not with me, is against me.' "

"He just told people not to talk to the police," said Rebecka thoughtfully. "He wants the church to shut itself off."

Anna-Maria looked at Rebecka in amazement as she thought of her colleagues who had spent the day knocking on doors and speaking to members of the congregation. During the course of their inquiries every single officer had complained that it had been impossible to get people to talk to them at all.

During the prayers of intercession the collection was taken.

"If you had intended to give only ten kronor, wrap it in a hundred-kronor note!" shouted Pastor Gunnar Isaksson.

Curt Bäckström also spoke.

"What shall we talk about?" he asked the congregation, just as Viktor Strandgård used to do.

Is he mad? thought Rebecka.

People squirmed uncomfortably. Nobody spoke. Finally Thomas Söderberg saved the situation.

"Talk about the power of intercession," he said.

Anna-Maria nodded toward the television, where Curt was instructing the congregation.

"He was in the church praying when we were speaking to the pastors," she said. "I know you used to be a member of the church. Did you know the pastors and the congregation?"

"Yes," said Rebecka in a reluctant tone of voice, making it clear that this was something she didn't want to go into.

Some of them in the purely biblical sense, she thought, and suddenly the camera angle altered and Thomas Söderberg was looking straight into the lens and into her eyes.

Rebecka is sitting in the visitors' armchair in Thomas Söderberg's office; she is crying. The midseason sales are on. The town is full of people. Handwritten signs in red proclaiming big reductions plaster the shop windows. The atmosphere makes you feel hollow inside.

"It feels as though He doesn't love me," she sobs.

She is talking about God.

"I feel like His stepchild," she says. "A changeling."

Thomas Söderberg smiles carefully and passes her a handkerchief. She blows her nose and snivels. Just turned eighteen and crying like a baby.

"Why can't I hear His voice?" She sniffs. "You can hear Him and talk to Him every day. Sanna can hear Him. Viktor has even met Him. . . ."

"But Viktor is special," interjects Thomas Söderberg.

"Exactly," howls Rebecka. "I'd just like to feel as if I were a little bit special too."

Thomas Söderberg sits without speaking for a little while, as if he were listening inside himself for the right words.

"It's all a matter of training, Rebecka," he says. "You must believe me. In the beginning when I thought I could hear His voice, it was only my own imagination I heard."

He puts his hands together before his breast, raises his eyes and says in a childish voice:

"Do you love me, God?"

Then he answers himself in a deep voice:

"Yes, Thomas, you know I do. Very, very much."

Rebecka laughs through her tears. There is almost too much laughter. It bubbles over because she has cried so much she has created an empty space, ready to be filled by another feeling. Thomas joins in and laughs too. Then all of a sudden he becomes serious and gazes into her eyes for a long time.

"And you are special, Rebecka. Believe me, you are special."

Then the tears come again. They roll silently down her cheeks. Thomas Söderberg reaches out and wipes them away. Strokes her lips with the palm of his hand. Rebecka is totally still. She didn't want to frighten him away, she thinks later.

Thomas Söderberg stretches out his other hand and wipes away the rest of her tears with his thumb, while his fingers take hold of her hair. All at once his breath is very close. It flows over her face like warm water. There is the slightly acrid smell of coffee, the sweetness of gingerbread and something else that is just him.

Then everything happens so quickly. His tongue is inside her mouth. His fingers are tangled in her hair. She clasps the back of his head with one hand

and with the other tries in vain to undo at least one button on his shirt. His hands fumble at her breasts and try to find their way in under her skirt. They are in a hurry. They rush over each other's bodies before reason catches up with them. Before the shame comes.

She locks her arms around his neck and he raises her up out of the chair, lifts her onto the desk and pushes up her skirt with a single movement. She wants to get inside him. Presses him against her body. When he pulls off her tights he scratches the outside of her thigh, but she doesn't notice until later. He can't get her knickers off. There isn't time. Pushes the crotch to one side at the same time as he undoes his trousers. Over his shoulder she can see the key in the door. She thinks that they should lock it, but now he is inside her. Her mouth is open against his ear and she gasps for breath with every thrust. She clings to him like a baby monkey to its mother. He comes silently, controlled, with a final convulsion. He leans over her; she has to support herself on the desk with one hand so that she doesn't fall backwards.

Then he backs away from her. Takes several steps, until he bumps into the door. He looks at her with no expression, and shakes his head. Then he turns his back on her and looks out through the window. Rebecka slides off the desk. She pulls on her tights and straightens her skirt. Thomas Söderberg's back is like a wall.

"I'm sorry," she says in a small voice. "I didn't mean to do that."

"Please go," he says roughly. "Just go."

She runs all the way home to the flat she shares with Sanna. Runs straight across roads without looking. It is the middle of an icy January. The cold stabs at her and hurts her throat. The inside of her thighs is sticky.

The door burst open and Prosecutor Carl von Post's furious face appeared.

"What the hell is going on here?" he asked. When he got no answer, he turned to Anna-Maria and went on:

"What are you up to? You're not going through preliminary investigation material with her, surely?"

He jerked his head toward Rebecka.

"None of this is classified information," said Anna-Maria loudly. "You can buy the tapes in the church bookshop. We were just having a chat. If that's okay with you?"

"I suppose so!" snapped von Post. "But you need to talk to me now! My office. Five minutes."

He slammed the door shut.

The two women looked at each other.

"The journalist who accused you of assault has withdrawn her complaint," said Anna-Maria Mella.

Her voice was casual, as if to demonstrate that she'd changed track, and that what she was saying had nothing whatsoever to do with Carl von Post. But the message got through.

He's livid about it, of course, thought Rebecka.

"She said she'd slipped, and it can't possibly have been your intention to knock her over," Anna-Maria went on as she slowly stood up. "I must go. Was there anything you wanted?"

Thoughts whirled around in Rebecka's head. From Måns, who must have spoken to the journalist, to Viktor's Bible.

"The Bible," she said to Anna-Maria. "Viktor's Bible, have you got it here?"

"No, they haven't finished with it in Linköping. They'll be hanging on to it for the time being. Why?"

"I'd like to have a look at it if possible. Would they be able to photocopy it down there? Not all of it, of course, but all the pages where there are notes. And copies of all the scraps of paper, photographs, cards, that sort of thing."

"Of course," said Anna-Maria thoughtfully. "That shouldn't be a problem. In return maybe you'd be prepared to talk to me about the church if I have any questions."

"As long as it's not to do with Sanna," said Rebecka, looking at her watch.

It was time to fetch Sara and Lova. She said good-bye to Anna-Maria Mella, but before she went out to the car she sat down on the sofa in reception, opened up her laptop and connected it to her cell phone. She keyed in Maria Taube's e-mail address and wrote:

Hi, Maria.
Isn't there an investigator at the tax office who's got a soft spot for you? Can you ask him to check out a couple of constitutions and a nonprofit-making organization for me?

She sent the message, and the answer was on the screen before she managed to log off.

Hi, kid. I can ask him to check on anything as long as it's not classified. M

That was the whole point, thought Rebecka with a feeling of disappointment as she logged off. Anything that isn't classified I can check out for myself.

She'd only just shut down the computer when her phone rang; it was Maria Taube.

"You're not as clever as people might think," she said.

"What?" said Rebecka, surprised.

"Don't you realize that all e-mails at work can be monitored? An employer can go into the server and read all incoming and outgoing messages. Do you want the partners to know you're asking me to fish for classified information from the tax office? Do you really think I want them to know that?"

"No," replied Rebecka in a small voice.

"What is it you want to find out?"

Rebecka gathered her thoughts and babbled:

"Ask him to go into the LT and CT and check out—"

"Hang on, I need to write this down," said Maria. "LT and CT, what's that?"

"The Local and Central Transaction Systems. Ask him to check out the church of The Source of All Our Strength and the pastors employed there: Thomas Söderberg, Vesa Larsson and Gunnar Isaksson. Ask him to check up on Viktor Strandgård as well. I want the balance sheet and the proceeds for the church. And I want to know a bit about the pastors' financial situation, and Viktor's. Salaries, how much, from whom. What property they own. What stocks or bonds they own. Other assets."

"Okay," said Maria, making notes.

"One more thing. Can you get into PRV and check out the organization surrounding the church? Everything on the Net is so slow when you link up through a cell phone. Check if the church owns shares in any company that isn't listed on the stock market, or has any financial interest in a trading company or anything like that. Check out the pastors and Viktor too."

"May one ask why?"

"I don't know," said Rebecka. "Just an idea. I might as well do something while I'm hanging about up here."

"What is it they say in English?" said Maria. "Shake the tree. See what falls down. Something like that?"

"Maybe," said Rebecka.

Outside it had already begun to grow dark. Rebecka let Virku out of the car. The dog hurtled over to a pile of snow and squatted down. The streetlights were on, and shone down on something square and white tucked under the Audi's windscreen wiper. At first Rebecka thought she'd got a parking ticket, then she realized that her name was printed in big letters on an envelope. She let Virku into the front passenger seat, got into the car and opened the envelope. Inside was a handwritten message. The writing was sprawling and clumsy. As if the person who'd written it had been wearing gloves, or had used the wrong hand.

"When I say to the wicked, 'You will surely DIE,' and you do not warn him or speak out to warn the wicked from his wicked ways that he may live, that wicked man shall DIE in his iniquity, but his BLOOD I will require at your hand. Yet if you have warned the wicked and he does not turn from his wickedness or from his wicked ways, he shall die in his iniquity, but you have delivered yourself."

YOU HAVE BEEN WARNED!

Rebecka could feel the fear clutching at her stomach. The hairs stood up on the back of her neck and on her arms, but she resisted the urge to turn her head to see if anyone was watching her. She screwed the piece of paper into a little ball and dropped it on the floor in front of the passenger seat.

"Show yourselves, you bloody cowards," she said out loud as she drove out of the car park.

All the way to the school she had the feeling that she was being followed.

The head teacher of the local primary school, preschool and nursery looked at Rebecka across the desk with open dislike. She was a dumpy woman of around fifty. Her thick hair was dyed the color of a black tulip and was molded like a helmet around her square face. Her glasses, shaped like a cat's eyes, hung on a cord around her neck, tangled up with a necklace made up of leather, feathers and bits of china.

"I really don't understand what it is you think the school can do in this particular situation," she said, picking a hair off her cardigan with its striking pattern.

"I have already explained," said Rebecka, trying to hide her impatience. "The staff are not to allow Sara and Lova to leave with anyone but me."

The head smiled indulgently.

"We do actually prefer not to get involved in family matters, and I have already explained this to the girls' mother, Sanna Strandgård."

Rebecka stood up and leaned over the desk.

"I couldn't give a toss what you prefer or don't prefer," she said loudly. "It's your bloody responsibility as head teacher to make sure the children are safe during school hours and until they are handed over to their parents or to the person who has responsibility for them. If you don't do as I say, and make absolutely clear to your staff that they are to release the girls only to me, your name is going to be plastered all over the media as an accessory to inappropriate interference with children. Trust me, they'll love it. My cell phone is absolutely stuffed with messages from journalists who want to talk about Sanna Strandgård."

The skin was stretched tightly around the head's mouth and jawline.

"Is this what happens when you live in Stockholm and work for some smart law firm?"

"No," said Rebecka deliberately. "This is what happens when I have to deal with people like you."

They looked at each other in silence until the head gave up with a shrug of her shoulders.

"It isn't exactly easy to know what's supposed to be happening with those particular children," she snapped. "First of all, they can be collected by both the grandparents and the brother. Then all of a sudden last week Sanna Strandgård came marching in here and said they weren't to go with anyone but her, and now they can't go with anyone but you."

"Sanna said last week that the children weren't to go with anyone but her?" asked Rebecka. "Did she say why?"

"No idea. As far as I know, her parents are the most considerate people you could wish to meet. They've always supported her."

"As far as you know," said Rebecka crossly. "Now I'm going to fetch the girls."

At six o'clock that evening Rebecka was sitting in her grandmother's kitchen in Kurravaara. Sivving was at the stove with his sleeves rolled up, frying reindeer steaks in the heavy, black cast-iron pan. When the potatoes were ready he used the electric whisk in the aluminum pan to turn them into creamy mash with milk, butter and two egg yolks. Finally he seasoned the whole lot with salt and pepper. Virku and Bella sat at his feet like trained circus dogs, hypnotized by the wonderful smells coming from the stove. Lova and Sara were lying on a mattress on the floor, doing a jigsaw puzzle.

"I brought some videos, if you want to have a look," said Sivving to the girls. "There's *The Lion King* and a couple of cartoons. They're in that bag."

Rebecka was leafing distractedly through an old magazine. The kitchen was crowded but cozy, with Sivving spreading himself out in front of the stove. When she went to borrow the key for the second time in one day, he'd immediately asked if they were hungry, and offered to cook a meal. The fire was crackling cheerfully and the wind soughed in the chimney.

Something very strange has happened in the Strandgård family, she thought. And tomorrow I want to know from Sanna exactly what it is.

She looked at Sara. Sivving didn't seem bothered by the fact that she was silent, her face turned away.

I'm not going to wear myself out over her, she thought. Just let her be.

"I thought they might need something to pass the time with," said Sivving, nodding toward the girls. "Although these days it seems as if some youngsters don't know how to play outside, what with all these videos and computer games. You know Manfred, over on the other side of the river? He said his grandchildren came to visit in the summer. In the end he had to force them to go outside and play. 'You can only stay inside if it pours down in the summer,' he said to them. And they went outside. But they hadn't got a clue how to play—just stood there in the garden, completely lost. After a while Manfred noticed they were standing in a circle with their hands clasped in front of them. When he asked them what they were doing, they said they were praying to God to make it pour with rain."

He took the pan off the stove.

"Okay, everybody, food!"

He put the meat, mashed potato and tub of ice cream with jam on the table.

"Those kids," he laughed. "Manfred didn't know what to say."

Måns Wenngren was sitting on a stool in the hallway of his flat, listening to a message on the answering machine. It was from Rebecka. He was still wearing his coat, and hadn't even switched on the light. He played the message three times. Listened to her voice. It sounded different. As if she wasn't quite in control. At work her voice was always very obedient, walking to heel. It was never allowed to go scampering off after her feelings, giving away what was really going on inside her head.

"Thanks for sorting out that business with the reporter," she said. "It can't have taken you long to find a horse's head, or did you come up with something else? I'm keeping my phone switched off all the time, because so many journalists are ringing. But I keep checking my voice mail and e-mail. Thanks again. Good night."

He wondered if she looked different as well. Like the time he met her in reception at five o'clock in the morning. He'd been sitting in an all-night meeting, and she'd just arrived for work. She'd walked. Her hair was tousled, and one strand was stuck to her cheek. Her cheeks were rosy from the cold wind, and her eyes were sparkling and almost happy. He remembered how surprised she'd looked. And almost embarrassed. He'd tried to stop and chat, but she'd made some brief comment and slid past him into her office.

"Good night," he said out loud, into the silent flat.

And evening came and morning came, the third day

At quarter past three in the morning it begins to snow. Just a few flakes at first, then more and more. Above the dense clouds the Aurora Borealis hurls herself recklessly across the heavens. Writhing like a snake. Opening herself up to the constellations.

Kristina Strandgård is sitting in her husband's metallic gray Volvo in the garage beneath the house. It is dark in the garage. Only the map-reading light inside the car is lit. Kristina is wearing a shiny quilted dressing gown and slippers. Her left hand is resting on her knee, and her right hand is clutching the car keys. She has rolled up several rag rugs and stuffed them along the bottom of the garage door. The door leading into the house is closed and locked. The gaps between the door and the frame are covered with tape.

I ought to cry, she thinks. I ought to be like Rachel: "A voice was heard in Ramah, wailing and loud lamentation: Rachel weeping for her children; she refused to be comforted, for they were no more." But I don't feel anything. It's as if all I have inside is rustling white paper. I'm the one in this family who's sick. I didn't think that was the problem, but I'm the one who's sick.

She puts the key in the ignition. But the tears won't come now either.

Sanna Strandgård is standing in her cell, her forehead pressed against the cold steel bars in front of the reinforced glass window. She is looking out at the pavement in front of the green metal façades on Konduktörsgatan. In the glow of a street lamp, Viktor is standing in the snow. He is naked, apart from the enormous dove-gray wings that he has wrapped around his body in order to cover himself a little. The snowflakes fall around him like stardust. Sparkle in the light of the street lamp. They do not melt when they land on his naked skin. He raises his eyes and looks up at Sanna.

"I can't forgive you," she whispers, drawing on the window with her finger. "But forgiveness is a miracle that happens in the heart. So if you forgive me, then perhaps . . ."

She closes her eyes and sees Rebecka. Rebecka's hands and arms are covered in blood, right up to her elbows. She stretches out her arms and places one hand protectively above Sara's head, the other above Lova's.

I'm so sorry, Rebecka, thinks Sanna. But you're the one who has to do it.

When the town hall clock strikes five, Kristina Strandgård takes the key out of the ignition and gets out of the car. She takes the rugs away from the garage door. She rips the tape off the door to the house, screws it up and puts it in the pocket of her dressing gown. Then she goes up to the kitchen and begins to make bread. She adds some linseed to the flour; Olof's stomach can be a little sluggish.

Wednesday, February 19

Early in the morning the telephone rang at Anna-Maria Mella's house.

"Leave it," said Robert hoarsely.

But with the conditioning of many years, Anna-Maria's hand had already reached out and lifted the receiver.

It was Sven-Erik Stålnacke.

"It's me," he said tersely. "You sound out of breath."

"I've just come upstairs."

"Have you looked outside yet? It's been snowing like mad all night."

"Mmm."

"We've had an answer from Linköping," said Sven-Erik. "No finger-prints on the knife. It's been washed and dried. But it is the murder weapon. Traces of Viktor Strandgård's blood were found at the base of the blade close to the handle. And traces of Viktor Strandgård's blood were also found in Sanna Strandgård's kitchen sink."

Anna-Maria clicked her tongue thoughtfully.

"And von Post is going absolutely crazy. He knew, of course, that we were going to find absolute technical proof. He rang me at about half five, howling about motives and insisting we find the blunt instrument that was used on the back of the lad's head."

"Well, he's right," replied Anna-Maria.

"Do you think she did it?" asked Sven-Erik.

"It seems very odd if she did. But then, I'm no psychologist."

"Von Pisspot is intending to have another go at her anyway."

Anna-Maria inhaled sharply through her nose.

"What do you mean, 'have another go'?"

"How should I know?" replied Sven-Erik. "I presume he's going to interview her again. And he was talking about moving her to Luleå when she's arrested."

"Bloody hell," Anna-Maria burst out. "Doesn't he understand that frightening her won't help at all. We ought to get somebody professional up here, somebody who can talk to her. And I'm going to talk to Sanna myself. It's pointless just sitting in and listening to von Post interviewing her."

"Just be careful," Sven-Erik warned her. "Don't start interrogating her behind his back, or the shit really will hit the fan."

"I can make up some excuse. It's better if I push the boundaries a bit than if you do."

"When are you coming in?" asked Sven-Erik. "You've got a load of faxes from Linköping to deal with as well. The office girls are running around here like lemmings. They're wondering if everything's supposed to be recorded officially, and they're hacked off because the fax has been busy all morning."

"It's copies of pages from Viktor's Bible. Tell them they don't need to make a record of them."

"So when are you coming in?" Sven-Erik asked again.

"It'll be a while," said Anna-Maria evasively. "Robert's got to dig the car out and so on."

"Okay," said Sven-Erik. "See you when I see you."

He put the phone down.

"Now, where were we?" smiled Anna-Maria, looking down at Robert.

"Here," said Robert with laughter in his voice.

He was lying naked on his back underneath her, his hands caressing her enormous stomach and tracing a path toward her breasts.

"We were just here," he said, his fingers circling the brown nipples. "Just here."

Rebecka Martinsson was standing in the yard outside her grandmother's house brushing snow off the car with a broom. It had snowed heavily during the night, and clearing the car was hard work. She was sweating under her hat. It was still dark, and the snow was whirling down. There was a thick layer of fresh snow on the road, and zero vision. Driving into town wasn't going to be much fun. That's if she could actually get the car out. Sara and Lova were sitting at the kitchen window looking down at her. There was no point in letting them stand outside to get covered in snow, or sit in the car and freeze. Virku had raced off around the side of the house and was nowhere to be seen. Her cell phone rang; she pushed in her earpiece and answered impatiently:

"Rebecka."

It was Maria Taube.

"Hi," she said cheerfully. "You're answering the phone, then. I thought I'd be talking to your voice mail."

"I've just rung my neighbor and asked him to help me get the car out of the yard," panted Rebecka. "I've got to get the kids to nursery and school, and it's snowing like mad. I can't get the car out."

" 'I've got to get the kids to nursery,' " mimicked Maria. "Am I really talking to Rebecka Martinsson? It sounds more like a worn-out working mother to me. One foot in the nursery, the other at work, and thank God it's nearly Friday so you can collapse with a packet of chips and a glass of wine in front of the TV."

Rebecka laughed. Virku and Bella came hurtling toward her, snow spraying up all around them. Bella was in the lead. The deep snow was more of a handicap for Virku, who had shorter legs. Sivving must be on his way.

"I've got the information you wanted about the church," said Maria. "And I promised Johan Dahlström a dinner to say thank you, so you owe me a night out or something. I could do with going to the Sturehof and getting a little bit of male attention."

"Sounds like you're coming out of this pretty well," puffed Rebecka as she swept the bonnet of the car. "First of all, your Johan is bound to insist on paying for this thank-you-for-your-help dinner, and then I treat you to a night out so you can kick your heels up."

"He isn't 'my' Johan. Nice and grateful now, otherwise you won't find out a thing."

"I am nice and grateful," said Rebecka meekly. "Tell me."

"Okay, he said the church had only ticked the box to indicate that it's a nonprofit-making organization."

"Damn," said Rebecka.

"I've never had anything to do with nonprofit-making organizations and foundations and that sort of stuff. What does it mean?" asked Maria.

"It means it's a nonprofit-making organization that exists for the public good, so it isn't liable for income or capital tax. So it doesn't have to submit a tax declaration, nor a statement of accounts. It's impossible to get any kind of access to its affairs."

"With regard to Viktor Strandgård, he had a very modest salary from the church. Johan checked back two years. No other income. No capital. No property, and no shares."

Sivving was coming across the yard. His fur hat was pulled well down over his eyes, and he was dragging a snow rake behind him. The dogs raced to meet him and scampered playfully around his feet. Rebecka waved, but he had his eyes fixed on the ground and didn't see her.

"The pastors take forty-five thousand kronor a month."

"That's a damn good salary for a pastor," said Rebecka.

"Thomas Söderberg has quite a large share portfolio, about half a million. And he owns some land out on Värmdö."

"Värmdö Stockholm?" asked Rebecka.

"Yes, value for tax purposes four hundred and twenty. But it could be worth just about anything. The taxation value of Vesa Larsson's house is one point two million. It's quite new. The value was set last year in a specific property taxation arrangement. He's got a loan of a million. Presumably on the house."

"What about Gunnar Isaksson?" asked Rebecka.

"Nothing special. A few bonds, some savings in the bank."

"Okay," said Rebecka. "Anything else as far as the church goes? Does it own any companies or anything?"

Sivving appeared behind Rebecka.

"Hello there!" he boomed. "Talking to yourself?"

"Hang on a minute," said Rebecka to Maria.

She turned to Sivving. Only a tiny part of his face was visible above his scarf. A little snowdrift had already formed on the top of his cap.

"I'm on the phone," she said, pointing at the wire to her earpiece. "I can't get the car out. The wheels were just spinning around when I tried to start it."

"You're on the phone on that wire thing?" he asked. "Good Lord, soon they'll be operating to put a telephone inside your head the second you're born. You carry on, I'll start clearing."

He started dragging the rake across the ground in front of the car.

"Hi," said Rebecka into the phone.

"I'm still here," replied Maria. "The church owns nothing, but I checked out the pastors and their families. The wives are part owners in a trading company. Victory Print."

"Did you check it out?"

"No, but its tax records are in the public domain, so you can call the local tax office. I didn't want to ask Johan again. He wasn't that keen on asking for information from another tax authority's transaction network."

"Thanks a million," said Rebecka. "I've got to give Sivving a hand now. I'll call you."

"Be careful," said Maria, and hung up.

Slowly the night abandoned Sanna Strandgård. Slipped away. Out through the reinforced window and the heavy steel door, leaving room for the unforgiving day. It would be a while before it grew light outside. A faint glow from the street lamps outside pushed its way in through the window and hovered like a shadow beneath the ceiling. Sanna lay motionless on her bunk.

Just a little bit longer, she prayed, but merciful sleep was gone.

She felt as if her face was completely numb. Her hand crept out from under the blanket and she caressed her lips. Pretended her hand was Sara's soft hair. Let her nose remember the scent of Lova. She still smelled like a child, although she was turning into a big girl. Her body relaxed and sank into her memories. The bedroom at home in the flat. All four of them in the bed. Lova, with her arms around Sanna's neck. Sara, curled up behind her back. And Virku lying on Sara's feet. The little black paws, galloping in her sleep. Every single thing was tattooed on her skin, imprinted on the insides of her hands and her lips. Whatever happened, her body would remember.

Rebecka, she thought. I won't lose them. Rebecka will fix it. I won't cry. There's no point.

An hour later the cell door was tentatively pushed open a fraction. Light poured in through the gap, and someone whispered:

"Are you awake?"

It was Anna-Maria Mella. The policewoman with the long plait and the huge stomach.

Sanna answered, and Anna-Maria's face appeared in the doorway.

"I just thought I'd see if you wanted some breakfast. Tea and a sandwich?"

Sanna said yes, and Anna-Maria disappeared. She left the cell door slightly ajar.

From the corridor Sanna heard the guard's resigned voice:

"For God's sake, Mella!"

Then she heard Anna-Maria's reply:

"Oh, come on. What do you think she's going to do? Come out here and blast her way through the security door?"

I'll bet she's a good mother, thought Sanna. The sort who leaves the door open a bit so the children can hear her moving about in the kitchen. The sort who leaves a light on by the bed if they're scared of the dark.

After a while Anna-Maria Mella came back with two gherkin sandwiches in one hand and a mug of tea in the other. She had a file clamped under one arm, and pushed the door shut with her foot. The mug was chipped, and once upon a time had belonged to "The Best Grandmother in the World."

"Wow," said Sanna gratefully, sitting up. "I thought it was just bread and water in jail."

"This is bread and water," laughed Anna-Maria. "Do you mind if I sit down?"

Sanna gestured invitingly toward the foot of the bunk, and Anna-Maria sat down. She placed the file on the floor.

"It's dropped," said Sanna between mouthfuls of tea, nodding at Anna-Maria's stomach. "It's nearly time."

"Yes." Anna-Maria smiled.

There was a comfortable silence between them. Sanna took small bites of her sandwich. The gherkin crunched between her teeth. Anna-Maria gazed out of the window at the heavy snow.

"The murder of your brother was so—how shall I put it—religious," said Anna-Maria thoughtfully. "Ritualistic, somehow."

Sanna stopped chewing. The piece of sandwich stuck in her mouth like a huge lump.

"The gouged-out eyes, the severed hands, all the stab wounds," Anna-Maria went on. "The place where the body was lying. Right in the middle of the aisle, in front of the altar. And no sign of struggle or violence."

"Like a sacrificial lamb," said Sanna quietly.

"Exactly," agreed Anna-Maria. "It made me think of a place in the Bible, 'an eye for an eye, a tooth for a tooth.' "

"It's in one of the Books of Moses," said Sanna, reaching for her Bible, which was on the floor next to her bunk.

She searched for a moment, then she read out loud:

" 'And if any harm follow, then thou shalt give life for life, eye for eye, tooth for tooth . . .' "

She paused and read silently to herself before continuing:

" '. . . hand for hand, foot for foot, burning for burning, wound for wound, stripe for stripe.' "

"Who had a reason to take revenge on him?" asked Anna-Maria.

Sanna didn't reply, but flicked through the Bible, apparently aimlessly.

"They often put out people's eyes in the Old Testament," she said. "The Philistines put out Samson's eyes. The Ammonites offered the besieged people of Rabbah peace, on condition that they were allowed to put out the right eye of every single one."

She fell silent as the door was pushed wide open and the guard appeared with Rebecka Martinsson behind him. Rebecka's hair was lying on her shoulders in wet clumps. Her mascara had run into two black circles under her eyes. Her nose was an angry red dripping tap.

"Good morning," she said, glaring at the two smiling women on the bunk. "Don't ask!"

The guard disappeared and Rebecka remained standing in the doorway.

"What's this, morning prayers?" she asked.

"We were talking about eyes being put out in the Bible," said Sanna.

" 'An eye for an eye, a tooth for a tooth,' for example," added Anna-Maria.

"Mmm," said Rebecka. "And then there's that place in one of the gospels: 'if thine eye offend thee' and so on—where was it?"

Sanna flicked through the Bible.

"It's in Mark," she said. "Here it is, Mark 9:43 onward. 'And if your hand causes you to sin, cut it off. It is better for you to enter life maimed than with two hands to go into hell, where their worm does not die, and the fire is not quenched. And if your foot causes you to sin, cut it off. It is better for you to enter life crippled than to have two feet and be thrown into hell, where their worm does not die, and the fire is not quenched. And if your eye causes you to sin, pluck it out. It is better for you to enter the kingdom of God with one eye than to have two eyes and be thrown into hell, where their worm does not die, and the fire is not quenched.' "

"Good grief!" said Anna-Maria with feeling.

"What made you start talking about this?" asked Rebecka, struggling out of her coat.

Sanna put the Bible down.

"Anna-Maria said she thought Viktor's murder seemed so ritualistic," she replied.

A tense silence filled the little room. Rebecka looked grimly at Anna-Maria.

"I don't want you to talk to Sanna about the murder when I'm not present," she said sharply.

Anna-Maria leaned forward with difficulty and picked the file up off the floor. She stood up and looked steadily at Rebecka.

"I hadn't planned it," she said. "It just happened. I'll take you to a room where you can talk. Rebecka, can you ask the guard to take Sanna along to the shower when you've finished, then we'll all meet in the interview room in forty minutes."

She held the file out to Rebecka.

"Here," she said with a conciliatory smile. "The copies of Viktor's Bible you wanted. I really hope we can work well together."

No points to you, thought Rebecka as Anna-Maria walked ahead of them.

When they were alone Rebecka sank down on a chair and looked resolutely at Sanna, who was standing by the window looking out at the falling snow.

"Who could have put the murder weapon in your flat?" asked Rebecka.

"I can't think of anybody," said Sanna. "I don't know any more now than I did before. I was asleep. Viktor was standing by my bed. I put Lova in the sledge and took Sara by the hand and we went to the church. He was lying there."

They fell silent. Rebecka opened the file Anna-Maria had given her. The first sheet was a copy of the back of a postcard. There was no stamp. Rebecka stared at the handwriting. A chill went though her body. It was the same writing as the message on her car. Sprawling. As if the person who had written it had been wearing gloves, or had written it with the wrong hand. She read:

What we have done is not wrong in the eyes of God. I love you.

"What is it?" asked Sanna, terrified, as she watched the color drain from Rebecka's face.

I can't say anything about the note on the car, thought Rebecka. She'll go mad. She'll be terrified something will happen to the girls.

"Nothing," she replied, "but listen to this."

She read the postcard out loud.

"Who loved him, Sanna?" she asked.

Sanna looked down.

"I don't know," she said. "Loads of people."

"You really don't know a thing," said Rebecka crossly.

She felt upset. Something wasn't right, but she couldn't work out what it was.

"Had you fallen out with Viktor when he died?" she asked. "Why weren't he and your parents allowed to pick up the girls?"

"I've explained all that," said Sanna impatiently. "Viktor would just have given them to my parents."

Rebecka didn't speak, she just gazed out of the window. She was thinking about Patrik Mattsson. On the video from the church service he'd grabbed at Viktor's hands. And Viktor had snatched them away.

"I need to go for a shower now if I'm going to fit it in before the interview," said Sanna.

Rebecka nodded absently.

I'll talk to Patrik Mattsson, she thought.

She was jerked back to the present by Sanna running her hand quickly over Rebecka's hair.

"I love you, Rebecka," she said softly. "My dearest, dearest sister."

It's just amazing how everybody loves me, thought Rebecka. They lie, deceive and eat you up for breakfast, all out of love.

Rebecka and Sanna are sitting at the kitchen table. Sara is lying on a bean-bag in the living room listening to Jojje Wadenius. It's her morning routine. Porridge and Jojje on the beanbag. In the kitchen the radio is turned to P1. The orange Advent star is still hanging in the window, although it's February. But you need to hang on to a little bit of Christmas, its decorations and its light, just to keep you going until the spring arrives. Sanna is standing by the stove making sandwiches. The coffee percolator gurgles one last time, then falls silent. She pours two mugs and places them on the kitchen table.

Nausea floods through Rebecka like an enormous wave. She jumps up from the table and rushes into the bathroom. She doesn't even manage to lift the lid properly. Most of the vomit ends up all over the lid and the floor.

Sanna follows her. She stands in the doorway in her tatty green fluffy dressing gown, looking at Rebecka with anxious eyes. Rebecka wipes away a strand of mucus and vomit from her mouth with the back of her hand. When she turns her face up toward Sanna, she can see that Sanna has realized.

"Who?" asks Sanna. "Is it Viktor?"

"He has the right to know," says Sanna.*

They are sitting at the kitchen table again. The coffee has been thrown away.

"Why?" says Rebecka harshly.

She feels as if she is trapped inside thick glass. It's been like this for a while now. Her body wakes long before she does in the mornings. Her mouth opens for the toothbrush. Her hands make the bed. Her legs make their way to the Hjalmar Lundbohm school. Sometimes she stops dead in the middle of the street, wondering whether it's Saturday. If she has to go to school at all. But it's remarkable. Her legs are always right. She arrives in the right room on the right day at the right time. Her body can manage perfectly well without her. She's avoided going to church. Blamed schoolwork and the flu and gone to visit her grandmother in Kurravaara. And Thomas Söderberg hasn't asked about her, or phoned.

"Because it's his child," says Sanna. "He's bound to realize, in any case. I mean, it'll show in a few months."

"No," says Rebecka tonelessly. "It won't."

She sees how the meaning of what she has just said sinks in.

"No, Rebecka," says Sanna, shaking her head.

Tears well up in her eyes and she reaches for Rebecka's hand, but Rebecka gets up and puts on her shoes and padded jacket.

"I love you, Rebecka," pleads Sanna. "Don't you understand that it's a gift? I'll help you to . . ."

She stops speaking as Rebecka looks at her with contempt.

"I know," she says quietly. "You don't think I'm even capable of looking after myself and Sara."

Sanna buries her head in her hands and begins to weep inconsolably.

Rebecka leaves the flat. Rage is pounding through her body. Her fists are clenched inside her gloves. It feels as if she could kill someone. Anyone.

When Rebecka has gone, Sanna picks up the telephone and dials. It is Thomas Söderberg's wife, Maja, who answers.

Patrik Mattsson was woken at quarter past eleven in the morning by the sound of a key being turned in the outside door of his flat. Then his mother's voice. Fragile as ice in the autumn. Full of anxiety. She called his name, and he heard her go through the hall and past the bathroom where he was lying. She stopped at the door of the living room and called again. After a while she knocked on the bathroom door.

"Hello! Patrik!"

I ought to answer, he thought.

He moved slightly, and the tiles on the floor laid their coolness against his face. He must have fallen asleep in the end. On the bathroom floor. Curled up like a fetus. He still had his clothes on.

His mother's voice again. Determined hammering on the door.

"Hello, Patrik, open the door, there's a good boy. Are you all right?"

No, I'm not all right, he thought. I'll never be all right again.

His lips formed the name. But no sound was allowed to pass his lips.

Viktor. Viktor. Viktor.

Now she was rattling the door handle.

"Patrik, either you open this door right now or I'm ringing the police and they can kick it in."

Oh, God. He managed to get to his knees. His head was pounding like a pneumatic drill. The hip that had been resting on the hard tiled floor was aching.

"I'm coming," he croaked. "I've . . . not been too well. Hang on."

She backed away as he opened the door.

"You look terrible," she burst out. "Are you ill?"

"Yes," he replied.

"Shall I ring up and say you're not coming in?"

"No, I've got to go now."

He looked at the clock.

She followed him into the lounge. Flowerpots lay smashed on the floor. The rug had ended up in one corner. One of the armchairs had been tipped upside down.

"What's been going on here?" she asked weakly.

He turned and put his arm around her shoulders.

"I did it myself, Mum. But it's nothing for you to worry about. I'm feeling better now."

She nodded in reply, but he could see that tears weren't far away. He turned away from her.

"I must get off to the mushroom farm," he said.

"I'll stay here and clean up for you," his mother said from behind him, bending down to pick up a glass from the floor.

Patrik Mattsson defended himself against her submissive concern.

"No, honestly, Mum, you don't need to do that," he said.

"For my sake," she whispered, trying to catch his eye.

She bit her lower lip in an attempt to keep the tears at bay.

"I know you don't want to confide in me," she went on. "But if you'd just let me tidy up, then . . ."

She swallowed once.

". . . then at least I'll have done something for you," she finished.

He dropped his shoulders and forced himself to give her a quick hug.

"Okay," he said. "That would be really kind."

Then he shot out through the door.

He got into his Golf and turned the key in the ignition. Let the engine race with the clutch down to drown out his thoughts.

No crying now, he told himself sternly.

He twisted the rearview mirror and looked at his face. His eyes were swollen. His lank hair was plastered to his head. He gave a short, joyless bark of laughter. It sounded more like a cough. Then he turned the mirror back sharply.

I'm never going to think about him again, he thought. Never again.

He screeched out onto Gruvvägen and accelerated down the hill toward Lappgatan. He was almost driving from memory, couldn't see a thing through the falling snow. The snowplow had been along the road in the morning, but since then more snow had fallen, and the fresh snow gave way treacherously beneath his tires. He increased the pressure on the accelerator. From time to time one of the wheels went into a spin and the car slid over to the opposite side of the road. It didn't matter.

At the crossroads with Lappgatan he didn't stand a chance, the car skidded helplessly straight across the road. Out of the corner of his eye he could see a woman with a kick sledge and a small child. She pushed the sledge over the mound of snow left by the plow, and raised her arm at him. Presumably she was giving him the finger. As he drove past the Laestadian chapel, the road surface altered. The snow had become packed together under the weight of the cars, but it was rutted, and the Golf wanted to go its own way. Afterward he couldn't remember how he'd got over the crossroads at Gruvvägen and Hjalmar Lundbohmsvägen. Had he stopped at the traffic lights?

Down by the mine he drove past the sentry box with a wave. The guard was buried in his newspaper and didn't even look up. He stopped by the barrier in front of the tunnel opening that led down into the mine. His whole body was shaking. His fingers wouldn't cooperate when he fumbled for a cigarette in his jacket pocket. He felt empty inside. That was good. For the last five minutes he hadn't thought about Viktor Strandgård once. He took a long pull on the cigarette and inhaled deeply.

Keep calm, he whispered reassuringly, just keep calm.

Maybe he should have stayed at home. But shut in the flat all day, he'd have jumped off the balcony, for sure.

Oh, who are you kidding, he sneered at himself. As if you'd dare. Smashing teacups and chucking flowerpots on the floor, that's all you can manage.

He wound down the window and stretched out his hand to insert his pass card into the machine.

A hand grabbed his wrist and he jumped, the hot ash from the cigarette falling on his knee. At first he couldn't see who it was, and his stomach cramped with fear. Then a familiar face appeared.

"Rebecka Martinsson," he said.

The snow was falling on her dark hair, the flakes melting against her nose.

"I want to talk to you," she said.

He nodded toward the passenger seat. "Hop in, then."

Rebecka hesitated. She was thinking about the message someone had left on her car. "You will surely die," "You have been warned."

"It's now or never, as The King says," said Patrik Mattsson, leaning over the seat and opening the car door.

Rebecka looked at the mine entrance in front of her. A black hole, down into the underworld.

"Okay, but I've got the dog in the car, I'll have to be back in an hour."

She walked around the car, got in and shut the door.

Nobody knows where I am, she thought as Patrik Mattsson stuck his card into the machine and the barrier that barred the way down into the mine slowly lifted.

He slipped the car into gear and they drove down into the mine.

Ahead of them they could see the reflectors shining on the walls; behind them a dense darkness descended like a black velvet curtain.

Rebecka tried to talk. It was like dragging a reluctant dog along on its lead.

"My ears are popping, why does that happen?"

"The difference in altitude."

"How far down are we going?"

"Five hundred forty meters."

"So you've started growing mushrooms, then?"

No reply.

"Shiitake, I've never actually tried those. Is it just you?"

"No."

"So there are a few of you, then? Anybody else there at the moment?"

No answer, driving fast, downward.

Patrik Mattsson parked the car in front of an underground workshop. There was no door, just a large opening in the side of the mine. Inside Rebecka could see men in overalls and helmets. They were holding tools. Huge drills from Atlas Copco were lined up ready for repair.

"This way," said Patrik Mattsson, and set off.

Rebecka followed him, looking at the men in the workshop and wishing one of them would turn around and see her.

Black primitive rock rose up on both sides of them. Here and there water was running out of the rocks and turning the walls green.

"It's the copper, the water turns it green," explained Patrik when she asked.

He stubbed out his cigarette under his foot and unlocked a heavy steel door in the wall.

"I thought you weren't allowed to smoke down here," said Rebecka.

"Why not?" asked Patrik. "There aren't any explosive gases or anything like that."

She laughed out loud.

"Brilliant. You can hide away down here, five hundred meters under the surface, and have a secret smoke!"

He held open the heavy door and held out his other hand, palm upward, indicating that she should go in ahead of him.

"I've never understood the list of commandments in the free church," she said, turning toward him so that she wouldn't have her back to him as they went in. "Thou shalt not smoke. Thou shalt not drink alcohol. Thou shalt not go to the disco. Where did they get it from? Gluttony, and not sharing what you have with those in need, sins that are actually mentioned in the Bible, they haven't got a word to say about those."

The door closed behind them. Patrick switched on the light. The room looked like a huge bunker. Steel shelves hung from the ceiling on bars. Something that looked like great big vacuum-packed sausages, or round logs, was lying on the shelves.

Rebecka asked, and Patrik Mattsson explained.

"Blocks of alder packed in plastic. They've been injected with spores. When they've been there for a certain amount of time, you can take off the plastic and just tap the wood with your hand. Then they start to grow, and after five days you harvest them."

He disappeared behind a large plastic curtain at the far end of the room. After a while he came back with several blocks of wood full of shiitake mushrooms. He placed the blocks on a table and began to pick the mushrooms with a practiced hand. As he picked, he dropped them into a box. The smell of mushrooms and damp wood permeated the room.

"It's the right climate for them down here," he said. "And the lights change automatically to give them very short nights and days. Enough of the small talk, Rebecka—what do you want?"

"I wanted to talk about Viktor."

He looked at her expressionlessly. Rebecka had the feeling that she should have dressed more simply. They were standing here on different planets, trying to talk. She had that damned coat on, and her fine, expensive gloves.

"When I used to live here, you were very close," she said.

"Yes."

"How was he? After I left, I mean."

Behind the curtain the watering system sprang to life with a muted hiss. Moisture sprayed from the roof and trickled down the stiff, transparent plastic.

"He was perfect. Handsome. Devoted. A gifted speaker. But he had a tough God. If he'd lived in the Middle Ages he'd have whipped himself with a scourge and walked to holy places in his bare, wounded feet."

He picked the mushrooms from the last block of wood and spread them evenly in the box.

"In what way did he punish himself?" she asked.

Patrik Mattsson carried on rearranging the mushrooms; it was as if he was talking to them rather than to her.

"You know. Strip away anything that doesn't come from God. No listening to anything other than Christian music, because then you'd expose yourself to the influence of evil spirits. He was really keen to get a dog once, but a dog takes up time, and that time belongs to God, so nothing came of it."

He shook his head.

"He should have got that dog," he said.

"But how was he?" asked Rebecka.

"I told you. Perfect. Everybody loved him."

"And you?"

Patrik Mattsson didn't answer her.

I didn't come here to learn about growing mushrooms, thought Rebecka.

"I think you loved him too," she said.

Patrik breathed in sharply through his nose, clamped his lips tightly together and gazed up at the ceiling.

"He was just a sham," he said violently. "Nothing matters any-more. And I'm glad he's dead."

"What do you mean? What sort of sham?"

"Leave it," he said. "Just leave it, Rebecka."

"Did you write him a card telling him you loved him, and that what you were doing wasn't wrong?"

Patrik Mattsson buried his face in his hands and shook his head.

"Did you have a relationship, or not?"

He started to cry.

"Ask Vesa Larsson," he sniveled. "Ask him about Viktor's sex life."

He broke off and fumbled in his pocket for a handkerchief. When he didn't find one, he wiped his nose on the sleeve of his sweater. Rebecka took a step toward him.

"Don't touch me!" he snapped.

She froze on the spot.

"Do you know what you're asking? You, who just ran away when things got difficult."

"Yes," she whispered.

He lifted his hands.

"Do you understand, I can raze the whole temple to the ground! There will be nothing but ash left of The Source of All Our Strength and the movement and the school and—all of it! The town will be able to turn the Crystal Church into an ice hockey rink."

" 'The truth shall set you free,' it says."

He fell silent.

"Free!" he spat. "Is that what you are?"

He looked around, seemed to be looking for something.

A knife—the thought went through Rebecka's head.

He made a gesture with his hand, the fingers together, palm facing her, which seemed to indicate that he wanted her to wait. Then he disappeared through a door farther down the room. There was a heavy click as it closed behind him, then silence. Just the sound of dripping from behind the plastic curtain. The electricity humming through the light cables.

A minute passed. She thought about the man who had disappeared in the mine in the 1960s. He'd gone down, but never came up again. His car was in the parking lot, but he was gone. Without a trace. No body. Nothing. Never found.

And Virku in the car in the big parking lot, how long would she cope if Rebecka didn't come back? Would she start barking, and be found by somebody passing by? Or just lie down and go to sleep in the snow-covered car?

She went to the door that led out to the road into the mine, and pushed it. To her relief, it wasn't locked. She had to control herself to stop herself from running toward the workshop. As soon as she saw the people inside and heard the noise of their tools and the sound of steel being bent and shaped, her fear started to ebb away.

A man came out of the workshop. He took off his helmet and went over to one of the cars parked outside.

"Are you going up?" asked Rebecka.

"Why?" He smiled. "Want a lift?"

She drove back up with the lad from the workshop. She could feel him looking at her from the side, amused and curious. Although of course he couldn't see much in the darkness.

"So," he said, "do you come here often?"

Virku was full of reproaches when Rebecka got back to the car in the parking lot at the mine.

"Sorry, sweetheart," said Rebecka, with a pang of guilt. "We're going to pick up Sara and Lova soon, then we'll play outside for a long time, I promise. We're just going to pop into the tax office first and check something on their computers, okay?"

She drove through the falling snow to the local tax office.

"I hope this is over soon," she said to Virku. "Although it's not looking too good. I can't make any sense of it."

Virku sat beside her on the front seat, listening carefully. She tilted her head anxiously to one side, and looked as if she understood every single word Rebecka said.

She's like Jussi, Grandmother's dog, thought Rebecka. The same clever expression.

She remembered how the men in the village used to sit and talk to Jussi, who was allowed to come and go as he pleased. "The only thing he can't do is talk," they used to sigh.

"Your mistress didn't feel too good during the interrogation today," Rebecka went on. "She sort of curls up and disappears through the window when they push her. Sounds far away, as if she doesn't care. She drives the prosecutor mad."

The tax office was in the same building as the police station. Rebecka looked around as she parked outside. The bad feeling from the previous day when she'd found the note on the car just wouldn't go away.

"Five minutes," she said to Virku, locking the car door behind her.

Ten minutes later she was back. She placed four computer printouts in the glove compartment and scratched the top of Virku's head.

"Right, that's it," she said triumphantly. "This time they'd better answer me when I start asking questions. We can fit in one more thing before we pick up the girls."

She drove up to the Crystal Church on Sandstensberget and let Virku jump out of the car in front of her.

I might need somebody who's on my side, she thought.

Her heart was pounding as she walked up the hill toward the café and the bookshop. The risk of bumping into somebody she knew was relatively high. Just as long as it wasn't one of the pastors or the elders.

It doesn't matter, she told herself. It might as well happen now as later.

Virku raced from one lamppost to the next, reading and replying to messages. A lot of male dogs had been along here, ones Virku didn't already know.

There wasn't a soul inside the bookshop, apart from the girl behind the counter. Rebecka had never met her before. She had short curly hair and a large cross covered in glass beads on a short chain around her neck. She smiled at Rebecka.

"Just let me know if you need any help," she trilled.

It was obvious that she vaguely recognized Rebecka, but couldn't place her.

She's seen me on television, thought Rebecka. She nodded at the girl, told Virku to stay by the door, brushed the snow off her coat and set off toward the nearest shelf.

Christian pop poured out of the loudspeakers, the volume low. Glass lights from IKEA hung from the ceiling, and spotlights illuminated the shelves on the walls, filled with books and CDs. The shelves in the middle of the shop were so low you couldn't hide behind them. Rebecka could see straight through the big glass doors leading into the café. The wooden floor was almost dry. Not many people with snowy shoes had come in here today.

"Isn't it quiet?" she said to the girl behind the counter.

"Everyone's at seminars," replied the girl. "The Miracle Conference is on at the moment."

"You decided to go ahead with it, even though Viktor Strandgård..."

"Yes," the girl answered quickly. "It's what he would have wanted. And God wanted it too. Yesterday and the day before there were loads of journalists in here, asking questions and buying tapes and books, but today it's quiet."

There it was. Rebecka found the shelf with Viktor's book. *Heaven and Back*. It was available in English, German and French. She turned it over. "Printed by Victory Print Ltd." She turned over some of the other books and pamphlets. They had also been printed by Victory Print Ltd. And on the videotapes: "Copyright Victory Print Ltd." Bingo.

At that moment she heard a voice right behind her.

"Rebecka Martinsson," it said, far too loudly. "It's been a long time."

When she swung around Pastor Gunnar Isaksson was right next to her. He was deliberately standing too close. His stomach was almost touching her.

It's a magnificent and serviceable stomach, thought Rebecka.

It protruded above his belt like an advance guard, able to penetrate other people's territory while Gunnar Isaksson himself sheltered behind it at a safe distance. She quelled the impulse to take a step backwards.

I tolerated your hands on my body when you prayed for me, she thought. So I can bloody well put up with you standing too close.

"Hi, Gunnar," she said casually.

"I've been waiting for you to show up," he said. "I thought you would have come to our evening services while you're in town."

Rebecka kept quiet. From a poster on the wall, Viktor Strandgård gazed down on them.

"What do you think of the bookshop?" Gunnar Isaksson went on, looking around proudly. "We did it up last year. Opened it up right through to the café, so you can sit and flick through a book while you're having coffee. You can hang your coat in there if you want to. I said we should put a sign above the coat hooks: 'Leave your common sense here.' "

Rebecka looked at him. He bore the marks of the halcyon days. Bigger stomach. Expensive shirt, expensive tie. His beard and hair were well groomed.

"What do I think of the bookshop?" she said. "I think the church should be digging wells and putting street children into school, instead of leaving them to work as prostitutes."

Gunnar Isaksson looked at her with a supercilious expression.

"God does not concern himself with artificial irrigation," he said loudly, with the emphasis on "God." "In this church community He has opened a spring of His abundance. Through our prayers such springs will open up all over the world."

He glanced at the girl behind the counter and noted with satisfaction that he had her full attention. It was more amusing to put Rebecka in her place when there was an audience.

"This," he said with a sweeping gesture that seemed to encompass the Crystal Church and all the success the church had enjoyed, "this is only the beginning."

"Absolute crap," said Rebecka dryly. "The poor can pray their own way to wealth, is that what you mean? Doesn't Jesus say: 'Truly, whatever you have done for the least of my children, you have done for me.' And what was it that was supposed to happen to those who left the little ones without help? 'They shall go forward to eternal damnation, but the righteous shall go forward to eternal life.' "

Gunnar Isaksson's cheeks were turning red. He leaned toward her and his breath thudded against her face. It smelled of menthol and oranges.

"And you think you belong to the righteous?" he whispered scornfully.

"No," Rebecka whispered back. "But maybe you should prepare yourself to keep me company in hell."

Before he could answer, she went on:

"I see that Victory Print Ltd. prints a lot of the things you sell here. Your wife is a partner in the firm."

"Yes," said Gunnar Isaksson suspiciously.

"I checked at the tax office. The company has reclaimed a huge amount of VAT from the state. I can't see any reason for that other than that enormous investments have been made in the company. How could you afford that? Does she earn a lot, your wife? She used to be a primary school teacher, didn't she?"

"You've no right to go snooping in Victory Print's affairs," hissed Gunnar Isaksson angrily.

"The tax records are in the public domain," replied Rebecka loudly. "I'd like you to answer some questions. Where does the money for the investments in Victory Print come from? Was anything in particular bothering Viktor before he died? Was he having a relationship with anyone? For example, one of the men in the church?"

Gunnar Isaksson took a step back and looked at her with disgust. Then he raised his index finger and pointed at the door.

"Out!" he yelled.

The girl behind the counter jumped and gave them a frightened look. Virku stood up and barked.

Gunnar Isaksson stepped menacingly toward Rebecka so that she was forced backwards.

"Don't you come here trying to threaten the work of God and the people of God," he roared. "In the name of Jesus and by the power of prayer I condemn thy evil plans. Do you hear what I say? Out!"

Rebecka turned on her heel and quickly left the bookshop. Her heart was in her mouth. Virku was right behind her.

The dark blue shades of evening were settling over Rebecka's grandmother's garden. Rebecka was sitting on a kick sledge watching Lova and Virku playing in the snow. Sara was reading on her bed upstairs. She hadn't even bothered to say no when Rebecka asked if they wanted to go outside, she'd just shut the door behind her and thrown herself on the bed.

"Rebecka, look at me!" shouted Lova. She was standing on the ridge on top of the cold store roof. She turned around and let herself fall backwards into the snow. It wasn't particularly high. She lay there in the snow, flapping her arms and legs to make the outline of an angel in the snow.

They'd been playing outside for almost an hour, building an obstacle course. It went along a tunnel through the bank of snow toward the barn, three times around the big birch tree, up on to the roof of the cold store, walk along the ridge without falling off, jump down into the snow, then back to the start. You had to run back-wards in the snow for the last bit, Lova had decided. She was busy marking out the track with pine branches. She had a problem with Virku, who felt it was her job to steal all the branches and take them off to secret places where the outdoor lights didn't reach.

"Stop it, I said!" Lova shouted breathlessly to Virku, who was just scampering off happily with another find in her mouth.

"Come on, what about some hot chocolate and a sandwich?" Re-becka tried for the third time.

She'd worn herself out tunneling through the snow. Now she'd stopped sweating and started to shiver. She wanted to go inside. It was still snowing.

But Lova protested furiously. Rebecka had to time her as she did the obstacle course.

"All right, but let's do it now," said Rebecka. "You can manage without the branches—you know the route."

It was difficult to run in the snow. Lova only managed twice around the birch tree, and she didn't run the last bit backwards. When she got to the end she collapsed in Rebecka's arms, exhausted.

"A new world record!" shouted Rebecka.

"Now it's your turn."

"In your dreams. Maybe tomorrow. Inside!"

"Virku!" called Lova as they walked toward the house.

But there was no sign of the dog.

"You go in," said Rebecka. "I'll give her a shout."

"And put your pajamas and socks on," she called after Lova as she disappeared up the stairs.

She closed the outside door and called again. Out into the dark-ness.

"Virku!"

It felt as if her voice reached only a few meters. The falling snow muffled every sound, and when she listened out into the darkness there was an eerie silence. She had to steel herself to shout again. It felt creepy, standing there exposed by the porch light, shouting into the silent, pitch-black forest all around her.

"Virku, here girl! Virku!"

Bloody dog. She took a step down from the porch to take a walk around the garden, but stopped herself.

Stop being so childish, she scolded herself, but still couldn't bring herself to leave the porch or to call out again. She couldn't get the image of the note on her car out of her head. The word "BLOOD" written in sprawling letters. She thought about Viktor. And about the children inside the house. She went backwards up the steps to the porch. Couldn't make herself turn her back on the unknown things that might be lurking out there. When she got inside she locked the door and ran upstairs.

She stopped in the hallway and rang Sivving. He turned up after five minutes.

"She's probably in heat," he said. "She won't come to any harm. Probably just the opposite."

"But it's so cold," said Rebecka.

"If it's too cold, she'll come home."

"You're probably right," sighed Rebecka. "It just feels a bit funny without her."

She hesitated for a moment, then said, "I want to show you something. Wait here, I don't want the girls to see it."

She ran out to the car and fetched the note that had been on the windscreen.

Sivving read it, a deep frown creasing his forehead.

"Have you shown this to the police?" he asked.

"No, what can they do?"

"How should I know—give you protection or something."

Rebecka laughed dryly.

"For this? No way, they don't have the resources to do that. But there's something else as well."

She told him about the postcard in Viktor's Bible.

"What if the person who wrote the postcard was somebody who loved him?"

"Well?"

" 'What we have done is not wrong in the eyes of God.' I don't know, but Viktor never had a girlfriend. I'm just thinking that maybe . . . well, it just occurred to me that there might be somebody who loved him, but who wasn't allowed to. And maybe it's that person who's threatening me, because he feels threatened himself."

"A man?"

"Exactly. That would never be accepted within the church. He'd be out on his ear. And if that's the case, and Viktor wanted to keep it secret, I don't want to go running to the police and broadcasting it unnecessarily. You can just imagine the headlines."

Sivving grunted and ran his hand anxiously over his head.

"I don't like it," he said. "What if something happens to you?"

"Nothing's going to happen to me. But I'm worried about Virku."

"Do you want me and Bella to come and stay the night?"

Rebecka shook her head.

"She'll be back soon," said Sivving reassuringly. "I'm going to take Bella for a walk. I'll give her a shout."

But Sivving is wrong. Virku isn't coming back. She is lying on a rag rug in the trunk of a car. There is silver tape wound around her muzzle. And around her back and front paws. Her heart is pounding in her little chest and her eyes are staring out into the black darkness. She scrabbles around in the cramped trunk and pushes her face against the floor in a desperate attempt to get rid of the tape around her muzzle. One tooth has been partly knocked out, and bits of tooth and blood are in her throat. How can this dog be such an easy victim? A dog who was mistreated by her previous owner over and over again. Why doesn't she recognize evil when she runs straight into its arms? Because she has the ability to forget. Just like her mistress. She forgets. Burrows down into the feathery snow and is pleased to see anyone who stretches out a hand to her. And now she is lying here.

And evening came and morning came, the fourth day

Måns Wenngren wakes with a start. His heart is pounding like a clenched fist. His lungs are gasping for air. He gropes for the bedside light and switches it on; it's twenty past three. How the hell is he supposed to sleep when his brain is running a nonstop festival of horror films. First of all it was a car that went straight through the ice on the lake outside the summer cottage. He was standing on the shore watching, but couldn't do anything. In the rear window he saw Rebecka's pale, terrified face. And the last time he'd managed to go back to sleep, Rebecka had come to him in his dream and put her arms around him. When his hands moved over her back and up toward her hair, they had become wet and warm. The whole of the back of her head had been shot away.

He wriggles backwards in the bed and sits up, leaning against the headboard. It used to be different, once upon a time. The boys and the job took it out of him. You didn't get enough sleep, but at least it was proper sleep. These days it's hardly ever sleep that's waiting for him when he goes to bed in the small hours. Instead he falls into a deep, dreamless state of unconsciousness. And look what happens when he goes to bed sober. Keeps waking up with panic racing through his body, sweating like a pig.

The apartment is as silent as the grave. The only sound is his own breathing and the low drone of the air-conditioning. Apart from that, every other sound is outside. The humming of the electricity meter out in the stairwell. The practiced tread of the paperboy on the stairs. Every other step going up, every third step going down. The cars and people still out for the night down on the street. When the boys were little, their room used to be filled with the sounds they made. Little Johan's short, rapid breathing. Calle, snuffling under a mountain of cuddly toys. And Madelene, of course, who started snoring as soon as she had even a hint of a cold. Then it became quieter and quieter. The boys moved into their own room. Madelene lay quiet as a mouse, pretending to be asleep when he got home late.

No, that's it. He'll stick an old Clint movie in the video and pour himself a Macallan. Maybe he'll doze off in the armchair.

It is still snowing in the mountains. In Kurravaara cars and houses are buried under a thick white blanket. In the sofa bed in her grandmother's house, Rebecka lies awake.

I ought to get up and see if the dog's here, she thinks. She might be standing out there in the snow freezing her paws off.

It's impossible to get back to sleep. She closes her eyes and alters her position, shifts onto her side. But her brain is wide-awake inside her tired body.

There is something peculiar about the knife. Why had it been washed? If someone wanted to put the blame on Sanna, and put the knife in her drawer, then why did that person wash the blade? Surely it would have been better to clean the handle to get rid of any possible prints, and to leave the blade covered in blood. There was a risk they might not be able to tie the weapon to the murder. There is something she isn't seeing. Like one of those pictures that is made up of a jumble of dots. All of a sudden the image appears. That's how it feels now. All the little dots are there. It's just a question of finding the pattern that links them together.

She switches on the bedside light and gets up carefully. The bed creaks by way of an answer. She listens to make sure the children haven't woken up. Slides her feet into ice-cold shoes and goes out to shout for Virku.

She stands there in the falling snow, shouting for a dog that doesn't come.

When Rebecka comes back inside, Sara is standing in the middle of the kitchen. She turns stiffly toward Rebecka. Her thin body is swamped by the big woolly sweater and baggy pants.

"What's the matter?" asks Rebecka. "Have you been dreaming?"

At the same time she realizes Sara is crying. It is a terrible cry. Dry and hacking. Her lower jaw is working up and down, like a clattering puppet made of wood.

"What's the matter?" Rebecka asks again, kicking her shoes off quickly. "Is it because Virku's gone?"

There is no answer. Her face is still distorted by the strange crying. But her arms move forward slightly, as if she would have held them out to Rebecka, if only she could.

Rebecka picks her up. Sara doesn't resist. It is a small child Rebecka holds in her arms. Not someone who is almost a teenager. Just a little girl. And she is so light. Rebecka lays her down on the bed and crawls in behind her. She puts her arms around Sara's body, feeling it tense as if she is aching with tears that won't come. At last they fall asleep.

At around five Rebecka is woken by Lova, who comes tiptoeing in. She creeps into bed behind Rebecka, cuddles into her back, slips her arm under Rebecka's sweater and falls asleep.

It is as warm as toast under all the blankets, but Rebecka lies there wide-awake, as still as stone.

Thursday, February 20

At half past five in the morning Manne the cat decided to wake Sven-Erik Stålnacke. He padded to and fro across Sven-Erik's sleeping body, emitting a plaintive cry from time to time. When that didn't work, he made his way up to Sven-Erik's face and laid a tentative paw against his cheek. But Sven-Erik was in a deep sleep. Manne moved the paw to his hairline and unsheathed his claws just enough to catch the skin and scratch his master's scalp very gently. Sven-Erik opened his eyes at once and detached the claws from his head. He stroked the cat's gray striped back affectionately.

"Bloody cat," he said cheerfully. "Do you think it's time to get up, then?"

Manne meowed accusingly, jumped down from the bed and

disappeared through the bedroom door. Sven-Erik heard him run to the outside door and position himself there, wailing.

"I'm coming, I'm coming."

He'd taken over Manne from his daughter when she and her partner had moved to Luleå. "He's used to his freedom," she'd said, "you know how miserable he'd be in an apartment in the middle of town. He's like you, Dad. Needs the forest around him to be able to live."

Sven-Erik got up and opened the outside door for the cat. But Manne just poked his nose out into the snow, then turned and padded back into the hall. As soon as Sven-Erik closed the door, the cat let out another long, drawn-out howl.

"Well, what do you want me to do?" asked Sven-Erik. "I can't help it if it's snowing and you don't like it. Either you go out, or you stay in and keep quiet."

He went into the kitchen and got out a tin of cat food. Manne made encouraging noises, winding himself around Sven-Erik's legs until the food was safely in the bowl. Then he put the coffee percolator on, and it gurgled into action. When Anna-Maria Mella rang he'd just taken his first bite of a sandwich.

"Listen to this," she said, her voice crackling with energy. "I was talking to Sanna Strandgård yesterday morning and we were discussing the fact that the murder seemed so ritualistic and about passages in the Bible where it talks about hands being cut off and eyes put out and all that sort of thing."

Sven-Erik grunted between mouthfuls, and Anna-Maria went on:

"Sanna quoted Mark 9:43: 'And if your hand causes you to sin, cut it off. It is better for you to enter life maimed than with two hands to go into hell, where their worm does not die, and the fire is not quenched. And if your foot causes you to sin, cut it off. It is better for you to enter life crippled than to have two feet and be thrown into hell, where their worm does not die, and the fire is not quenched. And if your eye causes you to sin, pluck it out. It is better for you to enter the kingdom of God with one eye than to have two eyes and be thrown into hell, where their worm does not die, and the fire is not quenched.' "

"And?" said Sven-Erik, with the feeling that he was being rather slow.

"But she didn't read the beginning of the text!" Anna-Maria went on excitedly. "This is what it says in Mark 9:42: 'And if anyone causes one of these little ones who believe in me to sin, it would be better for him to be thrown into the sea with a millstone around his neck.' "

Sven-Erik clamped the receiver between his shoulder and his ear and picked up Manne, who was rubbing against his legs.

"There are parallel passages in the gospels of both Luke and Matthew," said Anna-Maria. "In Matthew it says that a child's angels in heaven always see the face of God. And when I checked in my confirmation Bible, there was a note explaining that this was a very clear expression of the fact that children are under God's special protection. According to Hebrew belief at that time, each individual has their own angel who speaks for them before God, and only the most elevated angels were believed to have access to the throne of God."

"So you mean somebody killed him because he caused one of these little ones to sin," said Sven-Erik thoughtfully. "Do you mean he . . . ?"

He broke off, feeling distaste wash over him before he went on.

"With Sanna's girls, then."

"Why did she miss the beginning?" said Anna-Maria. "Von Post is right, in any case. We have to talk to Sanna Strandgård's children. She might have had a damned good reason to hate her brother. We need to get in touch with the child protection unit. They can help us talk to the girls."

When they'd hung up, Sven-Erik stayed at the kitchen table with the cat on his knee.

Shit, he thought. Anything but that.

It was the pastors' secretary Ann-Gull Kyrö who answered the office telephone at the church when Rebecka rang at quarter past eight in the morning. Rebecka had just dropped the children off and was on her way back to the car. When she asked for Thomas Söderberg, she heard the woman on the other end of the phone inhale sharply.

"Unfortunately," said Ann-Gull, "he and Gunnar Isaksson are busy with the morning service and cannot be disturbed."

"Where's Vesa Larsson?"

"He's not well today, he's not to be disturbed either."

"Perhaps I could leave a message for Thomas Söderberg. I'd like him to ring me; the number is—"

"I'm sorry," Ann-Gull interrupted her politely. "But during the Miracle Conference the pastors are extremely busy and won't have time to ring people who are trying to get hold of them."

"But if I could just explain," said Rebecka, "I'm representing Sanna Strandgård and—"

The woman on the other end of the line interrupted her again. This time there was a certain element of sharpness beneath the polite tones.

"I know exactly who you are, Rebecka Martinsson," she said. "But as I said, the pastors have no time during the conference."

Rebecka clenched her hands.

"You can tell the pastors that I'm not going to disappear just because they're ignoring me," she said furiously. "I—"

"I have no intention of telling them anything," Ann-Gull Kyrö interjected. "And there's no point in threatening me. This conversation is over. Good-bye."

Rebecka pulled out her earpiece and pushed it into her coat pocket. She had reached the car. She turned her face up to the sky and let the snowflakes land on her cheeks. After a few seconds she was wet and cold.

You bastards, she thought. I'm not about to slink away like a dog that's afraid of being beaten. You will talk to me about Viktor. You say I've got nothing to threaten you with. We'll see about that.

Thomas Söderberg lived with his wife, Maja, and their two daughters in an apartment in the middle of town, above a clothes shop. Rebecka's footsteps echoed on the stairs as she made her way up to the top floor. Shell-colored fossils were inlaid in the brown stone. The nameplates were all made of brass, and etched in the same neat, italic script. It was the kind of silent stairwell where you can just imagine the elderly residents inside their stuffy apartments, ears pressed to the door, wondering who's there.

Pull yourself together, Rebecka said to herself. There's no point in wondering whether you want to do this or not. You've just got to get it over with. Like a visit to the dentist. Open wide and it'll soon be over. She pressed the bell on the door marked "Söderberg." For a split second she thought that Thomas might open the door, and suppressed the urge to turn tail and run down the stairs.

It was Maja Söderberg's sister, Magdalena, who opened the door.

"Rebecka" was all she said. She didn't look surprised. Rebecka got the feeling she was expected. Perhaps Thomas had asked his sister-in-law to take some time off work, and installed her as a guard dog to protect his little family. Magdalena hadn't changed. Her hair was cut in the same practical pageboy bob as it had been ten years ago. She was wearing unfashionable jeans tucked into a pair of hand-knitted woolen kneesocks.

She's sticking to her own special style, thought Rebecka. If there's anyone who isn't about to fall for the idea of dressing for success and slipping on a pair of high heels, it's Magdalena. If she'd been born in the nineteenth century she'd have worn her well-starched nurse's uniform all the time and paddled her own canoe along the rivers to the godforsaken villages with her super-size syringe in her bag.

"I've come to talk to Maja," said Rebecka.

"I don't think you've got anything to talk about," said Magdalena, holding firmly onto the door handle with one hand and resting the other on the doorjamb so that Rebecka wouldn't be able to get past her.

Rebecka raised her voice so that it could be heard in the flat.

"Tell Maja I want to talk to her about Victory Print. I want to give her the chance to persuade me not to go to the police."

"Right, I'm closing the door," said Magdalena angrily.

Rebecka placed her hand on the door frame.

"You'll break my fingers if you do," she said so loudly that it bounced off the walls of the stairwell. "Come on, Magdalena. See if Maja wants to talk to me. Tell her it's about her holdings in the company."

"I'm closing it," said Magdalena threateningly, pulling the door back slightly as if she were going to slam it. "If your hand's still there, you've only yourself to blame."

You won't do it, thought Rebecka. You're a nurse.

———

Rebecka sits down and flicks through a magazine. It's from last year. It doesn't matter. She isn't reading it anyway. After a while the nurse who first saw her comes back and closes the door behind her. Rosita is her name.

"You're pregnant, Rebecka," says Rosita. "If you've decided to have an abortion, we need to book you in for a D & C."

D & C. That means they're going to scrape Johanna out of her womb.

It's when Rebecka is on her way out that it happens. Before she manages to get past reception, she bumps into Magdalena. Magdalena stops in the corridor to say hello. Rebecka stops and returns her greeting. Magdalena asks if Rebecka is coming to choir practice on Thursday, and Rebecka looks uncomfortable, makes excuses.

Magdalena doesn't ask what Rebecka is doing at the hospital. That's how Rebecka realizes that Magdalena knows. It's the things you don't say. That's what always gives a person away.

"Let her in. The neighbors must be wondering what the hell's going on."

Maja appeared behind Magdalena. The years had etched two hard lines around the corners of her mouth. They grew even deeper as she contemplated Rebecka.

"You can keep your coat on," said Maja. "You won't be staying long."

They sat down in the kitchen. It was spacious, with new white cupboards and a central island. Rebecka wondered whether the children were in school. Rakel must be in her early teens, and Anna should be at high school by now. Time had passed here too.

"Shall I make some tea?" asked Magdalena.

"No, thank you," replied Maja.

Magdalena sank back onto her chair. Her hands moved to the cloth and brushed away nonexistent crumbs.

You poor thing, thought Rebecka, looking at Magdalena. You ought to get your own life, instead of being one of this family's possessions.

Maja stared stonily at Rebecka.

"What do you want with me?" she asked.

"I want to ask you about Viktor," said Rebecka. "He—"

"Just now you were standing out there showing us up in front of the neighbors and playing hell about Victory Print. What did you want to say about it?"

Rebecka took a deep breath.

"I'll tell you what I think I know. And then you can tell me if I'm right."

Maja snorted.

"According to the tax records I've seen, Victory Print has reclaimed VAT from the state," said Rebecka. "A great deal of VAT. That indicates that considerable investments have been made in the company."

"There's nothing wrong with that," snapped Maja.

Rebecka's gaze was icy as she looked at the two sisters.

"The church of The Source of All Our Strength has informed the tax authorities that it is a nonprofit-making organization that is therefore exempt from income tax and VAT. That's brilliant for the church, because it presumably rakes in a ton of money. The profit from the sales of books, pamphlets and videos alone must be huge. No translation costs, people do it as a service to God. No royalties to the author, at least not to Viktor, so the whole of the profit must have gone to the church."

Rebecka paused briefly. Maja didn't take her eyes off her. Her face was set, like a mask. Magdalena was gazing out through the window. In a tree just outside, a great tit was pecking eagerly at a bit of bacon rind. Rebecka went on:

"The only problem is that when the church is exempt from tax, it isn't allowed to make deductions for its costs either. Nor can you reclaim VAT on those costs. So what do you do? Well, the smart solution is to set up a company and put all the costs and expenses that can give you back your VAT into that company. So when the church decides it's a good idea to print books and pamphlets and copy videotapes itself, it sets up a trading company. The wives of the pastors are designated the owners of the company. The company buys all the necessary equipment. And it costs a lot of money. You get twenty percent of your outgoings back from the state. That's a tidy sum in the pockets of the pastors' families. The company sells services, printing and so on, cheaply to the church, and runs at a loss. That's good, because then there's no profit to be taxed. And there's another good thing. The partners can claim up to a hundred thousand kronor each of those losses against their earned income for the first five years. I noticed that you, Maja, were paying zero tax this year and last year. Vesa Larsson's wife and Gunnar Isaksson's wife had minimal taxed income from employment. I think you've used the company's losses to make your wages disappear, to avoid paying tax on them."

"Yes, what about it?" said Maja crossly. "It's perfectly legal. I don't understand what you want, Rebecka. You of all people ought to know that tax management—"

"I haven't finished," Rebecka cut her off sharply. "I think the company has been selling its services to the church below the market price, and has therefore deliberately created losses. I'm also wondering where the money to invest in the company has come from. As far as I know, none of the partners has a fortune hidden away. Perhaps you took out a massive bank loan, but I don't think so. I didn't actually see any deficit in capital earnings for any of you. I think the money to buy the printing works and other things comes from the church, but it isn't on record. And that means it isn't a matter of tax management. That means we're talking about tax fraud. If the tax authorities and the Economic Crimes prosecutor start poking about in all this, then this is what will happen: If the partners can't account for where the investment money has come from, you will be taxed on that money at the business rate. The church has made an advance payment, which should have been recorded as revenue."

Rebecka leaned forward and fixed Maja Söderberg with her eyes.

"Do you understand, Maja," she said. "About half of the money you have received from the church has to be paid in taxes. Then there's national insurance and supplementary tax. You personally will be declared bankrupt, and you'll have the authorities after you for the rest of your life. On top of which you'll end up in jail for quite some time. Society takes dubious financial dealings very seriously. And if the pastors are behind the whole thing, as I believe they are, then Thomas is guilty of both fraud and a breach of trust against his principals, and God knows what else. Siphoned money from the church into his wife's company. If he's sent to jail as well, who's going to look after the children? They'll be able to come and visit you. Some depressing visitors' room for a few hours at the weekend. And when you get out, where are you going to find a job?"

Maja stared at Rebecka.

"What is it you want? You come here, into my home, with your speculation and your threats. Threatening me. The whole family. The children."

She stopped speaking and covered her mouth with her hand.

"If you want revenge, Rebecka, then take it out on me," said Magdalena.

"Shut the fuck up!" snapped Rebecka, and saw how the sisters jumped when she swore.

It made her feel like swearing again.

"Too fucking right I want revenge," she went on, "but that's not why I'm here."

Rebecka is at home alone when the doorbell rings. Thomas Söderberg is standing outside. Maja and Magdalena are with him.

Now Rebecka understands why Sanna was in such a hurry to go out. And why she insisted Rebecka should stay at home and study. Sanna knew they were coming.

Afterward Rebecka thinks that she should never have let them in. That she should have slammed the door in their well-meaning faces. She knows why they're here. Can see it in their faces. In Thomas's serious and concerned expression. In Maja's pursed lips. And in Magdalena, who can't quite bring herself to meet Rebecka's eyes.

They don't want anything to drink. But then Thomas changes his mind and asks for a glass of water. During the ensuing conversation he pauses from time to time to drink from the glass.

When they sit down in the living room Thomas takes control. He asks Rebecka to sit on the wicker chair, and steers his wife and sister-in-law to opposite ends of the L-shaped sofa. He places himself in the corner of the sofa. This enables him to maintain eye contact with all three of them at the same time. Rebecka has to keep turning her head to look at Maja and Magdalena.

Thomas Söderberg goes right to the heart of the matter.

"Magdalena told us she met you at the hospital," he says, looking into Rebecka's eyes. "She's also told us why you were there. We've come here to persuade you not to go through with it."

When Rebecka doesn't respond, he goes on.

"I understand that things are difficult for you, but you really have to think of the child. You have a life inside you, Rebecka. You have no right to snuff it out. Maja and I have talked about this, and she has forgiven me."

He pauses, gazing at Maja with his eyes full of love and gratitude.

"We want to look after the child," he says. "Adopt it. Do you understand, Rebecka? It would have the same status in our family as Rakel and Anna. A little brother."

Maja glances at him.

"If it's a boy, of course," he adds.

After a while he asks:

"What's your answer, Rebecka?"

Rebecka looks up from the table and stares hard at Maja.

"What's my answer," she says, shaking her head slowly.

"I looked at your notes and broke confidentiality," says Magdalena. "You're perfectly entitled to report me to the authorities."

"Sometimes we have to choose whether to follow the laws of Caesar or of God," says Thomas. "I've told Magdalena that you'll understand. Isn't that right, Rebecka? Or are you going to report her?"

Rebecka shakes her head. Magdalena looks relieved. She is almost smiling. Maja isn't smiling. Her eyes are black when she looks at Rebecka. Rebecka feels the nausea welling up. She ought to eat something, it usually eases off then.

They want her to bring up my child? thinks Rebecka.

"So what do you say, Rebecka?" Thomas persists. "Can I leave here with your promise to cancel that hospital appointment?"

Now the nausea suddenly floods through her body. Rebecka bangs her knee on the table as she leaps out of the wicker chair and runs to the bathroom. She brings up the contents of her stomach with such force that it hurts. When she hears them getting up in the lounge, she closes the door and locks it behind her.

The next moment all three of them are standing outside the door. They knock. Ask how she is, and beg her to open the door. It's deafening. Her legs feel weak and she slumps down on the toilet seat.

At first the voices outside sound anxious, and they plead with her to come out. Even Maja is sent to the door.

"I've forgiven you, Rebecka," she says. "We only want to help you."

Rebecka doesn't answer. She reaches out and turns the taps full-on. The water thunders into the bath, the pipes bang and drown out their voices. At first Thomas is merely irritated. Then he gets angry.

"Open this door!" he shouts, hammering on it. "It's my child, Rebecka. You have no right, do you hear me? I have no intention of allowing you to murder my child. Open the door before I break it down!"

In the background she can hear Maja and Magdalena trying to calm him. They pull him away from the door. At last she hears the door to the flat close, and their footsteps disappearing down the stairs. Rebecka lowers herself into the bath and closes her eyes.

Much later the door of the flat opens again. Sanna is home. The bathwater has been cold for a long time. Rebecka climbs out and goes into the kitchen.

"You knew," she says to Sanna.

Sanna looks guiltily at her.

"Can you forgive me?" she says. "I did it because I love you, you do understand that?"

"Why are you here?" asked Maja.

"I want to know why Viktor died," said Rebecka harshly. "Sanna is a suspect, she's being held for questioning and nobody seems to give a shit. The people in the church are dancing and singing hymns and refusing to cooperate with the police."

"But I don't know anything about it," exclaimed Maja. "Do you think I killed him? Or Thomas? Chopped off his hands and gouged out his eyes? Have you gone mad?"

"How should I know?" replied Rebecka. "Was Thomas at home the night Viktor was murdered?"

"That's enough, Rebecka," Magdalena interjected.

"Something was going on with Viktor before he died," said Rebecka. "He seemed to have fallen out with Sanna. Patrik Mattsson was angry with him. I want to know why. Was he having a relationship with somebody in the church? A man, perhaps? Is that why it's so quiet you can hear a pin drop in the house of God?"

Maja Söderberg stood up.

"Didn't you hear what I said?" Maja screamed. "I have no idea! Thomas was Viktor's spiritual mentor. And Thomas would never pass on anything he was told in confidence in his capacity as pastor. Not to me, nor to the police."

"But Viktor's dead!" hissed Rebecka. "So I imagine he couldn't give a shit whether Thomas breaks a confidence or not. I think you all know more than you're prepared to say. And I'm ready to go to the police with what I know, then we'll see what else comes out in a preliminary investigation."

Maja stared at her.

"You've taken leave of your senses," she exclaimed. "Why do you hate me? Did you think he'd leave me and the girls for you, is that what it is?"

"I don't hate you," said Rebecka tiredly, getting up. "I feel sorry for you. I never thought he'd leave you. I never imagined I was the only one, it was just bad luck that you found out. Am I the only one you know about, or were there . . . ?"

Maja swayed slightly. Then she pointed her finger at Rebecka.

"You," she said furiously. "You child murderer! Get out of here!"

Magdalena followed Rebecka to the door.

"Don't do it, Rebecka," she pleaded. "Don't go to the police and stir things up. What's the point? Think of the children."

"Well, help me, then," snapped Rebecka. "Sanna's on her way to jail, and nobody will say a bloody word. And you want me to be nice."

Magdalena pushed Rebecka out onto the landing in front of her, then closed the door behind them.

"You're right," she said. "There was something the matter with Viktor recently. He'd changed. Become aggressive."

"What do you mean?" asked Rebecka, pressing the glowing red button so that the lights came on.

"Well, you know, his whole manner, how he prayed and spoke to the congregation. It's hard to put your finger on it. He was restless, somehow. Often used to pray at night in the church, and didn't want any company. He never used to be like that. He used to like other people to pray with him. He was fasting and he was always busy. I thought he looked haggard."

She's right, thought Rebecka, remembering how he'd looked on the video. Hollow-eyed. Strained.

"Why was he fasting?" she asked.

Magdalena shrugged her shoulders.

"How should I know," she said. "It does say that certain demons can be driven out only by prayer and fasting. But I wonder if anyone knows what was wrong with him. I'm sure Thomas doesn't know, they hadn't been getting on very well recently."

"What was the problem between them?" asked Rebecka.

"Well, nothing that was going to make Thomas murder Viktor, at any rate," said Magdalena. "But seriously, Rebecka, you can't really believe that? It seemed as if Viktor had withdrawn from everybody. Including Thomas. I just think you should leave this family in peace. Neither Thomas nor Maja has anything to tell you."

"Who has, then?" asked Rebecka.

When Magdalena didn't reply, she went on:

"Vesa Larsson, maybe?"

When Rebecka reached the street it occurred to her that she'd better let Virku out of the car for a pee, before she remembered that the dog had disappeared. What if something had happened to her? In her mind's eye she could see Virku's little body lying in the snow, frozen to death. Her eyes had been pecked out by crows or ravens, and a fox had eaten the tastiest parts of her stomach.

I'll have to tell Sanna, she thought, and her heart felt heavy in her breast.

A couple pushing a pram passed by. The girl was young. Maybe not even twenty. Rebecka noticed her glance enviously at Rebecka's boots. She was passing the old Palladium. Ice and snow sculptures still stood there, left over from the Snow Festival at the end of January. There were three half-meter-high concrete ptarmigans in the middle of Geologgatan to stop cars driving down it. They had little hoods of snow on their heads.

It was an unpleasant feeling, getting into the empty car. She realized she'd already got used to the children and the dog.

Pack it in, she told herself sharply.

She looked at her watch. It was already half past twelve. In two hours it would be time to pick up Sara and Lova. She'd promised them they'd go swimming this afternoon. She ought to get something to eat. This morning she'd given the girls sandwiches and hot chocolate, but she'd just gulped down two mugs of coffee. And she wanted to fit Vesa Larsson in as well. And she ought to try and do a bit of work. She could feel the pain in her midriff kick in when she thought about the memo on the new regulations for small companies that she still hadn't finished.

She nipped into The Black Bear and grabbed a bar of chocolate, a banana and a Coke. An advertising board for one of the evening papers screamed, "Viktor Strandgård Murdered by Satanists." Above the headline in almost illegible print it said, "Anonymous Member of the Church Claims."

"What a cold hand," said the woman who took her money.

She wrapped her warm, dry hand around Rebecka's fingers and squeezed them briefly before she let go.

Rebecka smiled at her in surprise.

I'm not used to it anymore, she thought, chatting to strangers.

The car was icy cold. She ripped off the skin and gobbled the banana. Her fingers were getting colder and colder. She thought about the woman in the newsagent's. She was around sixty. Powerful arms and plump bust in a pink mohair cardigan. Home-permed hair, cut short in a style that was fashionable in the eighties. She'd had kind eyes. Then she thought about Sara and Lova. About how warm their bodies were when they slept. And about Virku. Virku with her velvety eyes and her soft woolly coat. Misery suddenly overwhelmed her. She turned her face up to the roof of the car and wiped the tears from her eyelashes with her index finger so that she wouldn't get mascara under her eyes.

Pull yourself together, she told herself, and turned the ignition key.

Virku is lying in darkness. Then the lid above her is opened and the light of a torch dazzles her. Her heart shrinks with fear, but she does not try to resist when two rough hands reach in and lift her up. Dehydration has made her passive and obedient. But she still turns her face up toward the man who is lifting her out of the trunk of his car. Shows him as much submission as she can, with silver tape bound tightly around her muzzle and paws. In vain she exposes her throat and presses her tail between her back legs. For there is no mercy to be had.

P astor Vesa Larsson's newly built modern villa was behind the Folk High School. Rebecka parked the car and looked up at the impressive building. The white geometric blocks of stone blended in with the white landscape all around. In snowy weather it would have been easy to drive straight past without realizing there was a house here, if it hadn't been for the connecting sections, which glowed in glorious bright red, yellow and blue. It was obvious the architect had been thinking of the white mountains and the colors of the Sami people.

Vesa Larsson's wife, Astrid, opened the door.

Behind her stood a small Shetland sheepdog, barking frantically at Rebecka. Astrid's eyes narrowed and the corners of her mouth curved downward in a grimace of distaste when she saw who was at the door.

"And what do you want?" she asked.

She must have put on thirty pounds since Rebecka last saw her. Her hair was tied back messily, and she was wearing Adidas tracksuit bottoms and a washed-out sweatshirt. In an instant she had registered Rebecka's long camel coat, the soft Max Mara scarf and the new Audi parked outside. A hint of uncertainty flickered across her face.

I knew it, thought Rebecka nastily. I knew she'd lose the plot as soon as they had their first child.

In those days Astrid had been a little on the plump side, but pretty. Like a chubby little cherub on a fluffy cloud. And Vesa Larsson was the unmarried pastor, fought over by all the prettiest girls in the Pentecostal church who were desperate to get married.

It's very liberating not to have to try to love everybody, thought Rebecka. I never did like her.

"I've come to see Vesa," said Rebecka, walking into the house before Astrid had time to reply.

The dog backed away, but was now barking so hysterically that it was making itself hoarse with the effort. It sounded as if it had a hacking cough.

There was no hallway and no porch. The whole of the ground floor was open plan, and from her position in the doorway Rebecka could see the kitchen, the dining area, the seating around the big open fireplace and the impressive picture windows looking out at the snow. On a clear day you would have been able to see Vittangivaara, Luossavaara and the Crystal Church up on Sandstensberget through those windows.

"Is he in?" asked Rebecka, trying to speak over the sound of the dog without shouting.

Astrid snapped back: "Yes, he is. Will you shut up!"

This last remark was directed at the furiously barking dog. She rummaged in her pocket and found a handful of reddish brown dog treats, which she threw onto the floor. The dog stopped yapping and scurried after them.

Rebecka hung her coat on a hook and pushed her hat and gloves into her pocket. They'd be soaking wet when it was time to put them on again, but that couldn't be helped. Astrid opened her mouth as if to protest, but closed it again.

"I don't know if he'll see you," she said sourly. "He's got the flu."

"Well, I'm not leaving here until I've spoken to him," said Rebecka calmly. "It's important."

The dog had now eaten all its treats and come back to its mistress, grabbed her leg and started rubbing itself against her, once again yapping excitedly.

"Don't do that, Baloo," Astrid protested halfheartedly. "I'm not a bitch."

She tried to push the dog off, but it clung frantically to her leg with its front paws.

Good God, you can see who's in charge in this house, thought Rebecka.

"I mean it," said Rebecka. "I'll sleep on the sofa. You'll have to call the police to get rid of me."

Astrid gave up. The combination of the dog and Rebecka was just too much for her.

"He's in the studio," she said. "Up the stairs, first on the left."

Rebecka took the stairs in five long strides

"Knock first," Astrid called after her.

Vesa Larsson was sitting in front of the big white-tiled stove on a sheepskin-covered stool. On one of the tiles "The Lord Is My Shepherd" was written in elegant letters the color of birch leaves. It was pretty. Presumably Vesa Larsson had written it himself. He wasn't dressed, but was wearing a thick toweling dressing gown over flannelette pajamas. His tired eyes looked at Rebecka from two gray hollows above his stubble.

He feels bad, all right, thought Rebecka, but it's not the flu.

"So you've come to threaten me," he said. "Go home, Rebecka. Leave all of this alone."

Aha, thought Rebecka. They didn't waste any time ringing to warn you.

"Nice studio," she said, instead of answering.

"Mmm," he said. "The architect nearly had a stroke when I said I wanted an untreated wooden floor in here. He said it would be ruined in no time by paint and ink and all the rest of it. But that was the idea. I wanted the floor to have a patina, from everything I'd created."

Rebecka looked around. The studio was large. Despite the gloomy snowy weather outside, the daylight flooded in through the huge windows. Everything was tidy. On an easel in front of the picture window stood a covered canvas. There wasn't the least speck of color on the floor as far as she could see. It had been a bit different in the days when he used to work in the cellar of the Pentecostal church. There were sheets of drawings all over the floor, and you could hardly move for fear of knocking over one of the many jars of turpentine and brushes. The smell of turpentine gave you a slight headache after a while. In this room there was just the faint smell of smoke from the stove. Vesa Larsson saw her inquiring look and gave a crooked smile.

"I know," he said. "When you finally get the studio other people can only dream about, you ..."

He finished the sentence with a shrug of his shoulders.

"My father used to paint in oils, you know," he went on. "The Aurora Borealis, Lapporten, the cottage in Merasjärvi. He never grew tired of it. Refused to take an ordinary job, sat drinking with his mates instead. Then he'd pat me on the head and say: 'The lad thinks he's going to be a truck driver and all sorts of things, but I've told him, you can't get away from art.' But I don't know, these days it just seems pathetic, sitting here with my dreams of being a painter. It wasn't so hard to get away from art after all."

They looked at each other in silence. Without knowing it, they were both thinking about the other one's hair. That it used to look better. When it was allowed to grow more freely, go its own way. When it was obvious it was friends who were wielding the scissors.

"Nice view," said Rebecka, and added: "Although maybe not just at the moment."

All you could see outside was a curtain of falling snow.

"Why not?" said Vesa Larsson. "Maybe this is the best view of all. It's beautiful, the winter and the snow. Everything's simpler. Less to take in. Fewer colors. Fewer smells. Shorter days. Your head can have a rest."

"What was going on with Viktor?" asked Rebecka.

Vesa Larsson shook his head.

"What's Sanna's told you?" he asked.

"Nothing," replied Rebecka.

"What do you mean, nothing?" said Vesa Larsson suspiciously.

"Nobody's telling me a damned thing," said Rebecka angrily. "But I don't believe she did it. She's on another planet sometimes, but she can't have done this."

Vesa Larsson sat in silence, gazing at the falling snow.

"Why did Patrik Mattsson say I should ask you about Viktor's sexual inclinations?" asked Rebecka.

When Vesa Larsson didn't answer, she went on:

"Did you have a relationship with him? Did you send him a card?"

Did you put a threatening note on my car? she thought.

Vesa Larsson replied without meeting her eyes.

"I'm not even going to comment on that."

"Right," she said harshly. "Soon I'll be thinking it was you three pastors who killed him. Because he wanted to blow the whistle on your dubious financial dealings. Or maybe because he was threatening to tell your wife about the two of you."

Vesa Larsson hid his face in his hands.

"I didn't do it," he mumbled. "I didn't kill him."

I'm losing it, thought Rebecka. Running around accusing people.

She rubbed her fist across her forehead in an attempt to force a sensible thought out of her brain.

"I don't understand," she said. "I don't understand why you're all keeping quiet. I don't understand why somebody put the knife in Sanna's kitchen drawer."

Vesa Larsson turned and looked at her in horror.

"What do you mean?" he said. "What knife?"

Rebecka could have bitten off her tongue.

"The police haven't told the press yet," she said. "But they found the murder weapon in Sanna's kitchen. In the drawer under the sofa bed."

Vesa Larsson stared at her.

"Oh, my God," he said. "Oh, God!"

"What is it?"

Vesa Larsson's face changed to a stiff mask.

"I've broken the vow of silence once too often," he said.

"Fuck the vow of silence," exclaimed Rebecka. "Viktor's dead. He couldn't give a shit if you break the vow of silence as far as he's concerned."

"I have a vow of silence toward Sanna."

"Fine!" Rebecka exploded. "Don't bother talking to me, then! But I'm prepared to turn over every last stone to see what crawls out. And I'm starting with the church and your financial affairs. Then I'm going to find out who loved Viktor. And I'm going to get the truth out of Sanna this afternoon."

Vesa Larsson looked at her, his expression tortured.

"Can't you just leave it, Rebecka? Go home. Don't let yourself be used."

"What do you mean by that?"

He shook his head with an air of resignation.

"Do what you think you have to do," he said. "But you can't take anything from me that I haven't already lost."

"Screw the lot of you," said Rebecka, but she hadn't the strength to inject any emotion into the words.

" 'Let he who is without sin . . .' " said Vesa Larsson.

Oh, yes, thought Rebecka. I'm a murderer after all. A child killer.

Rebecka is standing in her grandmother's woodshed chopping wood. No, "chopping" isn't the right word. She has picked out the thickest and heaviest logs and is splitting them in a kind of feverish frenzy. Brings the axe down onto the reluctant wood with every ounce of her strength. Lifts the axe with the log hanging from its blade and slams the back of it down onto the chopping block with all her might. The weight and the force drive the axe in like a wedge. Now she must pry it apart and work at it. At last the log is split in two. She splits the halves in two again, then places the next log on the chopping block. Sweat is pouring down her back. Her shoulders and arms are aching from the effort, but she doesn't spare herself. If she's lucky the child will come out. Nobody has said that she shouldn't chop wood. Perhaps then Thomas will say that it was not God's will that she should be born.

It, Rebecka corrects herself. That it was not meant to be born. The child. And yet, she knows deep within herself that it's a girl. Johanna.

When she hears Viktor's voice behind her, the tape inside her head rewinds and she realizes that he has been standing behind her for some while and has said her name several times without her hearing him.

It feels strange to see him sitting there on the broken wooden chair that never quite makes it to the fire. The back of the chair is missing, and there are holes at the back of the seat where the wooden staves used to be. It's been standing there for years, waiting to be turned into firewood.

"Who told you?" asks Rebecka.

"Sanna," he replies. "She said you'd be furious."

Rebecka shrugs her shoulders. She hasn't the strength to be angry.

"Who else knows?" she asks.

Now it's Viktor's turn to shrug his shoulders. The news has got around, then. Of course. What did she expect? He's wearing his secondhand leather jacket and a long scarf that some girl has knitted for him. His hair is neatly parted in the center, and is tucked into his scarf.

"Marry me," he says.

Rebecka looks at him in amazement.

"Are you out of your mind?"

"I love you," he says. "I love the child."

The air smells of sawdust and wood. Outside she can hear water dripping from the roof. The tears are stuck in her throat, and it hurts.

"Just like you love all your brothers and sisters, friends and enemies?" she says.

Like the love of God. The same for everyone. Prepacked and issued to everyone who joins the queue. Maybe that's the kind of love for her. Maybe she should take what she can get.

He looks so tired.

Where have you gone, Viktor? she thinks. After your journey to God, there are so very many people queueing up for a little bit of you.

"I'd never abandon you," he says. "You know that."

"You don't understand anything," says Rebecka; tears and snot are *pouring down her face, and she can't stop herself. "As soon as I answer, I've already been abandoned."*

At half past six in the evening Rebecka arrived at the police station with Sara and Lova. They had spent the afternoon at the swimming baths.

Sanna came into the meeting room and looked at Rebecka as if she had stolen something from her.

"Oh, so here you are," she said. "I was beginning to think you'd forgotten about me."

The girls took off their outdoor clothes and each climbed up onto a chair. Lova was laughing, because a piece of her hair that had been sticking out from under her hat was frozen solid.

"Look, Mummy," she said, shaking her head so that the clumps of ice in her hair made a tinkling noise.

"We had sausage and mash after swimming," she went on. "And ice cream. Ida and me are meeting up on Saturday, aren't we, Rebecka?"

"Ida was a little girl about the same age that she met in the small pool," Rebecka explained.

Sanna gave Rebecka an odd look, and Rebecka didn't bother to add that Ida's mother was a former classmate of hers.

Why do I feel as if I have to apologize and explain? she thought angrily. I haven't done anything wrong.

"I dived from the three-meter board," said Sara, creeping onto Sanna's knee. "Rebecka showed me how."

"Oh, yes," said Sanna indifferently.

She had already disappeared. It was as if just the shell of her remained there on the chair. She didn't even seem to react when they told her Virku had vanished. The girls noticed and started babbling. Rebecka squirmed uncomfortably. After a while Lova stood up and started to jump up and down on her chair, shouting:

"Ida on Saturday, Ida on Saturday."

Up and down, up and down she jumped. Sometimes she came dangerously close to falling. Rebecka got very anxious. If she fell, she could easily hit her head on the concrete windowsill. Then she'd really hurt herself. Sanna didn't seem to notice.

I'm not going to interfere, Rebecka told herself.

Finally Sara grabbed her younger sister's arm and snapped:

"Will you pack that in!"

But Lova just pulled her arm away and carried on blithely jumping up and down.

"Are you sad, Mummy?" asked Sara anxiously, putting her arms around Sanna's neck.

Sanna avoided looking Sara in the eye when she replied. She stroked her daughter's blond, shining hair. Tidied up the parting with her fingers, tucked her hair behind her ears.

"Yes," she said quietly, "I am sad. You know that I might have to go to jail, and not be your mummy anymore. I'm sad about that."

Sara's face turned ashen. Her eyes enormous with fear.

"But you're coming home soon," she said.

Sanna put her hand under Sara's chin and looked into her eyes.

"Not if I'm convicted, Sara. Then I'll get life, and I won't come out until you're grown up and don't need a mummy anymore. Or I'll get sick and die in jail, and then I'll never come out."

The last sentence was added with a laugh that wasn't a laugh at all.

Sara's lips were a thin, strained line.

"But who's going to look after us?" she whispered.

Then she suddenly yelled at Lova, who was still bouncing up and down on the chair like a lunatic.

"I told you to pack that in!"

Lova stopped at once and slumped down on the chair. She pushed half of her hand into her mouth.

Rebecka's eyes were shooting flashes of lightning at Sanna.

"Sanna's upset," she said to Lova, who was sitting there like a little mouse, watching her older sister and her mother.

She turned to Sara and went on:

"That's why she's saying those things. I promise you she's not going to jail. She'll soon be back home."

She regretted it the moment she opened her mouth. How the hell could she promise something like that?

When it was time to leave, Rebecka asked the girls to go out and wait by the car. She was grinding her teeth with suppressed rage.

"How could you," she hissed. "They'd been out and been swimming and had a nice time for a little while, but you..."

She shook her head, unable to find the right words.

"I've spoken to Maja, Magdalena and Vesa today. I know there was something going on with Viktor. And I know that you know what it was. Come on, Sanna. You have to tell me."

Sanna didn't say a word. She leaned against the mint green concrete wall and chewed on her thumbnail, already bitten down to the quick. Her face was closed.

"You've got to tell me, for Christ's sake," said Rebecka threateningly. "What was going on with Viktor? Vesa said he couldn't break his vow of silence to you."

Sanna remained silent. She gnawed and gnawed at her thumbnail. Bit the skin at the side and pulled it off so that it started to bleed. Rebecka started to sweat. She had the urge to grab hold of Sanna by the hair and bang her head against the concrete wall. More or less like Ronny Björnström, Sara's father, had done. Until in the end he got fed up of that as well, and cleared off.

The girls were waiting by the car. Rebecka thought of Lova, who didn't have any gloves with her.

"Fuck you, then," she said in the end, turned on her heel and left.

Sanna is no longer in her cell. She has disappeared through the concrete ceiling. Forced her way through atoms and molecules and floated out into the firmament above the snow clouds. She has already forgotten the visit. She has no children. She is just a little girl. And God is her Great Mother, who lifts her up under the arms, raising her up to the light so that she has butterflies in her tummy. But She doesn't let go. God doesn't let go of Her little girl. There is no need for Sanna to be afraid. She isn't going to fall.

Curt Bäckström is standing in front of the long mirror on the living room wall, carefully examining his naked body. Light floods over him from a number of small lamps that he has covered with pieces of transparent red fabric, and from dozens of candles. He has pinned black sheets over the windows so that no one can see in.

The room is sparsely furnished. There is no television in the apartment, no radio, no microwave. The radiation and the signals they emitted used to make him ill. He used to be woken in the middle of the night by voices from the electrical equipment, although it was switched off. Nowadays nothing like that can harm him, and he has plugged in the refrigerator and the freezer again. But he has no need of television or radio. They only broadcast godless rubbish, in any case. Messages from Satan, day in and day out.

He can see that he has changed. In the last few days he has become a decimeter taller. And his hair has grown very quickly; soon he'll be able to tie it back. He has parted it in the center, and leans toward the mirror. He looks frighteningly like Viktor Strandgård.

For a moment he tries to see if he can find himself in the mirror. His old self. Perhaps there is a glimpse of something in the eyes, but then it's gone. The image in the mirror disperses and grows blurred. He is completely transformed.

He turns his hands and holds them up to the mirror. In the red glow he can see blood and oil seeping from the wounds on his palms.

Sanna Strandgård should be here. She should be kneeling naked before him, gathering the oil that runs from his palms in a small glass bottle.

He can see her in front of him. How she slowly screws the cork into the shimmering green bottle. Her eyes are fixed on his the whole time, and her lips form the word *"rabbuni."*

True, he has sometimes doubted. Doubted that he is really chosen. Or his ability to contain all of God's might. The last communion service was almost impossible to endure. People all around him, cackling and dancing like chickens. While he was becoming more and more a part of God. The words came thundering toward him: "This is my BODY; this is my BLOOD." He had staggered back to his seat, hearing nothing. Didn't hear the choir. His hands were filled with such strength that they grew thicker. The skin covering his fingers stretched like a balloon, became completely smooth and shiny. He was afraid his fingers would split, like sausages in a frying pan.

The next day he bought some gloves in the biggest size available. He will have to wear them indoors now and again. Until the time comes for people to see.

When he paid for the gloves he suddenly had a feeling of intense distaste. The woman behind the counter smiled at him. For a long time he had had the ability to distinguish between souls, and as he took his change she was transformed before his eyes. Her teeth went yellow, her eyes were turned inside out and became opaque, like frosted glass. The red nails on the fingers handing over the coins grew into long claws.

He waited behind the shop for several hours. But then he received a message telling him that he need not kill her, but must save his strength for something more important.

Curt goes into the bathroom. In the glow of the candles the steam rising from the bath curls upward and forms a dripping layer of moisture on the white tiles. The air is thick with the coppery stench of blood and the harsh smell of damp wool.

On a white plastic clothes drier above him hangs Virku's lifeless body. Her back paws are tied to the clothesline. Blood is dripping slowly into the water. Her head lies on the floor beside the bath. Her muzzle is still bound with silver tape.

As he sinks down into the crimson water, he can immediately feel how his body is suffused with the qualities of the dog. His legs become agile and quick. They twitch restlessly as he lies there. He could jump out and set a world record in the hundred meters.

And he can feel Sanna. Can feel her lips against the dog's ear. Now it is his ear they are touching. She whispers, *"I love you."*

He has already taken her rabbit, her cat and even two gerbils. And all the time her love for him has grown.

He drinks the crimson bathwater in great gulps. His hands begin to shake. He loses all control over them when God takes over.

Then God takes his hand and lifts it. Dips the fingers in blood as if it were ink, and writes on the tiles in sprawling letters. The letters spell out a name. And then:

THE WHORE SHALL DIE.

And evening came and morning came, the fifth day

Maja Söderberg is sitting at the kitchen table in the middle of the night. Well, maybe "sitting" is not the right word. Her bottom is certainly on the chair, but her upper body is sprawled across the table and her legs are dangling beneath the chair. Her cheek is resting on one hand, and she is staring at the pattern on the wallpaper as it grows and shrinks, fades and returns. In front of her is a bottle of vodka. It hasn't been easy for an unpracticed drinker like her to get so much down. But she did it. First of all she cried and sniveled. But now it's better. Some kind soul has injected the stuff the dentist uses straight into her brain.

Then she hears Thomas coming up the stairs. The evening services during the Miracle Conference are long, drawn-out affairs. The services go on until late. Then people sit in the café and chat. And then there are always a few ardent souls who stay on and pray until the small hours. It's important for Thomas to be there then. She understands that. She understands everything.

She can hear him treading carefully on the stairs so as not to disturb the neighbors in the middle of the night. He's so damned considerate. Of the neighbors.

His footsteps rouse her fury.

Hush, she says. But the fury won't go back to sleep. It has woken up and is pulling at its chain. Let me loose, it gurgles in a muffled voice. Let me loose and I'll finish him off.

And then he is standing there beside the kitchen table. His eyes and his mouth are open wide with horror. He looks totally ridiculous. Three gaping holes below his fur hat. She smiles a crooked smile. Has to feel for her mouth with her hand. Yes, her mouth is crooked. How did it end up like that?

"What are you doing?" he asks.

What is she doing? Can't he see? Drinking, of course. She marched down to the liquor store and spent the whole week's housekeeping on booze.

He is full of accusations and questions. Where are the children? Does she realize how small this town is? How is he going to explain away his wife buying spirits at the liquor store?

Then her mouth opens and she begins to howl. The numbness in her mouth and her head wears off immediately.

"Shut your fucking mouth!" she screams. "Rebecka's been here. Do you get it? I'm going to end up in jail."

He tells her to calm down. To think of the neighbors. That they're a team, a family. That they'll get through this together. But she can't stop screaming now. Curses and swear words that she's never uttered before come pouring out of her mouth. You bastard. You hypocritical fucking bastard.

Much later, when he is certain that Maja is sleeping like the dead, Thomas picks up the telephone and makes a call.

"It's Rebecka," he says. "I can't allow her to carry on like this."

Friday, February 21

It had stopped snowing and begun to blow. A piercing, ice-cold wind raced across the forests and the roads. It swept the snow along with it, smoothing out the whole landscape with a white, even cover. The morning train to Luleå was delayed by several hours, and the neat piles of snow shoveled to one side by the owners of the villas were pushed back onto their driveways, blocking their garage doors. It whistled round the corners of the house in its quest for more snow, and found its way inside the collars of cursing paperboys.

Rebecka Martinsson was plodding over to Sivving's house. Her shoulders were hunched against the wind, and she kept her head down like a charging animal. Snow was blowing up into her face so that she could hardly see. She was carrying Lova under one arm like a bundle, and in the other hand she was carrying the child's pink denim rucksack.

"I can walk by myself," whined Lova.

"I know, honey," said Rebecka. "But we haven't got time. It's quicker if I carry you."

She pushed Sivving's door open with her elbow and dropped Lova in a heap on the hall floor.

"Hello," she called, and Bella answered at once with an excited bark.

Sivving appeared in the doorway leading down to the cellar.

"Thanks for taking her," said Rebecka breathlessly, trying in vain to pull Lova's shoes off without undoing them. "Useless idiots. They could at least have told me yesterday when I picked her up."

When she had arrived at nursery with Lova, she'd been informed that the staff had a training day and that none of the children were to attend. That had been exactly one hour before the hearing about Sanna's arrest, and now she was really pushed for time. Before long the wind would have blown so much snow up against the car that she might not be able to get out. And then she'd never make it in time.

She pulled at Lova's shoelaces, but Sara had tied double knots when she helped her little sister get dressed.

"Let me do it," said Sivving. "You're in a hurry."

He picked Lova up and sat with her on his knee on a little green wooden chair that completely disappeared under his bulk. Patiently he started to undo the knots.

Rebecka looked gratefully at him. The route march from the nursery to the car and from the car to Sivving had made her hot and sweaty. She could feel her blouse sticking to her body, but there wasn't a snowball's chance in hell that she would have time to shower and change her clothes. She had half an hour.

"Now, you're going to stay here with Sivving, and I'll be back soon to pick you up, okay?" she said to Lova.

Lova nodded and turned her face up toward Sivving so that she was looking at the underside of his chin.

"Why are you called Sivving?" she asked. "It's a funny name."

"Yes, it is," laughed Sivving. "My real name is Erik."

Rebecka looked at him in surprise, and forgot that she was in a hurry.

"What?" she said. "Isn't your name Sivving? Why are you called that, then?"

"Don't you know?" Sivving smiled. "It was my mother. I was at college in Stockholm, studying to be a mining engineer. Then I moved back home, and was due to start work with LKAB, the mining company. And my mother got a bit above herself. She was proud of me, of course. And she'd had to put up with a lot of nonsense from other people in the village when she sent me away to study. It was really only posh people who sent their children away to study, and they thought there was no call for her to start getting big ideas about herself."

The memory brought a wry smile to his lips, and he went on:

"Anyway, I rented a room on Arent Grapegatan and my mother sorted out a telephone subscription. And she wrote down my title, and it ended up in the phone book. Civ.eng, civil engineer. Well, you can imagine what they all said to start with: 'Oh look, it's civ.eng himself calling to see us.' But after a while people forgot where the name came from, and I just ended up being called Sivving. And I got used to it. Even Maj-Lis called me Sivving."

Rebecka looked at him, smiling in amazement.

"Well, I'll be damned," she said.

"Weren't you in a hurry?" asked Sivving.

She gave a start and shot out through the door.

"Don't you go killing yourself in that car, you hear?" he called after her through the gale.

"Don't go putting ideas in my head," she yelled back, and jumped into the car.

What do I look like, she thought as the car slithered up the tortuous road into town. If only I'd had another half hour to have a shower and put something different on.

She was beginning to know her way into town now. Didn't need to concentrate a hundred percent, could let her thoughts drift away instead.

Rebecka is lying on her bed with her hands pressed against her stomach.

It wasn't too bad, she says to herself. And now it's over.

Strangers dressed in white with soft, impersonal hands. ("Hi, Rebecka, I'm just going to put a cannula in your arm for the drip," a wad of cold cotton wool against her skin, the nurse's fingers are cold too, maybe she's taken a minute to have a quick cigarette out on the balcony in the spring sunshine, "just a sharp prick, that's it, all done.")

She had been lying there looking out at the sun as it poured down onto the snow and made the world outside almost unbearably bright. Happiness came floating along down a plastic tube, straight into her arm. All her worries and difficulties drained away, and after a little while two of the people dressed in white came and wheeled her away for the operation.

That was yesterday morning. Now she is lying here with a searing pain in her stomach. She has taken several painkillers, but it doesn't help. She can't stop shivering. If she has a shower she'll get warm. Perhaps it will ease the cramps in her stomach.

In the shower, gouts of blood spurt out of her. She watches them run down her leg, horrified.

She has to go back to the hospital. Another drip in her arm, and she has to stay overnight.

"You're not in any danger," says one of the sisters when she notices the thin line of Rebecka's lips. "An abortion can sometimes lead to an infection afterward. It's nothing to do with poor hygiene, or anything you've done. The antibiotics will sort it out."

Rebecka tries to smile back at her, but all she can manage is a peculiar grimace.

It isn't a punishment, she thinks. He isn't like that. It isn't a punishment.

Sanna Strandgård was arrested on Friday, February 21, at 10:25, on the basis that there was sufficient reason to suspect her of the murder of Viktor Strandgård. The press and television gobbled up the decision like a pack of hungry foxes. The corridor outside the courtroom was illuminated by camera flashes and film lights as Assistant Chief Prosecutor Carl von Post addressed the media.

Rebecka Martinsson stood with Sanna in the arrest room just inside the court. Two guards were waiting to escort Sanna to the car and back to the station.

"We'll appeal, of course," said Rebecka.

Sanna twirled a lock of her hair absentmindedly between her thumb and forefinger.

"That young lad who was taking the minutes was really staring at me. Did you notice?"

"You do want me to lodge an appeal, don't you?"

"He was looking at me as if we knew each other, but I didn't know him."

Rebecka slammed her briefcase shut.

"Sanna, you're a murder suspect. Every single person in the courtroom was looking at you. Shall I file an appeal on your behalf, or not?"

"Yes, of course," said Sanna, and looked at the guards. "Shall we go?"

When they had gone Rebecka stood there staring at the door leading out to the car park. The door of the courtroom behind her opened. When she turned round she met Anna-Maria Mella's inquiring gaze.

"How are things?"

"So-so," said Rebecka with a grimace. "What about you?"

"Oh, you know . . . so-so."

Anna-Maria flopped down on a chair. She unzipped her thick padded jacket and let her stomach out. Then she pulled off her grayish white woolly hat without bothering to tidy her hair afterward.

"I can honestly say that I'm dying to be a real person again."

" 'To be a real person,' what does that mean?" asked Rebecka with a little smile.

"To be able to sneeze and drink coffee like ordinary people," laughed Anna-Maria.

A young lad in his twenties appeared in the doorway with a notebook in his hand.

"Rebecka Martinsson?" he asked. "Have you got a minute?"

"In a while," said Anna-Maria pleasantly.

She got up and closed the door.

"We're going to interview Sanna's girls," said Anna-Maria without preamble when she had sat down again.

"No, you . . . you're joking," groaned Rebecka. "They don't know anything. They were asleep in bed when he was murdered. Is that . . . Is von Post going to practice his macho interrogation technique on two little girls of eleven and four? Who's going to take care of them afterward? You?"

Anna-Maria leaned back in her chair and pressed her right hand just below her ribs.

"I can understand your reaction to the way he spoke to Sanna..."

"Well, be fair, didn't you feel the same?"

"...but I'll make sure the interview with the girls goes as smoothly as possible. A doctor from the Child Psych team will be there."

"Why?" asked Rebecka. "Why are they being interviewed?"

"You have to understand that we don't have a choice. One murder weapon has been found in Sanna's apartment, but technically it can't be linked directly to her. We haven't found the other one. So we have only circumstantial evidence. Sanna has told us that Sara was with her when she found Viktor, and that Lova was asleep in her sledge. The girls might have seen something important."

"Seen their mother murder Viktor, you mean?"

"At the very least we have to be able to rule them out of our inquiries," said Anna-Maria dryly.

"I want to be there," said Rebecka.

"Of course," said Anna-Maria courteously. "I'll tell Sanna, I'm going to the station now anyway. She looked very calm, I thought."

"She wasn't even here," said Rebecka with a heavy heart.

"It's difficult to imagine what she's going through. To be facing jail."

"Yes," said Rebecka.

They have gathered at Gunnar Isaksson's house. The pastors, the church elders and Rebecka. Rebecka is the last to arrive, although she is ten minutes early. She hears how the conversation in the living room comes to an abrupt stop when Gunnar opens the door.

Neither Gunnar's wife, Karin, nor the children are at home, but in the kitchen there are two large thermos flasks on the round table. One of coffee, one of hot water for tea. On a round silver-colored dish there are cakes and buns covered with a small white-and-yellow-checked cloth. Karin has left out cups, saucers and spoons. There is even milk in a little jug. But they will eat and drink later. First they are going to talk.

"You'll be wondering why we've asked you to come here, of course."

Frans Zachrisson starts the discussion. He is one of the elders. In normal circumstances he hardly looks at her. He doesn't like Sanna or Rebecka. But now his gaze is troubled and gentle. His voice is full of warmth and consideration. It terrifies Rebecka. She doesn't answer, just sits down when he asks her to.

Some of the other elders are looking at her seriously. They are all middle-aged or older. Vesa Larsson and Thomas Söderberg are the youngest, barely thirty.

Vesa Larsson is looking down at the table. Thomas Söderberg is leaning forward in his chair, his elbows on his knees. His forehead is resting on his clasped hands and his eyes are closed.

"Thomas has handed in his resignation," says Frans Zachrisson. "After what's happened he doesn't feel that he can continue as pastor in the same church as you, Rebecka."

The elders nod supportively, and Frans Zachrisson continues:

"I regard what's happened with the utmost seriousness. But I also believe in forgiveness. Forgiveness from both God and man. I know that God has forgiven Thomas, and I myself have forgiven him. We all have."

He falls silent. Wonders for a moment whether he ought to speak of forgiveness in connection with her, Rebecka, perhaps. But it's a tricky business. She went through with the abortion despite Thomas Söderberg's unselfish appeal. And she shows no sign of repentance. Can there be forgiveness without repentance?

Rebecka tries to force herself to look up and meet Frans Zachrisson's eyes. But she can't. There are too many of them. They overpower her.

"We have tried to persuade Thomas to withdraw his resignation, but he has not done so. It is difficult for him to move on here, because he would always be reminded of his mistake. . . ."

He stops speaking again and Pastor Gunnar Isaksson takes the opportunity to say a few words. Rebecka sneaks a glance in his direction. Gunnar is leaning back on the leather sofa. His expression is, well, almost greedy. He looks as if he might stretch out his fat little hand at any second, grab hold of her and eat her all up. She realizes that he's glad Thomas Söderberg is in trouble. Thomas is far too intellectual for his taste. Speaks Greek, and is always pointing out what the original text says. Read theology at university. Gunnar only went to high school. He must have been like the cat that's got the cream recently, being able to discuss Thomas Söderberg's "weakness" with his brothers.

Gunnar Isaksson points out that he too has been tempted, but it is in these circumstances that one's relationship with God is tested. He says that when he was asked by the elders whether he still had faith in Thomas Söderberg, he asked for a day to think about it before he said yes. He wanted his decision to be firmly anchored in God. He hoped Rebecka understood that it was.

"We believe God has great plans for Kiruna," Alf Hedman, another of the elders, interrupts, "and we believe Thomas has a key role to play in those plans."

Rebecka understands exactly why they have asked her to come. Thomas cannot remain in the church if she is a member of the congregation, for then he will be constantly reminded of his sin. And everybody wants Thomas to stay. She immediately does what they want.

"He doesn't need to move," she says. "I'm going to ask to be released from the church, in any case, because I'm moving to Uppsala to study."

They congratulate her on her decision. And besides, there is a very good church in Uppsala that she will be able to join.

Now they want to pray for her. Rebecka and Thomas have to sit on two chairs beside each other and the rest stand in a circle around them and place their hands upon them in prayer. Soon the sound of speaking in tongues is pouring out through the windows and up to heaven.

Their hands are like insects crawling all over her body. Everywhere. No, they're like red-hot stones burning holes right through her clothes and her skin. Her soul pours out through the holes. She feels ill. She wants to be sick. But she can't. She's trapped beneath all these men who have laid their hands upon her body. One thing she does do. She refuses to close her eyes. You're supposed to close your eyes when receiving intercession. Open yourself.

Inward and upward. But she keeps her eyes open. Clings to reality by star-ing at her knees. At an almost invisible mark on her skirt.

"You'll stay for coffee," says Gunnar Isaksson when they've finished.

And she stays, obediently. The pastors and the elders munch on Karin's homemade cakes with sensual enjoyment. Except for Thomas, who disap-pears immediately after the intercession. The others talk about the weather and about the services to come during the Easter season.

No one speaks to Rebecka. It's as if she isn't there. She chews on a choco-late marshmallow. It's dry and turns to dust in her mouth, and she takes great gulps of coffee to try and sluice it down. When she has eaten the cake she puts down her cup, mumbles a good-bye and sneaks out through the front door. Like a thief.

Anna-Maria Mella plodded up to her house. A snowdrift had covered the drive, and the car had got stuck just inside the gate.

She kicked away the snow that had collected in front of the door and yanked it open. Yelled into the house.

"Robert!"

No answer. From Marcus's room upstairs she could hear music. No point in asking him to go out and clear the snow. That would just mean half an hour's discussion, in which case she might as well do it herself. But she couldn't manage it. The snow had wedged itself in the door frame and she had to slam the door to shut it. Robert had probably gone off somewhere with Jenny and Petter. To his mother's, perhaps.

Marcus had friends round. Presumably some of the hockey team. His sports bag was lying on the hall floor swimming in melted snow from his outdoor shoes, along with two bags she didn't recognize.

She climbed over their indoor hockey sticks and carried the wet sports bags into the bathroom. Took Marcus's sports gear out of his bag. Dried the hall floor and placed the shoes and sticks in a neat row by the door.

On the way to the laundry room with her arms full of wet sports kit she passed the kitchen. On the table stood a carton of milk and a tin of O'boy chocolate. From this morning? Or Marcus and his mates? She shook the milk carton carefully and sniffed at it. It was okay. She put it in the fridge. Just looking at the overloaded draining board made her feel tired, and she went down to the cellar. Two banana boxes full of Christmas decorations were just inside the door to the cellar stairs. Robert was supposed to be carrying them downstairs to put away.

She went down to the cellar. Kicked dirty clothes chucked down the stairs by the family in front of her as she went, carried them into the laundry room and sighed. It felt like a lifetime since she'd had the strength to stand there ironing and folding everything. The mountain of clean laundry as high as Tolpagorni in front of the workbench. Dirty laundry in stale heaps on the floor in front of the washing machine. Fluff in every corner. Well established, perfectly happy there. Wet, black, grubby suds around the drain.

When I'm on maternity leave, she thought. Then I'll have time.

She stuffed a load of white kneesocks, underclothes, some sheets and hand towels into the machine. Turned it to sixty degrees, program B. The washing machine began to hum with exertion, and Anna-Maria waited for the usual click, like a short burst of Morse code, as the program started up, followed by the sound of the water gushing into the drum, but nothing happened. The machine kept up its monotonous hum.

"Oh, come on!" she said, banging the top of it with her fist.

Not a new washing machine. That would cost thousands.

The machine hummed painfully. Anna-Maria switched it off and then back on again. Tried a different program. In the end, she kicked it. Then the tears came.

When Robert went down to the laundry room an hour later she

was sitting in front of the workbench. Folding clothes like a mad thing, tears pouring down her face.

His gentle hands moving over her back and her hair.

"What's wrong, Mia-Mia?"

"Leave me alone!" she snapped.

But then, when he put his arms around her, she sobbed into his shoulder and told him about the washing machine.

"And everything's such a bloody tip," she sniveled. "As soon as I get through the door all I can see is things that need doing. And now this . . ." She fished a pair of blue-and-white-striped rompers out of the pile of clean washing. The blue had faded and frequent washing had made the fabric bobbly.

"Poor kid. He's going to be wearing faded hand-me-downs for the rest of his life. He'll get bullied at school."

Robert smiled into her hair. After all, there hadn't been too many storms this time around. When she'd been expecting Petter things had been worse.

"And then there's this case," she went on. "We've got a list of everyone who's involved in the Miracle Conference. The idea was to blitz them all. But Sanna Strandgård was arrested today, and now von Post wants all resources concentrated on her. So I've promised Sven-Erik I'll go through the list, because officially I'm not part of the investigation. I just don't know when I'm going to get it done."

"Come on," said Robert. "Let's go up to the kitchen and I'll make some tea."

They sat opposite each other at the kitchen table. Anna-Maria moved her spoon around listlessly in her mug, watching the honey dissolve in the chamomile tea. Robert peeled an apple, cut it into small pieces and passed them to her. She pushed them in her mouth without even noticing.

"Everything will work out okay," he said.

"Don't say everything will work out okay."

"We'll move, then. You and me and the baby. We'll leave this untidy house. The kids'll be all right for a while. And then I'm sure society will intervene and find them some decent foster parents."

Anna-Maria laughed out loud, then blew her nose loudly on a rough piece of kitchen roll.

"Or we could ask my mother to move in here," said Robert.

"Never."

"She'd do the cleaning."

Anna-Maria laughed.

"Never in a million years."

"Empty the dishwasher. Iron my socks. Give you good advice."

Robert got up and threw the apple peel in the sink.

Why can't he just throw it straight in the bin? she thought tiredly.

"Come on, let's take the kids and go for a pizza. We can drop you at the station afterward and you can go through the Miracle lot this evening."

When Sara and Rebecka walked into Sivving's kitchen on Friday afternoon, he and Lova were busy waxing skis. Sivving was holding a white cake of paraffin wax up against a little travel iron, letting it drip onto the skis, which were held in a waxing clamp. Then he carefully spread the paraffin the whole length of the ski with the iron. He put the iron down and held his hand out to Lova without looking at her. Like a surgeon looking down at his patient.

"Scraper," he said.

Lova passed him the scraper.

"We're waxing skis," Lova explained to her older sister as Sivving shaved away the excess paraffin in white curly flakes.

"I can see that," said Sara, bending down to pat Bella, who was lying on the rag rug in front of the window and playing a tune on the radiator behind her as she wagged her tail.

"So," Rebecka said to Sivving, "you've moved into the kitchen."

"Well," he said, "this particular job takes up a lot of space. It might be an idea if you say hello to Bella as well before she wriggles out of her skin. I've told her to stay put, so she doesn't knock the skis over or run around among the flakes of paraffin. Okay, Lova, now you can pass me the glide wax."

He picked up the iron from the draining board and melted more paraffin onto the skis.

"Right, chicken, now you can take your skis and put on one layer of blue kick wax."

Rebecka stooped down to Bella and scratched under her chin.

"Are you hungry?" asked Sivving. "There's cinnamon buns and milk."

Rebecka and Sara sat on the wooden sofa with a glass of milk each, waiting for the microwave to ping.

"Are you going skiing?" asked Rebecka.

"No," said Sivving, "you are. The wind's going to drop tomorrow. I thought we could take the snowmobile and follow the river up to the cabin in Jiekajärvi. Then you can do a bit of skiing. You haven't been up there for years and years."

Rebecka took the cinnamon buns out of the microwave and placed them straight on the pine table in a pile. They were much too hot, but she and Sara tore off chunks and dunked them in the cold milk. Lova was rubbing away at her skis.

"I'd love to go up to Jiekajärvi, but I've got to do some work tomorrow as well," said Rebecka, blinking.

The headache was like being stabbed behind the eyes with a chisel. She pinched the bridge of her nose between her thumb and forefinger. Sivving glanced at her. Looked at the half-eaten bun next to her glass of milk. He passed Lova the cork and showed her how to smooth out the wax under her skis.

"Listen," he said to Rebecka, "you go upstairs and lie down for a bit. The girls and I will go out with Bella, then I'll sort out some food."

Rebecka went up to the bedroom. Sivving and Maj-Lis's double bed stood there in the silent room, neatly made and empty. The big rounded knobs on the pine headboard had grown dark and shiny with many years' use. She had the urge to place her hand on one of them. The gray sky was shutting out most of the daylight, and the room was dark. She lay down on top of the bed and pulled the woolen rug that was folded up at the bottom of the bed over her. She was tired and frozen and her head was pounding. Restlessly she fumbled for her cell phone and checked her messages. The first was from Måns Wenngren.

"I didn't need a horse's head," he drawled. "But I did promise that journalist first pop at the story if she dropped the complaint."

"What story?" snapped Rebecka.

She waited for him to say something else, but the message was over, and an expressionless voice in her ear was telling her the time of the next message.

What were you expecting? she sneered at herself. That he was going to whisper sweet nothings and make small talk?

The next message was from Sanna.

"Hi," said Sanna tersely. "I've just heard from Anna-Maria that the girls are going to be interviewed. And they're dragging somebody from the Child Psych team in. I don't want it to happen, and I'm surprised you haven't spoken to me about it. Unfortunately things don't seem to be working out with you and me, so I've decided that Mum and Dad can look after the girls for the time being."

Rebecka switched off the phone without listening to her other messages. There was a knock on the door, and Sivving popped his head round. He looked at her lying there, and stared at the telephone in her hand.

"I think we need to swap that for a proper teddy bear," he said. "It'll do you good to come out to Jiekajärvi. There's no reception there, so you might as well leave it at home. I was just going to say the food will be ready in an hour, and I'll come and wake you. Now get some sleep."

Rebecka looked at him.

"Don't go," she said. "Talk to me about my grandmother."

Sivving went over to the wardrobe, took out another woolen blanket and spread it over Rebecka. Then he took the telephone off her and placed it on the bedside table.

"People round here never used to think that Albert, your grandfather, would get married," he said. "He always used to sit in the corner with his cap in his hand when he went visiting, never said a word.

He was the only one of the brothers that stayed on the farm with his father. And his father, your grandfather's father, Emil, he was a real hard man. We lads were terrified of him. Hell, one time when he caught us playing poker in the sandpit, I thought he was going to pull my ear clean off my head. He was a really strict Laestadian. But anyway, Albert went off to a funeral in Junosuando, and when he came back there was something different about him. He still didn't say anything, just like before. But it was as if he was sitting there smiling to himself, although his mouth never moved, if you see what I mean. He'd met your grandmother. And that summer he went off several times to visit relatives in Kuoksu. Emil was furious when Albert disappeared right in the middle of the harvest. In the end she came to visit. And you know what Theresia was like. When it came to work, there was nobody to beat her. Anyway, I don't know how it came about, but suddenly she and Emil were out there cutting one half each of the old sheep pasture, you know, the meadow between the potato field and the river. It was like a competition. I remember it as if it were yesterday. It was quite late in the summer, the blackflies had arrived and it was just before supper, so they were biting well. We lads stood there watching. And Isak, Emil's brother, he was there too. You never got to meet him. Pity. They worked in silence, Emil and Theresia, each with their own scythe. The rest of us kept quiet too. All you could hear were the insects and the evening cry of the swallows."

"Did she win?" asked Rebecka.

"No, but in a way, neither did Emil. He finished first, but your grandmother wasn't far behind. And Isak ran his hand over the stubble on his chin and said, 'Well, Emil, we'd better put the ram out on your half.' Emil had rushed ahead with his scythe like a fury, but he hadn't made a very good job of it. But your grandmother's half looked as if she'd crawled over the meadow on her knees with a pair of nail scissors. So, now you know how she won the respect of your grandfather's father."

"Tell me some more," begged Rebecka.

"Another time." Sivving smiled. "Now you need to sleep for a while."

He closed the door behind him.

How am I supposed to sleep? thought Rebecka.

She had the distinct impression that Anna-Maria Mella had lied to her. Or maybe not lied, but kept something back. And why was Sanna lashing out now that the girls were going to be interviewed? Was it for the same reason as Rebecka, that she had no confidence in von Post? Or was it because a child psychologist was going to be involved? Why had somebody sent a card to Viktor saying that what they'd done wasn't wrong in the eyes of God? Why had the same person threatened Rebecka? Or maybe it wasn't a threat, maybe it was a warning? She tried to remember exactly what it had said on the note.

God, I can't possibly sleep, she thought, gazing up at the ceiling.

But the next minute she had fallen into a deep sleep.

She was woken by a thought, opened her eyes to the darkness beneath the ceiling and lay completely still so as not to frighten it away.

It was something Anna-Maria Mella had said. "We have only circumstantial evidence."

"If you only have circumstantial evidence, what is it you need?" she whispered to the ceiling.

Motive. And what kind of motive could you uncover by interviewing Sanna's daughters?

The realization dropped into her brain like a coin in a wishing well. It floated down through the water and settled on the bottom. The ripples on the surface died away, and the picture was crystal clear.

Viktor and the girls. Rebecka pushed the thought away. It just wasn't possible. And yet, it was horribly possible.

She remembered how things had been when she arrived in Kurravaara. Lova dousing herself and the dog with soap. And hadn't Sanna said she always carried on like that? Didn't that seem like a typical thing to do for children who . . .

She couldn't bring herself to finish the thought.

She suddenly thought of Sanna. Sanna, with her provocative clothes. And her heavy-handed, dangerous daddy.

How could I not have seen it, she thought. The family. The family secret. It can't be true. It must be true.

But still, Sanna couldn't have killed Viktor on her own. Sanna couldn't have managed it, even if she'd wanted to.

She remembered the time Sanna had bought a toaster that didn't work.

She couldn't bring herself to take it back, she thought. If I hadn't taken it she would have just kept quiet and held on to it.

She sat up on the bed, thinking. If Sanna didn't want the children interviewed, then her parents were probably on the way here already. Presumably they'd already been to her grandmother's house, rattling the door handle. And they were bound to be back any minute.

She picked up her cell phone and rang Anna-Maria Mella. She answered on her direct line at work. Sounded tired.

"I can't explain," said Rebecka, "but if you do want to interview the children, I can come in with them tomorrow. After that it's going to be difficult for you."

Anna-Maria kept her questions to herself.

"Fine" was all she said. "I'll sort it out."

They arranged a time for the following day, and Rebecka promised to bring the children in.

That's it, then, thought Rebecka as she got up. Sorry, Sanna, but I won't be checking my messages till tomorrow afternoon. So I still don't know that you want your parents to take the girls.

She had to keep out of the way until the following day. She couldn't stay here with the girls. Sanna had been to Sivving's house.

At the police station Anna-Maria Mella was sitting in front of the computer, going through the matches for the participants in the conference. The corridor outside her room was in darkness. Next to her on the desk lay a half-eaten tuna pizza in its greasy box. There were matches for a surprising number of those involved in the Miracle Conference on the criminal records register, the register of suspects and the antisocial-behavior records. Most were drug-related offenses linked to theft and violence.

Reformed junkies and thugs, thought Anna-Maria.

She had written down the names and ID numbers of a few people she thought were worth following up.

Just when she had decided to ring Robert, her eye caught a note on a murder case. The verdict had been returned by the court in Gävle. Twelve years ago. Sentence: placed in a secure psychiatric unit. Nothing since then.

I wonder, she thought. Is he out on parole, or has he been discharged? I must check up on him.

She picked up the phone and rang home. Marcus answered. Sounded disappointed when it was only his mother.

"Tell Dad I'll be late," she said.

Rebecka went down to the kitchen. Sivving was just laying the table for dinner. He was putting out the same Duralex glasses, the cutlery with the black Bakelite handles and the everyday china with the yellow flowers that she remembered from when she was little. She'd often sat here in the kitchen talking to Maj-Lis and Sivving.

"It's meatballs," he said.

"I'm absolutely starving," said Rebecka. "It smells terrific."

"Two-thirds elk mince and one-third beef."

"Where are the girls?"

He nodded toward the big room.

"Sivving," said Rebecka, "can I borrow your snowmobile and the sledge trailer? I'm going up to the cabin in Jiekajärvi with the girls this evening."

Sivving put the cast-iron pan on the table. He used a folded tea towel with Maj-Lis's initials embroidered on it in red cross-stitch as a table mat.

"Has something happened?" he asked.

Rebecka nodded.

"We're not in any danger," she said. "But we can't stay here. If Sanna's parents come here asking for us, you don't know where we are."

"I see," said Sivving. "There are padded scooter overalls here for both you and the children. And I'll give you some food and dry wood to take with you. Bella and I will follow you up early tomorrow morning. But I'm not letting you go without some food inside you."

Rebecka went into the other room. Lova and Sara had spread a newspaper out on the folding table and were painting stones with intense concentration. In the middle of the table lay a finished stone as an example. It was slightly bigger than a man's clenched fist, and on it was painted a curled-up cat with big turquoise eyes.

"My grandchildren enjoyed doing that last summer," said Sivving from the kitchen. "I thought it might be fun for Lova and Sara."

From the kitchen Bella gave a warning bark.

"Quiet!" growled Sivving.

"I don't know what's the matter with her," he said to Rebecka. "Half an hour ago she set off barking just like that. It must be a fox or something. She didn't wake you?"

Rebecka shook her head.

"Look, Rebecka, I'm painting Virku!" shouted Lova.

"Mmm, lovely," replied Rebecka absently. "You can take the stones and the paints with you, because we're going off on the snowmobile tonight—we're going to sleep in my grandmother's cabin."

At quarter past six in the evening Rebecka drove the snowmobile across the road from Sivving's on her way down to the river. She was wearing a balaclava and a fur hat, but she still had to blink fiercely to keep out the snow that was being whipped up against her face. The headlights were reflected back at her by the whirling snow, and she couldn't see more than a meter or so in front of her. Sara and Lova were tucked up in the sledge trailer under rugs and reindeer skins, along with all their packages. You could just about see the tips of their noses.

She crossed her grandmother's yard and stopped outside the house. She really ought to run upstairs and fetch the children's pajamas. But there was every chance Sanna's parents would turn up at that very moment. No, it was best not to linger. If she could just keep the girls out of the way until the next day, then the psychiatrist would talk to them. Then Social Services could take over, or whoever the hell it might be. At least she would have done what she could for them.

She put her foot down and drove down toward the river. The darkness closed behind her like a curtain. And the wind immediately covered their tracks with snow.

Curt Bäckström is standing like a shadow in her grandmother's kitchen. He leans against the wall by the window and watches the headlights disappearing down toward the river. In his right hand he is holding a knife. He runs his forefinger cautiously along the blade to feel its sharpness. In one pocket of his snowsuit lie three black plastic sacks. In the other is the house key that he took out of Rebecka's coat pocket. He has been standing here in the darkness for a long time, waiting. Now he allows his eyes to close for a little while. It feels good. His eyes are dry and burning.

The fox has her lair and the birds of the air have their nests, but the Son of Man has no place to rest his head.

Anna-Maria Mella was driving along Österleden down toward Lombolo. It was quarter past ten at night. She was driving too fast. With a reflex action, Sven-Erik grabbed at the top of the glove compartment as the car skidded over the fresh snow on the road. His hand in its thick glove found nothing to hang on to.

The Obs department store on the right, a few pinpricks of light behind the curtain of snow. Stop at the roundabout, wheels spinning as she put her foot down. On the left the Space House, like a stranded silver alien spaceship. The signs glowing red. The residential area—Stenvägen, Klippvägen, Blockvägen, with their tenaciously cleared driveways and their well-stocked bird tables.

"His name is Curt Bäckström," said Anna-Maria. "Convicted of murder twelve years ago, then sent to a secure psychiatric unit, as they used to call it. No notes since then."

"Right. So tell me about the murder."

"He stabbed his stepfather. Several times. His mother was watching and testified against her son. In the witness box she admitted she was scared of the boy."

"Boy?"

"He was only nineteen. And he's not here as a visitor at the conference. He lives here, down in Lompis. Tallplan 5B. Somebody down at the station in Gävle knew somebody in the court office. She went there after work and faxed everything over to me. Some people are easy to deal with."

She pulled into the car park. Long rows of garages. Two-story wooden apartment blocks built in the late sixties. They got out of the car and started walking. Not a soul in sight, despite the fact that it was Friday night.

"The county court discharged him two years ago," Anna-Maria went on. "He was still in contact with a community care unit in Gävle. Had regular shots, held down a job. But according to the records he moved to Kiruna in January last year. And according to the duty doctor at the psychiatric unit in Gällivare, he hasn't had any contact with community care in Kiruna."

"So . . ."

"So I don't know, but presumably he hasn't had the medication he needs for a year. And is that so odd? I mean, you've seen those tapes from the church. 'Throw away your pills! God is your doctor!' "

They stood for a while outside the door. Two of the apartments were in darkness. Sven-Erik had his hand on the door handle. Anna-Maria lowered her voice.

"I asked the duty doctor what he thought might happen to a person who stopped their injections."

"And . . ."

"And you know what they're like . . . can't comment on this particular case . . . varies from one individual to another . . . but in the end he admitted that it was perhaps possibly likely that he might get worse. Bad, even. Do you know what he said when I told him there was a church that thought people should throw away all their medication?"

Sven-Erik shook his head.

"He said: 'Weak people are often drawn to the church. And people who want power over weak people are also drawn there.' "

They stood in silence for a few seconds. Anna-Maria watched as the wind filled their footprints on the porch with snow.

"Shall we go in, then?" she said.

Sven-Erik opened the door and they went into the dark stairwell. Anna-Maria switched on the light. A small plaque on the right showed that Bäckström lived on the next floor. They went up the stairs. They had both been to these apartments on many occasions in the past, when the neighbors had phoned to complain about some disturbance. There was the same smell as there always was in these places. Piss under the stairs. The acrid smell of cleaning fluid. Concrete.

They rang the bell, but no one answered. Listened at the door, but the only sound was music from the apartment opposite. There had been no light in the window. Anna-Maria opened the letter box and tried to look in. The flat was in darkness.

"We'll have to come back," she said.

And evening came and morning came, the sixth day

It is twenty past four in the morning. Rebecka is sitting at the small kitchen table in the cabin in Jiekajärvi. She looks toward the window and looks straight into her own great big eyes. Anybody could be standing right outside and looking in at her, and she wouldn't be able to see them. That person would suddenly press his face against the glass and the image of his face would melt into the reflection of her own.

Stop it, she says to herself. There's nothing out there. Who'd go out in the dark in a storm like this?

The fire is crackling in the stove and the draught in the chimney makes a long, lonely sound that is accompanied by the howling wind outside and the soft hissing of the kerosene gas lamp. She gets up and pushes in two more logs. When there's a storm like this it's important to keep the fire going. Otherwise the cabin will be chilled through by tomorrow morning.

The strong wind finds its way through gaps in the walls and between the door frame and the old ocher yellow mirrored door. Once upon a time, before Rebecka was born, it had been the door of the pigsty. Her grandmother had told her that. And before that it had been somewhere else. It is much too beautiful and too solid a door to have been made for the pigsty. Presumably it used to be in a house somewhere that had been pulled down. And somebody had decided to find a home for the door.

On the floor there are several layers of Grandmother's rag rugs. They insulate the house and keep the cold out. The snow that has been blown up against the walls insulates too. And the north-facing wall has a little extra protection from the stack of wood that has been covered with a tarpaulin to keep the snow off.

Next to the stove is the enamel water bucket with the ladle made of stainless steel, and a big basket of wood. Right beside it are Sara and Lova's painted cat stones on top of a pile of old magazines. Although of course Lova's stone represents a dog. It is curled up with its muzzle between its paws, gazing at Rebecka all the time. Just to be on the safe side Lova has written "Virku" on its painted black back. Both the girls are fast asleep in the same bed now, their fingers spattered with paint and a double layer of blankets right up to their ears. Before they went to bed all three of them worked together, rolling up the mattresses to press all the cold air out of them. Sara is sleeping with her mouth open, and Lova is curled up in the curve of her big sister's arm. Their cheeks are rosy. Rebecka takes off one blanket and puts it up on the shelf.

It's not my job to protect them, she tells herself. After tomorrow there will be nothing more I can do for them.

Anna-Maria sits up in bed with the bedside lamp lit. Robert is sleeping beside her. She has two pillows behind her back, and is leaning against the headboard. On her knee she has Kristina Strandgård's album of newspaper cuttings and pictures of Viktor Strandgård. The child moves in her stomach. She can feel a foot pressing against her.

"Hello, pest," she says, rubbing the hard lump under her skin that is the foot. "You shouldn't kick your old mum."

She looks at a picture of Viktor Strandgård sitting on the steps in front of the Crystal Church in the middle of winter. He is wearing an indescribably ugly green crocheted hat. His long hair is lying over his left shoulder. He is holding his book up toward the camera, *Heaven and Back*. Laughing. Looks open and relaxed.

Did he do something to Sanna's children? wonders Anna-Maria. He's just a boy.

She is dreading tomorrow and the interview with Sanna Strandgård's daughters.

At least you're going to have a nice daddy, she tells the child in her belly.

All of a sudden she is deeply moved. Thinks of that small life. Capable of survival, perfect, with ten fingers and ten toes and a personality all its own. Why does she always get so tearful and over-the-top? Can't even watch a Disney film without howling at the really sad part just before everything turns out all right in the end. Is it really fourteen years since Marcus was lying in her stomach? And Jenny and Petter, they're so big too. Life goes so incredibly quickly. She is filled with a deep sense of gratitude.

I really haven't got anything to complain about, she thinks, turning to someone out there in the universe. A wonderful family and a good life. I've already had more than anyone has a right to ask for.

"Thank you," she says out loud.

Robert changes position, turns onto his side, wraps himself in his blanket so that he looks like a stuffed cabbage roll.

"You're welcome," he answers in his sleep.

Saturday, February 22

Rebecka pours coffee from the thermos flask and puts it down on the kitchen table.

What if Viktor did something to Sanna's girls, she thinks. Could Sanna have been so furious that she killed him? Maybe she went looking for him to confront him, and . . .

And what? she interrupts herself. And she lost the plot and whipped out a hunting knife from nowhere and stabbed him to death? And smashed him over the head as well, with something heavy she just happened to have in her pocket?

No, it didn't make sense.

And who wrote that postcard to Viktor that was in his Bible? "What we have done is not wrong in the eyes of God."

She gets the tins of paint the girls have been using and spreads an old newspaper out on the table. Then she paints a picture of Sanna. It looks more like the woman who lived in the gingerbread house than anything else, with long, curly hair. Underneath Sanna, she writes "Sara" and "Lova." She draws Viktor beside them. She paints a halo around his head; it has slipped slightly. Then she joins the girls' names to Viktor with a line. She draws a line between Viktor and Sanna as well.

But that relationship was broken, she thinks, and scribbles out the lines linking Viktor to Sanna and the girls.

She leans back in her chair and allows her gaze to range over the sparse furniture, the hand-carved green beds, the kitchen table with its four odd chairs, the sink with the red plastic bowl and the little stool that just fits into the corner by the door.

Once upon a time, when the cabin was used on hunting trips, Uncle Affe used to stand his rifle on the stool, leaning against the wall. She remembers her grandfather's frown of displeasure. Her grandfather himself always placed his gun carefully in its case and pushed it under the bed.

Nowadays the axe for chopping wood stands on the stool, and the handsaw hangs above it on a hook.

Sanna, thinks Rebecka, and looks back at her painting.

She draws curly little spirals and stars above Sanna's head.

Silly-billy Sanna. Who can't manage anything by herself. All her life a series of idiots have leapt in and sorted things out for her. I'm one of them. She didn't even have to ask me to come up here. I came scampering up anyway, like a damned puppy.

She makes Sanna's arms and hands disappear by painting over them in black. There, now she can't do anything. Then she paints herself and writes "IDIOT" above.

Comprehension rises out of the picture. The brush shakily traces the figures she has painted on the newspaper. Sanna can't manage anything by herself. There she stands, no arms, no hands. When Sanna needs something, some idiot leaps in and sorts things out for her. Rebecka Martinsson is an example of such an idiot.

If Viktor is doing something to her children . . .

...and she gets so angry she wants to kill him, what happens then?

Then some idiot is going to kill Viktor for her.

Can that be what happened? It has to be what happened.

The Bible. The murderer put Viktor's Bible in Sanna's kitchen drawer.

Of course. Not to frame Sanna. It was a present for her. The message, the postcard with the sprawling handwriting, was written to Sanna, not to Viktor. "What we have done is not wrong in the eyes of God." Killing Viktor was not wrong in the eyes of God.

"Who?" says Rebecka to herself, drawing an empty heart next to the picture of Sanna. Inside the heart she draws a question mark.

She listens. Tries to make out a sound through the storm. A sound that doesn't belong here. And then suddenly she hears it, the noise of a snowmobile.

Curt. Curt Bäckström, who sat on his snowmobile under the window, gazing up at Sanna.

She gets up and looks around.

The axe, she thinks in a panic. I'll get the axe.

But she can't hear the noise of the engine anymore.

It was just your imagination, calm down, she reassures herself. Sit down. You're stressed and scared and you imagined you heard something. There's nothing out there.

She sits down, but can't take her eyes off the doorknob. She ought to get up and lock it.

Don't start, she thinks, like some kind of spell. There's nothing out there.

The next moment the doorknob begins to turn. The door opens. The moaning of the storm bursts in, along with a rush of cold air, and a man dressed in a dark blue snowsuit steps quickly inside. Pushes the door shut behind him. At first she can't make out who it is. Then he takes off his hood and balaclava.

It isn't Curt Bäckström. It's Vesa Larsson.

Anna-Maria Mella is dreaming. She jumps out of a police car and runs with her colleagues along the E10 between Kiruna and Gällivare. They are on their way to a crashed car lying upside down ten meters from the carriageway. It's such hard work. Her colleagues are already standing next to the crumpled car and yelling at her.

"Get a move on! You're the one with the saw! We've got to get them out!"

She carries on running with the chainsaw in her hand. Somewhere she can hear a woman; her screams are heartrending.

She's there at last. She starts up the chainsaw. It shrieks through the metal of the car. She catches sight of the child seat hanging upside down in the car, but she can't see if there's a child in it. The saw gives a shrill howl, but suddenly it makes a loud piercing ringing sound. Like a telephone.

Robert nudges Anna-Maria in the side and goes back to sleep as soon as she has picked up the receiver. Sven-Erik Stålnacke's voice comes down the line.

"It's me," he says. "Listen, I went back to Curt Bäckström's yesterday. But he hasn't been there all night, at least nobody's answering the door."

"Mmm," mumbles Anna-Maria.

The nastiness of her dream lingers on. She squints at the clock radio beside the bed. Twenty-five to five. She shuffles backwards in the bed and leans against the headboard.

"You didn't go there on your own?"

"Don't make a fuss, Mella, just listen. When he didn't seem to be at home, or wasn't opening the door, or whatever, I went to the Crystal Church to see if there was some sort of all-night hallelujah carry-on, but there wasn't. Then I rang the pastors—Thomas Söderberg, Vesa Larsson and Gunnar Isaksson, in that order. I thought maybe they kept an eye on their flock and might know if this Curt Bäckström was in the habit of spending his free time during the day anywhere other than in his flat."

"And?"

"Thomas Söderberg and Vesa Larsson weren't at home. Their wives insisted they must still be at the church because of this conference, but I swear to you, Anna-Maria, there was nobody in that church. I mean, they could have been sitting there hiding in the dark, quiet as mice, but I find that difficult to believe. Pastor Gunnar Isaksson was at home, answered after ten rings and rambled on—he'd obviously had a nightcap."

Anna-Maria ponders for a while. She feels befuddled and slightly unwell.

"I wonder if we've got enough for a search warrant," she says. "I'd like to get into Curt Bäckström's apartment. Ring von Post and ask him."

Sven-Erik sighs at the other end of the phone.

"He's completely hung up on Sanna Strandgård," he says. "And we haven't got a shred of evidence. But still, I've got a really bad feeling about this guy. I'm going to go in."

"Into his apartment? Just stop right there."

"I'm going to ring Benny the locksmith. He won't ask any questions if I tell him he can send the bill to the police."

"You're out of your mind."

Anna-Maria lowers her feet to the floor.

"Wait for me," she says. "Robert can dig the car out."

"Take it easy now, Rebecka," says Vesa Larsson. "We only want to talk. Don't do anything stupid."

Without taking his eyes off her he fumbles behind with his hand, grabs hold of the door handle and presses it downward.

We, she thinks. Who are "we"?

All at once she realizes that he is not alone. He just came in first to make sure the situation was under control.

Vesa Larsson opens the door and two other men come into the room. The door closes behind them. They are dressed in dark clothes. No skin visible anywhere. Balaclavas. Goggles.

Rebecka tries to get up from the chair, but her legs will not obey her. It is as if her whole body is ceasing to function. Her lungs are incapable of taking in any air. The blood that has flowed through her veins since she was born is stopping. Like the river when a dam has been built. Her stomach is turning into a solid knot.

No, no, fuck, fuck . . .

One of the two men takes off his hood and reveals his dark shiny curls. It is Curt Bäckström. His snowsuit is black and shiny. On his feet he has sturdy biker's boots with steel toe-caps. Over his shoulder he is carrying a shotgun, double barreled. His nostrils and pupils are flared, like a warhorse. She looks straight into his glazed eyes. Sees the fever in them.

Be very careful with him, she thinks.

She sneaks a glance at the girls. They are fast asleep.

She sees who the other man is before he removes his hood and goggles. It doesn't matter what he's wearing, she would recognize him anywhere. Thomas Söderberg. The way he moves. Dominates the room. It's almost as if they had rehearsed. Curt Bäckström and Vesa Larsson take up positions on either side of the door to the pigsty.

Vesa Larsson looks past her. Or maybe straight through her. He has the same look as the parents of small children in the supermarket. The muscles beneath the skin of the face have given up. They can't hide the tiredness anymore. The dead expression. The parents haul their trolleys up and down the aisles like donkeys beaten to the limit of their endurance, deaf to their children's crying or their agitated chatter.

Thomas Söderberg takes a step forward. At first he doesn't look at her. With tense, watchful movements he unzips his leathers and takes out his glasses. They are new since she last saw him, but that's a long time ago. He looks around the room like a commander in a science-fiction film, registers everything, the children, the axe in the corner and Rebecka, by the kitchen table. Then he relaxes. His shoulders drop. His movements become softer, like a lion padding over the savannah.

He turns to Rebecka.

"Do you remember that Easter when you invited Maja and me here?" he asks. "It feels like another lifetime. For a while I thought I wouldn't be able to find it. In the dark and the storm."

Rebecka looks at him. He takes off his hood and his gloves and pushes them into the pockets of his leathers. His hair has got thinner. The odd gray streak among the brown, otherwise he is just the same. As if time had stood still. Maybe he has put on a little weight, but it's hard to tell.

Vesa Larsson leans against the door frame. He is breathing with his mouth open and his face is turned slightly upward, as if he were feeling carsick. His gaze wanders from Curt to Thomas, and to Rebecka herself. But he doesn't look at the children.

Why doesn't he look at the children?

Curt sways to and fro a little. His gaze is firmly fixed, sometimes on Rebecka, sometimes on Thomas.

What's going to happen now? Is Curt going to take the shotgun from his shoulder and shoot her? One, two, three, and it's all over. Black. She must gain time. Talk, woman. Think of Sara and Lova.

Rebecka uses her hands to support her; leaning on the edge of the table, she raises herself from the chair.

"Sit down!" barks Thomas, and she slumps back down like a beaten dog.

Sara whimpers slightly but doesn't wake. She turns over and her breathing once again becomes deep and calm.

"Was it you?" croaks Rebecka. "Why?"

"It was God himself, Rebecka," says Thomas earnestly.

She recognizes the serious tone of voice and the attitude. This is how he looks and sounds when he wants to impress important matters upon his listeners. His whole being is transformed. It is as if he were a block of stone that has thrust up through the earth from under the ground, with its roots in the earth's core. Gravity, strength and power through and through. And yet, at the same time, humility before God.

Why is he putting on this performance for her? No, it isn't for her benefit. It's for Curt. He's . . . he's handling Curt.

"What about the children?" she asks.

Thomas bows his head. Now there is something fragile in his tone. Something frail. It's as if his voice can barely manage the words.

"If you hadn't . . ." he begins. ". . . I don't know if I'll ever be able to forgive you for forcing me to do this, Rebecka."

As if he has been given an invisible sign, Curt removes his right glove and takes a coil of rope from his pocket.

She turns to Curt. Forces her voice past the lump blocking her throat.

"But you love Sanna," she says. "How can you love her and kill her children?"

Curt closes his eyes. He continues to sway gently to and fro as if he doesn't hear her. Then his lips move silently for a while before he answers.

"They are shadow children," he says. "They must be put aside."

If she can just get him talking. Gain some time. She has to think. Follow his thread. Thomas is letting him talk, he daren't do anything else.

" 'Shadow children'? What do you mean?"

She tilts her head to one side and rests her cheek on her hand just as Sanna does, makes a real effort to keep her voice calm.

Curt speaks straight out into the room with his eyes fixed on the kerosene lamp. As if he were alone. Or as if there were some being inside the light itself, listening to him.

"The sun is behind me," he says. "My shadow falls before me. It walks in front of me. But when I step into it, the shadow must give way. Sanna will have new children. She will bear me two sons."

I'm going to be sick, thinks Rebecka, and she can taste minced elk meat and bile surging up through her body.

She gets up. Her face is as white as snow. Her legs are trembling under her. Her body is so heavy. It weighs several tons. Her legs are like spindly toothpicks.

In a second Curt is in front of her. His face is twisted with rage. He screams at her so loudly that he has to draw breath after each word.

"You . . . were . . . told . . . to . . . sit . . . down!"

He hits her in the stomach with enormous force and she folds forward like a clasp knife. Her legs lose their last vestige of strength. The floor comes rushing up to meet her face. Grandmother's rag rug against her cheek. Unbearable pain in her stomach. A long way above her, agitated voices. A rushing, ringing noise in her ears.

She has to close her eyes for a little while. Just for a little while. Then she'll open her eyes. That's a promise. Sara and Lova. Sara and Lova. Who's screaming? Is it Lova, screaming like that? Just for a little while . . .

Benny the locksmith unlocks the door to Curt Bäckström's apartment and disappears. Sven-Erik Stålnacke and Anna-Maria Mella stand there on the dark staircase. Only the lights from outside shine in through the window facing the yard. Silence. They look at each other and nod. Anna-Maria has undone the safety catch on her pistol, a Sig Sauer.

Sven-Erik goes in. She hears his tentative hello. Anna-Maria stands guard outside the open door.

I must be out of my mind, she thinks.

The bottom of her back is aching. She leans against the wall and takes deep breaths. What if he's in there in the dark. He might be dead. Or lying in wait somewhere. He could rush her from inside and knock her down the stairs.

Sven-Erik switches on the light in the hallway.

She peers in. It's a one-room apartment. You can see straight into the combined living room and bedroom from the hall. It's a peculiar place. Does someone really live here?

There isn't a stick of furniture in the hall. No desk with bits and pieces and the mail. No mat. Nothing hanging on the coat stand below the hat pegs. The living room is empty too. Almost. There are some lamps standing on the floor, and a huge mirror hangs on the wall. The windows are covered with black sheets. Nothing on the windowsills. No curtains. A single pine bed up against the wall. The coverlet is pale blue machine-quilted nylon.

Sven-Erik comes out of the kitchen. He shakes his head imperceptibly. Their eyes meet. Full of questions and foreboding. He walks over to the bathroom door and opens it. The light switch is on the inside. He stretches out his hand. She hears the click, but the light doesn't come on. Sven-Erik remains standing in the doorway. She can see him from the side. His hand taking out his key ring. He has a small torch on it. The narrow beam of light in through the door. The eyes narrowing so that they can see better.

Perhaps she makes a movement that he sees out of the corner of his eye, because his hand flies up to stop her. He takes one step into the room. One foot over the threshold. Her back is tense and aching again. She clenches her fist and presses it against her spine.

He comes out of the bathroom. Rapid steps. Mouth open. Pupils like black holes in a face made of ice.

"Ring," he says hoarsely.

"Ring who?" she asks.

"Everybody! Wake up the whole bloody lot of them!"

Rebecka opens her eyes. How much time has passed? Thomas Söderberg's face is floating just below the ceiling. He looks like the eclipse of the sun. His face is in the shadows, and the kerosene lamp hanging behind his head forms a corona around his brown curls.

Her stomach is still hurting. Worse than before. And over and above the pain, outside the pain, is something warm and wet. Blood. She realizes with terror that Curt didn't punch her.

He stabbed her with a knife.

"This isn't exactly what we planned," says Thomas Söderberg firmly. "We must reconsider."

She turns her head. Sara and Lova are lying head to tail on the bed. Their hands are tied to the bedposts. Bits of white cloth are sticking out of their mouths. On the floor by the bed lies a torn-up sheet. That's what they've got in their mouths. She can see their chests moving up and down rapidly as they fight to take in enough air through their noses.

Lova has a cold. But she's breathing.

Keep calm, she's breathing. Fuck, fuck.

"The idea was," says Thomas Söderberg thoughtfully, "the idea was to set fire to the cabin. And we were going to give you the keys to your snowmobile so you could get away, just in your nightdress or a T-shirt. You'd take the chance, of course; who wouldn't? With the storm and the windchill factor when you're traveling by snow-mobile, I reckon you'd have got about a hundred meters at the most. Then you'd have fallen off and frozen to death in a matter of min-utes. It would have shown up as a simple accident on the police re-port. The cabin catches fire. You panic, leave the kids and rush out just as you are. You try to escape and freeze to death just a little dis-tance away. No major investigation, no questions. Now it's going to be more difficult."

"Are you intending to let the children burn to death?"

Thomas bites his lip thoughtfully as if he hasn't heard her.

"I think we'll have to take you with us," he says. "Even if your body burns, the mark of the stab wound might still be there. I can't risk that."

He breaks off and turns his head as Vesa Larsson comes in with a red plastic gasoline can in his hand.

"No gasoline," says Thomas angrily. "No accelerants and no chemicals. Anything like that will show up in a technical examina-tion. We'll set fire to the curtains and the bedclothes with matches."

He nods at Rebecka.

"We'll take her with us," he continues. "You two go and spread a tarpaulin over the trailer."

Vesa Larsson and Curt disappear through the door. The storm roars, then falls silent as the door closes. Now she is alone with him. Her heart is pounding. She must hurry. She knows that. Otherwise her body will fail her.

Did Curt put the gun down by the door? Difficult to spread out a heavy tarpaulin in a storm with a gun slung on your back. Come closer.

"I can't understand how you could do this," says Rebecka. "Doesn't it say 'Thou shalt not kill'?"

Thomas sighs. He is squatting by her side.

"And yet, the Bible is full of examples of when God has taken life," he says. "Don't you understand, Rebecka? He is allowed to break his own laws. And I couldn't do it. I told him that. Then he sent me Curt. It was more than a sign. I had to obey him."

He stops to wipe away the snot running from his nose. His face is beginning to redden in the heat from the stove. It must be warm in that suit.

"I don't have the right to allow you to destroy God's work. The media would have blown these financial difficulties up into a full-scale scandal, and then it would all have been over. What has happened in Kiruna is something great. And yet, God has made me understand that this is only the beginning."

"Did Viktor threaten you?"

"In the end he was a threat to everyone. Not least to himself. But I know that he is with God."

"Tell me what happened."

Thomas shakes his head impatiently.

"There is neither the time nor any reason to do so, Rebecka."

"And what about the girls?"

"They can tell people things about their uncle that ... We still need Viktor. His name must not be dragged through the dirt. Do you know how many people we help to come off drugs every year? Do you know how many children are reunited with their lost mummies and daddies? Do you know how many find faith? Job opportunities? A decent life? Marriages saved? In the night God has talked to me about all this again and again."

He breaks off and stretches out his hand to her. Lets his fingers trail over her mouth and down to her throat.

"I loved you just as much as I love my own daughter. And you ..."

"I know," she squeaks. "Forgive me."

Come closer.

"But what about now?" she sobs. "Do you love me now?"

His face becomes as hard as stone.

"You killed my child."

The man who has only daughters. Who wanted a son.

"I know. I think about him every day. But it wasn't..."

She turns her head to the side and coughs and presses her hand against her stomach. Then she looks up at him again.

There it was. She could see it. Thirty centimeters from her head. The stone Lova had painted Virku on. When he's close enough. Grab it and hit him. Don't think. Don't hesitate. Grab it and hit him.

"There was someone else as well. It wasn't..."

Her voice tails away in an exhausted whisper. He leans toward her. Like a fox listening for voles under the snow.

Her lips form words he cannot hear.

Finally he bends over her. Don't hesitate, count to three.

"Pray for me..." she whispers in his ear.

One...

"...you weren't the only one I..."

Two...

"...it wasn't your child."

Three!

He stiffens for a second and it's enough. Her arm shoots out like a striking cobra, grabs the stone. She shuts her eyes and hits him with every ounce of strength she has. On the temple. In her mind's eye she sees the stone shooting like a missile straight through his skull and out through the wall. But when she opens her eyes the stone is still in her hand. Thomas is lying on his side next to her. Perhaps his hands are making an attempt to shield his head. She doesn't really know. She is already up on her knees and she hits him again. And again. On the head every time.

That's enough. Now she's in a hurry.

She drops the stone and tries to get to her feet, but her legs won't bear her weight. She crawls across the floor to the corner by the door. Curt's shotgun is next to the axe. She drags herself along on her knees, using her right hand. She keeps her left hand pressed against her stomach.

If she can only manage it in time. If they come in now it's all over.

She grabs hold of the weapon. Gets to her knees. Fumbles. Her hands are shaky and clumsy. Slips the bolt. Breaks the gun. It's loaded. Snaps it shut and releases the safety catch. Scrabbles backwards toward the middle of the floor. The rag rugs are spattered with blood. Drops of her own blood as big as a one-krona coin. Blurred prints from her right hand, the hand that held the stone.

If they go around the house they'll be able to see her through the window. They won't do that. Why would they go tramping off round there? She feels ill. Mustn't throw up. How is she going to manage to hold on to the gun?

She shuffles farther back in a half-sitting position, one hand pressed against her stomach. Moves the other hand toward the table and pushes with her legs. Gets hold of the gun and drags it along with her. Sits with the table leg supporting her back. Legs slightly drawn up. Lays the gun along her thighs so that it is pointing upward at the door. And waits.

"Keep calm," she says to Lova and Sara without taking her eyes off the door. "Shut your eyes and keep calm."

Curt is the first to come in through the door. Just behind him she can see Vesa. Curt catches sight of her with the gun. Registers the two black holes pointing at him. For a fraction of a second his face alters. From irritation with the cold, the wind and the stiff tarpaulin into—not fear, but something else. First of all, the realization that he can't get to her in time. Then his gaze becomes dull. Empty and expressionless.

She doesn't lift the gun high enough and the recoil cracks her lower rib when she blasts a hole in Curt's stomach. He falls back against the door. The snow comes whirling in through the opening.

Vesa stands frozen to the spot. His whole body is a single scream.

"In!" she snaps, and points the gun at him. "And bring him with you. Sit down!"

He does as she says and squats on his haunches by the door.

"On your backside!" she orders.

He slumps down. His suit is bulky. He can't easily get to his feet from that position. Without her telling him to, he links his hands behind his head. Curt is lying between them. In the silence that follows when the door has closed against the storm, they can hear Curt's labored breathing: short, panting whistles.

She leans her head back. Tired. Very tired.

"Now," she says to Vesa Larsson, "you are going to tell me everything. And as long as you keep talking and keep telling the truth, you can stay alive."

"Sanna Strandgård came to me," says Vesa hoarsely. "She was . . . in floods of tears. I know that's a ridiculous expression, but you should have seen her."

Oh, I can see her, all right, thinks Rebecka. Hair all fluffed out like a dandelion clock. Nobody suits snot and tears better than Sanna.

"She said Viktor had interfered with her girls."

Rebecka steals a glance at the girls; they are still tied to the bed with rags in their mouths. She's afraid she'll faint if she crawls over to them. And if she tells Vesa to untie them, he can kick the gun out of her hand in a second. She must wait a little while.

They're breathing. They're alive. She'll soon work out what to do.

"What do you mean, 'interfered with'?"

"I don't know, it was something Sara had said that made her realize. I didn't really get a clear idea of what had happened. But I promised to speak to Viktor. I . . ."

He breaks off in confusion.

She does confuse people, thinks Rebecka. Lures them into the forest and steals their compass.

"Yes?"

"I was such a fool," he whines. "I asked her not to go to the police or the authorities. She'd spoken to Patrik Mattsson. I rang him and said Sanna had made a mistake. Threatened to throw him out of the church if he spread the rumor around."

"Get on with it," said Rebecka impatiently. "Did you speak to Viktor?"

The gun resting on her legs is getting heavier and heavier.

"He wouldn't listen to me. It wasn't even a conversation. He leaned across my desk and threatened me—said my days as a pastor in this church were numbered. Said he had no intention of putting up with the fact that the pastors were lining their own pockets through the business."

"The trading company?"

"Yes. When we started Victory Print, I thought it was all above-board. Or maybe it was just that I didn't think too hard about it. A member of the church who owned his own company gave us the idea. He said it was all perfectly legal. We put the costs down to the company, and reclaimed the VAT from the state. Of course, the church gave us money to make the investments on the quiet, but in our eyes everything in the company belonged to our church anyway. As I saw it, we weren't deceiving anybody. It wasn't until I broke the vow of confidentiality and told Thomas about Sanna's suspicions, and that Viktor had threatened me, that I realized we were in trouble. Thomas got scared. Do you understand? Within the space of three hours, the whole world began to shake. Viktor was aggressive and a danger to children. Viktor, who had always loved children. Used to help out in Sunday school and so on . . . It made me feel sick. And Thomas was afraid. Thomas, who'd always been as solid as a rock. And I was a criminal. Can I take my hands down from my neck? My head and shoulders are aching."

She nods.

"We decided to speak to him together," he goes on. "Thomas said Viktor needed help, and he would get that help within the church. So that evening . . ."

He stops speaking and they both look at Curt, lying on the floor between them. The rug has turned red beneath him. His breathing changes from a whistling rattle to a quiet wheezing. And then he stops breathing. Silence.

Vesa Larsson stares at him, his pupils dilated with fear. Then he looks at Rebecka and at the shotgun on her knee.

Rebecka blinks. She is beginning to feel listless and uninterested. It is as if Vesa's story no longer has anything to do with her. But now he needs no encouragement to keep talking. Suddenly he is babbling at top speed.

"Viktor wouldn't listen to us. He said he had fasted and prayed, and that it was time for the church to be cleansed. All of a sudden we were the ones standing there being accused. He said we were hawkers who should be driven from the temple. That this was God's work, yet we were prepared to hand it over to Mammon. And then...oh, God... then all at once Curt was there. I don't know if he'd been standing there listening all the time, or if he'd just come into the church."

Vesa screws up his eyes and his mouth contorts into a grimace.

"Viktor pointed at Thomas and screamed, I don't remember what. Curt had an unopened wine bottle in his hand. We had celebrated communion during the service. He hit Viktor on the back of the head. Viktor fell to his knees. Curt was wearing a big padded jacket. He slipped the bottle into his inside pocket. Then he took the knife out of his belt and stabbed him. Two or three blows. Viktor fell backwards and stayed still, lying on his back."

"And you stood there watching," whispers Rebecka.

"I tried to intervene, but Thomas stopped me."

He pushes his fists against his eyes.

"No, that isn't true," he goes on. "I think I took a step forward. But Thomas just made a small movement with his hand. And I stopped. Just like a well-trained dog. Then Curt turned and came over to us. Suddenly I was terrified that he was going to kill me too. Thomas stood completely still with no expression on his face. I remember looking at him and thinking I'd read that's what you're meant to do if you're attacked by a rabid dog. Don't run, don't scream, just stay calm and stand still. We stood there. Curt didn't say anything either, just looked at us with the knife in his hand. Then he turned on his heel and went back to Viktor. He..."

Vesa makes a keening noise through his teeth.

"...stabbed him again, over and over. Dug into his eyes with the knife. Then he stuck his fingers into the sockets and smeared the blood over his own eyes. 'All that he has seen, I have now seen,' he cried out. He licked the knife like ... an animal! I think he cut his tongue, because there was blood trickling down the side of his mouth. And then he cut off the hands. Hacking and twisting. He pushed one in his jacket pocket, but there wasn't room for the other one, and he dropped it on the floor, and ... I don't really remember after that. Thomas drove me along Norgevägen in his car. I stood out in the cold in the middle of the night throwing up. And all the time Thomas was going on and on. About our families. About the church. Saying the best thing we could do now was to keep quiet. Afterward, I wondered whether he knew Curt was there. Or whether he'd actually seen him standing there."

"And Gunnar Isaksson?"

"He didn't know anything. He's a waste of space."

"You cowardly bastard," said Rebecka, exhausted.

"I've got children," he whines. "Everything will be different now. You'll see."

"Don't even bother," she says. "When Sanna came to you. That's when you should have gone to the police and Social Services. But no—you didn't want the scandal. You didn't want to lose your nice house and your well-paying job."

Soon she won't be able to keep her right leg drawn up any longer. If she puts the gun down on the floor he'll have time to get up and kick her in the head before she's even had time to raise it into the firing position. She can't see properly. Black spots are clouding her vision. As if somebody had fired paintballs at a shop window.

She's going to faint. There's no time.

She points the gun at him.

"Don't do it, Rebecka," he says. "You won't be able to live with yourself. I never wanted this, Rebecka. It's over now."

She wishes he would do something. Make a move to get up. Reach for the axe.

Maybe she can trust him. Maybe he'll put her and the children in the sledge and take them back. Give himself up to the police.

Or maybe not. And then—roaring fire. The terrified eyes of the girls as they tug at the ropes binding their hands and feet to the bed.

The flames melting the flesh on their bones. If Vesa sets the place on fire, there's nobody to tell. Thomas and Curt will get the blame, and he'll walk free.

He came here to kill us, she says to herself. Just remember that.

He is weeping now, Vesa Larsson. Just a moment ago Rebecka was sixteen, sitting in the cellar of the Pentecostal church in the middle of all his painting gear, talking about God, life, love and art.

"Think of my children, Rebecka."

It's him or the girls.

She closes her eyes as her finger squeezes the trigger. The report is deafening. When she opens her eyes he is still sitting there in the same position. But he no longer has a face. A second passes, then the body falls to one side.

Don't look at it. Don't think. Sara and Lova.

She drops the gun and hauls herself up onto all fours. Her whole body shakes from the exertion as she crawls toward the bed, inch by inch. A ringing, howling noise fills her ears.

Sara's hand. One hand is enough. If she can free one hand . . .

She crawls over Curt's lifeless body. Fumbles with his belt. Gropes under his body with her hand. There's the knife. She undoes the sheath, draws it out. It looks as if she has dipped her hand in blood. She's reached the bed.

Steady hand, now. Don't cut Sara.

She cuts through the hemp rope and pulls it off Sara's wrist. Places the knife in Sara's free hand and sees her fingers close around the handle.

Now rest.

She slumps down on the floor.

After a little while Lova and Sara's faces appear above her. She grabs Sara's sleeve.

"Remember," she croaks. "Stay inside the cabin. Keep the door shut and put on your snowsuits and all the blankets. Sivving and Bella are coming in the morning. Wait for them. Are you listening, Sara? I'm just going to have a little rest."

Nothing hurts anymore. But her hands are ice cold. She loses her grip on Sara's sleeve. Their faces drift away. She is sinking down into a well; they are standing at the top in the sun, looking down at her. And all the time it's getting darker and colder.

Sara and Lova crouch down on either side of Rebecka. Lova turns to her older sister.

"What did she say?" she asks.

"I thought it sounded like 'Will you receive me?' " replies Sara.

The winter wind was tearing frantically at the spindly birch trees outside the hospital in Kiruna. Pulling at their gnarled arms, reaching up into the blue black sky. Snapping their spindly, frozen fingers.

Måns Wenngren hurtled straight past the intensive care reception desk. The cold glare of the fluorescent lights bounced off the polished surface of the floor and the pallid cream walls of the corridor, with their indescribably ugly pattern in wine red. His whole being was revolted by the impression. The smell of disinfectant and cleaning fluid mixed with the stale, creeping stench of crumbling bodies. The constant clatter of metal trollies delivering food, samples or Lord knows what.

At least it isn't Christmas, he thought.

His father had had his final heart attack on Christmas day. It was many years ago now, but Måns could still see the hospital staff's unfortunate and unsuccessful attempts to create a festive atmosphere on the ward. Cheap, mass-produced ginger biscuits served with afternoon tea on paper serviettes with a Christmas motif. A plastic tree at the far end of the corridor, its needles pointing the wrong way and squashed flat after a long year in its box up on a shelf in the storeroom. Odd baubles dangling from the branches on a piece of thread. And beneath the lower branches, gaudy packages that you knew had nothing in them.

He shook off the memories before they got as far as his parents. Swung around without pausing, his wool coat streaming out behind him like a cloak.

"I'm looking for Rebecka Martinsson," he roared. "Is anybody working here, or what?"

That morning he had been woken by the telephone. It was the police in Kiruna, wondering if it was true that he was Rebecka Martinsson's boss. Yes, it was true. They hadn't managed to find any records of close relatives. Perhaps the firm knew if she had a partner or boyfriend? No, the firm didn't know that. He had asked what had happened. The police had finally told him Rebecka was undergoing an operation, but they refused to part with any more information.

He had phoned the hospital in Kiruna. They hadn't even been prepared to confirm that she'd been admitted. "Classified" was the only word he could get out of them.

Then he'd phoned one of the two female partners in the firm.

"Måns, darling," she'd said, "Rebecka is your assistant."

In the end he'd taken a taxi to the airport at Arlanda.

Halfway down the corridor a nurse caught up with him. She followed him, a torrent of words spilling out as he opened various doors and looked in. He registered only fragments of her babble. Classified. Unauthorized. Security.

"I'm her partner," he bluffed as he carried on opening doors and looking in.

He found Rebecka alone in a four-bed room. Next to the bed was a drip with a plastic bag half full of clear fluid. Eyes closed. Face deathly white, even her lips.

He pulled a stool up to the bed, but didn't sit down. Instead he turned and growled at the little woman who was pursuing him. She disappeared at once, her Birkenstocks clattering frantically down the corridor.

After a moment another woman wearing a white coat and white trousers came in. In two strides he was right in front of her, reading the small name badge pinned to her breast pocket.

"Right, Sister Frida," he said aggressively, before she'd even managed to open her mouth, "would you be so kind as to explain this to me?"

He pointed at Rebecka's hands. Both were securely tied to the sides of the bed with gauze bandage.

Sister Frida blinked in surprise before she answered.

"Come out here with me," she said softly. "Then we can calm down and have a little chat."

Måns waved his hand in front of him as if she'd been a fly.

"Fetch the doctor who's responsible for her," he said angrily.

Sister Frida was attractive. She was a natural blonde. She had high cheekbones, and her mouth was subtly painted with pink lip gloss. She was used to people obeying her soft voice. She was known for it. She'd never been a fly before. She wondered whether to call security. Or maybe the police, in view of these particular circumstances. But then she looked at Måns Wenngren. Her gaze swept over him, from the improbably well-ironed shirt collar, over the gray-and-black-striped tie, to the discreet black suit and the beautifully polished shoes.

"All right, come with me and you can speak to the doctor," she said brusquely, turned on her heel and stalked out with Måns trailing in her wake.

The doctor was a short man with thick, gray-blond hair. His face was sunburned and his nose had begun to peel slightly. Presumably he'd recently had a little holiday abroad. His white coat was left casually unbuttoned over jeans and a turquoise T-shirt. The pocket of his coat was stuffed with several pens, a notebook and a pair of glasses.

Middle-aged angst with traces of hippie syndrome, thought Måns, standing just a little too close when they shook hands so that the doctor was forced to look upward like a stargazer.

They went into the consulting room together.

"It's for her own good," the doctor explained to Måns. "When she woke up she pulled the cannula out of her arm. We've given her a mild sedative, but—"

"Is she being held for questioning?" asked Måns. "Or has she been arrested?"

"Not as far as I know."

"Has any decision been taken about compulsory care? Is there a care order?"

"No."

"Shit, it's like the Wild West up here," said Måns contemptuously. "You've got her lying here, tied up, with no order from the police, the prosecutor or the chief medical officer. That's illegal curtailment of liberty. Prosecution, fines and a slap on the wrist from the authorities for you. But I'm not here to cause trouble. Tell me what's happened, the police must have told you, untie her and get me a cup of coffee. In return I'll sit quietly in her room and make sure she doesn't do anything stupid when she wakes up. And I won't make trouble for the hospital either."

"But the information the police passed on to me is classified," said the doctor halfheartedly.

"Give some, get some," Måns replied laconically.

A little while later Måns was leaning back on the uncomfortable chair next to Rebecka's bed. His left hand was gently clasping her fingers, and in the other hand he had a cup of scalding coffee in a plastic cup in a brown holder.

"Bloody girl," he muttered. "Wake up so I can tell you off."

D arkness. Then darkness and pain. Rebecka opens her eyes carefully. On the wall above the door is a large clock. The minute hand quivers each time it jumps to the next mark. She screws up her eyes, but can't make out what it says, or if it's day or night. The light stabs at her eyes like knives. Burns a hole of pain into her head. It explodes in a thousand pieces. Every breath is pain and agony. Her tongue is stuck fast to the top of her mouth. She closes her eyes again and sees Vesa Larsson's terrified face before her. "Don't do it, Rebecka. You won't be able to live with yourself."

Back into the darkness. Down. Deeper. Downward. Away. The pain recedes. And she is dreaming. It's summer. The sun is blazing down from a blue sky. The bumblebees weave about drunkenly between the midsummer flowers and the yarrow. Her grandmother is kneeling on the jetty down by the river, scrubbing rag rugs. She has made the soap herself from lye and fat. The scrubbing brush moves back and forth over the stripes on the rug. The faint breeze from the river keeps the mosquitoes away. On the edge of the jetty sits a child with her feet in the water. She has caught a water boatman in a jam jar with a hole in the lid. She is fascinated, watching the large beetle swimming around inside the jar. Rebecka begins to walk down to the water. She is strangely aware that she is dreaming, and mumbles quietly to herself: "Let me see her face. Let me see what she looks like." Then Johanna turns and catches sight of her. She holds the jam jar triumphantly up to show Rebecka as her lips form the word "Mummy."

It was almost a Christmas card. But not really. Three wise men look-ing down at the sleeping child. But the child was Rebecka Martinsson and the men Assistant Chief Prosecutor Carl von Post, the lawyer Måns Wenngren and Inspector Sven-Erik Stålnacke.

"She's killed three people," said von Post. "I can't just let her go."

"It's a textbook example of self-defense," said Måns Wenngren. "Surely you can see that? Besides which, she's the hero of the hour. Believe me, the newspapers are already busy cooking up a real Mod-esty Blaise story. Saved two children, killed all the bad guys . . . You need to ask yourself what role you want to play. The heap of shit who goes after her and tries to put her behind bars? Or the nice guy who gets to join in and share the glory?"

The assistant chief prosecutor's gaze flickered away. Flew to Sven-Erik, where there was no support to be had, not even the smallest stick to lean on. Wandered back to the yellow hospital blanket, neatly tucked in under Rebecka's mattress.

"We had thought we'd try to keep the media out of it," he said tentatively. "I mean, the dead pastors had families. A certain amount of consideration . . ."

Beneath his moustache Sven-Erik Stålnacke sucked air in through his teeth.

"It's going to be difficult to keep the press and TV out of it," said Måns casually. "The truth has a way of leaking out somehow."

Von Post fastened his coat.

"All right, but she's got to be interrogated. She's going nowhere until then."

"Of course. As soon as the doctors say she's up to it. Anything else?"

"Call me when she's ready to be interviewed," said von Post to Sven-Erik, and disappeared through the door.

Sven-Erik Stålnacke took off his padded jacket.

"I'll go and sit in the corridor," he said. "Let me know when she wakes up. There's something I want to say to her. I was thinking of getting a coffee and a snack from the machine. Can I get you anything?"

Rebecka woke up. In less than a minute a doctor was leaning over her. Big nose and big hands. Broad back. Looked like a blacksmith in disguise in his white coat. He asked how she was feeling. She didn't reply. Behind him stood a nurse with a caring and not too broad smile on her face. Måns by the window. Looking out, although he couldn't possibly see anything other than a reflection of himself and the room behind him. Fiddled with the blind. Closed, opened. Closed, opened.

"You've gone through quite an ordeal," said the doctor. "Both physically and mentally. Sister Marie here is going to give you something to calm you down, and a little more pain relief if you need it."

The last remark was a question, but she didn't answer. The doctor got up, nodding to the nurse.

———

The injection worked after a while. She could breathe normally without it hurting.

Måns sat down by the bed and looked at her in silence.

"Thirsty," she whispered.

"You're not allowed to drink properly yet. You're getting what you need through the drip, but just wait a while."

He got up. She brushed his hand.

"Don't be angry," she croaked.

"Don't start," he said as he walked toward the door. "I'm bloody furious."

After a while he came back with two white plastic cups. In one of them was water so that she could rinse her mouth. In the other two ice cubes.

"You're allowed to suck these," he said, rattling the ice cubes. "There's a policeman here who wants to talk to you. Are you up to it?"

She nodded.

Måns waved Sven-Erik in, and he sat down by her bed.

"The girls?" she asked.

"They're fine," said Sven-Erik. "We got to the cabin quite soon after . . . after it was all over."

"How?"

"We went into Curt Bäckström's apartment and realized we had to find you. We can talk about all that later, but we found a number of rather unpleasant things. In his refrigerator and freezer, among other places. So we went to the house in Kurravaara, the address you'd given the police. But there was nobody there. We actually broke in. Then we went to the nearest neighbor."

"Sivving."

"He was able to lead us to the cabin. The eldest girl told us what happened."

"But the girls are all right?"

"Definitely. Sara's cheek was frostbitten. She'd been outside try-ing to start the snowmobile."

Rebecka whimpered. "But I told her."

"It's nothing serious. They're here in the hospital with their mother."

Rebecka closed her eyes.

"I want to see the girls."

Sven-Erik rubbed his chin and looked at Måns. Måns shrugged his shoulders.

"She did save their lives after all."

"Okay," said Sven-Erik. "We'll have a word with the nice doctor and we won't bother having a word with the nice prosecutor, and we'll see."

Sven-Erik Stålnacke pushed Rebecka's bed in front of him along the corridor. Måns was one step behind with the rickety drip.

"That reporter who dropped the assault complaint has been sticking to me like a tick," said Måns to Rebecka.

The corridor outside Sanna and the girls' room was almost eerily empty. It was half past ten at night. From the dayroom farther along they could see the bluish glow of a television, but no sound. Sven-Erik knocked on the door and backed away a few meters, along with Måns.

It was Olof Strandgård who opened the door. His face contorted in an expression of distaste when he saw Rebecka. They glimpsed Kristina and Sanna behind him. There was no sign of the children. Perhaps they were sleeping.

"It's okay, Daddy," said Sanna, stepping out of the room. "You stay here with Mummy and the girls."

She closed the door behind her and went to stand beside Rebecka. Through the door they heard Olof Strandgård's voice:

"I mean, she was the one who endangered the girls' lives," he said. "Is she supposed to be some sort of hero now?"

Then they heard Kristina Strandgård, couldn't make out any words, just a soothing mumble.

"What?" Olof Strandgård again. "So if I chuck somebody through a hole in the ice and then pull him out, I've saved his life, have I?"

Sanna pulled a face at Rebecka. Don't bother about him, we're all a bit shaken up and tired, it said.

"Sara," said Rebecka. "And Lova."

"They're asleep, I don't want to wake them up. I'll tell them you were here."

She's not going to let me see them, thought Rebecka, biting her lip.

Sanna reached out her hand and stroked Rebecka's cheek.

"I'm not angry with you," she said gently. "I know you did what you thought was best for them."

Rebecka's hand clenched into a fist under the blanket. Then it shot out and fastened itself around Sanna's wrist like a pine marten grabbing a ptarmigan by the back of the neck.

"You . . ." hissed Rebecka.

Sanna tried to pull her hand away, but Rebecka hung on to her.

"What is it?" asked Sanna. "What have I done?"

Måns and Sven-Erik Stålnacke carried on talking to each other a little distance away down the corridor, but it was obvious they had completely lost the thread of their own conversation. All their attention was fixed on Rebecka and Sanna.

Sanna crumpled.

"What have I done?" she whimpered again.

"I don't know," said Rebecka, holding on to Sanna's hand as tightly as she could. "You tell me what you've done. Curt loved you, didn't he? In his own twisted way. Maybe you told him about your suspicions of Viktor? Maybe you did the whole helpless-little-girl bit, told him you didn't know what you were going to do? Maybe you cried a little and said you wished Viktor would just disappear out of your life?"

Sanna jerked back as if someone had slapped her. For a second something dark and alien passed across her eyes. Rage. She looked as if she wished her nails would grow into claws of iron so that she could dig them into Rebecka and rip out her insides. Then the moment was gone and her lower lip began to tremble. Big tears welled up in her eyes.

"I really didn't know . . ." she stammered. "How could I know what Curt would do . . . how can you think . . . ?"

"I'm not even sure it was Viktor," said Rebecka. "It might just have been Olof. All the time. But you can't get the better of him. And now you're taking the girls back to him. I'm going to put in a complaint. Ask Social Services to carry out an investigation."

They had met on the spring ice. On an ice floe, the remains of something that no longer existed. And now the ice was cracking, splitting in two. They were floating away in different directions. Irrevocably.

Rebecka turned her head away and released her hold on Sanna, almost threw the white hand away from her.

"Tired," she said.

In a flash Måns and Sven-Erik were by the bed. Each of them bade a silent farewell to Sanna. Måns jerked his head. Sven-Erik gave a brief nod, and smiled. They swapped places. Måns grabbed hold of the bed and Sven-Erik took the drip. Without a word they pushed Rebecka off down the corridor.

Sanna Strandgård stood there watching them as they disappeared around the corner. She leaned against the closed door.

In the summer, thought Sanna, I'll take the girls on a cycling holiday. I'll borrow a trailer for Lova. Sara will be all right on her own bike. We can cycle down through Tornedalen, they'd like that.

Sven-Erik said good-bye and disappeared in the opposite direction. Måns pressed the elevator button, and the door slid open with a ping. He swore as he banged the bed against one of the walls. He stretched out for the drip, keeping one leg in front of the electronic eye at the same time so the door wouldn't close. The unaccustomed gymnastics made him breathless. He was dying for a Scotch. He looked at Rebecka. Her eyes were closed. Maybe she'd fallen asleep.

"Do you think you can put up with this?" he asked with a crooked smile. "Being pushed around by an old man?"

From a loudspeaker in the ceiling a metallic voice announced "Third floor," and the elevator door slid open.

Rebecka didn't open her eyes.

You carry on pushing, she thought. I can't afford to be choosy. I'll take what I can get.

And evening came and morning came, the seventh day

Anna-Maria Mella is kneeling on the bed in the delivery room. She is hanging on to the steel bars of the headboard so tightly that her knuckles are white. She pushes her face into the gas mask and breathes deeply. Robert is stroking her sweat-drenched hair.

"Now," she yells. "It's coming now!"

The labor pains are like an avalanche rushing down the side of a mountain. All she can do is go with them. She squeezes and pushes and bears down.

Two midwives are standing behind her. They are shouting and cheering as if she were their winning horse in a trotting race.

"Come on, Anna-Maria! One more time! Just once more! You're such a good girl!"

It burns like fire when the child's head starts to emerge. And then, when the head is finally out, the child slides out of her like a slippery salmon in a stream.

She hasn't the energy to turn around. But she hears the furious, demanding cry.

Robert takes hold of her head in both his hands and kisses her smack in the middle of her face. He is crying.

"You did it!" he laughs through his tears. "It's a little boy!"

AUTHOR'S ACKNOWLEDGMENTS

Rebecka Martinsson will be back, she's not that easy to get rid of. Just give her a little time.

Remember that this story is made up, and so are the characters. Some places in the book are also invented: for example, the Crystal Church and the stairwell in the Söderberg family house.

There are many people to thank, and I would like to mention some of them here. Jur. Kand. Karina Lundström, who in her former life was a police investigator and used to be known as Kritan. I asked her about guns and police databases, for example. Deputy Magistrate Viktoria Lindgren and Councillor Maria Widebäck. Senior doctor Jan Lindberg and autopsy technician Kjell Edh, who contributed to the description of the dead man and the autopsy room. Birgitta Holmgren, for information about psychiatric care in Kiruna. Shiitake grower Sven-Ivan Mella, for all the stuff about mushrooms and the mine and the man who disappeared.

Any errors in the book are mine. There are certain things I didn't ask the people named above, certain things I've misunderstood, and sometimes I just decided to go my own way. For me the most important thing has been to make my lies credible, and when there was a conflict between the story and reality, the story won—every time.

Thanks also to: the literary surgical team—Hans-Olov Öberg, Marcus Tull and Sören Bondeson (who have sighed, groaned, shaken their heads and on the odd occasion grunted approvingly). Publisher Gunnar Nirstedt, for his opinions. Thanks to Elisabeth Ohlson-Wallin and John Eyre. My mother and Eva Jensen, who kept shouting, "Write faster," and thought EVERYTHING was BRILLIANT. Lena Andersson and Thomas Karlsen Andersson, for friendship and hospitality whenever I've been in Kiruna.

And finally: Per. Lead the tiger away. . . .

ASA LARSSON

THE BLOOD SPILT

07921
7/8205

BY ASA LARSSON

THE SECOND REBECKA MARTINSSON THRILLER

Under the midnight sun murder will be done ...

Midsummer in Sweden, the sun never sets and the only darkness lies in the recesses of the human mind. For a priest – Matilda Nilsson – has been brutally killed and lawyer Rebecka Martinsson, who thought she'd done with Kiruna the little town of her birth, is dragged back there to stop a killing spree. Yet the shadows that surrounded Matilda – the hurt and healing, sin and sexuality, lethal sacrifice – will come to engulf those like Rebecka who seek the truth.

COMING SOON